KT-459-887

Paul Stewart is a well-established and award-winning author of children's books – everything from picture books to fantasy, sci-fi and horror.

Chris Riddell is an accomplished artist and political cartoonist for the *Observer*. His books have won many awards, including the Kate Greenaway Medal, the Nestlé Children's Book Prize and the Red House Children's Book Award.

Paul and Chris first met at their sons' nursery school and decided to work together (they can't remember why!). Since then their books have included the Blobheads series, The Edge Chronicles, the Far-Flung Adventures and the Muddle Earth books.

'Paul Stewart and Chris Riddell's The Edge Chronicles series has built a seriously solid fan base of children and young-at-heart fantasy-fevered adults. *Muddle Earth* will delight them all' amazon.co.uk

'I laughed from cover to cover . . . an excellent book' Donald Carrick, 12, *Herald*

Also by Paul Stewart and Chris Riddell

Muddle Earth

Blobheads
Blobheads Go Boing!

The Rabbit and Hedgehog books

The Edge Chronicles

The Far-Flung Adventures

And by Chris Riddell

Ottoline and the Yellow Cat
Ottoline Goes to School
Ottoline at Sea

www.panmacmillan.com/chrisriddell

Paul Stewart & Chris Riddell

MACMILLAN CHILDREN'S BOOKS

COVENTRY SCHOOLS LIBRARY SERVICE

3 8002 01972 7264

21-Oct-2011	JF
PETERS	

First published 2011 by Macmillan Children's Books
a division of Macmillan Publishers Limited
20 New Wharf Road, London N1 9RR
Basingstoke and Oxford
Associated companies throughout the world
www.panmacmillan.com

ISBN 978-0-230-74767-8 (HB)
ISBN 978-0-230-75452-2 (TPB)

Text and illustrations copyright © Paul Stewart and Chris Riddell 2011

The right of Paul Stewart and Chris Riddell to be identified as the authors
of this work has been asserted by them in accordance with the
Copyright, Designs and Patents Act 1988.

All rights reserved. No part of this publication may be
reproduced, stored in or introduced into a retrieval system, or
transmitted, in any form or by any means (electronic, mechanical,
photocopying, recording or otherwise), without the prior written
permission of the publisher. Any person who does any unauthorized
act in relation to this publication may be liable to criminal
prosecution and civil claims for damages.

1 3 5 7 9 8 6 4 2

A CIP catalogue record for this book is available from
the British Library.

Printed and bound in the UK by CPI Mackays, Chatham ME5 8TD

This book is sold subject to the condition that it shall not,
by way of trade or otherwise, be lent, resold, hired out,
or otherwise circulated without the publisher's prior consent
in any form of binding or cover other than that in which
it is published and without a similar condition including this
condition being imposed on the subsequent purchaser.

For Julie
PS

For Jo
CR

NAME: Joe Jefferson

OCCUPATION: Schoolboy

HOBBIES: Football, TV, arguing with his sister

FAVOURITE FOOD: Anything not cooked by Norbert

NAME: Randalf the Wise, Muddle Earth's . . . er, leading wizard?

OCCUPATION: Wizard Headmaster of Stinkyhogs School of Wizardry

HOBBIES: Performing spells (I think you'll find that's spell! – Veronica)

FAVOURITE FOOD: Norbert's squashed tadpole fritters

NAME: Ella Jefferson

OCCUPATION: Moody big sister to her brother, Joe – and a barbarian princess

HOBBIES: See 'Occupation', plus painting her nails black

FAVOURITE FOOD: Cheeseburger and fries

NAME: Norbert the
Not-Very-Big

OCCUPATION: School cook

HOBBIES: Thumb-sucking,
cooking – especially
cake-decorating

FAVOURITE FOOD: Everything

NAME: Veronica

OCCUPATION: Familiar to the
great wizard, Randalf the Wise

HOBBIES: Being sarcastic

FAVOURITE FOOD: Anything not
cooked by Norbert

NAME: Walter, once The Horned
Baron, now retired

OCCUPATION: Retired Ruler
of Muddle Earth

HOBBIES: Wooing Fifi the Fair in
their love nest in Trollbridge

FAVOURITE FOOD: Bad-breath
porridge

NAME: Lord Asbow

OCCUPATION: Dean of
University of Whatever

HOBBIES: Repelling invaders,
discussing the meaning of life
with his pet Labrador

FAVOURITE FOOD: Sunrise dust,
dog food

name: Edward Gorgeous

Occupation: Student and
barbarian

Hobbies: Broomball, brooding,
looking gorgeous

Favourite food: Tomatoes
(sort of)

name: Edwina Lovely

Occupation: Queen Susan's
lady-in-waiting (sometimes)

Hobbies: Looking lovely,
obsessing over Edward
Gorgeous

Favourite food: Royal blood

name: Eraguff the
Eager-to-Please

Occupation: Dragon

Hobbies: Nest decorating,
flower picking, knitting

Favourite food: Definitely
NOT wizard

NAME: Eudora Pinkwhistle,
one of Muddle Earth's
leading witches

OCCUPATION: Potions
teacher, Stinkyhogs

HOBBIES: Spells, and crushing
on a certain wizard headmaster

FAVOURITE FOOD: Tea and
fairy-cake

NAME: Mr Fluffy

OCCUPATION: Woodwork
teacher, Stinkyhogs

HOBBIES: Storing food in his
chubby cheeks, howling at
Muddle Earth's three moons

FAVOURITE FOOD: Nuts

NAME: Kings Peter and
Edmund and Queens Susan
and Lucy

OCCUPATION: Er . . . Kings
and Queens

HOBBIES: Bossing people about

FAVOURITE FOOD: As long as
it's expensive, anything!

NAME: Pesticide and
Nettle, Thistle and
Briar Rose

OCCUPATION: Flower fairies

HOBBIES: Jeer-leading,
causing trouble

FAVOURITE FOOD:
Pollen pizza

Book One

Down with Stinkyhogs!

Prologue

Day was dawning over Muddle Earth and, as usual, things were getting in a muddle. Two of the three moons had forgotten to set. They shone down – one purple, one yellow – on the Ogre Hills, which rumbled with the snores of sleeping ogres, and the rattle and clink of the milk-elf delivering bottles of stiltmouse milk to the steps of every cave.

Meanwhile, the sun was rising over the Musty Mountains, sending flocks of tatty batbirds flapping off to roost. High above the Perfumed Bog they collided with sleepy lazybirds that were just waking up and taking to the air like overstuffed pillowcases looking for a pillow-fight.

The noise roused a wallowing pink stinky hog that looked up wearily, and an exploding gas frog that inflated in alarm, and blew up. After a good deal of honking and hooting, flapping and plumping, the birds settled their differences and all headed for Elfwood, where it still seemed to be the middle of the afternoon.

'Here they come, Sandra, bold as you please,' a spreading chestnut tree grumbled, 'perching in our branches without so much as a by-your-leave.'

'Oh, the batbirds and lazybirds are nothing, Trevor,' his neighbour, a dumpy sycamore, replied with a shudder. 'It's the woodpeckers you've got to watch out for . . .'

In Goblintown, the city that never sleeps, the goblins were going about their business as usual. Sausage makers were sausage making, bakers were baking and bankers were going out for enormous lunches on expenses.

Meanwhile in nearby Trollbridge, the city that never sweeps, the trolls were knee-deep in rotten cabbage leaves and mouldy turnip tops, but didn't seem to mind. Below their bridge, the Enchanted River flowed past.

'Toffee trousers, watering cans, *tinkle-tinkle*, April showers . . .' it babbled enchantedly as it meandered through fields and orchards, before rising up into the air like a big wet mushroom to form the Enchanted Lake.

Bobbing upon its magical waters were the seven houseboats belonging to the seven wizards of Muddle Earth. Six were in darkness, their owners still fast asleep, while the seventh was aglow with lamplight. This, the largest and grandest of them all, was the residence of Roger the Wrinkled, who was pacing up and down the deck in a purple chiffon dressing gown and pink fluffy mules, dictating a letter to his enchanted quill.

He was working late, or working early. He wasn't sure which.

'With our ruler the Horned Baron having stepped down from the throne *comma* and the wizards in charge of Muddle Earth *comma* . . .' Roger intoned in his thin, reedy voice, 'it is more important than ever that the highest standards of . . .'

He paused to allow the quill to dip itself in the ink pot that hovered beside the floating parchment.

'. . . the highest standards of . . .'

'You've said that already,' wheezed the quill in a scratchy-sounding whisper.

'... the highest standards of wizardry,' Roger continued, ignoring it, 'should be maintained at all costs. *Full stop*. It is therefore my duty to inform you that unless Stinkyhogs School of Wizardry triumphs in the forthcoming tournament ...'

He paused to clear his throat importantly.

Ahem! wrote the quill.

'... then you will leave me no alternative but to close the school. *Full stop*. In that unfortunate event you'll have let not only me down *comma* my fellow wizards down *comma* but worst of all you will have let yourself down – *double exclamation mark*.'

Roger the Wrinkled waved an immaculately varnished fingernail at the parchment, which immediately folded itself into a neat envelope.

'And,' whispered the quill, as it fluttered up and lodged itself behind its master's wrinkled ear, 'Muddle Earth too!'

The hulking cave trog shuffled down the corridor, his horny bare feet sending dust flying up from the varnished floorboards.

Ting-a-ling-a-ling . . .

Attached to his cap was a tiny brass bell which bounced about on the end of a spring.

Ting-a-ling-a-ling . . . Ting-a-ling-a-ling . . .

The wooden panels strapped to his front and back had various bits of tattered parchment pinned to them that flapped as he went.

SIGN UP FOR GLUM CLUB, read one; *Weeping and Wailing Experience Not Essential.*

Elf Computer Class – After School in the Dungeon, read another.

Why not try FANTASY ROLE PLAY? Join our Accountants and Bank Managers Group. (See Mr Mild for details.)

The cave trog paused.

Ting-a-ling-a-ling . . .

A loosely attached piece of parchment fluttered to the floor and, tutting loudly, the cave trog bent to pick it up.

Ting-a-ling-a-CLUNK.

Straightening up, he adjusted his cap and scrutinized the parchment. He ran the filthy nail of a fat finger along the words, his lips moving as he read.

Stinkyhogs School of Wizardry Broomball Team for the Goblet of Porridge Match.

Under this was a list of names.

Coach: Thragar Warspanner
Centre Spoon: Thrasher
Mid-Broom: Charlie Battlepants
Graters: Olga Onionbreath & Rufus Hairyear
Chimney Sweeper: Edward Gorgeous.
GO, PERFUMED PORKERS!

With the exception of Edward Gorgeous, all the names had been crossed out.

The cave trog unwrinkled the parchment. Going cross-eyed as he squinted down at his front, he carefully pinned the notice back on his board.

Ting-a-ling-a-ling.

The cave trog got to the end of the corridor and turned. The doors that lined it remained resolutely closed and the corridor was so silent you could hear a pin drop – which it did, and another notice fluttered to the floor. It was pink and covered in poorly applied glitter.

Jeer-leading Practice Today at . . . You call those pom-poms? . . . Oh, shut up!

The cave trog ignored it. *Ting-a-ling-a-ling* went his tiny bell. He sighed forlornly. Then, raising his two great hams of hands and cupping them round his mouth, he bellowed so loudly the door frames rattled and the oak panelling shook.

'*TING – ER – LING – ER – **LING!***'

There was a brief pause. Then, with a *bang-bang-bang-bang*, the doors on both sides of the corridor flew open and the pupils of Stinkyhogs School of Wizardry came pouring out.

Young trolls and goblins, ogres and barbarians, each one wearing ill-fitting blazers of pink and even pinker stripes, and pointy hats that were either too big or too small, pushed past each other in a swirling scrum of elbows and shoulder barges as they made their way from classrooms on one side of the corridor to classrooms on the other. The air throbbed with feverish noise. There was shouting. Laughter. Hustle-bustle and harum-scarum.

The pupils kicked the cave trog's shins as they shoved past. 'Ouch! Ouch! Ouch!' he exclaimed.

Frowning, he reached behind his back and pulled a notice from the board.

Kick me, it read.

'Yeah, yeah, very funny,' he murmured mournfully to no one in particular. 'You should try being a noticeboard and the school bell, all at the same time.'

'Not to mention janitor,' came an exasperated voice from just behind the trog. 'The toilets are blocked in the East Tower, Tinklebell.'

Bang! Bang! Bang! Bang! Bang! The doors slammed shut.

Silence fell as swiftly and suddenly as it had been shattered. Another drawing pin clattered to the wooden floor.

'Remind me to have a word with Norbert about serving prune curry for breakfast.'

Tinklebell the cave trog, school bell, noticeboard and janitor turned to see a short, portly figure with thick white hair and a bushy white beard staring up at him. He wore a voluminous black cape around his shoulders and a tall pointy wizard's hat on his head. A budgie was perched upon its brim.

'Remind him yourself. I'm not your secretary!' the budgie exclaimed. 'She's the one upstairs, remember? Got you wrapped around her little finger, at her constant beck and call. "No, Mrs Horned Baron. Yes, Mrs Horned Baron. Three bags full, Mrs Horned Baron . . ."'

'Shut up, Veronica,' headmaster Randalfus Rumblebore hissed through gritted teeth as he tried to swat the budgie away.

'Randalf! Randalf!' came a loud and piercing voice from the top of the stairs. 'What *is* that awful smell? Do something, Randalf! *Do* something!'

'All under control, Mrs Horned Baron,' the headmaster called back meekly. 'I'm taking care of it.'

'Well, just make sure you do!' Ingrid bellowed back.

'And have my afternoon tea sent up. I'm absolutely parched!'

Looking down, an exasperated Randalf noticed a piece of parchment lying on the floor. He picked it up, turned it over and found himself looking at the broomball notice with the names crossed off.

'Oh, for crying out loud,' he muttered woefully.

'So he's left,' Veronica commented disdainfully, 'and taken the team with him.' She tutted. 'Well, you can't say I didn't warn you. Turning down his request for a pay rise was just asking for trouble. That's barbarians for you – never trust anyone with wings on their helmet. I mean, it's just not natural . . .'

'Shut *up*, Veronica,' Randalf snapped.

Just then, Norbert the Not-Very-Big appeared at the far end of the corridor. He minced carefully over the creaking floorboards on great stocky ogre legs, his three eyes blinking with concentration as he balanced a tray of afternoon tea and half a dozen snugglemuffins on an upraised hand.

'Wish they'd make their minds up,' he was grumbling. 'Moons rising. Sun setting. I don't know whether I'm coming or going. What time of day is it, anyway?'

He had just reached the stairs that led up to Ingrid's chambers when a lazybird came flopping through the open window opposite and perched on the tea tray – slopping the tea and squashing one of the snugglemuffins as it landed – and promptly fell asleep. There was a crumpled letter clamped in its beak.

'Clear off,' Norbert said, brushing the bird aside with his free arm.

The lazybird squawked, dropped the letter and flapped off. Norbert righted the crockery, daubed at the spilt milk and tea, pushed the crumbs of the damaged snugglemuffin into his mouth and, tray held high, continued up the stairs.

'Take me for granted, they do,' the cave trog was muttering to himself as he turned on his calloused heels and blundered back along the corridor to deal with the blocked toilet.

Randalf stared down at the folded letter that lay at his feet, a sinking feeling in his stomach. It was from Roger the Wrinkled. He could tell that from the blob of red sealing wax with its oh-so-familiar imprint of a stiletto-heeled shoe.

'What now?' he groaned.

'Only one way to find out,' said Veronica.

Randalf sighed, then grunted as he stooped down and picked up the letter. He broke the seal, opened the letter and started reading – then sighed again, long and loud and heartfelt.

'Oh, Veronica,' he said. 'That's all I need. Roger is threatening to close the school if we don't win the Goblet of Porridge, which is in three days' time – and now we don't even have a broomball team!'

Before Veronica could answer, there came the most

extraordinary sound from somewhere outside, in the school grounds. It was low-pitched and mournful, rising to a spine-tingling but chewy wail, like a wolf howling at the moon with its mouth full. At the window, a green moon had risen, round and full, and was hanging in the air like a giant glowing cabbage.

'What on Muddle Earth was that?' exclaimed Randalf.

'No idea,' said Veronica, with a shrug. 'But whatever it was, it didn't sound very happy.'

It was an odd day in the Jefferson household. For a start it was quiet. There was no vacuum cleaner whirring or noisy dusting because Mrs Jefferson was at work. There was no hammering or buzzing of power tools because Mr Jefferson was at the DIY store buying more materials for the extension he was building on to the back of the house. And there were no wild shrieks and cries of 'Mum! Mum! Where are my trainers?' because the twins were playing football over at the park.

Odder still was where Joe was. He couldn't remember the last time he'd set foot inside his sister Ella's bedroom. Normally Joe, like everyone else in the family, was forbidden to enter. A sign in threatening black letters – *KEEP OUT . . . OR ELSE!* – written beneath a sinister skull and crossbones emphasized the point.

Yet that was where Joe was now. In Ella's bedroom. He was kneeling on the floor beside a heap of wooden boards, pieces of dowelling, screws and hinges. Before him were instructions on how to assemble a wardrobe.

The *Tumnus* claimed to be 'a stylish, easy-to-assemble bedroom unit' from somewhere unpronounceable in 'Binland' – or was that 'Fimland'? Joe couldn't be sure. The instructions seemed to be written in Elvish.

'I can't find the thing for tightening the screws,' he grumbled.

Ella, who was sitting on her bed, flicking through a magazine called *Goth Idol* while painting her toenails black, reached up and pulled a headphone from her ear.

'Did you say something?' she asked.

'Call this a wardrobe?' Joe shook his head. 'Where on earth does Dad find this stuff?'

'The internet, probably. Dead cheap, but who knows where it's from? And who cares? Just follow the instructions.'

Joe smoothed them out, then turned them upside down.

'Perhaps this is it,' he said, picking up an odd-looking bit of flat metal shaped like an acorn. With a shrug, he took a plank of wood and tried slotting it into place with another. 'Do you think these go together?' he asked tentatively.

Ella shrugged. 'Whatever,' she said, without taking her eyes off the magazine.

Joe glared at his big sister. Oh yes, it was a change being allowed into her precious bedroom, but there was no change in Ella herself. She was still as moody and temperamental as ever – or 'artistic and sensitive' as she called it. Here he was, trying to be helpful, and this was all the thanks he got.

Joe fitted the two bits of wood together and picked up another. He squinted at the smudgy printed diagram. He would not give up. He would not be beaten.

'If this goes in there . . . then this must go there . . .' he muttered.

Slowly, as Joe persevered, the wardrobe started to take shape. Sides. Back. Bottom, with pedestal feet. Shelves, side drawers, hanger rail. Top. Finally all that needed to be done was the front. He had the door. He had the hinges. But where were the screws?

He upended the cardboard box with the word *Tumnus* and a drawing of an impressive-looking wardrobe on the side, and shook it. It was empty. He looked beneath the unfinished wardrobe. He rummaged under Ella's bed, through her waste-paper basket; he checked his own pockets. But the screws were nowhere to be found.

'They're not here!' he complained loudly.

Ella removed her headphones. 'Pardon?' she said.

'The screws,' he said. 'I can't find the hinge screws anywhere, and I need them to . . .'

And then he saw them. They were in the small clear plastic envelope that Ella was idly fiddling with as she pored over a two-page spread about how black was the new black.

'There!' Joe said, outraged.

'Where?' said Ella.

'You're holding them.'

Ella looked down at her hand and frowned, as if seeing the screws for the first time. 'Oh, are these what you were looking for?'

'Yes,' said Joe as calmly as he could manage. 'But you're going to have to give me a hand.'

'But *you're* meant to be doing *me* a favour . . .'

'I can't fix the door on my own,' he said. 'What do you want to do, hold the door or screw the hinges into place?'

Ella climbed from the bed. 'I'll do the hinges,' she said. 'Some favour this is. You're the one who claims to be good at fixing things. I'm artistic, sensitive . . .'

Joe bit his tongue and handed Ella the flat metal acorn-shaped tool.

While he held the door in place, Ella climbed inside the wardrobe and, one by one, attached the hinges, tightening the screws, first at the top and then at the bottom . . .

'Last one,' Ella said. 'Just a bit tighter. There we are . . .' She slipped the screw-tightening tool into the pocket of her black cut-off jeans. 'All done!'

Joe giggled. 'Artistic', 'sensitive' . . . He pushed the door shut and leaned against it. There was a scrabbling noise as Ella climbed to her feet and a *thump thump thump* as she pounded on the door.

'Let me out, Joe!' came her muffled voice. 'It's not funny. Open the door and stop mucking around . . .'

'Whatever!' said Joe, laughing as he leaned against the rattling door.

It went silent. Joe smiled. He knew what she was up to. She was pretending to be calm, then when he did open the door, she'd leap out at him.

'So you're artistic and sensitive?' he said.

Nothing.

'Is that why you paint your toenails black?'

Still nothing.

'Ella?

He straightened up and pulled the door open. He peered inside.

'Ella?' The wardrobe was empty. 'Ella, where are you?'

Joe frowned, baffled. The *Tumnus* was a flat-pack wardrobe, not a magic trick.

So where was she?

Joe climbed warily inside. The door closed behind him, plunging the inside of the wardrobe into darkness. He reached out with his hands – and felt something there. Clothes, on hangers, smelling of old ladies and banana skins. Fur coats, dozens of them.

He took a step forward. The soft fur rubbed against his face. He took another step, and another. The *Tumnus* was huge inside, so much larger than it had looked in the drawing on the cardboard box. He took another step . . .

His feet crunched on something underfoot. Twigs and fir cones. The fur coats prickled against his face as they turned into the branches of trees – Christmas trees. Up ahead was a faint yellow light. And as Joe made his way towards it, the trees thinned out and the air was filled with white flakes that swirled around him and settled on the ground.

Like snow – except it wasn't snow at all. It was ash.

Boom came a soft, half-hearted sound, and the air grew thick with a musty smell like unwashed socks.

Joe stopped. In front of him was a lamp-post. It was short – barely taller than Joe himself – and black and made of cast iron, with a fluted column and a hexagonal glass lantern at the top which gave out a soft yellow light.

Just then there was a loud scream. Joe froze, his stomach churning.

'Ella!' he called out. 'Ella, is that you?'

Joe dashed headlong towards the sound of the scream. He stumbled and skidded, sending great clouds of musty white ash into the air. As he rounded a large boulder, he saw Ella lying in the middle of a large field, which was covered in strange markings and had a fireplace with a crooked chimney at each end of it.

He halted in his tracks.

Ella was swathed in a large fur coat, and a figure was crouched down beside her, cradling her in his muscular arms. As Joe ran over, Ella opened her eyes. She looked up.

'Wh . . . Where am I?' she whispered. Her frightened expression softened. 'And who are *you*?'

The handsome stranger stared down at her hands, then took one in his own. 'Hush, now,' he said. 'My name is Edward. Edward Gorgeous. You've had a bad fright.'

'I was in . . . in the wardrobe,' said Ella dreamily, gazing up into the stranger's eyes. 'And then I was walking . . . walking through Christmas trees towards a lamp-post.

Then this . . . this *thing* appeared . . .'

'"Thing"?' the gorgeous barbarian said, his dark eyes staring intently at the hand he was stroking.

'It was horrible,' Ella went on, 'with huge red eyes and bulging cheeks . . .'

'There, there,' Edward Gorgeous said, his voice soft and soothing. 'It's all right. You're safe now, *I'm* here.'

He raised Ella's hand to his mouth, his gaze fixed upon her thumb. His lips parted . . .

'Edward! Edward! *There* you are!' came a voice, and a portly, bearded wizard came strutting across the field, a budgie on his shoulder and a three-eyed ogre in tow. 'I've been looking for you everywhere. Tell me, Edward, is it really true that Coach Warspanner has left, and taken the rest of the team with him?' Then he paused, frowned, put his podgy hands on his broad hips and nodded down at the girl in Edward Gorgeous's arms. 'And who, pray, is this?'

Joe stepped forward. 'Randalf?' he said. 'Randalf, is that you?'

The portly wizard, the dusty budgie and the three-eyed, not very big ogre spun round.

'JOE!' they exclaimed as one.

'Joe the Barbarian,' said Randalf. 'As I live and breathe. I never thought I . . . *Oooof!*'

'Joe!' bellowed Norbert, a huge grin on his face as he inadvertantly shouldered Randalf out of the way. He wrapped his meaty arms around the boy and lifted him high in the air. 'Joe, it's *you!*' he said.

'It's an omen,' Randalf said, climbing to his feet and dusting himself down. 'Joe the Barbarian has returned!'

'Omen? You wouldn't know an omen from an oven glove, you old fraud!' said Veronica scornfully. She flew over and landed on Joe's shoulder as Norbert put him gently down. 'Joe, how nice to see you,' she tweeted sweetly. 'What brings you back to Muddle Earth?'

'A wardrobe,' said Joe, trying to gather his thoughts. It had been nearly a year since Joe had last been in Muddle Earth. On that occasion, Randalf the wizard had accidentally summoned Joe's dog Henry with his warrior-hero-summoning spell – and Joe, who had been holding Henry's lead, had been dragged along too. Now, here he was again. Only this time Henry was curled up in his basket by the fire at home, and he was here with his sulky, lazy, good-for-nothing big sister! 'One minute I was getting into a wardrobe. The next, I was here . . . You haven't been using your warrior-hero-summoning spell again, have you, Randalf?' Joe asked.

'No, no. Certainly not,' said Randalf hotly.

Norbert patted Joe affectionately on his head. 'But it's lovely to see you – isn't it, sir? It's lovely to see him, isn't it?'

Randalf scratched his head thoughtfully. 'You got into a wardrobe, you say?' he said. 'Well, that explains it.'

'It does?' said Joe, even more confused than he already was.

'Cross-worlds contamination. It's quite common . . .'

'It is?' said Joe.

'And of course you wouldn't have anything to do with it, would you, Randalf?' said Veronica tartly.

'Shut up, Veronica,' said Randalf, going distinctly red in the face. He put an arm round Joe's shoulders comfortingly. 'You see, Joe, magic is a funny old business. Trust me, I'm a wizard. Magic's like sawdust, or dandruff, or . . .'

He paused to brush the dust from Joe's shoulders.

'Or ash from Mount Boom. It can stick to you.'

'I don't understand,' said Joe.

'What Fatso's trying to say,' Veronica broke in, 'is that you must have picked up bits of magic from the last time you visited us here in Muddle Earth.'

Joe remembered his last time in Muddle Earth only

too well, when he'd had to pretend to be a warrior-hero to help Randalf out. He'd battled sheep-squeezing ogres, ridden antique-collecting dragons and even foiled the dastardly Dr Cuddles's plans to take over Muddle Earth. Flying wardrobes. Talking teddy bears. Barbarian princesses riding battlecats . . . Come to think of it, it had all been rather good fun.

'I didn't *visit* exactly,' Joe said. 'Randalf brought me here with that warrior-hero-summoning spell of his.'

'Exactly,' said Randalf apologetically. 'That's when you were sprinkled with magic. Very hard to get rid of – like dandruff . . . Little bits of it, you see, they fall off, and strange effects occur. Things transmogrify. Portals open up from one world to another – such as this wardrobe you spoke of.' His face grew serious. 'It's a good job you weren't unblocking the toilet, Joe. That's no way to enter another world!'

'As Sebastian the Smelly can testify,' sniffed Veronica.

Randalf frowned. 'And who is your charming companion, Joe? A barbarian princess?'

'That's not a barbarian princess,' Joe said. 'That's my big sister Ella.'

Cradled in Edward Gorgeous's arms, Ella ignored them as she gazed into her rescuer's eyes.

'Don't get me wrong, Randalf. It is great to see you again, but we really can't stay,' said Joe. 'The twins will be back from the park soon, and they haven't got a key . . . Can you send us home with that spell you used last time?'

'I'm afraid not,' said Randalf, scratching his head. 'You see, the problem is, I didn't summon you with a spell this time, so I can't send you back with a spell. It simply wouldn't work. Trust me, I'm a wizard.'

Joe glanced round at Ella. Luckily she was so taken with the handsome barbarian that she didn't seem to have heard a word they'd said. And thank goodness for that, Joe thought. His big sister could be very awkward when she wanted to be.

'Then how *do* we get back?' Joe whispered.

'Oh, that's easy,' said Randalf. 'In these sorts of cases, there's usually some sort of marker or other . . .'

'There was a lamp-post,' Joe said uncertainly.

'Well, that'll be it,' said Randalf. 'Just go back to the lamp-post and you'll find the portal.'

Joe turned and sprinted back the short distance to the spot where the lamp-post had been standing, only to find that it was no longer there. Little footprints led away up the mountainside, then disappeared.

'Oh, dear,' said Randalf, when Joe returned, covered in ash and even greater confusion. 'A wandering lamp-post. What appalling luck. Still, all you have to do is wait around a while and it should be back along this way soon.'

'How soon, Randalf?' panted Joe. 'I mean, I don't mind staying here in Muddle Earth a little longer.' He nodded towards Ella. 'It's her,' he whispered. 'My big sister. I don't think she'll be very good with ogres and dragons . . .'

'She seems to like barbarians,' Randalf said with a smile. He paused and rubbed a hand thoughtfully over his snow-white beard. 'And in the meantime, since you're with us—'

'Here we go,' twittered Veronica from her perch on the brim of Randalf's hat.

Randalf took no notice. He clapped an arm round Joe's shoulders. 'You see, I've got this teeny-weeny problem, Joe.'

'It isn't fighting ogres or foiling teddy bears, is it?' said Joe uncertainly.

'Oh, no. Nothing like that,' said Randalf airily.

Edward Gorgeous helped Joe's sister to her feet and dusted down her fur coat. 'Are you OK?' he asked her.

'*Mmm?*' she said dreamily. 'I think so.'

'Excellent, excellent,' said Randalf, and clapped his hands together. 'In that case, everyone follow me.'

'If it's all the same to you, sir, I think I'll get back to my sweeping practice,' said Edward Gorgeous.

'Marvellous idea,' said Randalf. 'You do that. Go, porkers!'

Ella gazed into Edward's dark, brooding eyes. 'Could you show me how to play?' she asked.

Edward flicked his hair off his forehead. 'If you'd like me to,' he said, gazing back at her.

'Yes, well,' said Randalf, 'let's leave them to it.' He took Joe by the arm and steered him across the playing field and down a path that led to a large, pointy-turreted castle. 'The Horned Baron's castle is a school now,' Randalf explained. 'Stinkyhogs School of Wizardry. And I,' he added, puffing out his chest proudly, 'Randalfus Rumblebore, Professor of the Magical Arts, am the headmaster.'

'It was all Fatso's idea,' said Veronica. 'Roger the Wrinkled said he could open the school so long as he stayed out of trouble and didn't bring wizardry into disrepute. Fat chance!'

'Ignore her,' said Randalf, as he led Joe across the courtyard, up the steps and through the heavy oak doors of the castle. 'You see, the Horned Baron has retired to Trollbridge, so the place really wasn't being used for much and I spotted an opportunity – though the headmaster's lot isn't always an easy one . . .'

They crossed the hallway and climbed the stairs.

'Randalf!' came a shrill yet booming voice from high up in the castle. 'My teapot's getting cold. The tea cosy, Randalf! Now!'

'Certainly, Mrs Horned Baron, sir,' Randalf

shouted up the stairs.

He turned to Joe. 'Unfortunately, the castle still belongs to the Horned Baron's ex-wife, Ingrid.' He rolled his eyes. 'As I was saying, the headmaster's lot isn't always an easy one.' He took off his pointy hat and gave it to Norbert. 'Take it to her.'

He sighed as a disgruntled Veronica settled on top of his bald head.

'Goggle, goggle, goggle, goggle, goggle . . .' came a squeaky voice, and Joe glanced round to see a tiny, wiry elf. 'Average length of a turnip,' it was muttering. 'Average length of a turnip . . .'

'That's the inter-elf,' Randalf said proudly, striding down the long, door-lined corridor. 'We're connected up to the Muddle-Wide-Web here at Stinkyhogs. Wands, broomsticks, wizards' staffs – we've got all the latest technology. Step this way.'

'Where are you taking me?' asked Joe.

'To meet the staff,' said Randalf, gesturing ahead, and Joe noticed the plaque on the door they were approaching.

Staff room, it said.

Joe seized the handle and pulled the door open. The next moment, there was a clatter and a crash as dozens of staffs – large, crooked and nobbly – tumbled out into the corridor. Randalf leaped forward and between them, they managed to shove the door back into place.

'Not that one,' said Randalf. He pointed to the adjacent

door, which bore the word *Teachers* on it. '*That* one!'

This time, when Joe turned the handle, the door opened to reveal a broad, high-ceiling room that was filled with chairs and sofas of all types, from broad-winged leather armchairs to stout chintz-covered settees. The only thing they had in common was their age, for they were all old, with faded covers, torn upholstery and protruding springs. That and the fact that most of them were occupied by the teachers of Stinkyhogs School of Wizardry who were perched, slumped or slouching upon them.

'Welcome, Joe, to our little family,' said Randalf grandly. 'A band of dedicated and enthusiastic educators.'

Joe looked around. Apart from a pointy-faced woman in black robes and a witch's hat, not one of the teachers had so much as glanced up when they'd entered the room.

Randalf cleared his throat. 'Good morning, staff,' he said.

'Good morning to *you*, Professor Rumblebore,' said the witch brightly, fluttering her eyelashes. 'How *lovely* to see you.'

No one else spoke, though a few more looked their way.

'Dedicated . . . and . . . enthusiastic,' said Randalf, with a fixed smile. He turned to Joe. 'That's Mr Chiaroscuro, our art master. And Miss Balsamic, who takes Good Wizardkeeping.'

Joe nodded greetings at the moustachioed lady goblin in the stripy overalls. And then at Mr Chiaroscuro, a flamboyant troll in a long paint-spattered apron.

'That's Mr Polly,' Randalf continued, pointing to a tearful, one-eyed cyclops who was holding a large spotted handkerchief. On a chain around his neck were spectacles – or to be more precise, *a* spectacle, for the frame contained a single lens of magnifying glass. 'And over there by the window are Mr Shaggymane and Mr Shinyhoof.'

Joe tried not to stare. Both teachers were half man, half horse – though in Mr Shaggymane's case, the horse was the top half, and in Mr Shinyhoof's the opposite was true.

'Those were *my* chocolate brownies!' Mr Shaggymane whinnied, tossing his head and stamping his feet.

'Well, how was I to know?' Mr Shinyhoof retorted. 'Besides, you had my oatcakes the other day, you . . .'

'And this,' said Randalf, turning hurriedly away, 'is Miss Eudora Pinkwhistle, one of Muddle Earth's leading witches.'

'Oh, Professor,' said Eudora, blushing furiously behind her lank black hair and batting her eyelids again. 'You flatterer!'

A corpulent black cat appeared from beneath her

tattered skirts and gazed up at the budgie on Randalf's head.

'He licked his lips, Randalf!' said Veronica shrilly. 'I saw him. That cat licked his lips and looked straight at me!'

'You're overreacting, Veronica,' said Randalf with an indulgent chuckle. 'Forgive my familiar, Miss Pinkwhistle,' he said, bowing to the witch and causing Veronica to tumble from his bald head and cling on to his beard for dear life.

'Not at all, headmaster,' gushed the witch, picking up the cat and stroking it. 'Slocum wouldn't hurt a fly, would you, Slocum?'

The cat burped extravagantly.

Joe's attention fell on a small, slightly hunchbacked, bespectacled individual sitting in a rocking chair in the corner. He was wearing a tweed jacket with leather patches at the elbows, a brown tie and baggy corduroy trousers – and looked absolutely exhausted. A cup of tea rested on the arm of the chair, while in his hands was a copy of *Dove-Tail Joints for Beginners*, which had clearly been nibbled at the corners.

'That's Mr Fluffy,' said Randalf, noticing where Joe was looking.

'The woodwork master. Doesn't say much, tends to keep himself to himself. . .'

He turned and clapped his hands together. No one paid him a blind bit of notice. He clapped his hands again.

'Staff!' Randalf said loudly. 'I regret to announce that Coach Warspanner has moved on to pastures new . . .'

'He quit!' squawked Veronica.

'But I should like to take this opportunity to introduce to you Joe the Barbarian, who is visiting, and who has agreed to help our broomball team in the Goblet of Porridge match!'

'I have?' said Joe, turning on Randalf. 'But . . . but I don't know anything about broomball!'

'Oh, a warrior-hero like you, Joe,' he said. 'You'll pick it up in no time.' Randalf smiled warmly. 'Trust me, I'm a wizard!'

Just then, the teachers' room door creaked open and Tinklebell's huge head peered through.

'*BONG!* he boomed. '*BONG! BONG!*'

'Excellent,' said Randalf. 'Time for dinner!' He patted his stomach. 'I could eat a horse.'

'How dare he!' whinnied Mr Shaggymane.

'The cheek!' snorted Mr Shinyhoof.

The magnificent Throne Room of the Horned Baron's castle had seen better days.

Once, the Horned Baron himself had perched upon the high throne – his stubby legs not quite reaching the expensively tiled floor – and bossed people about. Above his large horn-helmeted head, the vaulted ceilings had been bedecked with tatty goblin tapestries, soggy ogre snuggly-wugglies and humorously shaped root vegetables from Trollbridge – all tributes from the grateful peoples of Muddle Earth to their glorious and beloved leader.

But not any more. Ingrid had had them all thrown in the moat when the Horned Baron had run off with Mucky Maud to Trollbridge.

Now, the cavernous hall was laid out quite differently. Four enormous dining tables, with rough-hewn benches on either side of them, had been placed in a row upon the tiled floor, from one side wall to the other, while the throne itself stood at the top end of a high table beneath a pair of majestic arched windows. On the far wall was a large, gaudy painting of a purple blob with four eyes, twelve arms and what appeared to be dollops of pink stinky hog dung covered in glitter stuck randomly across its surface. The plaque on the wall below the gold frame read, *Randalfus Rumblebore, Headmaster.*

'It was Benson who talked me into it,' Randalf was saying, as he led Joe across the great hall, the rest of the staff shuffling along behind.

'Benson?' said Joe. 'The Horned Baron's butler?'

'That's the one,' said Randalf. He paused. The teachers paused behind him. 'Benson felt Mrs Horned Baron needed something to take her mind off her –' Randalf's voice dropped to a hushed whisper – '... *troubles.*'

Veronica snorted.

'And what could be better than the pitter-patter of tiny feet and the happy voices of little wizards-to-be?' Randalf went on. 'At least, that's what Benson said as he was leaving ...'

'Couldn't wait to get out the door,' said Veronica.

'And now, with him gone, poor old Fatso here is at Ingrid's beck and call.'

'Anyway,' said Randalf, with a sweep of his podgy arm that knocked Veronica accidently-on-purpose from the brim of his pointy hat, 'as you can see, the transformation from throne room to dining hall has been a great success . . .'

He walked over to the high throne and patted an ornately carved arm proprietorially. 'This is where I sit.'

So saying, Randalf heaved himself up on to the seat of the high, gilded, straight-backed throne, where he perched, his stubby legs not quite reaching the floor.

Some things hadn't changed.

Taking his lead, the other teachers made a beeline for their seats.

'You sit here, Joe,' said Randalf, patting the chair to his right.

Joe sat down. Eudora Pinkwhistle, who was clearly used to having that place herself, scooted round to the chair on the left of Randalf, only to find that Mr Chiaroscuro had beaten her to it. He had pulled a voluminous silk handkerchief from his sleeve and was flicking dust from the chair cushion.

'This seat's taken,' he announced, sweeping back his voluminous purple cloak and plonking himself down next to the headmaster. 'This really is the best angle to view my masterpiece,' he added, gazing up at the portrait of Randalf.

'And smell it!' Eudora grumbled, as she sat down further along the table next to Mr Fluffy, who was nibbling on a small pile of nuts, his cheeks bulging as he did so. The other teachers took their places at the table – all apart from Mr Shinyhoof, who seemed to find it easier to remain standing.

'*BONG! BONG! BONG!*'

The sound of Tinklebell's booming voice echoed from the corridors outside. It was followed by the *bang-bang-bang* of doors, and suddenly the air was filled with the excited clamour of hungry young goblins, trolls, ogres and barbarians as the pupils of Stinkyhogs poured out from their classrooms and hurried to the dining hall.

'Ah, look at them,' Randalf said fondly, his eyes twinkling as, with a loud *crash*, the door slammed back and they streamed through the doorway and into the hall. 'The future of Muddle Earth . . .'

'Heaven help us.' Veronica sniffed and flapped her wings.

Jostling and shoving one another, the pupils headed for their tables in the middle of the hall, the goblins on one, the trolls, ogres and barbarians on the others. The babble of voices grew louder.

'Here at Stinkyhogs,' Randalf shouted above the din, 'our young wizards-to-be each belong to a hovel. There are four hovels . . .'

'Don't you mean *houses*?' said Joe.

'No, definitely hovels,' said Randalf. 'We don't go in for luxuries here at Stinkyhogs.' He pointed at each of the tables in turn. 'There's Brillig, Mimsy, Borogove and Wabe.'

He climbed down from the throne. Then, realizing that he was in fact shorter standing, he sat down again.

'Now, if we're all here,' he said loudly, 'let us raise our voices in the school song.'

'*Stinkyhogs! O Stinkyhogs! . . .*'

Just then, there was a second *crash* as the door of the dining hall burst open again, and Norbert, wearing a soup-spattered apron, came trundling into the hall. He was pushing a supermarket trolley that contained a huge steaming cauldron, struggling to keep it moving in a straight line. It wasn't easy. The front wheel on the left saw to that. Squeaking and squealing, it seemed determined to go back the way it had come.

The pupils, who had ignored Randalf and the school song, now picked up their spoons and banged them rhythmically on the table before them.

'*Food, disgusting food!*' they sang at the top of their voices. '*Slops, lumps and gristle! . . .*'

As Norbert pushed the wayward trolley from table to table, the members of Brillig, Mimsy, Borogove and Wabe hovels raised their bowls and received ladlefuls of mushy, lumpy stew.

'*Food . . . disgusting . . . foo . . .*'

Slurp!

The singing died away and the hall was filled with the sounds of slopping, slurping and burping as all the young wizards-to-be tucked in.

Norbert approached the top table and winked his three eyes at Joe. Reaching down, he unhooked a grubby sack from the handle of the trolley and, reaching inside, began to serve the teachers. Mr Shaggymane and Mr Shinyhoof shared a bundle of hay, while the rest of the teachers each got a cheese sandwich and an apple. Mr Fluffy ignored his and reached instead into the pocket of his tweed jacket for another handful of nuts.

Joe picked up his sandwich and took a small bite. It tasted of soggy cardboard and unwashed feet.

'How do you like it?' asked Norbert expectantly.

'Not bad,' Joe said, trying to swallow and smile at the same time.

'Oh, I'm so pleased!' said Norbert. 'I'll just serve thirds, and then I'll be back with the next course.'

'Thirds?' said Joe, putting down the sandwich

and picking up the apple.

'Nobody ever wants seconds,' Norbert explained patiently, 'so I give them thirds instead.'

He turned and wheeled the shopping trolley back past the tables, slopping more stew into bowls, on to heads, and down the back of necks until the cauldron was empty.

Looking across at the Brillig table, Joe saw his sister, Ella. She still seemed to be in a daze, staring adoringly up at the handsome barbarian Edward Gorgeous, who was holding her hand and staring back at her.

Ella was distracted for now, but how long would it be before she was back to her usual sulky, moody self and demanding explanations? Joe wondered. Hopefully it wouldn't be too soon. Joe loved sport. All sport. Cricket, football, basketball. He'd never heard of this broomball that Randalf wanted him to play, but it sounded like it might be fun. It certainly beat battling ogres! But then, what if the lamp-post turned up? They could return home, but then he'd never find out what broomball was . . .

Lost in thought, Joe raised the apple to his mouth, only for Mr Shaggymane to reach out a hand and knock it from his grasp. The apple soared high in the air before Mr Shaggymane caught it in his mouth and began crunching it noisily. Around him, the other teachers chuckled.

'You'll have to be quicker than that to play broomball,' said Mr Chiaroscuro, smiling.

'What exactly *is* broomball?' said Joe.

'Broomball,' said Randalf, 'is Muddle Earth's most popular sport.'

'After elf-throwing and sheep-squeezing,' chirruped Veronica. 'Not to mention troll-tag, barbarian wrestling and competitive flatulence . . .'

'Ignore Veronica,' said Randalf, biting into Joe's sandwich. 'We take broomball very seriously here at Stinkyhogs. After all, it is the sport of wizards!'

'But how do you actually play it?' said Joe.

'Simple,' said Randalf, finishing Joe's sandwich and sitting back. 'There are two muddles, five players per muddle. Centre spoon, mid-broom, two graters and the chimney sweeper.' He squinted at Joe thoughtfully. 'I see you as a mid-broom. Just the position for a warrior-hero, I'd say. You get your own broom,' he added.

'A *flying* broom?' said Joe excitedly.

Suddenly broomball was sounding even more interesting. He could see himself now, swooping down through the air on a magical broomstick, the crowd whooping and cheering as he homed in on the opponents' goal . . .

'Don't be ridiculous!' said Randalf. 'What on Muddle Earth would we want flying brooms for?'

'To ride around on?' suggested Joe. 'Chasing the ball and scoring goals? After all, you said it was the sport of wizards.'

'Dear me, no, Joe,' said Randalf. 'Flying brooms, indeed! I don't know what you do with them in *your* world, Joe, but here in Muddle Earth we use brooms for sweeping.'

'Sweeping,' Joe repeated, unable to keep the disappointment from his voice.

'Sweeping the cheese,' said Randalf enthusiastically. 'Finest Gorgonzola. You see, the centre spoon scoops the cheese, throws it to the graters, who scatter it for the mid-broom, who sweeps the cheese ready for the chimney sweeper to score. Simple!'

'Cheese?' said Joe, baffled. 'Isn't there a ball in broomball?'

'Of course there's a ball,' said Randalf. 'What crazy sort of game would it be without a ball? *And*, of course, a stiltmouse.'

Joe shook his head. 'A stiltmouse,' he repeated quietly. It sounded preposterous. He was beginning to understand why broomball was Muddle Earth's most popular game.

'The stiltmouse inside the ball,' said Randalf, nodding vigorously. 'You see, there are tiny perforations all round the ball, too tiny for the stilt-mouse to see out of, but adequate for it to sniff . . .'

'. . . the cheese,' said Joe.

'Exactly!' said Randalf. 'I told you it was simple. A few practice sessions and you'll take to broomball like a stiltmouse to cheese. Trust me, Joe, I'm a wizard!'

Joe was far from convinced. Still, he'd give it a go. It would pass the time until the lamp-post turned up . . .

'Ta-da!'

It was Norbert, back from the kitchens. Now his supermarket shopping trolley was piled high with stripy pink-iced snugglemuffins. A cheer went up and, as Norbert gave them out, the sound of happy chewing filled the air.

Randalf raised his arms. 'When the school bell rings, afternoon lessons will begin . . .'

Tinklebell put down the snugglemuffin Norbert had just given him with a little sigh, and put his hat with the bell on his head.

Tinkle, tinkle, tinkle . . .

Outside the window, two of the three moons of Muddle Earth rose up in a decidedly dark sky.

'Well I never!' said Randalf. 'Is that the time already?' He frowned. 'It appears that today there is no afternoon. In which case . . .'

'*TING – ER – LING – ER – LING!*' roared Tinklebell at the top of his voice.

Randalf cupped his hands to his mouth and called to the pupils, who were just climbing to their feet, their mouths full of snugglemuffin. 'School's over!' he announced. 'Time for bed!'

He turned back to Joe. 'Sleep well, Joe the Barbarian, warrior-hero,' he said as he jumped down from the throne. 'Broomball practice first thing tomorrow morning.'

'And the wandering lamp-post?' said Joe.

But Randalf had already gone.

Pffffwwp.

Randalf shook his silver whistle and tried again.

Pffffwwp.

'Shall I, sir?' said Tinklebell.

'If you wouldn't mind,' said Randalf.

'*PEEEEEEP!*'

Tinklebell's bellow echoed round Brillig Hovel, rudely awakening the sleeping young barbarians. Joe sat bolt upright and, bleary-eyed, looked up at the wizard standing over him.

'Is it morning already?' he muttered sleepily.

'Certainly is,' said Randalf brightly. 'Sleep well?'

Joe groaned. 'When you said "time for bed" last night, I thought there would be an actual bed to sleep on . . .'

'Excellent, excellent,' said Randalf, who wasn't really listening.

Brillig Hovel's dormitory was in the third pointy tower on the left at the top of the castle. Spread across its dusty floorboards were a collection of fur rugs on which the young barbarians slept – or, in Joe's case, tried to sleep. His rug – which looked as though it had come from a large goat, or a small yak – smelled of barnyards and itched like crazy. What was more, all through the night he'd had to contend with the snoring of the young barbarians around him.

They'd slept all right, all of them, their mouths open and making a raucous cacophony of snorts and snarks – and the occasional burst of sleep-singing. Gabbled bursts of *Food, Disgusting Food, A Dragon-Prodding We Will Go* and *I'm Too Sexy For My Winged Helmet* had woken Joe at regular intervals throughout the night.

Edward Gorgeous, meanwhile, had risen above it all. Literally. He had wrapped himself in a cloak and hung upside down by his ankles from a rafter in the pointy tower's ceiling.

'Come on then, Joe,' Randalf was saying. 'Up you get. Broomball practice before breakfast.'

Joe climbed to his feet and looked around bleary-eyed. The other barbarians snuggled further into their sheepskins and fur rugs and fell back to sleep.

'All set, Joe?' said Randalf. 'Now, where's Edward?'

Joe pointed up at the ceiling, but was surprised to see no sign of him.

'All set, sir,' said a brooding voice directly behind them that made Randalf and Joe both jump.

'As if the helmets weren't bad enough, you have to go

sneaking about like that,' squawked Veronica, who was perched on Randalf's shoulder. 'You barbarians give me the creeps.'

Randalf seemed unconcerned. 'There you are, Edward,' he said. 'Now, come with me over to the broomball pitch and meet your new team-mates. Since Coach Warspanner has left the Perfumed Porkers,' he added, slapping them both on the back, 'I've decided to coach the team myself!'

'Well, we can give up on the Goblet of Porridge then,' said Veronica.

'Shut up, Veronica!' said Randalf, as he turned and bustled out of the dormitory.

Joe and Edward Gorgeous followed him down the windy stairs of the pointy tower. When they reached the first landing, they saw the door to the girls' dormitory was open. Joe glanced inside.

Ella was sitting cross-legged in the middle of the room on a thick, luxuriant fleece, surrounded by entranced barbarian maidens. A battlecat – or possibly a battle*rabbit* – lay on the floor beside them. Ella looked up and smiled dreamily, and Joe saw that she was painting the toenails of the maidens who encircled her with her black nail varnish.

'Joe, it's you,' she said. 'This is the strangest dream I've ever had. And I just can't seem to wake up . . .'

She paused as her gaze met Edward's intense, longing stare.

'Not that I ever want it to end,' Ella breathed. She

smiled. 'You're gorgeous . . .'

'*Edward* Gorgeous,' said Edward, with a little bow. 'We met yesterday, fair maiden.'

'"Fair maiden",' swooned Ella, and around her the barbarian maidens broke into fits of giggles.

Joe had never seen his sister act this way before. But then she'd never travelled through a self-assembly wardrobe into another world before – especially a world like Muddle Earth which, as he knew only too well, could take a little getting used to.

Still, until the lamp-post came back, he and his sister were stuck here, however long that might be. But come to think about it, that shouldn't matter. After all, time moved differently in Muddle Earth. He'd spent ages and ages here the last time, yet when Randalf had finally managed to send him back, only half an hour had passed at home, Joe remembered. So they might as well make the most of it – and if that meant barbarian maidens with black toenails and broomball practice, then so be it . . .

'Come on, you two.' Randalf's voice sailed up from below. 'Last one on the pitch is a pink stinky hoglet!'

Joe and Edward turned and continued down the stairs. They left the tower, crossed the courtyard and walked slap-bang into a group of hunched, hooded figures.

'Watch where you're going, barbarian,' said a soft, menacing voice, and Joe found himself staring into a pair of intense green eyes.

The figures were all dressed the same, in black hoodies pulled down tight, stripy tights beneath ragged black tutus, thick mittens and big clumpy black boots. They barged past Joe and Edward and up the stairs of the pointy tower.

'Who are they?' said Joe.

Edward shrugged. 'They're the jeer-leaders,' he said. 'They keep themselves to themselves.'

Joe followed Edward across the courtyard, through the gate at the far end and on to the field beyond.

Now that the dust and ash from Mount Boom had cleared, Joe could see the broomball pitch more clearly. It was flat and made of clay, with tufts of grass poking up here and there. It had been marked out in a large pink rectangle and criss-crossed with pink wavy lines. At either end was a fireplace, complete with cast-iron grate and brick hearth and stack, and topped off with an earthenware chimney pot. Randalf and Veronica, together with Norbert and three pupils, were waiting for them.

'Norbert,' said Randalf, and snapped his fingers.

Norbert stepped forward. He had a couple of brooms under one arm and a large wicker hamper clamped to his chest, which he set down on the ground with a loud grunt. He unbuckled the lid and pulled it open.

'As I believe I told you, Joe, you're to play mid-broom,' said Randalf and, reaching into the hamper, he pulled out a pink apron, a pair of pink bristle-studded boots and a helmet made out of a triangular wedge of cheese. 'And here's your broom.'

Joe took the broomball kit and put it on. Edward did the same. His kit was the same as Joe's, but the broom Randalf handed him was the type that a chimney sweep would use up a chimney, with a circle of horizontal bristles.

When Joe was changed, Randalf took him by the arm. 'Let me introduce you to your other team-mates. This is Bradley the Big-For-His-Age,' he said, gesturing towards a huge, if rather knock-kneed ogre, whose apron was too short, and who looked as though he was about to burst

into tears. 'This is Percy Throwback,' Randalf continued, indicating the second player. A gap-toothed troll grinned at them eagerly. 'Bradley and Percy are our graters,' said Randalf.

Joe noticed they were both wearing curious pink gloves with cheese-graters stitched into the palms.

Randalf turned to the third team-member. 'And this is our centre spoon, Smutley. With Thragar Warspanner's handpicked team gone, I've handpicked my own team . . .'

'Sure you didn't use your feet?' said Veronica, fluffing up her feathers.

Joe looked at the young goblin called Smutley. Like the others, he wore a pink apron, but instead of a broom, he was holding an extremely long-handled wooden spoon, almost as tall as he was.

'Smutley's from Goblintown,' said Randalf. 'He's old Grubber's son . . .'

'That's Mr Grubley to you,' said Smutley snootily. 'Sir,' he added, his tone insolent.

Joe stifled a laugh. He remembered Grubley and his Discount Garment Store in Goblintown only too well from his last visit to Muddle Earth. It was where he'd been kitted out in clothes that looked almost as ridiculous as those that his son, Smutley, was now wearing.

'Right, let's all warm up.' Randalf jogged on the spot enthusiastically, but within seconds he was red-faced and glistening with sweat.

'You get much warmer, Fatso, and you're going to melt,' Veronica commented, fanning him with a feathered wing.

'Shut *up*, Veronica,' Randalf wheezed. 'Now, I want a dozen sit-downs, a dozen push-overs, and two dozen doodly-squats – and I want to see you working!'

Joe looked round at the others and did as they did, repeatedly sitting down and standing up again, shoving each other in the chest, and then doing a funny little dance that entailed shuffling their feet and looking down at their pink bristle-studded boots.

'Whoops!' Percy exclaimed, as he tripped over his

own feet and landed heavily on his backside. '*Ouch!*' He looked up cheerfully. 'I'm such an oaf.'

'No, you're not,' said Bradley the Big-For-His-Age earnestly. 'You're a troll. Oafs are much squatter. And hairier. One stole my snuggly-wuggly once,' he said, patting the bulge in the pocket of his shorts. 'Anyway, it's me who's the clumsy one.' He sighed. 'I mean, I try my best, but . . .' Tears welled up in his eyes. 'But it's never quite good enough.'

'You said it,' sniffed Smutley, and Joe realized that if Bradley was under-confident, then Smutley was the opposite. The goblin centre spoon clearly considered himself far too good for all of this. The young goblin turned to Randalf. 'When are we going to get down to some real practice?' he demanded.

Randalf ignored him and put his whistle to his mouth. *Pffffwwp.*

'To your positions, everyone!' he called. 'Let's practise some moves.'

Edward, his chimney-sweep brush raised high, walked across to the chimney. Bradley and Percy stopped on a wavy line some distance in front of him and clapped their cheese-grater gloves together. Smutley – who was clutching his long-handled spoon – trotted over to a circle in the middle of the pitch.

'Your position is there, Joe,' said Randalf, pointing to a spot halfway between Smutley and the two graters.

Joe trotted across the pitch, reaching up to stop the cheese helmet slipping over his eyes as he did so.

'Joe, hold your position. Smutley, prepare to scoop. And graters, get ready . . .'

Randalf put his whistle to his mouth again.

Pffffwwp.

Smutley reached out from the centre circle, plunged his spoon into the cheese on Joe's head and dug out a small divot of cheese. He spun round and lobbed it towards Bradley.

'Oh, no,' muttered Bradley as the lump of cheese came flying towards him. 'I'm going to drop it. I'm going to drop it. I know I am. I . . .'

It landed it his hands. He didn't drop it.

Smutley repeated the manoeuvre, lobbing a lump of

cheese at Percy. Percy ran this way, that way, arms raised as the piece of cheese came towards him – then, right at the last moment, tripped and fell. His chin thudded against the hard pitch. The cheese landed in front of him.

'Whoops,' he said, seizing the cheese and scrambling to his feet.

Pffffwwp.

'Get grating!'

Percy and Bradley began rubbing their gloved hands back and forward over their pieces of cheese, sending little grated chips flying into the air.

Pffffwwp.

'Joe, get sweeping!'

Joe raised his broom and dashed towards them.

'Nice tidy little piles of cheese,' Randalf instructed.

Joe stooped down and began sweeping the specks of cheese into a pile.

'Towards the chimney, Joe,' Randalf called out. 'Sweep towards the chimney.'

Joe did his best, as Percy and Bradley grated their lumps of cheese to powder.

Pffffwwp.

'Not bad,' Randalf called out. 'But Smutley, bigger chunks, please, and work on your throw. Bradley, I expect more vigorous grating from you, and Percy, try not to fall over. Joe, that wasn't bad for a first attempt. Back to your positions and let's try that again . . .'

Pffffwwp.

They repeated the moves another five times but, as Smutley scooped cheese from Joe's helmet, whittling it down in size, they actually seemed to be getting worse. Smutley's throws became wilder and Bradley's grating became slower and slower, while Percy seemed to spend most of his time sprawling on the ground saying 'whoops'.

Of all the Perfumed Porkers, only Joe seemed to be improving. Gradually, he was getting the hang of this crazy game, managing to sweep the grated cheese into two, then three, and finally half a dozen of the tiny piles that led towards the chimney place where Edward Gorgeous stood leaning against the mantelpiece and gazing off into the distance, a faraway look in his red-tinged eyes.

'This is hopeless,' Randalf conceded after their sixth attempt, as Smutley's lumps of cheese sailed over their heads, and Bradley and Percy ran into each other and fell over.

'You're not wrong there,' said Veronica. 'I blame the coach.'

Just then, Norbert appeared on the touchline. He had a large ball under one arm and a bell-shaped cage dangled from his outstretched hand.

Pffffwwp.

'At last! The broomball! What kept you, Norbert?' Randalf asked, bustling across to the not very big ogre, and taking the large ball with a small hinged door from him. He frowned. 'And why the glum face?'

Norbert raised the cage high and tapped at the bars

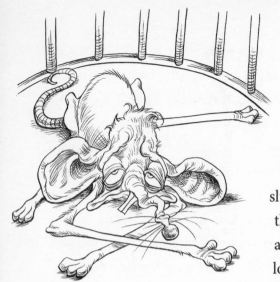

with a finger.

'It's the stiltmouse,' he said tearfully.

Everyone looked at the stiltmouse. It was slumped at the back of the cage, legs splayed and head down. It looked listless and drained of energy.

Randalf sighed. 'Edward . . .' he said.

'What? What?' said Edward Gorgeous, his face turning pink. 'I was somewhere else and you can't prove I wasn't, and anyone who says anything different is telling fibs . . .'

Puzzled, Randalf frowned. 'My dear boy, I was merely going to say that you'll have to practise your chimney sweeping with an empty ball until our stiltmouse recovers.'

'Oh, yes, headmaster,' said Edward Gorgeous, blushing even more furiously.

Randalf turned to Joe and examined what was left of his cheese helmet.

'That's the end of the first truckle,' he announced to the team. 'Norbert, where are the half-time snugglemuffins?'

'Randalf?'

'Yes, Joe?'

The rest of the broomball team had gone off to their lessons, and Joe and Randalf were standing outside the headmaster's study.

'Do we have to wait for the lamp-post to come back?' Joe asked, 'or would this be a good time to go looking for it?'

'Look for it?' said Randalf absent-mindedly, opening the study door.

'Yes,' said Joe. 'Perhaps we could go on a quest, Randalf. In search of the lamp-post. It would be like the old days. We could visit Goblintown, Trollbridge, Elfwood . . .'

'But Joe,' said Randalf, 'first things first. You've got to work on your broom handling. The big match is only two days away . . .'

Joe was about to protest that getting back home was more important to him than sweeping cheese into neat little piles when they were interrupted by a flustered-looking Mr Fluffy, the woodwork teacher.

'Headmaster, headmaster,' he squeaked, chips of wood fluttering to the floor as he shook his head. 'I've been looking for you everywhere . . .'

'No accounting for taste,' sniffed Veronica, who was perched on Randalf's shoulder.

'Well, you've found me now, Mr Fluffy,' said Randalf, ignoring the budgie. 'What is it?'

'I need a word,' he said, his voice low and confidential. 'It's most important.'

'Important?' said Randalf.

'Yes,' said Mr Fluffy, adjusting his small round glasses and smoothing the combed-over hair on his balding head. 'It's a personal matter.' He looked at Joe, and his small moustache twitched with agitation. 'An extremely personal matter . . .'

'My dear Mr Fluffy,' said Randalf, patting the teacher on the shoulder, 'calm yourself and step into my study.' He glanced round at Joe. 'I was just about to show Joe round our little educational establishment, but I'm sure he will excuse me.' He paused. 'Veronica, I don't suppose that *you*—'

'It would be my absolute pleasure,' said the budgie, flapping across to Joe and perching on his shoulder.

'Excellent, excellent,' said Randalf.

He ushered Mr Fluffy into his study, and Joe peeked inside. There was a lumpy-looking sofa in one corner, and an enormous desk with carved lion's feet in the other. Above it was a sign in lopsided writing that read, *You don't have to be mud to wink here, but it helps!*

'Now, do calm down, my dear chap,' Randalf was saying to Mr Fluffy as he followed him inside. 'Come and tell me all about it . . .'

The door closed.

Veronica chirruped happily from Joe's shoulder. 'It's so nice to see you, Joe! We've all missed you – especially old Fatso. Bitten off more than he can chew with this place, I can tell you.' She launched herself from Joe's shoulder and fluttered before him. 'Come with me and I'll show you what I mean.'

Joe followed the budgie along the corridor. They stopped next to a door with a small sign nailed to it. *Magical Manipulation and Deportment*, it said.

'As good a place to start as any,' said Veronica.

Joe turned the door handle and stepped inside.

The room must once have been some sort of games room. There was a dartboard on one wall, a wooden ball and a pile of skittles against another, and a punchbag hanging from the ceiling in the corner. They all had primitive faces drawn on them, together with the name *Ingrid* scrawled underneath.

'What's that *smell*?' said Joe, screwing up his nose.

'That'll be the ping-pong table, I expect,' said Veronica, nodding towards a battered-looking table with two mud-spattered table-tennis bats lying on it.

'Just don't ask what the ping-pong balls are made out of.'

Games room it might once have been, but for the current occupants of the room, the fun and games were clearly over. They were milling about in two groups on either side of the room, their faces blank with boredom, as Mr Shaggymane and Mr Shinyhoof whinnied instructions at them.

'Not like that, Lavinia,' Mr Shaggymane was complaining. 'Shoulders *back*. *Back!* And point your toes. Good heavens, stop hunching, girl!'

Lavinia – an ungainly troll with large tusks – was placing one foot carefully in front of the other as she endeavoured to walk in a graceful straight line without dislodging the heavy book that perched on her head.

'Swish!' Mr Shinyhoof commanded at the other end of the room, 'I want to see you swishing that wizard's gown like you really mean it, Boris. *That's* the way! And a little more elegance with that wand-waving, if you please. You're supposed to be a trainee wizard, not a stallholder at Trollbridge market.'

Boris the Slightly

Bloated, who was draped in a voluminous pink cape and with a small pointy hat perched on his oversized head, looked close to tears.

'I'm trying to swish, sir,' he said. 'I really am.'

'Then try harder, Boris,' said Mr Shinyhoof. 'And Pustule,' he added to a small, tubby goblin. 'How's that beard-combing coming along?'

'It would be a lot easier if I had a beard,' Pustule muttered sulkily, as he mimed a combing motion from his chin to his chest.

Joe watched with bemusement.

'Joe the Barbarian,' Mr Shinyhoof said brightly, trotting over to Joe. 'To what do we owe this honour?'

'Just showing him around, hay-breath,' said Veronica.

'So good of you to take an interest in our little efforts,' said Mr Shaggymane, with a friendly whinny. 'I don't suppose you've got a sugar lump?'

Joe shook his head. 'Sorry,' he said.

Suddenly, there was a loud crash and a distressed 'Whoops-a-daisy!' and everyone looked round to see Boris and Lavinia lying on the floor, their limbs entangled. The heavy book from Lavinia's head landed on Boris the Slightly Bloated's foot, and he burst into tears.

'My toe,' he wailed. 'My poor toe!'

Mr Shinyhoof and Mr Shaggymane glared at one another. Mr Shinyhoof pawed at the floor. Mr Shaggymane tossed his head.

'*If* you could keep your deportment class on your side

of the room, I should be *most* grateful,' Mr Shinyhoof said, his words clipped and sibilant.

'Certainly, Mr Shinyhoof,' said Mr Shaggymane. 'And I'd be most grateful if you could keep your wand-waving and gown-swishing class on *your* side of the room . . .'

Joe and Veronica left the two centaurs glaring at each other as their two classes became entangled in an increasingly chaotic scrum in the middle of the room.

'They'll probably settle it over a game of ping-pong,' Veronica cheeped in Joe's ear as they slipped out of the classroom. 'And we definitely don't want to stay for that!'

Joe closed the door behind him.

'Over there next,' said Veronica, flapping a wing at the door opposite.

There was a single word written on it: *Divination*.

'Divination?' said Joe.

'Don't ask me,' said Veronica. 'All they ever seem to do is sit about and try to see into the future.'

The pair of them stepped inside, and Joe looked around. A scuffed leather chair stood behind a desk to the right of the door, upon it, a gold and green reading lamp, while behind it the wall was lined with rows and rows of oak bookshelves, almost all of them empty. The Horned Baron had clearly not been much of a reader, for there were only four books that Joe could see.

Mucky Maud's Songbook. *The Horned Helmet Autumn Catalogue*. A well-thumbed picture book called *Binky the Bunny's Big Birthday Surprise*. And a small battered book with a green cover and no title.

The class in progress looked about as exciting as the books. Mr Polly the cyclops, who was dressed in a sparkly waistcoat and a stripy gown, was dabbing his eye with a large spotted handkerchief and pleading for quiet.

'Hush now, everyone,' he said tearfully. 'Now tell me, Gretchen, what can you see?'

The small goblin looked around. 'Nuffing,' she said. 'I can't see nuffing.' She poked at the large crystal ball that stood on a small table before her. 'Not a sausage!'

'Ah, maybe that's the problem,' said Mr Polly. 'Don't restrict yourself to looking for savoury titbits . . .'

'There's nuffing there at all,' said Gretchen stubbornly, as she stared fixedly into the glass ball.

The other pupils clustered about her were becoming restless. Mr Polly dabbed agitatedly at his eye.

'Do stop shoving, Bernard,' he said. 'You'll have your chance. And Flotsam, stop picking Felicity's nose . . .' He turned his attention back to Gretchen. 'Try polishing it,' he said, and handed her his handkerchief.

Gretchen wiped the moist cloth over the glass. 'Still nuffing,' she said a moment later, and handed it back.

'Bernard,' Mr Polly complained. 'I won't tell you again. And Igor—'

'It's Hagar,' said Hagar.

'Well, whatever you name is, put it away at once. It smells.' He frowned bleakly. 'Perhaps if we move the crystal ball closer to the light.'

He stepped forward and, with a grunt of effort, picked up the table, the stand, the crystal ball and all, and heaved it over to the window. The pupils went with him, shoving and sniggering as they went.

'Can anyone see anything now?'

A chorus of bored *no*s filled the air. The sniggering grew louder.

'Hagar, I told you to put that stinky hoglet away,' said Mr Polly. 'You know the rule about pets.'

'But it's the school mascot, sir,' said Hagar.

Mr Polly sighed and dabbed at his eye. 'Are you *sure* there's nothing there?'

'Yes,' came the chorus of voices. 'Nothing.'

'Oh, this is too much,' Mr Polly whimpered tearfully, emotion getting the better of him. 'I suppose it's my fault really.' He sniffed. 'I just don't have the gift ... Completely useless. I should give up and go back to my cave ...'

'Not such a bad idea,' Veronica whispered in Joe's ear. 'Though he's so short-sighted, he probably couldn't find his way back there if he wanted to.'

'Sir, sir,' said Gretchen enthusiastically, 'I think I *can* see something.'

'You can?' said Mr Polly keenly. 'But that's wonderful! Are the mists clearing? Is the future being revealed? *What* can you see?'

'A barbarian boy with a budgie on his shoulder,' said Gretchen. 'And they're standing over there.'

Mr Polly shook his head mournfully as he caught sight of Joe and Veronica.

'Hello,' he said gloomily.

'This is Joe,' said Veronica. 'Joe the Barbarian. I'm just showing him round.'

'Yes, well,' said Mr Polly, turning back to the crystal ball with a shrug and a barely stifled sob. 'There's nothing much to see here.'

Nobody noticed Joe or Veronica leave the classroom. Joe quietly closed the door and they crossed the corridor to the door opposite, which had the word *ART* painted on it in lopsided writing.

The room inside was long and thin and high-ceilinged. It had clearly once been some kind of armoury, for there were shields on the walls, and a collection of blunt axes, stubby spears, rusting chain-mail and broken swords piled in a heap in the corner.

A large piece of cloth had been unrolled and laid out upon the floor. Kneeling along its length were the young ogres, trolls, goblins and barbarians of Mr Chiaroscuro's art class, with brushes in their hands and paint pots by their sides.

Mr Chiaroscuro the art master was standing over

them, directing their every movement with flamboyant movements of his own. 'Put more expression into your brush strokes, Sprinkle!' he commanded. 'And don't drip, Grizelda!'

He noticed Joe and his eyebrows shot up. 'Ah, if it isn't the headmaster's favourite barbarian,' he said, flouncing towards him. 'We're making a banner for the Goblet of Porridge match.' Mr Chiaroscuro frowned and put his hands on his hips. 'Ogbert, will you *stop* drinking the paint.'

'No wonder we have problems with the toilets,' Veronica observed.

Mr Chiaroscuro reached into his pockets and sprinkled a handful of glitter on to the wet paint, before surveying the banner. 'Go, Perfumed Porkers!' he read out loud, and smiled at Joe. 'With this minimalist yet profound and intricately chromatic design, I feel I have captured the very essence of sporting conflict.' His voice dropped to a reverent whisper. 'I may well have created my greatest work . . .'

Joe looked at the banner.

GOO, BARFUMB DORKLERS, it read in lopsided glittery letters.

'It's very . . . very . . .' Joe struggled to find something to say.

'Glittery,' said Veronica. 'Come on, Joe. Let's leave Mr Chiaroscuro to his masterpiece.'

They crossed the corridor again and came to a door with the words *Good Wizardkeeping* written in tiny, neat handwriting on the doorknob. Joe pulled the door open, and was about to enter. But couldn't. There simply wasn't room.

Twenty-two pupils and Miss Balsamic, Stinkyhogs's Good Wizardkeeping teacher, were crammed inside a space no bigger than a broom cupboard. In fact, judging by the brooms that lined the walls and hung down from the ceiling, it *was* a broom cupboard.

'To harness the true power of the broom, young wizards-to-be,' Miss Balsamic was saying, her voice shrill and downy top lip quivering, 'one needs an incantation of rare and unsurpassed power . . . which, unfortunately, I do not possess. So for now, take the broom by the handle and introduce a sweeping motion, thus . . .'

Joe closed the door quietly. He looked at Veronica. 'Next,' he said, then almost tripped over the wiry inter-elf as it went scurrying past them.

'Goggle, goggle, goggle . . .' it was squeaking. 'The capital of Gothslavia. The capital of Gothslavia . . .'

Joe and Veronica went back across the corridor and Joe opened a door marked *Poultices and Potions*. Miss Eudora Pinkwhistle was standing in the centre of a glass conservatory, surrounded by her class and swathed in the steam that coiled up from a huge bubbling cauldron in front of her. Behind her, two huge earthenware pots held great writhing plants which, as Joe stared, gulped and snatched at the air with serrated mouths, as lazy bumblebees buzzed around them.

Eudora Pinkwhistle was concentrating so hard she didn't notice them. Dressed in a flapping black gown decorated with various silver squiggles, she was plucking the ingredients from a collection of jars beside her.

'*Eye of newt and toe of frog,*' she chanted, sprinkling things into the pot and stirring it with a long wooden spoon. '*Hair of cat and whisker of sheep, accountant's dandruff and bank manager's navel fluff . . .*'

The cauldron hissed and steamed as more items plopped down into the bubbling concoction. Joe watched, fascinated.

'She looks like a real witch,' he said, impressed.

'If you take my advice, Joe,' said Veronica, 'you'll avoid witches. They're nothing but bubble, bubble, toil and trouble!' She eyed Slocum warily as Eudora Pinkwhistle's black cat performed slinky figures-of-eight around her mistress's ankles. 'And you should see where she lives! A horrible little house in the middle of Elfwood made of cake . . .'

'What, like a fairy-tale gingerbread house,' said Joe, 'with barley-sugar windows and a candy roof?'

'Sort of,' said Veronica. 'Only her gingerbread is stale and decorated with cough sweets and throat lozenges . . .'

Joe was impressed nevertheless. Unlike any of the other teachers, Eudora Pinkwhistle actually seemed to know what she was doing.

'*Bubble, bubble, toil and trouble!*' she cackled, stirring the pot as her class stared down into it.

'Told you,' said Veronica. 'Come on, Joe, I've had enough of this.'

Behind them, one of the carnivorous plants caught a bumblebee and swallowed it noisily. Joe seized the door handle, then hesitated.

'What kind of magical potion is she making, anyway?' he asked, fascinated.

'Magical potion?' Veronica snorted. 'That's no magical potion. That's a face pack for Ingrid!'

Back outside, they were about to cross the corridor again when Randalf's study door opened, and he and Mr Fluffy emerged.

'I'm absolutely sure there's nothing to worry about, my dear fellow,' Randalf was saying, patting Mr Fluffy on the shoulder. 'And if you should start to feel a little twitchy, then come and see me. My door is always open.'

'Well, don't say I didn't warn you,' said Mr Fluffy as he turned away and shuffled off along the corridor.

Joe watched him. In his tweed jacket with the leather

patches at the elbows, his baggy grey corduroy trousers, brown tie and sensible shoes, the woodwork teacher looked as if he belonged in Joe's world rather than here in Muddle Earth.

'I don't know,' said Randalf, closing his study door and locking it. 'There's something not quite right about that man.' Sweeping back his cloak and adjusting his broad-brimmed pointy hat, Randalf turned to Joe. 'I mean, just look at the outlandish outfit he's wearing!'

'So, if I'm *not* dreaming,' Ella said, her voice rising in alarm, 'then . . . then I must be in a coma! Yes, that's it!' She jumped on to the table, scattering bowls of lumpy stew in all directions. 'I'm in a *coma*!'

Her hair was braided and she was wearing a fur cape and had various bangles on her wrists, heavy twists of plaited silver that were decorated with writhing dragons and snarling wolves. Around her, the barbarian maidens of Brillig Hovel gasped and stifled their giggles behind their black-fingernailed hands.

'That stupid wardrobe must have collapsed on top of me and knocked me out,' Ella was saying. 'I'm in a hospital bed hooked up to a machine with blinking lights and bleeping sounds! This is all a figment of my imagination! None of this is . . . *Blurrghh!*'

A dollop of steaming stew hit Ella full in the face.

'Thirds!' called Norbert happily, as he wheeled his shopping trolley between the tables, throwing stew

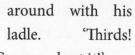

around with his ladle. 'Thirds! Come and get it!'

It was lunchtime. With the tour of the school over, Joe had been sitting at high table along with the staff of Stinkyhogs – apart from Mr Fluffy, whose chair was empty, and who Joe had last seen half an hour earlier, sneaking furtively down the corridor with an armful of timber. When he'd spotted Ella, she had beckoned to him agitatedly and, with a deep sigh and a sinking feeling, Joe had gone to talk to her.

'Calm down, Ella,' Joe told his sister now, taking her hand and helping her from the table.

A dollop of stew flew through the air towards him, only to be intercepted by an open-mouthed troll who bobbed up at the last moment and swallowed it.

'You're not in a coma,' Joe reassured Ella. 'You're in Muddle Earth.'

Beneath the mask of dripping stew, Ella's lower lip trembled. 'But I don't *want* to be in Muddle Earth, Joe,' she said. 'I want to be back home. I've got stuff to do. People to see . . .'

'I know, I know,' Joe said soothingly, patting her hand. 'And I've spoken to Randalf. If we can just track down the wandering lamp-post, then we'll find the portal, which'll lead us back into the wardrobe – and home.'

But Ella was no longer listening. Instead, she was staring at the barbarian maidens, who were sloshing stew into each other's faces and looking up at her expectantly.

'This place is totally weird,' she muttered.

'Things *are* a bit different here,' Joe conceded.

'You're not kidding.' Ella scowled. 'This lot follow me around everywhere and copy whatever I do.'

'They think you're cool,' said Joe, hoping to change the subject. 'Which you are. You're their style icon, Ella. A cool barbarian princess.'

'Barbarian princess?' said Ella, her face brightening beneath the dripping stew. 'Mmm . . . I think I like the sound of that . . .'

'Me too,' said Edward Gorgeous, who had just entered the hall.

He stopped before her, performed a small bow and offered her his handkerchief. Ella gave him a soppy smile.

'Edward,' she said.

She took the handkerchief and wiped the stew off her face, while Edward stared intently, his eyes smouldering from beneath a brooding, furrowed brow. He looked pale and his dark-ringed eyes had a reddish tinge.

Ella held out the handkerchief. Edward trembled, leaning forward as if to kiss Ella's outstretched hand. But before he could, he was interrupted by a barbarian maiden, who snatched the handkerchief away and wiped her own face with it, giggling as she did so. The other barbarian maidens scrambled over one another as, each in turn, they tried to snatch the handkerchief to wipe their own faces, just like Ella had done.

Ignoring them, Edward sat down on the bench and Ella sat beside him. He took a tomato from his pocket and put it to his lips, and began to slowly suck on it, his expression more brooding than ever.

'Is something the matter?' asked Ella, all thoughts of getting home seemingly vanished from her head.

Edward squeezed the tomato and sucked hard for a moment before replying.

'It's those Galloping Unicorns,' he said darkly.

'Galloping unicorns?' said Joe.

Edward nodded. 'The broomball team from Golden Towers Finishing School for Little Princes and Princesses,' he said, his top lip curling with distaste. 'They think they're better than everyone else – wafting around in their flowing robes and glittery crowns, putting on airs and graces, paying barbarians to play on their team for them . . .'

He raised his head and dropped the sucked-dry remains of the tomato on to the table.

'I really thought the Porkers had a chance of beating them this year,' Edward continued. 'You see, I recruited the biggest, brawniest barbarians I knew to play on the Stinkyhogs team with me. We were unbeatable. That's why I talked the headmaster into issuing the challenge to Golden Towers . . .' He shook his head. 'I should have known those snobs wouldn't play fair. They poached my barbarian team-mates by offering them bags of gold rather than the free wizardry and woodwork lessons that I'd persuaded the headmaster to offer them. Now we're going to lose,' he said bitterly. 'And it's all my fault!'

Ella reached out and took his hand. 'You'll do your best, Edward,' she said. 'I know you will. And I'll be there to support you,' she added. 'You can count on me.'

'I can?' said Edward, smiling. He looked down at her hand and trembled as he pulled his own hand away. He thrust it into his pocket and pulled out a second tomato, and the sound of slurping filled the air as he moodily sucked it dry.

Bang! Bang! Bang!

'What is that awful racket?'

Bang! Bang! Clatter!

'Him.' A gloved hand pointed. 'That crackpot woodwork teacher. Old wossisname . . .'

'Mr Fluffy.'

CRASH!

'Ouch!'

'Mr Butterfingers, more like!'

The four jeer-leaders were sitting on the ground on the far side of the courtyard, their backs against the wall. Their hoods were up and their faces were in shadow.

'I'll tell you what,' said Thistle. 'If I have to sit through another lesson about dovetail joints and dowelling, I'm going to get extra prickly.'

'It's that witch I can't bear,' said Nettle. 'I'll bring her out in a nasty rash if she's not careful.'

'And Mr Polly!' said Briar-Rose, who was idly plucking red and purple wallflowers one by one. 'What a crybaby!' She shook her head. 'I'd like to give him a thorny problem he'll never forget.'

'Hold on to your petals,' said Pesticide, her voice calm and determined. 'None of this will be for much longer.'

'Too long for my liking,' said Nettle gruffly.

'All this jeer-leading is getting me down,' said Thistle. 'I think I'm going to scream if I have to wave another pink stinky hoglet about. I mean, as if the smell's not bad enough, that squealing . . .'

'Like I said,' Pesticide told her. 'It's not for much longer. The Goblet of Porridge match is the day after tomorrow.'

Briar-Rose plucked a tall yellow flower, sniffed it, then added it to the rest. 'What about that new barbarian boy and his sister?' she said.

'They won't give us any trouble,' Pesticide assured her. 'As soon as the match begins, we can make our move.'

The banging and clattering stopped for a moment. There was a sound of sawing. Then the banging started up again.

'And you don't think anyone suspects?' said Thistle.

Pesticide shook her head. 'Nah,' she said, pulling down her hood. 'Not in these disguises. Besides,' she added, 'if anyone stands in our way . . .'

She pulled off one of her mittens and touched a fingertip to the flowers in Briar-Rose's hand. Instantly, the flowers wilted. Their leaves turned brown. Their petals dropped. A moment later, the whole bunch had turned to mush.

Pesticide giggled unpleasantly. 'They'll get a nasty surprise.'

Pffffwwp.

'Gather round, team! Now for some chimney-sweeping practice. Edward, take up your position. The rest of you, observe closely.'

Randalf removed the stiltmouse from the cage he was holding. It wriggled in his grasp, its long nose twitching.

'Eeek,' it squeaked.

'Hear that?' said Randalf. 'It's fully recovered and can't wait to get at that cheese!'

He put down the cage, and Norbert stepped forward with the large round broomball in his hand. The door in the side of the ball was open. Randalf pushed the stiltmouse inside the ball and clicked the little door back into place.

Joe looked round to see that Edward Gorgeous had already taken up his position beside the chimney. He was leaning nonchalantly against the fireplace, an elbow on the mantelpiece, his broom resting on his shoulder.

Bang! Bang! Bang!

Bang! Bang! . . . Crunch!

Joe turned in the direction of the noise and caught sight of Mr Fluffy. The woodwork teacher was standing on the far side of the courtyard surrounded by timber, which he was furiously nailing together to construct what looked like a primitive Ferris wheel.

'What's he *doing*?' said Joe.

'Making a cartwheel by the look of it,' said Randalf. 'For a very large cart . . .' He shrugged. 'Highly strung, our Mr Fluffy,' he added, placing the ball gently down on the ground. 'Hasn't been feeling himself lately. Still, good to see he's keeping busy.'

He raised his whistle to his mouth and blew.

Pffffwwp.

At first nothing happened. Then nothing happened again. But then the ball started to tremble as the stiltmouse inside took its first tentative steps.

'Eeek,' it squeaked as it picked up the scent of the trail of grated cheese that snaked across the broomball pitch towards the chimney, where Edward stood languidly examining his fingernails.

'Eeek. Eeek.'

The stiltmouse trotted on its thin, spindly legs, following the smell of the cheese and propelling the ball towards the chimney.

'Eeek!'

The ball trundled into the fireplace . . .

All at once, with the agility of a cat, Edward dropped to his knees and swept the broomball up the chimney with his chimney-sweeping brush.

'Eeek! Eeek!'

Reaching behind him, Edward took three extra lengths of the brush handle. He clicked one, then another, then the third dexterously into place, all the while sweeping the broomball higher and higher up the chimney.

'*Eeeeeeeek!*'

In a flurry of soot, the broomball flew out of the top of the chimney pot and up into the air. Edward let go of the brush, jumped to his feet and, as the ball came down, he caught it in one hand. Then, with a smile on his handsome face, he held it up.

'Bravo!' Randalf exclaimed. He strode across the field. 'Excellent sweeping, Edward,' he said. 'Well done! The rest of you, you need to brush up on your moves. There's only one day to go to the big match, and I know you won't let me down! Go, Perfumed Porkers!'

'Give me a *B*. Give me an *O*. Give me another *O*. What have we got?'

'*BOO!*'

A row of four hunched and hooded figures in black tutus, stripy tights and big clumpy boots had sidled out of the courtyard, and now stood at the edge of the pitch. Each held a pair of pink stinky hoglets in their gloved hands, which they were waving half-heartedly above their heads.

'You're rubbish, and you know you are!' they jeered.

'They've got a point,' said Smutley, the centre spoon, nudging Bradley the grater as the broomball team trudged from the field and headed back towards the courtyard.

In the sky above them, the yellow moon of Muddle Earth rose and poured down its light like melted butter. It was followed by the purple moon and, moments later, the sudden appearance of the third moon of Muddle Earth – the green one – which peeked up uncertainly over the horizon for a moment, before rising slowly and deliberately into the sky. It came to rest next to the others. The three of them formed a perfect equilateral triangle.

'*Aaaiiiooowww!*'

An unearthly howl split the air. Bradley the grater cried out and hugged his snuggly-wuggly tight. Percy, the other grater, tripped over his own feet and went sprawling. All eyes turned towards the courtyard where the strangulated, high-pitched howling seemed to be coming from.

Joe gasped.

'*Aaaaiiiioooowwww . . .*'

'It's Mr Fluffy!' Joe exclaimed.

Randalf and the others turned to the courtyard and squinted into the yellow, purple and green moonlight.

'*Aaaiiiooowww!*'

'Randalf?' Ingrid's voice rang out from the top of the castle. 'Randalf! What *is* that appalling racket?'

But Randalf was lost for words. There in the courtyard, next to the strange homemade Ferris wheel, stood Mr Fluffy. At least, what passed for Mr Fluffy. For, as the broomball team and the jeer-leaders watched open-mouthed, the mild-mannered woodwork teacher was transforming before their eyes. He'd thrown off his tweed jacket and was now down on all fours, arching his back and howling at the triple moons.

'Poor chap told me he was feeling a little peculiar,' Randalf babbled, finding his voice. 'Talked about his urge to make nests and chew chair legs.' He shook his head. 'But I didn't realize things were quite *this* bad . . .'

'*Aaaiiiooowww!*'

The yellow, purple and green light gleamed on Mr Fluffy's contorted features.

'I don't like the look of him,' chirruped Veronica, fluttering above Randalf's head. 'But then again, I never did.'

As Joe watched, Mr Fluffy's eyes began to change. They shrank in size and darkened, until they were as small and bright as two black pebbles, then seemed to shift round to the sides of his head. His nose thrust forward into a quivering snout, his cheeks swelled to an enormous size and his front teeth grew incredibly long. Mr Fluffy buried his head in his paws, which had become dainty and downy, with little claws at the tips.

There were gasps of astonishment.

The woodwork teacher's face was now covered in thick golden fur. Fine whiskers glinted in the coloured light as his nose twitched. His beady eyes looked around furtively and his teeth snapped at the air. Ripples of movement pulsed inside his shirt and down the legs of his trousers. Then there was a long, loud ripping sound as Mr Fluffy burst out of his clothes, to reveal the thick golden fur that now covered him, back and front, from stubby neck to swollen belly.

'I want my mummy!' cried Bradley the grater and burst into tears.

Joe stared at Mr Fluffy. He was furry and stout, with protruding front teeth and a stubby tail. He had transformed into . . .

'A hamster,' Joe murmured.

'A *were*hamster,' said Edward Gorgeous quietly.

'What, like a werewolf?' said Joe.

'Yes,' said Edward darkly. 'But fatter and sleepier.'

'That's as may be,' said Randalf, shaking his head, 'but I'm not sure such a creature has a place in a modern educational establishment . . .'

'Just as well he turned up in this dump, then,' said Veronica.

At that moment, Mr Fluffy scurried over to the wooden construction – which Joe now saw was a giant hamster wheel – and started running.

The wheel turned. Mr Fluffy went faster – and faster, his stubby legs becoming a blur as the wheel spun. He ran as though his very life depended on it. Then he opened his mouth, raised his head to the triple moons and . . .

'*AAAIIIOOOWWW!!!*' he howled.

'They're still at it,' King Peter noted. 'You've got to hand it to that barbarian chap Warspanner, he certainly knows his broomball. Worth every single muckle we're paying him.'

Queen Susan, who was reclining on an upholstered velvet couch, carefully peeling a grape, grimaced. 'Oh, but he's so uncouth, Peter. His fingernails are filthy and I'll wager a comb has never even been *near* his hair.'

'All barbawians are twuly howwid,' Queen Lucy said

primly, her nose wrinkling with distaste. '*And* they smell.'

'Whffffll mfflshlmm,' King Edmund mumbled, either in agreement or not, as he pushed a large lump of Turkish delight into his mouth.

'Block and sweep!' coach Thragar Warspanner was bellowing at his mid-broom, Charlie Battlepants. 'Use that spoon like you really mean it!' he shouted at Thrasher, the centre spoon. '*Destroy* the cheese! And you two!' he hollered at Olga Onionbreath and Rufus Hairyear. 'Grate and shove! Grate and shove!'

For all his bluster, Thragar Warspanner could see that the Galloping Unicorns were looking good. But then they did have the best coach money could buy . . .

Thragar puffed out his big barbarian chest and pushed his winged helmet to a jaunty angle on his head.

When that old fraud Randalfus Rumblebore had recruited him as the games master at that crackpot school of his, he had no idea what an excellent broomball team Thragar would build. Of course, Edward Gorgeous had helped, and Thragar was disappointed when his star chimney-sweeper had resolutely refused to leave Stinkyhogs and come with him and the rest of the team to Golden Towers.

He'd had to replace him with a minotaur from the castle kitchens, Tiny Bighorn, who was big on brawn but short on brains. Not that Thragar Warspanner was worried. Edward Gorgeous or Tiny Bighorn – either way, the Galloping Unicorns would wipe the floor with whatever team Stinkyhogs could find to put up against them.

'Use the *broom*, Tiny,' Thragar bellowed as the minotaur shoved his horned head up the chimney. 'And try not to squash the stiltmouse again!'

King Peter turned from the window of the opulent throne room, with its gilt-framed mirrors, its tapestries and rugs and glittering chandelier. He surveyed his brother and two sisters, who were lounging on three of the ornate plush velvet thrones.

'Looks quite good fun. I'm almost tempted to join in myself . . .' He patted his yawning mouth. 'If I could be bothered.' He sighed. 'Which I can't.'

'Just as well, I say,' Queen Susan said. 'You'd only get yourself all dirty, Peter. And you know how difficult cheese stains are to remove . . .'

'It's such a fwightful bore having those barbawians here,' Lucy commented, as a pair of fauns fanned her with white feathers on the end of sticks.

'We had no choice, Lucy,' said Peter. 'Not if we're going to win the broomball match . . .'

'Oh, bwoomball,' said Queen Lucy. She rang the small bell that stood by her side to summon one of the attendant centaurs to minister to her sudden desire for camomile tea. 'Such a wough, vulgar game,' she said. 'All that sweating and gwunting and gwoaning. And all for what? A Goblet of Powwidge. I don't even *like* powwidge . . .'

'Mfflll bwwlch,' said King Edmund enthusiastically,

and patted his enormous stomach.

'Yes, we all know *you* do, Edmund,' said Queen Susan with a little laugh.

'It isn't just the Goblet of Porridge, Lucy, as you well know,' said Peter. 'It's the prestige. Golden Towers *always* wins the Goblet of Porridge. It's traditional. We beat the Muckspreader Agricultural College of Trollbridge last year, Goblintown's Sir Bartleby Snot's Uncomprehensive the year before that, St Keef's Ogre School of Rock the year before that . . .' He smiled. 'We beat any school that challenges us.'

Queen Lucy shrugged listlessly. 'Only because you bwing in howwid smelly barbawians,' she said.

King Peter plucked at his cuffs and inspected his nails. 'Well, you surely don't expect our little princes and princesses to get all dirty, do you?'

'They might graze their knees,' said Queen Susan, popping the peeled grape into her mouth. 'Or hurt their hair.'

Golden Towers Finishing School for Little Princes and Princesses prided itself on its standards. Only the most exquisite individuals met the strict entry requirements of beauty, languor and general wonderfulness. Those who were accepted were educated by handpicked teachers in the subjects of indolent lolling, divine reclining, sighing, pouting and being exquisite. Broomball was not their thing. It was much too rough – at least, it was too rough the way Thragar Warspanner and his barbarian team played it.

'This year, the Stinkyhogs School of Wizardry challenged us,' King Peter told her. 'I tell you, Lucy,' he went on, 'I've been a trifle concerned of late. With the Horned Baron gone, those wizards think they're in charge, and they need to be put in their place. Luckily, Warspanner understands my point of view. When the Galloping Unicorns are finished with them, Stinkyhogs School of Wizardry will be a laughing stock!'

He sighed and put a silk sleeve to his brow as though exhausted by his mild outburst.

'Wwmmff bllokk,' mumbled King Edmund, stuffing the last piece of Turkish delight into his mouth, and reaching out for another box.

'Well said, Edmund,' King Peter chuckled, then glanced back out of the window, to see that coach Warspanner had brought the practice session to a close.

The broomball team were tramping back to their modest quarters in the east wing at the back of the castle, passing rowdily through the scented gardens as they went.

'I say, you chaps,' King Peter called out. 'Be careful of those roses . . .'

'Oh, they're not twampling the woses, are they?' Lucy said indignantly. 'This is too much. The chwysanthemums still haven't wecovered fwom last time . . .'

'As long as they don't teach the princes and princesses any more of those dreadful songs of theirs. I caught Edwina Lovely singing *Beowulf's Biggest Bottom-Burp* just this morning,' said Queen Susan, climbing slowly to her feet and joining King Peter at the window.

The pair of them looked down fondly at the gathering of pupils who, under the watchful eye of Big Lady Fauntleroy, were in the middle of a moonlit swanning-about lesson. Princes Caspian, Adrian and Toby were sniffing flowers. Princess Camilla was reclining in the gazebo, her empty ambrosia glass being topped up by a centaur in a black cummerbund and bow-tie, while her friend, Princess Guinevere sat beside her, languidly running her fingers through her long auburn hair. To the left of the gardens, Prince Rupert was strolling along one of the narrow winding paths, his nose buried in a book of romantic verse.

'Poo, what's that howwid pong?' Queen Lucy exclaimed, getting the fauns to fan her all the more vigorously.

The next moment, the door to the chamber burst

open. King Peter and Queen Lucy turned to see Thragar Warspanner standing in the doorway.

'Might have known,' Queen Lucy said, her voice muffled by the silken handkerchief she had pressed to her dainty nose. 'Thwagar . . .'

King Peter waved airily. 'Thragar Warspanner,' he said. 'How goes it?'

'Coming along very nicely, sire!' Thragar bellowed back, then chuckled. 'The Perfumed Porkers don't stand a chance.'

Queen Lucy winced and clamped her hands over her ears. 'He's an absolute bwute,' she mouthed to Queen Susan.

King Edmund rolled his great big fat body over to one side, and shoved two more lumps of Turkish delight into his mouth.

'Excellent,' said King Peter, as he crossed the room and stood in front of an exquisitely carved, glass-fronted trophy case and gazed at the rather battered little cup

The Goblet of Porridge

with a broad base inside. 'In that case, the day after tomorrow, when we've won the match, the Goblet of Porridge will return to where it belongs.' A little smile plucked at the corners of his mouth. 'Here. With those who have the taste and refinement to appreciate it.'

Behind him, King Edmund belched noisily.

The three moons of Muddle Earth were setting over the Musty Mountains. The sun was getting ready to rise.

Back at the Stinkyhogs School of Wizardry, a soft whiffling snore came from the corner of the courtyard, where a portly man in a pair of spotty underpants curled up in a nest of straw. A tweed jacket with leather patches at the sleeves was neatly folded by his side.

'Faster,' he murmured in his sleep. 'Faster . . .'

'Might I have a word, headmaster?' said Mr Polly.
The cyclops looked on the verge of tears – but then that was nothing new.

'A word?' said Randalf, who had been hurrying along the corridor with Joe when Mr Polly had stepped out of the teachers' room and blocked his path.

'Well, several words, actually,' said Mr Polly, his voice cracking with emotion. 'We're all terribly, terribly worried, not to mention upset . . .'

'Yes, well, we're awfully busy with broomball practice, aren't we, Joe?' Randalf blustered. 'Big match tomorrow and plenty to brush up on!'

'You're not kidding, Fatso,' chirruped Veronica from her perch on Randalf's pointy hat.

'That's what we'd like to talk to you about; the staff, I mean,' said Mr Polly, his eye welling up with tears. 'If you wouldn't mind, headmaster.'

The massive cyclops ushered Randalf into the teachers' room. Joe followed. The teachers of Stinkyhogs School of Wizardry were waiting, grim-faced. Eudora Pinkwhistle stepped forward and held out a crumpled piece of paper which seemed to have been nibbled at the edges.

'Mr Fluffy came across this in a waste-paper basket, headmaster,' the witch said.

'I was looking for nesting materials,' Mr Fluffy explained, stroking the stiltmouse that was poking its head out of the breast pocket of his tweed jacket. 'I'm afraid it's a little chewed. I couldn't help myself . . .'

'But perfectly legible,' said Eudora Pinkwhistle, clamping her black cat, Slocum, firmly under one arm and proceeding to read: '. . . *unless Stinkyhogs School of Wizardry triumphs in the forthcoming tournament . . . Ahem! . . . then you will leave me no alternative but to close the school. In that unfortunate event you'll have let not only me down, my fellow wizards down, but worst of all you will have let yourself down!! And Muddle Earth too! Yours sincerely, Roger the Wrink.*'

'Roger the Wrink?' said Randalf, going red in the face. 'I'm not sure I know a Roger the Wrink.'

'Roger the Wrinkled,' said Mr Fluffy. 'I'm afraid I nibbled the last bit.'

Joe nodded. He knew all about Roger the Wrinkled. He was head wizard of Muddle Earth, and Randalf's boss – and judging by the letter, he didn't seem happy. The broomball match was even more important than Joe had imagined. If the Perfumed Porkers didn't win the match, then the school would be closed! And Joe didn't want to let Randalf down.

Mr Polly looked up, tears in his eye. 'Close the school,' he repeated. 'I didn't see *this* coming.'

'None of us did,' said Miss Balsamic, who was clutching a broom which bucked and swayed in her grasp.

'And it comes straight from the horse's mouth,' said Mr Shinyhoof, snatching the broomball Mr Shaggymane was holding.

Mr Shaggymane rolled his eyes. 'Have I ever told you how much I hate that expression?' he whinnied, snatching it back.

'Anyway, we've put our heads together,' said Mr Shaggymane and Mr Shinyhoof in unison as they tussled over the broomball.

Tutting loudly, Mr Chiaroscuro wrested it from them and handed it to Mr Fluffy.

'And we've come up with a plan,' said Eudora Pinkwhistle, patting the pocket of the large black apron she was wearing. 'To the broomball pitch!' she announced, and strode towards the teachers' room door.

Intrigued, Randalf went with her, and the others followed.

They crossed the courtyard, where the jeer-leaders were huddled together, whispering furtively, and continued out on to the broomball pitch. Smutley, Bradley, Percy and Edward Gorgeous were waiting for them.

'Only one day to go,' said Edward broodingly.

'Yes, I know,' said Randalf in his most cheerful voice. 'And it seems my staff want to do their little bit to help.' He turned to the teachers. 'So, what do you have in mind? An uplifting banner, Mr Chiaroscuro? Or maybe a helpful premonition, Mr Polly?'

Mr Polly was standing stock-still and wide-eyed as he stared into the transparent hog bladder globe in his hands. 'The mists are clearing,' he was saying. 'I can see . . . see . . . a stiltmouse. A stiltmouse with beady eyes and a twitching nose . . .'

'That's the broomball, Mr Polly,' said Eudora Pinkwhistle, taking it away.

Mr Polly swallowed, then dabbed at his eye. 'I . . . I knew that,' he said, trying to sound dignified. 'I was just holding it for Mr Fluffy.'

'Eeek,' said the stiltmouse inside the broomball.

'Mr Fluffy,' said Eudora. 'If you wouldn't mind.'

Mr Fluffy stepped forward and took the ball from her.

He raised it and pressed his quivering, twitching nose to the transparent globe, his eyes staring deep into those of the stiltmouse.

'Eeeek,' he whispered. 'Eeeeeeeek.'

The broomball shook in his hands as the stiltmouse, its fur fluffed up and eyes bulging, jumped up and down on its long thin legs in a frenzy of excitement. Eudora Pinkwhistle stepped forward and, reaching into the pocket of her black apron, extracted a large wedge of green cheese with purple veins running through it.

'Finest Shreddar, organically enchanted and cauldron fresh,' she announced proudly. 'If I might borrow you, headmaster.'

Eudora swept Randalf's hat from his head, dislodging a furious Veronica in the process, and shoved the cheese helmet firmly down in its place.

'Allow me,' said Miss Balsamic, tugging the struggling broom forward. 'This is Dyson – a breakthrough in incantation-powered cleaning utensils. Hold on tight,' she instructed, handing Randalf the broom, 'and he'll do the rest.'

Randalf took the broom in both hands and . . .

'*WHOOOAHH!*' he cried, as the broom took off across the broomball pitch on its bristles, sending clouds of dust into the air. '*WHOOOOAAHHH!*' Randalf wailed as the green cheese on his head started to revolve and crumble, sending a shower of tiny flakes off in all directions.

At the same time, the broomball leaped out of Mr

Fluffy's hands and raced around the broomball pitch, the stiltmouse inside a blur of movement.

'Eeek! Eeek! Eeeek!'

'*WHOOOAHH!*'

Randalf shot past the astonished broomball team, clinging on to the broom, which dashed back and forth across the pitch as it swept the cheese into a great cheesedrift in the hearth of the chimney.

'Eeek!'

The broomball, which had been hurtling to and fro after the broom, suddenly plunged into the cheesedrift and shot up the chimney without the aid of a chimney-sweeper.

'*POUF!*'

The broomball burst out from the top of the chimney with such force that it sailed high into the sky and out over the Musty Mountains – where, far from Stinkyhog's School of Wizardry, it landed next to a short, stubby lamp-post with cast-iron legs.

With a little giggle, the lamp-post kicked the broomball off into the surrounding fir trees, which seemed to have fur coats hanging from their branches. Moments later, faraway voices sailed back to where the glowing lamp-post stood.

'Ella's not in her room . . . But there's a long-legged mouse in a funny cage in the middle of the floor . . . Mum! Dad! Come and see . . .'

With a shrug of its wrought-iron shoulders, the lamp-post turned and walked away.

Back at the broomball pitch, Randalf, shaken and covered in cheese dust but clearly excited, was just getting to his feet. Next to him, the broom was doing an enthusiastic little jig.

'Dyson! Heel!' commanded Miss Balsamic sternly.

Reluctantly the broom did as it was told.

'This is marvellous! Marvellous!' said Randalf delightedly, the revolving Shreddar cheese coming slowly to a halt on his head. 'Why, with this equipment, the Goblet of Porridge is as good as ours! Well done, Miss Pinkwhistle! Miss Balsamic! Mr Fluffy!'

Joe and the rest of the broomball team exchanged looks.

'But isn't this cheating?' Joe asked. This might be Muddle Earth, but he knew the difference between right and wrong. 'I mean, I know how important winning this broomball match is. Nobody wants the school to be shut down . . .

'School shut down?!' the rest of the team exclaimed, looking puzzled.

'. . . but cheating is just plain wrong,' Joe protested.

'Cheating?' said Randalf. 'Whatever do you mean?'

'Enchanted cheese, mesmerized stiltmice,' said Joe.

'Bewitched brooms.' He frowned. 'It seems like cheating to me.'

'Oh, my dear boy, I wouldn't worry about that if I were you,' said Randalf. 'All you and the team have to do is show up tomorrow and let these marvellous things win the match for you. It'll all work out perfectly.' He beamed with happiness. 'Trust me, I'm a wizard!'

'I haven't seen him this excited since the purple unicorn agreed to fertilize his prize roses,' said Veronica, fluttering down to land on Randalf's head as he removed the cheese helmet and handed it to Edward Gorgeous. 'Pfwooah!' she exclaimed. 'Your head smells worse than those roses ever did!'

'Shut up, Veronica!' said Randalf. 'Now, if you'll excuse me, I'm off to my study to decide where best to display the Goblet of Porridge when we win it from Golden Towers!'

As he strode off across the courtyard towards the castle, the jeer-leaders turned and watched him carefully.

Joe turned to the other Perfumed Porkers. 'I think we need to have a team meeting,' he said.

'Edward! Edward!'

It was Ella, hurrying in the opposite direction, a band of barbarian maidens in tow. She was wearing a ripped T-shirt on which she'd written the words *Battlecat, Not Copycat.*

The barbarian maidens tripping along behind her had the same slogan on their T-shirts. Ella ignored them.

'Edward, I've been looking for you everywhere,' she said. 'Do you want to get some breakfast?' She hesitated. 'Edward? Edward, what's wrong?'

Joe turned round. Mr Fluffy had been trying to organize the others into a hunt for the broomball in the Musty Mountains and Edward had been standing right next to Joe. Now Edward was lying on the ground. His eyes were closed and his skin looked like wax. His breath was coming in shallow, rasping gasps.

'What *is* it, Edward?' Joe knelt beside him. 'What's the matter?'

'Urgh . . . urgh . . .' Edward moaned, his voice so weak and faltering it could barely be heard.

Pushing Joe aside, Ella crouched down beside the chimney sweeper. 'Oh, Edward,' she said.

Edward's eyelids flickered. Ella cupped his face in her hands and he opened his eyes.

'What is it? Tell me . . .'

With a soft moan, Edward raised his head. 'Th . . . th . . .' he murmured.

Ella felt his cold breath as he whispered into her ear – and frowned.

'What did he say?' Joe asked.

~103~

Ella looked round. She seemed confused. 'He said, "*It's the cheese . . .*"' she told him.

Eudora Pinkwhistle stooped and picked up the cheese helmet that Edward had dropped, her eyes wide and anxious and her pointy nose twitching. 'But my Shreddar cheese is organically enchanted and cauldron fresh – made with the finest gas-frog milk, and mildew, and with just a pinch of garlic—'

'Garlic!' Edward gasped.

He let out a soft moan and slumped back in a dead faint.

Only one of the three moons had risen that night – the yellow one – and now the pointy towers of Stinkyhogs twinkled in the golden moonlight. Batbirds flapped about the turrets, hooting and bumping into each other, while in the distance, Mount Boom quietly smoked.

Not that Edward Gorgeous noticed any of this, for as usual, he was lost in brooding thought. He was wearing tight black trousers which tapered to his slim waist, and a large shirt, with even larger sleeves, that was open to the navel to reveal his pale yet muscular chest. His thick glossy hair was swept back from his handsome brooding brow, a stray lock giving his gleaming quiff a tousled, romantic look. Beneath his magnificently full and expressive eyebrows, his intense red-tinged eyes smouldered with a yearning passion.

Overhead, two batbirds bumped into each other and clattered on to the tiled roof of the pointy tower on whose balcony Edward Gorgeous was busy brooding.

'Dread creatures of the night,' he mused darkly, 'we are the same, you and I – condemned to haunt the twilight forever.'

The batbirds gave him a puzzled look, hooted quietly, and flapped off through the golden moonlight.

'They told me I'd find you here.'

Edward turned towards the voice. It was the barbarian princess with the beautiful eyes and black-painted fingernails. The one they called Ella.

'Who did?' he breathed, unable to take his eyes off her, so radiant in the golden moonlight.

'My brother Joe and the rest of the Porkers,' Ella explained in a tearful voice. 'They're having a team meeting in the dormitory . . . Are you feeling better? I missed you at breakfast, and at lunch, and at supper . . . It's almost as if you've been avoiding me.'

She reached out a black-fingernailed hand and touched him on the shoulder. He trembled.

'Why, Edward, you feel so cold,' Ella breathed, running her hand across his muscular chest. 'You should button up your shirt,' she said softly, 'or you'll catch your death . . .'

'I've already caught it,' Edward Gorgeous murmured, reaching up and taking Ella's hand in his. Beneath his dark eyebrows, his eyes glowed redder.

'What do you mean?' whispered Ella, as he pulled her close and squeezed her hand tightly.

'There is something you need to know about me,' Edward began, staring down at her hand. 'Something that means that I must fight these feelings I have for you, barbarian princess Ella . . .'

'What is it?' Ella asked breathlessly as Edward turned her hand over and examined her painted thumbnail. 'You can tell me, whatever it is.'

Edward's lips parted, and when he looked up, two sharpened front teeth glistened in the golden moonlight.

'It's these,' he said, running his tongue over the sharp fangs and raising Ella's thumb to his quivering lips.

'Oh, Edward, I understand,' said Ella softly as he trembled with suppressed emotion.

'You do?' he quivered, Ella's thumb inches from his mouth.

'Of course. But it's nothing to be ashamed of. Loads of my friends have had them, and quite frankly if you get them fitted now, you'll soon get used to them, and in a couple of years—'

'Get used to *what*?' Edward hesitated, a puzzled frown on his handsome face.

'Braces for those teeth of yours,' said Ella. 'I don't mind, honestly. We mustn't let a little bit of wire and metal come between us.' She laughed, but then stopped when she saw the intense emotion in Edward's red-tinged eyes.

'These fangs are who I am, Ella,' he said bitterly, gazing at her thumb, 'and the reason why we can never be together. Once upon a time – a long, long time ago – when I was young and carefree, I was invited to stay in my great-uncle Vlad's castle. Vlad the Tickler he was called, for he had a reputation for goosing his servants with a feather duster until they begged for mercy. It was there, in that terrible place, where the halls and dungeons echoed with screams of laughter, that I was bitten . . .'

'Bitten?' whispered Ella, hardly able to breathe.

Edward squeezed her hand even more intensely as his whole body shook. 'On the thumb,' he moaned. 'By a vampire – and turned into one of them. The most pathetic, miserable kind of vampire you can be . . . A thumbsucker.'

Ella pulled her hand away and stepped back.

'A thumbsucker?' she said uncertainly. 'Well, I suppose sucking your thumb *is* a bit babyish . . .'

'Not *my* thumb,' said Edward passionately, his fangs glinting menacingly in the moonlight, 'but the thumbs of others!'

His magnificent eyebrows knitted together and his

handsome face grew pale. A lock of his gorgeous hair flopped fetchingly forward across his beautiful brow. Despite herself, Ella fell into his muscular arms.

'Oh, Edward,' she groaned. 'What are we going to do?'

'I'm sorry to interrupt.'

Edward and Ella turned to see Joe standing in the doorway. The bewitched broom was standing beside him. Percy, Bradley and Smutley were behind him.

'We need to talk to you, Edward,' said Joe.

'What about?' said Edward, horrified that his words might have been overheard.

'It's all this magic business,' said Joe. 'Not only is it cheating, but it's far too risky as well. We've had a team meeting and we've decided that we can't use it.'

'*You* decided,' said Smutley darkly.

'We took a vote, remember?' said Percy.

'And Joe's right,' insisted Bradley. 'Magic is against the rules. When Roger the Wrinkled finds out we've used it – and he will! – we'll be disqualified for sure.'

'If we're going to win the Goblet of Porridge and save the school, then we're going to have to do it ourselves, by our own efforts, fairly and squarely,' said Joe. 'Which means, I'm afraid, no stiltmouse-whispering, no Shreddar cheese and,' he added, turning to the broom, 'no magic brooms. Besides, that way, win or lose, we can be proud that we didn't cheat. What do you say, Edward?'

Edward looked at the beautiful barbarian princess, Ella, then back at her little brother, and nodded grimly.

'Spoilsports,' muttered the broom.

The grounds of the Horned Baron's castle were buzzing – and not just because of the big purple and orange bees hovering over the pongweed flowers that decorated the newly built grandstand. Not since the Horned Baron's last helmet-polishing party had so many of Muddle Earth's residents flocked through the castle gates – except now they were school gates, and painted a fetching shade of pink.

Anyone who was anyone was there.

There were well-heeled Goblintown merchants in striped suits and spotty bow-ties walking arm in arm with their wives, who wore long dresses and broad-brimmed hats decorated with mouldy bananas and clusters of rotten tomatoes. There were happy Trollbridge gardeners in polished boots and freshly laundered smocks, with their favourite root vegetables under their arms. There were barbarians from the wilds of Muddle Earth: battle-scarred warriors and warrior maidens, armed with swords and dressed in sweeping fur cloaks and impressive winged helmets. There were bands of chattering elves from Elfwood getting under everyone's feet, and huge ogres from the Ogre Hills, clutching snuggly-wugglies and shielding their triple eyes from the bright sunshine, for it was a beautiful day.

Tiny clouds drifted across the bright blue sky like flocks of squeezed sheep on a warm breeze that set the pennants fluttering on top of the castle's pointy towers, and ruffled the brightly painted banner pointing the way to the grandstand erected by Mr Fluffy next to the broomball pitch.

POBWIT OF GOBBIGE MATCH THIS WEY the banner read, the words picked out in glittery lopsided writing, together with a splodgy pink blob with four legs and a curly tail.

'Note how I have expressed the intrinsic *perfumed* nature of the porker,' Mr Chiaroscuro was announcing proudly to a group of puzzled barbarian warriors in winged helmets, 'by my use of stippled pointilism and a rather Fauvist palette.'

'By the claws of Wotulf the Stormbringer, I know not of what you speak!' said a warrior, shaking his head.

'Oh, forget it. The grandstand is that way,' said Mr Chiaroscuro, sighing theatrically. 'Barbarians!'

The rest of the crowd followed, until the grandstand was full of excited spectators – at least, almost full, for two rows of stools with pink cushions, and the four golden thrones beside them, remained empty.

An expectant hush fell over the crowd as Randalfus Rumblebore, headmaster of Stinkyhogs School of Wizardry, bustled up the wooden steps of the grandstand, together with his teachers, and sat down. On the broomball pitch, Tinklebell raised a tiny golden trumpet to his lips and blew with all his might.

Hwooo! Hweeep!

Tinklebell tried again, his cheeks full and his face bright red with exertion.

Hwooo! Hweeep!

Giving up, he lowered the trumpet.

'Da. Da-da. Da-da-da – *dah*!' he bellowed. 'My lords, ladies and muddles,' he proclaimed. 'The Wizards of Muddle Earth!'

Cheers and applause broke out among the crowd, and everyone craned their necks to see the wizards make their

grand entrance through the courtyard and up the steps of the grandstand. They were each dressed in their finest clothes, flowing organza gowns, decorated with stars and crescent moons, and with tall pointy hats upon their heads.

'Roger the Wrinkled,' Tinklebell announced, as a small wizard with a white beard and a brow like a road map came tottering up the steps on shiny red patent leather court-shoes.

'Bertram the Incredibly Hairy,' Tinklebell intoned, as a larger wizard with beady black eyes lost in a dense thicket of ginger hair followed closely behind.

'Boris the Bald . . . Eric the Mottled . . . Ernie the Shrivelled . . . Melvyn the Mauve . . .!' Tinklebell continued as a bald, a mottled, a shrivelled and then a rather flamboyant wizard with a permed beard and winged spectacles strode up the steps and took their seats in the grandstand.

'And finally . . .' Tinklebell paused and stared at the bland-faced wizard with his black-rimmed glasses and neatly trimmed moustache who was standing next to him, waiting meekly for his name to be called. 'What did you say your name was?' he whispered.

The wizard leaned across and repeated his name, his voice nasal and flat and rather quiet.

'Wizard . . .' Tinklebell frowned. '. . . What's-his-name.'

Colin the Nondescript trotted after the others and sat down with a sigh.

Just then, bursting through the pink gates and throwing up clouds of dust, came a procession of huge pumpkin carriages pulled by galloping unicorns and driven by pairs of smartly uniformed beavers.

'Now, that's what I *call* a grand entrance!' said Veronica from her perch on Randalf's hat, as the carriage doors opened and the little princes and princesses stepped daintily out, followed by the kings and queens of Golden Towers.

'Da. Da-da. Da-da-da – *dah*!' Tinklebell bellowed at the top of his voice. 'The Kings and Queens of Golden Towers!'

There was more applause and more cheering from the crowd – but not from the wizards, who shifted uncomfortably on their stools and gazed into the middle distance.

'King Peter!' Tinklebell proclaimed as a tall, square-jawed monarch in purple robes trimmed with ermine,

and with a large jewel-encrusted crown upon his immaculately coiffured head, strode past him, waving graciously to the crowd.

'Queen Susan!' Tinklebell cried out, and a barbarian in the crowd wolf-whistled as she sashayed past. Her blouse was a little too flouncy, her heels a little too high, and her tiny bejewelled crown wobbled precariously atop her back-combed hairdo as she blew kisses to the crowd from lips that were a little too red.

'Queen Lucy!'

Following close on Queen Susan's extremely high heels, Queen Lucy walked stiffly, her crown pulled down firmly on her head as she kept her gaze held fixedly in front of her. She had a gold sceptre gripped in one hand, which she didn't look afraid to use. 'Wiff-waff,' she muttered under her breath.

'King Mff-wbb!' Tinklebell announced.

Sprawling on a cushioned couch carried by four wheezing, straining beavers, King Edmund eagerly stuffed a piece of Turkish delight into his mouth as he was carried up the steps of the grandstand.

'Brrmmppl,' he called, spraying bits of the half-chewed confection over the crowd as he sat down heavily in a golden throne next to his brother and sisters.

'Now, that's what I *call* a fatso!' said Veronica.

'Da. Da-da. Da-da-da – *dah*!'

It was Tinklebell again, and all eyes turned to the broomball pitch, where Prince Caspian and Princess

Camilla, who had stepped out of the last of the line of pumpkin carriages, were making their way towards a small golden marquee on the far touchline. Between them, on outstretched arms, they carried a large marble plinth. Upon it rested a plump velvet cushion, on top of which nestled a small, battered-looking drinking vessel.

'The Goblet of Porridge!' Tinklebell announced as the prince and princess placed the marble plinth inside the golden marquee and took up positions on either side of the curtained opening.

The crowd waved their arms about, whooping and cheering.

'Welcome, broomball fans!' a small, large-nosed goblin in a green visor shouted into a battered green loudhailer.

He was standing on a wooden box just in front of the grandstand, the word *Commentary* scrawled on it in black crayon. His fellow commentator, a portly troll, stood next to him, scratching his head as he tried to make out notes written on the grubby piece of parchment he clutched in his podgy fingers.

'You join us here on this sun-blessed afternoon for the annual Goblet of Porridge challenge match,' the goblin droned in an expressionless voice as he pulled the green visor low over his eyes.

The crowd whooped and cheered all the louder.

On the left-hand side of the pitch, behind the chimney, a row of little princes and princesses began a courtly dance to the accompaniment of lutes. At the opposite end, behind the other chimney, the four hunched, black-hooded jeer-leaders stood and scowled.

'I'm Spiff Spittle, and this is Turnip Mike,' the commentator droned on. 'Let's meet the teams!'

The troll scrutinized the parchment carefully, and whispered in the goblin's ear as the Galloping Unicorns emerged from the castle courtyard and charged on to the broomball pitch.

'For the Galloping Unicorns, with Number Three on his apron, mid-broom Charlie Battlepants,' Spiff Spittle announced, as a beefy young barbarian with a broom under one arm and two lumps of cheese impaled on the horns of his helmet took up his position, to roars of approval – and a little timid booing – from the crowd. 'Number Two, grater Rufus Hairyear. Number Four, grater Olga Onionbreath,' Spiff intoned, as a tall barbarian lad with pimples and a muscular girl with blonde pigtails and eyebrows raised their huge cheese-grater gloves and waved to the crowd. 'And wearing the Number One apron, chimney sweeper Tiny Bighorn . . .'

The hefty minotaur, who was busy headbutting the mantelpiece, turned and shook his chimney-sweep brush menacingly.

'And last but not least, wearing the Number Five apron, centre spoon and captain, let's hear it for Thrasher the Barbarian!'

The ground seemed to shake as the immense youth in an extravagantly winged helmet raised a fearsome-looking ladle and roared.

'My goodness, I'd forgotten just how big he is for his age!' Veronica said.

'Size isn't everything. We've got magic on our side,' said Randalf. 'The Galloping Unicorns don't stand a chance. Trust me—'

'I know, I know,' said Veronica with a sniff. 'You're a wizard!'

'*Biff them! Bash them! Biff! Bash! Bosh!*' sang the little princes and princesses demurely. '*They are common. We are posh!*'

'For the Perfumed Porkers,' Spiff Spittle intoned as the Stinkyhogs School team walked nervously on to the pitch. 'Centre spoon, Smutley Grubleyson. Graters,

Percy Spudbasher and Bradley the Big-For-His-Age . . .'

'Not compared to Thrasher! chirruped Veronica.

'Chimney sweeper, Edward Gorgeous,' Spiff continued. 'And captain and mid-broom, Joe the Barbarian!'

Polite applause broke out in the grandstand while, clearly unimpressed, the wizards turned and looked at Randalf. On his golden throne, King Peter smiled nonchalantly.

'*If you're rubbish and you know it,*' the jeer-leaders chorused from behind the chimney, raising their pink stinky hoglets high above their heads, '*and you're really going to show it, if you're rubbish and you know it, squeeze your hogs!*'

'Couldn't have put it better myself,' giggled Queen Susan.

Standing behind her throne, Queen Susan's lady-in-waiting, Edwina Lovely, stared down at the Perfumed Porkers' chimney sweeper, her lovely eyes burning with intensity and a twisted smile playing on her lovely lips. Down on the pitch, Edward Gorgeous returned her stare, his face even paler than usual.

Meanwhile, Joe strapped his cheese helmet to his

head and approached the centre circle, where a green-faced witch in a black-and-white-striped gown and a tall pointy hat with corks hanging from its brim was waiting. The huge form of Thrasher lumbered over. His muscular jaw was downy with the beginnings of a blond beard; his blue eyes were cold and brutal.

'Our referee today, Waltzing Matilda, the wicked witch of Oz, will toss the elf . . .' droned Spiff Spittle.

Down on the pitch, the wicked witch gripped a small nervous-looking elf in her hands. She looked at Thrasher. She looked at Joe.

'Who's going to call?' she asked.

'I will,' growled Thrasher, his hard blue eyes fixed on Joe.

Joe nodded.

The wicked witch tossed the elf into the air, where it spun round and round.

'Heads or snails?' she called out.

'Snails,' said Thrasher.

A moment later, and with a shrill 'Ouch', the elf fell to the ground, where it reached into its pocket, pulled out a small snail and held it out for everyone to see.

Thrasher smirked. 'Our ball!' he announced.

'So, there you have it, the Unicorns have won the toss,' Spiff Spittle announced, 'and will use their stiltmouse in the first half, which means that the Porkers will have to wait till the second half to use theirs. Now, as we wait for the hooter to signal the start of the match,' Spiff continued, his voice a flat monotone, 'you could cut the atmosphere with a cheese knife . . .'

Tinklebell stepped forward, cleared his throat, then bellowed.

'*HOOT!*'

Waltzing Matilda, the wicked witch of Oz, dropped the broomball into the centre circle of the pitch.

'Don't touch the ball, don't touch the ball,' Joe muttered to himself as he took up his position halfway between the circle and the Porkers' chimney. It was the first and most important rule of broomball, it seemed.

With a terrific roar, Thrasher sprang into action, clattering Smutley's long-handled spoon from his grasp with a sweep of his ladle, and rushing over to scoop a lump of cheese from Charlie Battlepants's horned helmet.

The crowd bellowed its approval.

Meanwhile, as Smutley had bent to retrieve his spoon, Olga Onionbreath had trampled over him and was now breathing down Joe's neck. The smell was terrible. Bradley the Big-For-His-Age stepped bravely forward to defend the mid-broom, only to be brought crashing to the ground by Olga's thunderous tackle.

'Oooh! That's got to hurt!' muttered Spiff Spittle from the commentary box.

Joe pushed his cheese helmet back from his eyes, just in time to see Olga jump to her feet and barrel into

Percy with a resounding thud.

'Biff and bosh!' Thragar Warspanner, the Unicorns' coach, bellowed from the touchline, his winged helmet quivering with excitement. 'Bosh and biff!'

Meanwhile, at the far end of the pitch, as Rufus Hairyear grated the lump of cheese with his big mittens, Charlie Battlepants was sweeping a perfect line of cheese crumbs towards the Unicorns' chimney. In the fireplace, Tiny Bighorn mooed and pawed the ground.

The stiltmouse in the broomball scuttled after the cheese towards the chimney. Joe ran forward, broom raised at the ready. If he could just sweep away the cheese trail . . .

'Oooof!!'

Appearing out of nowhere, Thrasher let out a roaring battle cry and crashed down on him with all his weight. A cloud of dust billowed up into the air.

It cleared to reveal Joe, a crumpled heap in the middle of the centre circle, with Thrasher standing over him, beating his chest and roaring. The crowd of spectators didn't notice. All eyes were on the broomball which, at that moment, reached the fireplace. Ignoring his chimney-sweeping brush, Tiny Bighorn butted it up the chimney with a throaty bellow.

The broomball shot out of the chimney pot with a loud *pop!* and a puff of soot.

'*POT!*' shouted the crowd.

'Is that allowed?' asked Joe, climbing unsteadily to his

feet and trying to catch his breath.

'Fair dinkum!' nodded Matilda, with a cackling laugh. 'One-nil.'

'*We are pretty, our blood is blue! We are, we are, better than you!*' the little princes and princesses behind the Unicorns' chimney chanted softly, and did a little dance that involved waving handkerchiefs about.

'I say, bad luck for your chaps,' smirked King Peter, turning to Roger the Wrinkled.

'They're not "my chaps",' said the wizard, staring coldly at Randalf, who was squirming awkwardly on his stool.

'As I always say, broomball's a game of two halves,' Randalf said, his face reddening. 'Isn't that right, Miss Pinkwhistle?'

Eudora Pinkwhistle shook her head. 'I don't understand it,' she said 'My cheese is organically enchanted and cauldron fresh . . .'

'And I don't know *what's* got into Dyson,' muttered Miss Balsamic distractedly.

A cheer went up from the crowd as the match restarted. Matilda the wicked witch dropped the ball.

This time, Joe was quick to run to the edge of the circle, where Smutley scooped a spoonful of cheese from his helmet and lobbed it to Percy. Joe turned, only for Thrasher to grab him by the waist and throw him at the broomball that was still sitting in the centre circle.

As Joe landed, his broom hit the see-through ball,

and sent it bouncing across the pitch.

'Eeek!' squeaked the stiltmouse.

'Penalty!' Matilda screeched. 'Joe the Barbarian has touched the ball! Clean sweep to the Unicorns!'

'But . . . but . . .' Joe protested. 'That's not fair. I didn't stand a chance . . .'

'Bit of a whingeing Pom, aren't you, dear?' said the witch, the corks on her hat dancing on the ends of their strings.

She pointed to the Unicorns' chimney.

While Joe and the Porkers watched, Charlie Battlepants swept a line of cheese to the chimney, unopposed, and the stiltmouse obediently trundled after it into the fireplace.

Thud!

The minotaur headbutted the broomball up the chimney.

'Two-nil!' roared the crowd.

The jeer-leaders turned away and shuffled along the touchline, heads down and staring at their big clumpy boots.

'*HOOT!*' bellowed Tinklebell.

'Half-time,' Matilda announced, and stroked her familiar – a small blue kangaroo that had just popped its head out of a pouch in her black-and-white-striped gown.

The Galloping Unicorns formed a huddle, with Thragar Warspanner at the middle of it. He handed out dainty little cupcakes with pink fondant icing to each of his barbarians in turn.

'We've got them exactly where we want them!' he roared. 'Now let's rip 'em to shreds!'

Joe joined the rest of the Porkers around the fireplace of their chimney. Percy was battered and bruised, Bradley was tearful, while Edward, looking more brooding than ever, was sending furtive glances up to the grandstand, where the kings and queens were seated on their golden thrones.

'Snugglemuffins!' Norbert cried out, beaming broadly as he pushed his shopping trolley over to them. 'These'll cheer you up,' he said, handing them out to each of the team.

Right behind him was a red-faced Randalf. 'What's going on?' he blustered. 'Where's the magic? The cheese, the broom . . .'

'Locked in a cupboard in the dorm,' said Joe, giving his snugglemuffin back to Norbert untouched. He stepped forward. 'Using magic is cheating. We want to win by our own efforts . . .'

'But they're wiping the floor with you!' protested Randalf.

'For once, I've got to agree with old Fatso, here,' said Veronica. 'You're being pulverized.'

'Actually, I think I'm getting the hang of broomball,' said Joe, as encouragingly as he could. 'If we work as a team, and with Edward as our chimney sweeper, we're still in with a chance. Isn't that right, Edward?'

But Edward Gorgeous didn't answer. Instead, he was gripping the mantelpiece and staring at Edwina Lovely, who was standing on the touchline, staring back at him.

Joe's sister Ella came running over, followed by a gaggle of giggling barbarian maidens. She stopped short when she saw the look on Edward's handsome face.

'Edward?' she breathed. 'What's the matter? . . . Who's this?'

'Oh,' said Edwina Lovely, smiling as she tossed back her long, lovely hair, 'we're old friends, aren't we, Edward?'

Just then, Waltzing Matilda strode to the centre circle, a broomball clasped in her hands.

'And with the half-time team talks over, it's back to the match,' droned Spiff Spittle from the commentary box, 'and the new ball!'

'*H*OOT!' bellowed Tinklebell.

Matilda the wicked witch of Oz dropped the broomball to the ground. On the touchline, Mr Fluffy gave an encouraging little wave.

'Eeek!' the stiltmouse squeaked as the broomball shot off down the pitch at a tremendous rate.

Joe and the rest of his team watched open-mouthed as it careered towards the Porkers' chimney.

'Oof!'

Joe was flattened by his opposite number, Charlie Battlepants.

'Oof!'

'Oof!'

'Ouch!'

Thrasher, Rufus Hairyear and Olga Onionbreath, who was panting furiously, crashed into Smutley, Percy and Bradley the Big-For-His-Age respectively, flattening each of them. Not that it did the Galloping

Unicorns any good . . .

The dust cleared and the crowd gasped as the broomball shot through Edward's legs and disappeared up the chimney.

'Eeek! Eeek!'

There was a sound of clattering, followed by a sooty *plopf!* as the broomball burst out of the top of the chimney pot, flew straight up into the air and came down into Edward Gorgeous's outstretched hands.

'*POT!*' roared the crowd, leaping to their feet and waving their arms in the air.

'Go, Perfumed Porkers!' they cheered.

'I knew the Porkers had it in them!' Randalf beamed, clapping his hands and jumping up and down.

'Looked like the ball did all the work to me,' Veronica chirped pointedly.

'Shut up, Veronica!' said Randalf, trying to swat the budgie off his hat, missing, and knocking Queen Lucy's crown into her lap.

'Oh, it's too fwightful for words,' exclaimed Queen Lucy, giving Randalf a filthy look. 'Why does bwoomball have to be so wough?'

'Looks like the plucky Perfumed Porkers' performance is peaking perfectly,' said Spiff Spittle from the commentary box, as Joe and the team climbed unsteadily to their feet.

'That's easy for you to say,' mumbled Turnip Mike, staring at his notes.

The wicked witch took the quivering broomball from Edward Gorgeous and strode back to the centre circle. On the touchline, Mr Fluffy let out a series of little squeaks, his nose quivering.

'*HOOT!*'

The next moment, the stiltmouse let out a shrill 'Eeeeek!' and the broomball jumped out of Matilda's hands and sailed high into the air.

'Ooh!' gasped the crowd.

It landed with a soft *clunk* yards from the Perfumed Porkers' chimney, and the stiltmouse inside pedalled furiously towards it.

'Aah!' went the crowd.

Thrasher and his team barged the Porkers out of the way and raced in the same direction, but the ball was too quick for them. As Edward Gorgeous stepped gracefully aside, his chimney-sweeping brush raised, the broomball shot up the chimney again.

Just in time.

With a bone-crunching crash, the barbarians of the Galloping Unicorns collided with the mantelpiece and landed in a heap in the fireplace.

'Eeek! Eeek! Eeek!' squeaked the stiltmouse – and, for a second time, the broomball burst from the top of the chimney, leaving Edward with nothing more exercising to do than hold out his hands and wait for it to drop into them.

'*POT!*'

The crowd went wild. The wizards were on their feet, applauding enthusiastically, while the kings and queens of Golden Towers sulked, and the little princes and princesses threw down their lutes and handkerchiefs and burst into tears.

'Oh, poo!' said Queen Susan.

'They're not only wough, they're wubbish,' said Queen Lucy dismissively as she surveyed the tangled pile of Galloping Unicorns in front of the chimney.

Thragar Warspanner was beside himself with rage, his winged helmet bouncing about on his head as he ran on to the pitch with a large bucket and a filthy-looking sponge.

'Call yourselves barbarians?' he roared, tipping the bucketful of water over the team. 'You're a disgrace! You're limper than a battlerabbit's half-chewed lettuce, and twice as wet!'

Thrasher got to his feet, the feathers on his winged helmet soggy and bedraggled. Beside him, Olga Onionbreath wrung out her pigtails, and Rufus Hairyear wiped his nose on his sleeve. Charlie Battlepants opened his mouth to say something, only to be hit in the face with the wet sponge.

'Pull yourselves together!' snarled Thragar as they formed a huddle. 'And remember what we're playing for – a battlecat each and all the Turkish delight we can eat! Except for him . . .' The team looked across the pitch at their chimney, where Tiny Bighorn was pawing the ground, mooing furiously and headbutting the mantelpiece. 'He plays for the fun of it.'

Meanwhile, Joe had gathered the Porkers into a huddle on the touchline.

'We've got a problem,' he whispered urgently. 'We got rid of the enchanted cheese and locked up the bewitched broomstick, but now someone's put a mesmerized stiltmouse in the ball! And a mesmerized stiltmouse is cheating. If we're caught out, we'll be disqualified.'

The other team members looked at one another.

'It wasn't me,' said Percy.

'Or me,' said Bradley.

'Or me,' said Smutley.

'It doesn't matter,' said Joe. 'The point is, we've been lucky so far.' He glanced over at Matilda the referee, who was over by the touchline, bouncing her blue kangaroo on her knee. 'But we can't risk using it any longer.'

Edward nodded, grim-faced. He opened the door in the ball and released the stiltmouse, which shot off across the pitch and into the top pocket of an astonished-looking Mr Fluffy.

'We'll use mine,' said Edward Gorgeous, producing a new stiltmouse from inside his flattering billowy open-necked shirt. 'I keep one with me in case . . .' His handsome eyes glittered broodingly. 'It doesn't matter,' he said, placing the creature in the broomball.

'OK,' said Joe. 'Remember what we talked about last night,' he told the team. 'We've got to use their strength against them. Percy, Bradley, you tease their graters – do whatever it takes. Smutley, you distract Charlie Battlepants. I'm counting on you. And Edward, the minotaur's yours. Think you can handle him?'

'Just try and stop me!' Edward grinned, handing Joe the broomball.

'*HOOT!*' bellowed Tinklebell.

The Porkers hurriedly took up their positions opposite the Unicorns, who didn't look *galloping* so much as fuming with barely suppressed rage. Matilda dropped the ball.

As the broomball jerked and started rolling, the Galloping Unicorns let out a menacing battle cry and hurtled towards their opposite numbers. Thrasher ran at Joe, Charlie Battlepants targeted Smutley, while Olga Onionbreath and Rufus Hairyear barrelled towards Bradley and Percy, their heads down and shoulders raised – only to stumble and fall as Joe stuck out his broom and tripped them up.

The crowd cheered.

Percy ran forward and tweaked Rufus Hairyear's hairy ear, while Bradley yanked Olga Onionbreath's pigtail, before both of them turned and ran, the enraged barbarians jumping to their feet and chasing after them.

Meanwhile, Joe swerved round a lumbering, bellowing Thrasher, who slammed head first into the hard ground, wedging his winged helmet down over his eyes as he did so. Smutley fell to his knees, causing Charlie Battlepants to trip over him, before raising his spoon and making a dash for Joe.

'You know what, Veronica,' Randalf said, 'I think Joe might have been right. He really *does* seem to be getting the hang of broomball . . .'

Randalf's pointy hat abruptly slumped down over his eyes as Veronica jumped up and down on the brim, flapping her wings and chirping encouragingly. Randalf reached up and pushed it back, but for once didn't complain.

'Go, Perfumed Porkers!' he shouted. 'Go!'

In the grandstand, all eyes were on the thrilling match unfolding on the broomball pitch, as the crowd *oohed* and *aahed* and clapped their hands. Nobody noticed the four hunched and hooded jeer-leaders making their way quietly along the touchline in the

direction of the golden marquee, where they stopped next to Prince Caspian and Princess Camilla.

'*Roses are red, violets are blue . . .*' chorused the jeer-leaders, closing in around the little prince and princess and bustling them inside the marquee. '*Daisies are weeds, and so are you!*'

'Ouch!' yelped Prince Caspian.

'That *stings!*' howled Princess Camilla, as the curtains closed behind them.

On the pitch, Smutley plunged his spoon into Joe's cheese helmet and tossed two divots of cheese upfield. Running at full pelt, Percy caught both of them in one glove, while behind him, Bradley the Big-For-His-Age dropped suddenly to his knees, sending Olga and Rufus somersaulting through the air as they tripped over him.

They landed on Thrasher with a crash that shook the grandstand.

Charlie Battlepants roared with rage and leaped at Joe, only to fall flat on his face, his baggy barbarian trousers suddenly down around his ankles. Behind him, Smutley smirked as he waved the barbarian's belt above his head.

The crowd was on its feet as Joe ran down the pitch, sweeping the cheese crumbs that Percy was busily grating into a line towards the Porkers' chimney.

'Eeek! Eeek!' the stiltmouse squeaked as its nose picked up the scent and it trundled the broomball after Joe's swept-up cheese and into the fireplace.

'Moo!'

All at once there came an enraged roar from behind Joe, who turned to see Tiny Bighorn charging down the pitch.

'*Ooohh!*' went the crowd.

'Leave this to me,' said Edward Gorgeous, gripping his large, flowing shirt and pulling it over his head to reveal his magnificently sculpted torso.

'*Aaaahhh!*' went the crowd.

'That's more like it,' said Queen Lucy.

'I agree,' said Roger the Wrinkled.

Edward tossed Joe his chimney-sweeping brush and stepped to the side, holding out his shirt as if it was a cape.

'I've got a blouse just like it,' said Roger the Wrinkled. 'Such a fetching shade of red.'

'Moo!' roared Tiny Bighorn, swerving away from the fireplace and charging at Edward's shirt instead.

But at the last moment, the brooding barbarian swept his shirt away, and the minotaur thundered into thin air. Skidding round on his heels, and in a cloud of dust, Tiny Bighorn lowered his horns and charged back – only for Edward to sidestep him again, his biceps rippling.

'*Ooohh!*' the crowd gasped.

'*Aaaahhh!*' they chorused.

Mesmerized, Tiny Bighorn charged yet again, and Edward wheeled him around and around with flourishes of his shirt, his abdominal muscles flexing as he did so.

'Moo! Moo! Moooo!'

Tiny launched himself at Edward, who pulled the shirt away one last time, sending the minotaur crashing into Thrasher and the rest of the Unicorns team, who had only just staggered to their feet again.

Meanwhile, as Edward distracted the minotaur, Joe grasped the chimney-sweeping brush and thrust the broomball up the chimney.

'Eeek! Eeek!'

Higher and higher the broomball went, as Joe added length after length to the handle.

'Eeek! Eeek! Eeek!'

With a final shove, Joe launched the broomball, stiltmouse and all, high up into the air.

The crowd erupted into wild cheering.

'They think it's all over,' said Spiff Spittle from the commentary box.

Throwing his shirt aside, Edward Gorgeous tossed his magnificent hair back, stepped elegantly forward, and caught the broomball in his hands.

'It is now!' said Spiff, falling off the box.

In the grandstand, Queen Lucy stood up and stamped her foot. 'Howwid, stupid game,' she said sulkily.

King Edmund stuffed a consoling lump of Turkish delight into his mouth and turned away, while King Peter and Queen Susan stared stonily ahead.

Roger the Wrinkled was on his feet, his hand outstretched to Randalf, who was busy bowing and waving to the ecstatic crowd.

'Well done, Randalf,' he said, tottering slightly on his high heels. 'You really pulled it off at the end!'

'It was looking a bit hairy for a moment,' said Bertram the Incredibly Hairy, shaking Randalf's hand. 'But you did it.'

'A close shave, if ever I saw one,' added Boris the Bald.

'You've spared our blushes,' said Eric the Mottled, glancing round smugly at the kings and queens.

'Rose to the occasion,' wheezed Ernie the Shrivelled.

'Superb six-pack,' observed Melvyn the Mauve.

'Many congratulations,' said Colin the Nondescript – though nobody heard him.

'As for Stinkyhogs School of Wizardry,' said Roger the Wrinkled, turning to the teachers, 'I think you've upheld the standards we wizards expect quite magnificently!' He turned to King Peter, his face a mass of smiling wrinkles. 'Now for the Award Ceremony!'

The wizards and the kings and queens, followed by the teachers, trooped down the steps of the grandstand. They made their way through the crowd to join the two teams, who were standing beside the small golden marquee on the far touchline.

Thragar Warspanner had taken off his winged helmet and stamped on it in a rage, while his barbarian team looked glum and distinctly tearful. Next to them, Joe tried not to look too triumphant, but Smutley kept punching the air and saying 'Yes! Yes! Yes!', while Percy

and Bradley did a little dance with the handkerchiefs the little princes and princesses had dropped.

Joe looked around for Edward, to give him back his chimney-sweeping brush, but he couldn't see him anywhere.

'Da. Da-da. Da-da-da – *dah*!' Tinklebell bellowed. He seized the cord that dangled from the side of the marquee and tugged. The golden curtains opened to reveal the marble plinth, velvet cushion and . . . Prince Caspian and Princess Camilla, tied up and gagged with knotted-together handkerchiefs.

A loud gasp echoed round the broomball pitch. The Goblet of Porridge was gone.

'It was those horrid jeer-leaders,' sobbed Princess Camilla, once Tinklebell had untied her.

'They called us names!' said Prince Caspian. 'And shrivelled our flowers.' He pointed to the brittle brown hoop on his head that had once been a garland of ninny-petals and trump-blossom.

'This is an outrage!' thundered King Peter.

'Something must be done!' agreed Queen Susan.

'Mmmph mmppll!' said King Edmund.

'And it's all the fault of you wizards!' said Queen Lucy. 'You've lost our Goblet of Powwidge!'

'Rest assured, your highnesses,' said Roger the Wrinkled, frowning severely, 'Randalfus Rumblebore will take full responsibility for recovering the missing trophy . . . Won't you, headmaster?'

'I . . . I . . . I . . .' Randalf blustered. 'Er . . . Of course we will.' He swallowed. 'Won't we, Joe?'

'Will we?' Joe exclaimed.

Just then, a gaggle of young barbarian maidens came barging through the crowd, waving their black-fingernailed hands about and gabbling excitedly.

'They've gone! They've gone!' they chorused. 'Edward Gorgeous and the princess Ella have taken a battlecat and ridden away!'

'A *getaway* battlecat,' said a lovely voice, and Edwina Lovely stepped from behind Queen Susan and wagged a lovely finger at Randalf. 'I should have guessed that Edward was behind this – the leader of the gang. Come, wizard,

I shall help you in your quest. We shall track him down and –' she turned her lovely eyes on Joe – 'his accomplices!'

Beneath Harmless Hill, the four flower fairies sat in the flickering candlelight, their gossamer wings fluttering at their backs. In front of them, on a small, moss-covered stone table, stood a tiny battered vessel.

'The fools! The fools!' laughed Pesticide. 'Goblet of Porridge, indeed! They really have no idea.' She reached out and stroked the object on the stone table with a gloved hand.

'What's next?' asked Nettle.

'And what do we have to do?' asked Thistle.

'And where do we have to go?' asked Briar-Rose.

Pesticide swept her green hair from her face and gave a pointy-toothed smile. Her wings fluttered.

'Nowhere,' she said.

Book Two

The Trouble with Big Sisters

Prologue

'Once upon a very long time ago, there lived a messy and muddled ruler, Marthur of the Round Kitchen Table. Bold of biscuit and light of sponge, his fondants were fancy and his buns were iced. Throughout the land of Muddle, his prowess with a waffle iron and his skill with a cake-slice were legendary and celebrated in song.

> 'Though his pots are burned and his pans are gritty,
> His cakes are fair and his pastries pretty;
> His kitchen's a shambles and his stove's a mess,
> But good King Marthur couldn't care less.

'But woe is me, gentle reader, for it came to pass that

the kitchen did fill up with a heap of cutlery and crockery and cooking utensils of every description. Verily was the floor strewn with baking trays and pots and pans, both short and long of handle, until there was, forsooth, a veritable mountain of washing-up.

'"Alas and alack!" cried King Marthur, attempting to find a clean plate. "I give up."

'He seized his sword and plunged it into a freshly baked scone of prodigious size and unparalleled deliciousness that he had just that moment pulled from the oven. As he strode from the kitchen, never to return, he spoke these immortal words:

'"Let he who pulls the sword from the scone do the washing-up and become the new and rightful ruler of the Round Kitchen Table . . . I'm off!"

'Many and varied were the bakers, the pastry-cooks and cake-decoraters who took up this legendary challenge, but all to no avail. Try as they might, none could pull the mighty sword from the floury dough-based teatime favourite. And they all lived happily ever after.

'Alas and alack! Alack and alas, dear reader. For this is a sad and sorry tale indeed, and had I hands to wring, I would surely wring them well and truly in the telling of it. But I have no hands. All I have are these beautifully written and magnificently illustrated pages that you see before you, and of course my mellifluous storytelling voice, with which to beguile and enchant you . . .

'Did I hear you right, gentle reader? You wish to hear my tale again? Very well! Once upon a very long time—'

'No, I don't!' said Joe, grabbing the book that was fluttering in the air above him like a moth over a candle, and slamming it shut. 'Fourteen times is quite enough. Will you please stay on your shelf and leave me alone. I'm trying to think!'

He climbed to his feet, crossed the room and placed the book firmly back on the shelf.

'Be like that then,' muttered the book huffily.

Joe turned away and was about to return to the wing-backed chair where he'd been sitting for the last half-hour, trying to collect his thoughts. Where was the Goblet of Porridge – and the lamp-post, for that matter? And where was *Ella*? Could she really be in league with Edward and the jeer-leaders in their dastardly scheme to steal the goblet? And as for the lamp-post, even if he did locate it, and the portal, how could he go back without Ella?

That was the trouble with big sisters. They were so unreliable: swooning over handsome strangers and disappearing with them on battlecats . . .

'*There* you are,' said Roger the Wrinkled, who had just walked into the library and spotted the book.

Not that that was difficult, since there were only three other books on the dusty bookshelves: *Mucky Maud's Songbook*, *The Horned Helmet Autumn Catalogue* and *Binky the Bunny's Big Birthday Surprise*.

'I've been looking for you everywhere,' said Roger as he picked the book up and placed it in the pocket of his flowery chemise. 'Oh, and what have we here?' he added, picking up *Binky the Bunny's Big Birthday Surprise*. 'I do enjoy a good thriller.'

Looking up, the wizard saw Joe and frowned. 'Still here?' he said. 'Shouldn't you and Randalf have set off on the quest to find the Goblet of Porridge by now? After all, there's no time to lose, you know. Not if you want the school to stay open . . .'

'Do *you* wish to hear my tale, gentle reader?' the book piped up.

'Oh, yes,' said Roger the Wrinkled enthusiastically, settling himself down in a chair. 'Let me get comfortable, then you can begin.'

The wind was up, whipping the sand and dust into the air and fuzzing the yellow and purple moons. The mighty battlecat flinched and yowled with unease, the fur at its neck and shoulders standing on end.

'Easy, Tiddles,' whispered the handsome youth upon its back, leaning forward and smoothing its ruffled fur.

The girl seated behind him shivered and tightened her black-fingernailed hold around his waist.

'Where are we?' she asked as lightning suddenly crackled and flashed above her head.

The youth turned. Another flash of lightning illuminated his high cheekbones, his sculpted jaw, and glinted in his red-tinged, almond-shaped eyes. He took the girl's hands in his and squeezed gently. He held her trembling gaze.

The howling wind and crashing thunder sounded like the clashing chords played upon a mighty organ.

'Nowhere,' he whispered.

'There you are!' said Roger the Wrinkled, frowning with irritation at Randalf, who was sitting at the top of the main staircase of Stinkyhogs, his faithful ogre servant, Norbert, seated on the stair below.

They were both dressed for travel, wearing cloaks and carrying luggage. Randalf had the stoutest staff from the staff room in his hand and a small backpack on his shoulders, while Norbert was holding a small leather satchel. Veronica the budgie was ready too, with a tiny scarf knotted at her neck, a miniature bobble hat on her head and a pair of little boots on her feet. She was perched in her favourite spot on the brim of Randalf's pointy hat.

'I've brought my recipe book *and* my findy bag,' said Norbert, his triple eyes blinking in sequence as he smiled down at Roger the Wrinkled and Joe at the foot of the staircase.

He unbuckled the small leather satchel and rootled

about inside it. 'This is where I keep my souvenirs,' he explained. 'Like this fabulous jewel of solid pebble,' he said, raising a small dull grey pebble between his finger and thumb. 'And this exquisite can of finest tin.' He held up a rusty tin can. 'And this—'

'I get the idea,' said Roger the Wrinkled, tapping the toe of his red high-heeled shoe impatiently. He looked up at Randalf. 'I can't tell you the fuss the kings and queens are making over this Goblet of Porridge business. It makes us wizards look so bad . . . I'm counting on you, Randalf, as headmaster of Stinkyhogs School of Wizardry, to put everything right. You've got the school holidays to find the goblet and bring it back to the school trophy-cabinet so we can put a stop to King Peter's petulant sighs and Queen Susan's sulky silences, not to mention Queen Lucy's filthy looks and King Edmund's flatulence . . .'

'Leave it to me, Roger, sir,' said Randalf confidently. He paused. 'There's just one thing . . .'

'Well?' said Roger wearily.

'It's this,' said Randalf. He tapped the brown stair-carpet on which he and Norbert were sitting. 'I think it's broken.'

'What do you mean, broken?'

'It won't fly,' said Randalf.

'It's a *magic* carpet,' said Roger. 'One that requires *magic* to make it fly.' He sighed. 'I can't think why *you* can't make it work.'

'No, sir, neither can I . . .'

'That was sarcasm.' Roger sighed again. 'I've worn petticoats with more talent for magic than you possess, Randalf.'

Randalf went red in the face. 'I . . . I employed an aeronautical betwitching spell of the highest calibre,' he blustered.

'I'm not sure that hitting it with your staff and shouting "Fly, you blasted thing!" counts,' said Veronica.

'Quite,' said Roger, rolling his eyes. 'What is required, Randalf – as you would know, if you had paid any attention when you were my apprentice – is a spell of transportation, a subtle and sensitive spell . . .' He stared down at the stair-carpet.

It was long and thin and frayed at the edges. Once it had been patterned. Now, grubby, worn and badly faded, it was brown. Plain brown. Apart from the stains.

'Let your weave be wafted and your weft upraised,' Roger intoned, sweeping back his sleeve and pointing at the rug. 'And your zephyr-light wool to the skies be praised!'

The carpet gave a soft put-upon sigh and seemed to shrug. Then, as Joe watched, it raised itself slowly into the air, a step at a time, until it hovered, kinked at right angles, above the staircase.

'Now what?' said Randalf from the top step of the floating stair-carpet.

'Flatter, signal, manoeuvre,' said Roger patiently.

'Do what?' said Randalf.

'Standard flying procedure,' said Roger, helping Joe up on to the carpet. 'Say something nice to it,' he instructed. 'Tap the bottom step lightly with your staff and give the command, "Fly!"'

Randalf nodded uncertainly.

'Ready?' Roger the Wrinkled asked.

'Leaving without me, you naughty, naughty wizard?' came a lovely voice.

Everyone turned to see Edwina Lovely walking down the school corridor in an ankle-length cloak with a fur-trimmed hood and matching handbag, her lovely eyes wide and her lovelier black hair tied back in a fetching ponytail. She stopped in front of the hovering stair-carpet and put her lovely hands on her lovely hips.

'I promised Queen Susan that I would help you in your quest, wizard,' she told Randalf, 'and help you I shall.'

She jumped on to the bottom step of the carpet and sat down next to Joe.

'Isn't this exciting?' she said, and gave a delightful tinkling laugh.

'If you're *quite* ready, Randalf,' said Roger the Wrinkled, an irritated edge to his voice.

'Ready and raring to go, sir,' Randalf confirmed unconvincingly. He cleared his throat, whacked the stair-carpet with his staff and roared, '*Fly!*'

The carpet reared up.

'*Whooooah!*'

A loud cry echoed round the hall as everyone was thrown violently back and had to hold on tightly to the frayed edges of the carpet as it flew down the corridor.

'*Waaaaah!*'

An even louder cry went up. The heavy oak doors they were heading for were closed. Roger the Wrinkled calmly raised a hand, clicked his fingers, and the doors burst open.

'*Wheeeee!*' squealed Norbert as the flying stair-carpet swept through the doorway and outside.

'Hold on to your hats!' Randalf shouted, doing just that with one hand while, with the other, he gripped the front of the stair-carpet.

The flying carpet shot up high into the sky, then swooped back down and began speeding round the walls of the Horned Baron's castle. In the castle doorway, Roger the Wrinkled's wrinkled face and flapping hands flashed past in a blur, once, twice, three times . . .

'We're going round in circles!' Randalf groaned. 'What's the matter with the stupid thing?'

Instantly, the flying carpet jerked back and sighed

a sort of if-you're-going-to-be-like-that kind of sigh, before rippling limply as it slowed to a halt and floated to the ground like a ribbon on the wind. It landed with a bump and a cloud of dust on the castle doorstep, where Roger the Wrinkled stood, clicking his red high-heels together in irritation.

'Flatter, signal, manoeuvre,' he said. 'You forgot to say something nice – and you were *far* too heavy with your staff. And as for your command . . .'

'*And* he called the carpet stupid,' said Veronica, smoothing down her feathers and adjusting her bobble hat.

'Now, perhaps you'd like to try that again, Randalf,' said Roger testily.

Randalf looked down at the carpet. 'Errm, "stupid"? Did I say "stupid"?' he said. 'A slip of the tongue. I meant . . . *stupendous*. I meant *superb*. I meant that you are a *superlative* carpet, beautifully woven, intelligent, graceful, and not at all stained . . .'

'All right, don't overdo it,' Veronica interrupted.

Not one to bear a grudge, the flying stair-carpet rose up in the air once more and its passengers gripped on tightly to their respective steps. Holding his staff gingerly by his fingertips, Randalf lightly tapped the stair-carpet and purred in a soft, sing-song voice, 'Fly!'

With a gentle that's-more-like-it kind of sigh, the stair-carpet flew back up into the sky and circled round the pointy towers of the castle.

'Now tell it where you want to go,' Roger called up to Randalf.

'Ogres love a good gossip,' said Edwina Lovely, snuggling up close to Joe on the bottom step. 'We're bound to find out something in the Ogre Hills.'

'That's just what I was thinking,' said Randalf, puffing out his chest importantly. 'Please take us to the Ogre Hills, fair rug of unparalleled loveliness.'

Instantly, the stair-carpet stopped circling the towers of the castle and set off across the sky towards the far horizon.

'And do feel free to take your time,' Randalf added, pulling his pointy hat down low over his eyes and folding his arms, 'O stair covering of legendary magnificence.' He yawned.

Once again, the stair-carpet did as it was requested. It slowed down to a soft, rippling speed and its passengers let out sighs of their own and began to relax.

'As I was saying to Queen Susan, it all seems perfectly clear to me,' said Edwina Lovely, slipping the red ribbon from her lovely hair and letting the dark tresses cascade over her shoulders. 'Edward Gorgeous planned the whole thing. It was his idea to challenge Golden Towers to the broomball match, just so we would bring the Goblet of Porridge to Stinkyhogs. And he recruited those jeer-leaders to steal the goblet while he kept us all distracted. Then he made his getaway on a stolen battlecat with that black-fingernailed lummox!'

'That wasn't a lummox,' said Norbert indignantly. 'That was Joe's big sister, Ella. She and Edward are an item – at least, that's what I heard Eloise Wolfbane say, who heard it from Sophie Skullsplitter, who said Lynda the Barbarianette told her . . .'

'You see,' said Edwina, with a petulant toss of her head. She turned away and Joe got a faceful of lovely hair. 'Ogres have all the best gossip. Even the stupidest ones like Numbutt here. In the Ogre Hills we're bound to find out something about Edward's whereabouts . . .'

'His name's Norbert,' spluttered Joe, pushing Edwina's hair aside and moving to the next step up, 'and he's right. Ella isn't a *lummox* – whatever that might be. She's just an ordinary girl. She isn't interested in the Goblet of Porridge . . . All I know is that I've got to find her, so that the pair of us can return home.'

But Edwina Lovely was no longer listening. Instead, her lovely hands were gripping the sides of the stair-carpet and her lovely face had a far from lovely sneer on it.

'Edward, Edward, Edward,' she muttered, gazing into the middle distance. 'Do you really think you can hide from me? Don't you know I will always find you in the end, wherever you run, whatever you do . . . whoever you're with! And when I do . . .' She trembled, her eyes sparkling and her face a deathly white. For a moment she sat still as a statue, before suddenly seeming to remember where she was. She looked over her shoulder at Joe and Norbert and gave that tinkling little laugh of hers. 'Sorry,' she said, 'I don't know what came over me.'

'You want to watch her,' Veronica whispered as she jumped on to Joe's shoulder. 'Not quite right in the head if you ask me.'

From the top stair, there came the sound of snoring. Randalf was fast asleep.

The flying carpet flew on, leaving the Musty Mountains far behind them, Mount Boom gently *boom-boom-boom*ing in the distance. Joe looked up. The Enchanted Lake was rapidly approaching and he could make out the seven houseboats belonging to the wizards of Muddle Earth bobbing on its sparkling surface. Floating in mid-air, the lake was an extraordinary sight, with the Enchanted River flowing down from it and looking like the stalk of a mighty mushroom.

'Only in Muddle Earth,' muttered Joe to himself, shaking his head.

A waft of pungent perfume filled the air with the scent of a thousand trampled rose petals mixed with the aroma of a million bruised violets, and the faintest whiff of pink stinky hog. Joe looked down. They were now passing over the Perfumed Bog. Far below, in the pink perfumed mist a pink stinky hog raised its curly tail and broke wind. Joe held his nose.

A while later, the bog gave way to flat, dusty ground, scattered with grassy mounds that gradually grew in size and number. Soon they were flying across an undulating landscape of barren hills.

'Wake up, sir. We're here,' said Norbert excitedly, shaking Randalf by the shoulders. 'The Ogre Hills!' His three eyes glistened as he looked at an endless expanse of dry, dusty hillocks. 'Isn't it beautiful!'

'Those aren't my pantaloons, and the cabbages are in the bath . . .' Randalf muttered sleepily. His eyes snapped open. 'Where am I?'

'The Ogre Hills, Fatso,' said Veronica, hopping from Joe's shoulder and on to Randalf's hat. 'Pull yourself together. We need you to land this thing . . . Politely!'

The wizard yawned and stretched extravagantly. 'O floor-tapestry of undreamt delight, if you'd be so good as to descend, I should be eternally grateful.'

With a little sigh, the stair-carpet swooped down out of the sky and came to a halt inches from the ground, maintaining its stair-like shape.

'Thank you, wondrous woven one,' said Randalf,

climbing to his feet and stepping down the stairs. 'Follow me, everyone.'

But Edwina Lovely had beaten him to it, and was already striding purposefully towards a group of gigantic figures in the distance. As she approached, the five ogres turned and glowered down at her, their triple eyes narrowing suspiciously.

'What's the word in the hills?' she said brightly, tossing back her mane of lovely hair.

'Who wants to know?' growled a massive ogre in a grubby custard-stained vest, a blue velveteen rabbit tucked under one hairy armpit.

'Oh, my, what an adorable bunny-wunny,' Edwina Lovely simpered. 'You must be so proud.'

'You mean Gilbert?' said the ogre, giving a shy, green-tusked smile. He raised the velveteen rabbit to his stubbled cheek and rubbed it up and down. 'He *is* very soft and snuggly.'

'And tell me, Gilbert,' said Edwina, perching daintily on a boulder and staring intently at the velveteen rabbit, 'with those lovely big ears of yours, have you heard any talk of a tall handsome stranger hiding in these parts?'

The ogre put the velveteen rabbit to his ear and listened intently. 'Gilbert says *he* hasn't heard anything,' he said, shaking his head solemnly. 'But he thinks that Elly-Welly might have.'

The even more enormous ogre next to him held the patchwork elephant he was cradling to his ear. 'Elly-

Welly ain't seen nuffink.'

'Maisie hasn't either,' announced a slightly smaller ogre with a misshapen knitted mouse in his hand.

'Nor has Sebastian,' said an ogre with a teddy bear.

'And Blanky keeps himself to himself,' said the smallest ogre of the bunch, who was clutching a small chewed-looking blanket.

'So much for gossiping ogres,' Veronica retorted from the brim of Randalf's hat, as the wizard came striding up to Edwina Lovely and stopped beside her, breathing hard.

Behind him, Norbert the Not-Very-Big ogre, suddenly all shy and bashful, squeezed Joe's hand and looked down at the ground.

'Oh, my goodness, what a magnificent snuggly-wuggly,' said the smallest ogre, who was still nearly twice as big as Norbert, as he stared at the rolled-up stair-carpet that Randalf was holding under his arm. 'Can I hold it? Can I stroke it? Oh, it looks so soft and cuddly . . .'

'No, *I* want to . . .'

'No, me . . . me . . .'

The ogres crowded in around them, their triple eyes wide and yellow-tinged tusks gleaming menacingly.

'Headmaster? Headmaster, is that you?'

'Bradley the Big-For-His-Age?' said Randalf as the Stinkyhogs School broomball player came bounding up to them. The young ogre stopped and frowned. 'Dorian the Dribbler! Leave the headmaster alone! And you, Nicholas the Nappy Filler, you wait till I tell your mummy! And the rest of you, you ought to be ashamed!'

The enormous ogres hung their heads and stroked their snuggly-wugglies furiously.

'Sorry . . . Sorry . . . Sorry . . .' came a chorus of deep ogre voices.

'So what brings you to the Ogre Hills?' Bradley asked

brightly, turning to Randalf and the others.

'We're searching for Edward Gorgeous,' said Edwina Lovely, stepping boldly towards him. 'He's a team-mate of yours,' she said accusingly. 'You're not hiding him, are you?'

'Of course not,' said Bradley, taken aback. 'I haven't seen Edward since just after Tinklebell shouted the final whistle and the crowd invaded the pitch.' He shrugged. 'After the game, I came home for the holidays. The last thing I remember is looking over the heads of the crowd and seeing him whisper something in Smutley's ear. The next moment, he was gone.' He blinked tearfully, once, twice, and then again. 'You don't really think that Edward stole the goblet, do you?'

'The Edward Gorgeous *I* know is capable of anything,' said Edwina darkly.

'Just how well *do* you know Edward Gorgeous?' asked Joe.

But Edwina Lovely ignored him. 'Come, wizard!' she announced bossily. 'Roll out that carpet of yours. We're off to find Smutley in Goblintown!'

~ 163 ~

A narrow, dusty road wound its way through a parched and empty landscape, heading north from the Musty Mountains. Far to the east, like a crazily over-decorated birthday cake topped with a thousand twisted candles, was the walled city of Goblintown with its tall towers and smoking chimneys. To the west, dark mountains rose on the distant horizon.

A lone serpent, high in the sky, flapped its ragged wings as it made its way over the jagged peaks. A little way to the left, another lone serpent flew slowly past. And a little way left of that, a third lone serpent lumbered laboriously across the sky. And a little way to the left of *that* was another and another and another – for here, and here, and here, be dragons.

The road continued northwards to the very edge of the map, where it petered out next to a small signpost, which bore the neatly painted words, *WELCOME TO NOWHERE – Twinned with WHATEVER*. Beyond, the uncharted barbarian lands of the north stretched as far as the eye could see.

'Left a bit. Left a bit. Right a bit. Throw! . . . By the twin orbs of Wotulf the Stormbringer, that was a fine effort for one so untutored.'

'Ooh, do you think so? Can I have another go?'

The barbarian princess reached out a black-fingernailed hand and picked up a second battleaxe. Bracing her legs at the knees, she raised the axe high above her head and took aim at the lemon drizzle cake propped up against the rock a little way off. Swinging her arm athletically, she let go of the axe, sending it spinning towards the target. With a heavy thud, the double-edged battleaxe embedded itself in the centre of the cake, scattering crumbs in all directions.

'Good shot, fair maiden!' exclaimed the hulking barbarian standing by her side. He scratched his thick ginger beard thoughtfully. 'Let's see, you've mastered battle-roaring, swordplay and axe-throwing, now what about a spot of battlecat taming?'

'Battlecats!' said Ella. 'I'd like that! But only if you think I'm ready, Deric.'

Deric the Red threw back his head and gave a roar of barbarian laughter, loud and hearty behind white clenched teeth.

'Ready? Why, by the whiskers of Freya the Beardy, you're a natural, young Ella. Follow me.'

They turned from the axe-range and made their way

along a track that led them through a wooded valley. Tall pine trees studded the rocky slopes to their right and left, a waterfall of crystal-clear mountain water cascaded down into a limpid pool before them, and beyond that lay alpine meadows dotted with yak-skin tents of various shapes and sizes. At the centre of the valley stood a magnificent wooden hall, with ornately carved lintels, onion-domed towers and a mighty pillared archway that framed two huge, black-hinged doors.

Ella followed Deric the Red round the edge of the pool and out across the meadow beyond, towards the tents. Deric paused beside a large patchwork yurt of stitched-together hides, some shaggy and new, some smooth and worn, but all smelling of damp yak.

'Excuse me for a moment,' he said, pulling aside a hairy tent-flap and disappearing inside. There came the sound of pots clattering and wooden chests being rummaged through. A minute later, Deric emerged with a jug and saucer in one hand and a large ball of yak wool in the other. 'This way,' he said cheerfully, his winged helmet wobbling on his head as he nodded towards the nearby meadow.

Ella followed him, catching her reflection in a burnished barbarian shield propped up against a neighbouring tent as she did so. She paused for a moment. She had to admit, she certainly looked the part, with her white-feathered helmet, blonde plaits, tooled-leather breastplate, short pleated barbarian skirt and barbarian sandals cross-laced to the knee.

'Here, kitty, kitty, kitty,' came Deric's bellowing voice.

Ella tore herself away from her reflection and hurried across to the barbarian. Deric the Red was pouring yak's milk from the jug into the saucer he'd placed on the ground at his feet. He stepped back.

'Here, kitty, kitty,' he bellowed.

Out from the dappled shadows of the wooded slopes came an excited roar and the sound of pounding feet as a huge pink-striped creature burst into the meadow. With its broad shoulders, rippling muscles and great sabre-toothed snarl, the cat was twice the size of Tiddles, the battlecat that Edward had 'borrowed' from the stables at Stinkyhogs.

'Careful now,' said Deric gravely. 'They can sense it if you're afraid.'

'I'm not afraid,' said Ella, smiling.

The huge cat came to a halt before them, a growl rumbling at the back of its throat. It fixed Ella with a fiery stare, before lowering its head and sniffing tentatively at the saucer. It shot out a long pink tongue, tasted the milk and began lapping. The growl turned to a purr.

Ella reached out and tickled the cat between the ears. The purr grew louder.

'You've got a way with battlecats,' said Deric approvingly. 'Here, try this.' He handed her the ball of yak wool.

The fearsome beast looked up, milk dripping from

its luxuriant whiskers. Behind it, its mighty tail swished to and fro. It raised a powerful paw and batted at the ball of wool, knocking it from Ella's hands and sending it rolling out across the meadow. With a roaring *miaow*, the pink-striped cat pounced on the unravelling wool, seized it in its claws and rolled on to its back. Ella laughed delightedly and rushed over to tickle its tummy.

'You're just a great big pussycat, aren't you?' she said, as the mighty battlecat's purr grew louder than ever.

'Now you've made friends,' said Deric the Red, 'why not go for a ride?'

'Really?' said Ella. 'Will it let me?'

'You're a barbarian princess with a way with battlecats,' said Deric. 'Why wouldn't it?'

Ella untangled the wool from the battlecat's claws, tickling its tummy as she did so. Climbing to its feet, the battlecat stared at her, its tail twitching expectantly.

'Go on,' said Deric. 'Jump on.'

Stroking the back of its ears, Ella pulled herself up on to the mighty creature's back. She put her arms around its neck and nuzzled its soft fur.

'Go, kitty, kitty. Go,' she whispered.

The battlecat's muscles rippled as it leaped up and galloped across the sunlit meadow. Gripping on tightly with her legs, Ella leaned forward and tickled the battlecat behind its right ear. In response, the creature turned to the right. She tickled the left ear and the creature turned left. They zigzagged round the meadow and then cantered back, coming to a stop in front of Deric as Ella pulled lightly on both the battlecat's ears at once.

'Quite astonishing.' Deric beamed, his white teeth flashing. 'Pinky's one of our biggest and fiercest battlecats. And you handled him like an expert. Well done, Ella!'

Ella slipped from the battlecat's back and stroked his soft pink fur. 'Like I said,' she giggled, 'he's just a great big pussycat. Aren't you, Pinky?'

The battlecat purred.

Just then, there came the sound of loud barbarian laughter and the drumming of galloping feet. A dozen battlecats emerged from the forest and slowed to a trot as they crossed the meadow and approached the tents. Pulling on their reins, their barbarian riders brought the battlecats to a halt and jumped from their saddles with hearty guffaws.

'By the Puddles of Asgard, my pancake batter shall not curdle this time!' said Rulf Son-of-Rulf, tying the reins of his battlecat to a tent-pole.

'Just don't ask to borrow my egg-whisk,' chuckled Glenda Daughter-of-Glenda and slapped him enthusiastically on the back.

'I've got big plans for a chocolate-chip meringue,' said Nigel Nephew-of-Nigel.

The voices of the other barbarians rose in good-natured banter as they patted their battlecats and unpacked their saddle-bags.

'Anyone seen my rolling-pin?'

'I've got a big spoon, if that'll help.'

'Last one to the Great Hall is a soggy crumpet!'

'Wait for me,' came a plaintive voice.

There was the sound of heavy *thud-thud-thud*ding and a giant lop-eared battlerabbit came hopping out of the trees and into the meadow. It paused and nibbled the grass despite the protestations of its rider, a rather weedy-looking barbarian with a wispy moustache. Wayne the Bunnyrider tugged hard on the reins.

'Come *on*, Benjamin,' he cried in frustration, 'or all the best oven gloves will be taken.'

The great black and white rabbit ignored him and continued to graze on the sweet meadow grass. With a petulant sigh, the barbarian jumped from the saddle and chased after the others.

Ella turned to Deric the Red. 'I didn't realize being a barbarian could be this much fun,' she said. 'Sword-fighting, axe-throwing and battlecat-riding out here in the middle of Nowhere . . .'

'Where no one can find us,' came a brooding voice.

Ella spun round. 'Edward!' she exclaimed. 'Where have you been?'

'Nowhere,' he said gloomily, staring up at the wooded mountains that surrounded the valley.

'Oh, Edward, cheer up. It's so beautiful here . . .'

'Beautiful,' said Edward, taking Ella in his muscular arms and staring deep into her eyes, 'but not as beautiful as you.'

'*Ahem*,' said Deric the Red, blushing. 'I've just remembered, I've got a cake in the oven that needs seeing to. If you two will excuse me . . .'

The ginger-bearded barbarian hurried off in the direction of his tent. With a low growl, Pinky the battlecat turned on his heel and loped back across the meadow and into the forest. Neither Ella nor Edward noticed them go.

'You're still so troubled,' said Ella. 'I can see it in your eyes.'

'I've been selfish,' said Edward, shaking his head. 'I should never have allowed you to come away with me.'

'You couldn't have stopped me,' Ella said passionately. 'There's a connection between us. I felt it the very first moment you looked into my eyes. And you felt it too, don't tell me you didn't.'

'Y . . . Yes, I did. But Ella, can't you see?' Edward protested. This thing between us, it can never work. I'm not normal . . .'

'Edward, you know I don't care about *that* . . .'

'How can you not care? I am a creature of the night. A vampire. Every time I take your hand, Ella, it's as much as I can do not to suck your thumb . . .'

'No, Edward,' she protested. 'You're not a creature of the night. It's a beautiful sunny afternoon, and you're here with me.'

'But tonight, Ella . . .' he said, his gorgeous face turning a deathly white, 'while you sleep, I shall be roaming these forests looking for thumbs to suck.'

'You only suck the thumbs of stiltmice and squirrels and little rabbits,' said Ella. 'And then only when you absolutely have to.'

'It's not just that,' said Edward bleakly. 'It's my past. It's come back to haunt me. And by being with me, you're putting yourself in great danger.'

Ella tightened her grip on his arms. 'Edward,' she said, 'who *was* that girl back at the broomball pitch, the pretty one with the lovely black hair?'

Edward flinched and looked away.

'Edward,' said Ella in exasperation, 'who is she? And what *is* this danger? Tell me! Tell me. How can I help you if you won't tell me?'

Edward looked back at her, his pale eyes blazing red. 'Her name, if you must know,' he said, his voice trembling with emotion, 'is Edwina Lovely.' He took a deep breath. 'We first met a very long time ago . . .'

3

Bong! Bong! Bong! Clunk . . .

The clock at the top of the clock-tower struck four o'clock.

Bing! Bing! Bing! The clock below it struck three.

Dongle! Dongle! Dongle! Dongle! Dongle! Dongle! Dongle! Dongle! Dongle! Dongle! Dongle! Dongle! Ping! The one below that struck thirteen.

Like a wobbly stack of children's building-blocks, the clock-tower of Goblintown was made up of clocks of every description. Some were large, some were small; some resembled oversized grandfather clocks, with swinging pendulums and Roman numerals; others looked like short, stout carriage clocks, with spinning cogs and battered brass cases. Some were round, and set in wood; some were square and set in stone. Some had thin, pointy hands and dials with no numbers, others had thick, stubby hands and numbers 1 to 13. Some had bells, some had whistles, some had klaxons and others

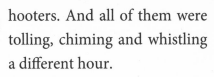

hooters. And all of them were tolling, chiming and whistling a different hour.

At the very top of the clock-tower, two small wooden doors burst open and an elf shot out at the end of a wooden spring. He put a megaphone to his mouth.

'*Cuckoo-cuckoo!*' he called in a small, slightly petulant voice. 'And all's well . . . as can be expected.'

A goblin in the square below paused, lowered the cart he was pushing and gazed up at the clock-tower.

'Is that the time?' he said.

'Don't ask me!' The elf pinged backwards and slammed the little wooden doors behind him.

'I was only asking,' the goblin muttered, picking up the wooden poles of his cart and setting off across the square to make the delivery he was probably already late for.

That was the thing about Goblintown, for the city that never slept was also the city that never kept the right time. Everyone was always late for everything. Or early. And even if they were perfectly on time, no one could ever tell.

The result was that the goblins of Goblintown ate whenever they were hungry, because they never knew when dinnertime was; slept whenever they felt like it, because they could never agree on bedtime, and smelt absolutely appalling – because bathtime was a dirty word. Whatever time of day it was, Goblintown's winding streets and narrow alleyways were filled with unwashed goblins eating snotbread sandwiches and sleeping on benches.

And as if telling the time wasn't difficult enough in Goblintown, finding space was even worse. There quite simply wasn't enough room inside the city walls, but no self-respecting goblin would dream of building his house or shop outside them. This meant that, like the clock-tower, the buildings of Goblintown were stacked one on top of the other to form tall, swaying towers, with winding stairs and crooked ladders linking one storey to the next. What's more, the towers were so tall that the cobbled streets and alleys below were cast in constant darkness and had to be lit by smelly oil-lamps.

The whole of Goblintown was full to bursting, and the pongy air rang out with a constant din of 'Ouch!' and 'Oof!' and 'Get your elbow out of my ear!' It was so cramped, there wasn't even room to swing a cat – which was a shame, since it had put paid to one of the goblins' favourite pastimes . . .

Far up at the top of the tallest tower of all, two goblin

builders were busy constructing the walls of yet another precarious dwelling. They were nailing floorboards to the roof, humming tunelessly, when one of the goblins looked up.

'What do you reckon that is?' he said, pushing his filthy flat-cap back on his head and scratching his scalp.

'What do I reckon *what* is?' said his workmate.

'*That.*' He pointed.

Both goblins laid down their tools, climbed to their feet and looked up at the sky. They squinted into the low sun of the late afternoon, where something small and ripply seemed to be flying straight towards them.

'Is it a bird? Is it a plane? . . .'

'Looks like a flying stair-carpet to me.'

'Flying a magic carpet isn't all plain sailing,' said Randalf sleepily from beneath his pointy hat.

A flock of lazybirds had just flown past, and several had landed on the carpet, yawning loudly. The wizard brushed one of them off his step with a sweep of his staff and shifted into a more comfortable position.

'How would you know when you're fast asleep most of the time?' said Veronica tartly. 'Oi! Buzz off and find your own perch!' she squawked as another lazybird flew in and attempted to settle on the brim of Randalf's hat.

The wizard began to snore.

Sitting next to Norbert on the step below, Joe looked

out across the landscape of Muddle Earth. The Perfumed Bog glistened pinkly far behind them, while in the distance, the mighty Enchanted River flowed through lushly wooded countryside on its way to Trollbridge. Joe could make out the curve of the great bridge and the outline of the buildings clustered along it. Beyond Trollbridge, the hazy hump of a high hill was just visible, a faint smudge on the horizon.

'Harmless Hill,' said Edwina Lovely from the bottom step, her eyes following Joe's gaze. 'The fairy folk live beneath it, ruled by their king and queen, Ron and Tania. Secretive folk, keep themselves to themselves as a general rule . . .'

She tossed back her lovely hair and gave a tinkling laugh.

'A little bit like you, Joe the Barbarian. Come . . .' She patted the carpet beside her. 'Sit here next to me and tell me a little bit about yourself.'

Reluctantly, Joe got up from his seat next to Norbert, who was busy examining the contents of his findy bag, stroking and cooing over each object in turn, and sat down next to Edwina. Perhaps it was her pale skin, cold and clammy to the touch, or her dark-eyed gaze, penetrating and unblinking, or that artificial little laugh of hers – Joe wasn't sure. Whatever the reason, Edwina Lovely made him distinctly uneasy.

'What do you want to know?' said Joe uncertainly.

'Everything,' said Edwina, reaching out and taking Joe's hand in a distinctly clammy grip. 'Such as, where do you come from? And what is your background?' She paused, her eyes growing wide. 'Are you of royal blood?'

'I don't think so,' said Joe, trying to get his hand back. He didn't entirely trust Edwina, and certainly wasn't going to tell her about the lamp-post and the wardrobe and where exactly it was he came from.

'Pity,' said Edwina, tightening her grip and giving him an intense stare. 'I'm a great admirer of royal blood. Take the kings and queens of Golden Towers, for example – so refined and delicate. Or the Sultans of the South – so full-bodied . . .'

'Yes, well, whatever,' said Joe, tugging harder on his hand.

'Aaah! So you're from Whatever!' said Edwina with a

tinkling laugh. 'Twinned with Nowhere!' Her face took on a thoughtful, faraway look. 'It's many years since I had the pleasure of visiting Whatever . . .'

Just then, the stair-carpet gave a shuddering lurch and swerved violently to one side to avoid an immense purple dragon that had flapped slowly into its path. Everyone woke up.

'Watch where you're going!' the dragon huffed smokily, before continuing on its lumbering way.

The stair-carpet gave a little well-pardon-me-for-existing sort of sigh and resumed its flight – but not before Joe had broken free of Edwina's icy grip and scuttled back to Norbert's step.

'Now, what will I find in Goblintown for my findy bag?' the ogre mused, stroking a bath plug on the end of a chain, and returning it to the leather satchel on his lap.

'Edward Gorgeous, with any luck,' said Edwina darkly.

They flew on in silence, the sun sinking low in the sky behind them. Far below, the shadows that streaked the undulating landscape grew longer. They passed over fields and valleys, hills and streams, and a sandpit in which half a dozen trolls with buckets and spades were happily building a sandcastle.

Mile after mile they went. And, as the rippling carpet flew on, its passengers grew drowsy.

Joe closed his eyes, Edwina's lovely head began to nod, while Randalf and Veronica both fell fast asleep, with the budgie on the wizard's shoulder, snuggled up against his beard and snoring. Soon, only Norbert's eyes were open – or rather, *one* of them was. And that was a bit heavy-lidded. The next moment, all three of them blinked with excitement as Norbert caught sight of the fabled walled city, with its glittering towers and smoking chimneys, looming up ahead.

'Goblintown,' he gasped. 'Goblintown, everyone!'

But there was no reply. The others were all fast asleep.

Tiptoeing clumsily to the top step, Norbert eased the staff from Randalf's clutches and raised it above his head. He hit the flying stair-carpet with a resounding *thwack*, sending a cloud of dust up into the air.

'Nice snuggly-wuggly rug,' he boomed in his politest voice. 'Land!'

He thwacked it a second time.

The carpet gave an ouch-that-hurt! kind of sigh and hurtled down towards the ground in a spiralling dive.

'What the . . . ?' shrieked Randalf, waking up and gripping the sides of the carpet in terror.

'Whoooaah!' Joe cried out.

'Waaaah!' screeched Edwina.

The carpet came to a shuddering halt inches from the ground, hovered for a moment, then flipped over, sending its passengers sprawling in the dust. With a that'll-teach-you sigh, it rolled itself up tightly and propped itself against a wall.

'Norbert!' Randalf stormed as he climbed shakily

to his feet. 'Give me that staff at once! What were you thinking of?'

'Sorry, sir,' said Norbert tearfully. 'You were all sleeping so peacefully, I didn't want to disturb you.'

'Well, you've certainly disturbed us now!' snapped Randalf. 'Joe? Are you all right? And how about you, Edwina? Here, let me help you up.'

'I'm fine, wizard,' said Edwina testily, brushing the dust from her lovely dress. 'No thanks to Numbutt here.'

'Sorry,' said Norbert, the tears welling up in his triple eyes.

'It's all right,' said Joe, patting the ogre on the back. 'No harm done. And look, we've landed in the perfect place.' He pointed at the building that the rolled-up stair-carpet was leaning against. Like all the buildings of Goblintown, it was tall and tottering, but this one also had a small wooden sign above the door which read, *Brinsley Blowfly's B & B – 8th Floor*. 'Perhaps we could get a bed for the night,' Joe suggested.

'Good idea,' said Randalf. 'I'm absolutely exhausted. What I need is a good night's sleep.'

'To go with the good *day's* sleep you've just had,' said Veronica.

'Shut up, Veronica!' said Randalf, picking up the stair-carpet and pushing open the door.

He stepped inside. The others followed, and together they climbed a rickety flight of stairs. Then another. And another. Then a ladder. Then a longer ladder. Then another three flights of stairs, until they came to a low wooden door with *Brinsley Blowfly's B & B* scrawled on it in red crayon.

'This looks like the place,' said Randalf.

'How can you tell?' said Veronica sarcastically.

Randalf reached into his robes and pulled out a small, misshapen silver coin. 'My last pipsqueak,' he said. 'Should be enough for a room for the night – but we can't expect a bed or breakfast.'

Joe frowned. 'So, what does the *B & B* stand for?'

'Bananas and Broccoli, of course,' said Randalf. 'To stuff in your ears if the snoring gets too loud.'

'Silly me,' Joe sighed. 'I should have guessed.'

Randalf raised his staff and rapped on the door, which was opened immediately by a small grubby-looking goblin.

'What do you want?' he mumbled.

'We seek shelter for the night, my good fellow,' said Randalf cheerily, waving the silver pipsqueak under the goblin's nose. 'Show us the finest accommodation this esteemed establishment has to offer.'

'So you want a room?' said the goblin.

'Indeed we do,' said Randalf.

'Follow me then.'

At the end of a dingy corridor that smelled of old socks and even older underwear, the goblin showed them into a low-ceilinged attic. There was a heap of straw on the floor covered with a sheet, and a threadbare blanket folded beside it. In one corner of the room was a wooden bowl filled with brown-flecked bananas and sprigs of wilting broccoli.

'We'll take it!' said Randalf, handing over the silver pipsqueak.

'Please yourself,' shrugged the goblin. He pocketed the coin and left.

What a dump, thought Joe, looking around the room.

The others didn't seem to notice. Edwina Lovely removed her cloak, spread it on the floor beneath the small attic window and sat down daintily upon it. Norbert plumped up the straw, smoothed out the sheet and laid the blanket over it.

'Your bed's ready for you, sir,' he announced. 'And you, Joe. I'm happy on the floor.'

'Pardon?' said Randalf, who had stuffed a peeled banana in one ear and a sprig of broccoli in the other. 'Ah, I see my bed's ready. Good night, everyone.'

The wizard flopped on to the straw, pulled his hat down over his eyes and started snoring. On the brim, Veronica put her head under her wing. Norbert rummaged in his findy bag, drew out a ragdoll and snuggled it against his cheek as he curled up on the floorboards.

'Good night, Angela,' he cooed, cuddling the ragdoll and closing his triple eyes.

Joe lay down. The straw beneath the sheet felt prickly, but at least it was better than the hard floorboards. Despite the gloom, he was uncomfortably aware of Edwina Lovely, who was still sitting beneath the window, gazing up at the two moons of Muddle Earth which had risen that night. The third was nowhere to be seen.

'Sweet dreams, Joe the Barbarian,' she whispered sweetly.

Joe closed his eyes. Goblintown, he thought. It hadn't changed a jot since the last time he was here. It was still noisy, smelly and overcrowded, and as for the hotel rooms . . .

Randalf was snoring thunderously, and Joe was almost tempted to stuff some of the bananas and broccoli into his own ears. But he was too weary to bother. Despite everything, he must have drifted off to sleep, for some time later something woke him. He opened his eyes and as they became accustomed to the gloom he saw that the attic window was ajar, and Edwina Lovely was nowhere to be seen.

Odd, he thought, and fell asleep again.

'Wakey-wakey, everyone!'

It was Edwina. She looked lovely. Her hair was glossy, her cheeks were rosy and her eyes sparkled.

'It's time to find this goblin, Smutley,' she announced, 'and get him to tell us everything he knows about Edward and his gang . . .'

'Why are you so sure it was Edward who stole the Goblet of Porridge anyway?' said Joe. 'Edward just doesn't strike me as the goblet-stealing type.'

Edwina glared at him. 'If you knew Edward the way I know Edward, you'd understand he's capable of *anything*.' She reached down and pulled the banana out of Randalf's ear. 'Wake up, wizard!' she shouted.

'And let's go and find Smutley.'

'Three and fourpence, and go easy on the jam . . .' said Randalf, sitting bolt upright. 'Where am I?'

'You're in a rundown flophouse in Goblintown being bossed about by a little madam,' said Veronica, *'that's* where.'

'Control your parrot, wizard,' snapped Edwina, turning on her heel and marching out of the room. 'Come *on!*' her voice echoed from the corridor.

'You heard her,' said Randalf, climbing to his feet. 'To Grubley's Discount Garment Store!'

Five minutes later, they were striding through the streets of Goblintown. Randalf was in front, staff under one arm and rolled-up carpet under the other, being urged on by a determined-looking Edwina Lovely. Joe followed, with Norbert lagging behind as he scanned the stalls and shopfronts, his hand hovering over the findy bag at his side. Veronica fluttered overhead, muttering under her breath and giving Edwina filthy looks.

'There it is,' said Randalf, stopping in front of a modest tower made up of four clothes shops, one on top of the other. 'Follow me.'

Here we go again, Joe thought as they marched through *Unction's Upmarket Outfitters*, climbed the stairs to *Mingletrip's Middle-of-the-Road Emporium*, took a spiral staircase to *Drool's Downmarket Depot*, and finally braved a flimsy ladder to *Grubley's Discount Garment Store*, where they were greeted by a smartly dressed shop assistant.

'Greetings, gentlemen, lady, budgie,' he said, nodding at each of them in turn and leading them inside the clothing store. 'The name's Smink. How might I facilitate your garment-purchasing needs this fabulous morning? A new gown for sir here?' he said, plucking a shimmering red cape trimmed with sequinned stars from a rail and handing it to Randalf. 'And a hat, perhaps,' he said, removing Randalf's pointy hat.

Veronica hopped on to Joe's shoulder with an indignant chirrup.

Smink placed a huge furry trilby on Randalf's head and steered him towards the mirror. 'And would sir like a tie to go with that? Kipper tie? Eel tie? Herring tie, knitted or unknitted? Halibut cravat? Haddock bow-tie? Oh, sir would look *marvellous* in a haddock bow-tie, if you don't mind me saying so.'

'Actually . . .' Randalf began.

'We're looking for Smutley,' Edwina butted in.

'What's he been up to now?' came a gruff voice, and a grim-faced goblin appeared from behind a rack of blouses. 'No, don't tell me, Randalf, not more exploding gas-frogs! Or have you caught him whittling in the staff room again? If I've told him once, I've told him a thousand times . . .'

'No, no, no, Grubbers,' said Randalf. 'He hasn't done anything wrong. We just want a word with him.' He frowned. 'Is he here?'

'It's "Mister Grubley" to you,' said Grubley, and his eyes narrowed as he noticed the cape and hat Randalf was wearing. 'And are you intending to buy those?'

'They do suit you, sir,' said Smink smarmily.

'OK, Smink, that'll do,' said Grubley, removing the fur trilby from Randalf's head. 'If I know Randalf here, he hasn't got two muckles to rub together.' He took the cape. 'If you want Smutley, you'll find him in Ladies Underwear upstairs.'

They climbed a rope ladder that went up through a hole in the ceiling and found themselves in a small, cramped room full of boxes and crates and bowed racks laden with frilly undergarments. Smutley was kneeling on the floor, a clipboard in one hand and a pencil in the other, busily ticking off items he was pulling from a large cardboard box.

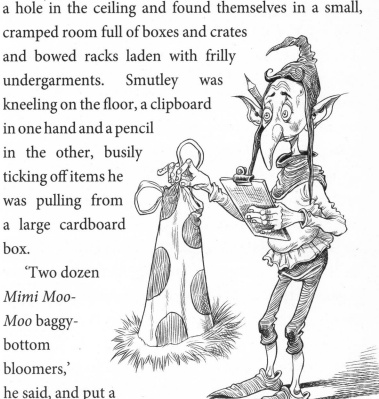

'Two dozen *Mimi Moo-Moo* baggy-bottom bloomers,' he said, and put a tick next to the order.

'Check. Three dozen pairs of *Twinkletoe* sparkle-tights, with reinforced gussets. Check. Six dozen *Big Bessie* feather-trimmed nighties . . .'

'Smutley?' said Randalf.

The goblin spun round. 'Headmaster?' he said, blushing a shade of red that matched the *Big Bessie* feather-trimmed nighties. 'What are you doing here? It's the school holidays, isn't it?'

He noticed Joe standing beside Randalf, and hid the nightie he was holding behind his back.

'Joe the Barbarian,' he said. 'Just helping out my dad with a spot of stocktaking,' he explained.

'And very nice stock it is too,' said Norbert. 'Lovely feathers . . .'

'When did you last see Edward Gorgeous?' Edwina interrupted, her lovely eyes flashing. 'He's your team-mate. You're not hiding him, are you?'

'Hiding him? Why would I do that?' said Smutley with a shrug. 'For your information, I've never liked him. Far too full of himself, if you ask me.'

'These really are quite fetching,' said Randalf, holding up a pair of the *Mimi Moo-Moo* baggy-bottom bloomers. 'I particularly like the sparkly cow jumping over the glittery moon on the back.'

'And judging by the size of them,' said Veronica, 'they might even fit you.'

'For crying out loud!' Edwina Lovely said. 'Smutley, when did you last see Edward Gorgeous?'

Smutley scratched his head. 'Last time I saw him, he and your sister – Ella, is it?'

Joe nodded.

'The pair of them were slipping out of the school gates on the back of that battlecat. I thought it was a bit odd at the time, seeing as how we were about to be presented with the Goblet of Porridge. Percy and I had just nipped off to change our shirts. We were hurrying back when Ella and Edward passed us on the battlecat. Percy was behind me, and I looked round to see Edward lean down and whisper in his ear. I didn't want to miss the presentation so I barged my way through the crowd to the tent, and you know the rest.'

'What did Edward whisper?' asked Joe.

'I dunno,' said Smutley with a shrug. 'You'll have to ask Percy that.'

'The troll!' Edwina Lovely exclaimed. 'You know what this means, don't you, wizard? We must go to Trollbridge.'

Randalf put down the baggy-bottomed bloomers and sighed. 'Must we?'

'If you wish to recover the Goblet of Porridge,' said Edwina sweetly.

Randalf shrugged. He laid the roll of carpet down on the floor and tapped it with his staff.

'O floor covering of supreme quality and superlative weave,' he said. 'If you'd be so good as to unroll.'

The stair-carpet obeyed.

'Climb aboard, everyone,' said Randalf. 'Not you, Smutley. The stair-carpet's quite full enough, thank you.' He tapped the flying carpet a second time. 'Take us to Trollbridge, O tufted transport of delight.'

Moments later, they were sweeping out through one of the narrow windows of the Discount Garment Store, and soaring up into the air. Before long, Goblintown was no more than a faint odour on the wind as the flying stair-carpet carried them across Muddle Earth towards Trollbridge.

Randalf, Joe and Edwina were sitting on their usual steps. Norbert was not. Randalf had just caught him red-handed – and redder-faced – pulling a *Big Bessie* feather-trimmed nightie out of his findy bag, and sent him straight to the naughty step right at the bottom of the carpet, where he would have time to think about just what a naughty thing he'd done.

'I knew it was wrong to take it, Joe,' said Norbert shamefacedly, 'but I just couldn't resist those snuggly feathers.'

But Joe wasn't listening. He was staring at Edwina Lovely, who, with her rosy cheeks and sparkling eyes, was looking lovelier than ever.

'Edwina?' he said.

'Yes, Joe?' she said, turning towards him and flashing him a lovely smile.

'Where did you go last night?'

'Go?' she said. 'I . . . I don't know what you're talking about?'

'I woke up,' said Joe. 'And when I looked over, you weren't there . . . And the window was open.'

'Oh, Joe, you silly barbarian, you must have been dreaming,' she said, and laughed that tinkly laugh of hers. 'I didn't go anywhere.'

It was market day in Trollbridge. In fact, every day was market day in Trollbridge.

As usual, trolls were coming from far and wide, from the turnip patches, the swede fields and the mangelwurzel plots which lined the banks of the Enchanted River. Pushing their rickety wheelbarrows piled high with extravagantly large root vegetables, the trolls raised their voices in happy song as they trundled towards the great arched bridge.

> *Ten fat turnips sitting on the bridge,*
> *Ten fat turnips sitting on the bridge,*
> *And if one fat turnip should accidently slip,*
> *There'll be . . . umm . . . errrm . . .*
>
> *Ten fat swedes sitting on the bridge,*
> *Ten fat swedes sitting on the bridge,*
> *And if one fat swede should accidently slip,*
> *There'll be . . . umm . . . errrm . . .*

Ten fat mangelwurzels sitting on the bridge,
Ten fat mangelwurzels sitting on the bridge . . .

Already on the crowded bridge, the market stalls and benches groaned beneath the weight of pumpkins, parsnips, cauliflowers, cabbages and purple-spotted potatoes of unfeasible size. Matrons in straw bonnets resembling buckets and watering cans mingled with troll maidens with beribboned plaits braided with marrow flowers. Stallholders in capacious aprons and impressive corduroy breeches juggled with knobbly vegetables and called out their wares.

'Sweetest sugar beets, two muckles a basket!'

'Finest potatoes, a pipsqueak a sack.'

'Amusing-shaped carrots, ten groats a snigger!'

Just another market day in Trollbridge. The sun was shining, birds were singing, buckets of manure were gently steaming . . .

'Help! Help! Help!' The cries from beneath the bridge grew louder and more desperate. 'For pity's sake, HELP!'

'Just take Norbert's hand, Randalf,' said Joe, 'and stop making such a fuss.'

'Shan't!' said Randalf. 'It's his fault we got dumped in the river in the first place. How many times do I have to tell you? Don't land the carpet on your own . . .'

'Sorry, sir,' Norbert sobbed. 'I forgot.'

'That's all very well, Norbert,' said Randalf, who was sitting waist-deep in the gently flowing waters of the

Enchanted River, his soggy pointy hat drooping, 'but look at the carpet. It's ruined.'

The flying stair-carpet was lying in a sodden heap on the riverbank, where Joe, Edwina and Norbert had hauled it. They too were soaking wet. From overhead came a smug chirp as Veronica fluttered down and landed on Joe's shoulder.

'Looks like the naughty step for you again, Norbert,' she giggled. 'If that thing ever flies again.'

'Stand up, Wizard,' said Edwina, dripping wet but still lovely. 'We haven't got time for this. Let's get on to the bridge and find that troll, Percy.'

Randalf climbed meekly to his feet and waded to the riverbank with as much dignity as he could muster. Edwina turned on her heel and marched up the path towards the magnificent gate-towers of Trollbridge. The others followed, with Norbert bringing up the rear, a crumpled mass of dripping carpet cradled in his arms. They approached the large wooden gateway that led on to the bridge, where a portly troll in patched dungarees was sitting on a three-legged stool. He put out a hand.

'Troll toll,' he said. 'Pay up.'

'Of course,' said Randalf, nodding. He made a great show of going through his pockets. 'Dear, dear,' he said at last. 'I seem to have spent my last pipsqueak. Edwina, I don't suppose . . .'

'Like Queen Susan,' she said snootily, 'I never carry money.'

Randalf sighed. 'Norbert?' he said.

'I've got that I.O.U. you gave me,' said the ogre, pulling a soggy piece of paper from his pocket. 'But the invisible ink seems to have been washed off.'

'Ah, yes. Well, never mind . . .' he said. 'How about you, Joe?'

Joe looked in his own pockets. He pulled out a laminated bus-pass, a packet of chewing gum and a rusty washer. The troll seized the dripping objects.

'That'll do nicely,' he said. 'I won't charge you for the parrot.'

'Budgerigar, *if* you don't mind,' said Veronica stiffly.

The troll heaved himself up off his stool, plodded across to the gate and pushed it open. 'Welcome to Trollbridge,' he said cheerfully, as Randalf, Norbert, Edwina and Joe filed past.

'Parrot indeed!' muttered Veronica as she fluttered down on to Randalf's hat. 'Does he look like a pirate?'

The gate slammed shut behind them.

'Trollbridge!' said Randalf, looking down at a pile

of rotten cabbage leaves. 'The city that never sweeps.' He stepped daintily over the cabbage leaves, and into a dollop of manure.

'I see what you mean,' said Edwina, wrinkling her lovely nose. 'Out of the way! Wizard on important business!'

She barged her way through the bustling crowd. It parted before her, the trolls giving the lovely stranger in the damp dress puzzled looks.

'Where do we find this Percy Throwback of yours?' Edwina called to Randalf over her shoulder.

'Percy Throwback?' said a hefty troll matron in a raffia bonnet shaped like a flowerpot. 'Why, that's old Nodding Ned and Lazy Susan's lad.' She shifted her trug of scallions from one arm to the other and gave Edwina a snaggle-tusked smile. 'They live under number 25, Southside Archway.' She pointed up ahead. 'First right after the marrow stall. You can't miss it.'

Edwina strode off.

'Thank you,' said Joe politely, and hurried after her, followed by Randalf and Norbert.

They reached a large trestle-table with a striped awning flapping above it, where a troll in a smock was busy polishing marrows. To the right of it, embedded in the cobblestones that ran along the balustrade of the bridge, were row upon row of numbered trapdoors.

'Here it is,' Edwina announced, briskly stamping her foot on a green trapdoor with the number 25 painted on it, and stepping back.

From below them came a gruff voice. 'If that's another one of those billy goats, tell him we're not interested.'

A moment later, the trapdoor opened and Percy's head appeared. He stared up at Edwina.

'Do I know you?' he said.

'Never mind that,' said Edwina, fixing him with a penetrating stare. 'I have good reason to be believe that you and that criminal, Edward Gorgeous, are in cahoots . . .'

'In cahoots? I'm not in cahoots. I'm in Trollbridge,' said Percy, perplexed. 'And I don't know where Edward Gorgeous is.'

He noticed the others, who had just caught up with Edwina and were now standing round the trapdoor.

'Headmaster?' Percy said. 'Joe!' He stepped up on to the bridge and shook Joe's hand delightedly. 'That was some broomball match!' he exclaimed. 'We really showed that snooty Golden Towers lot a thing or two. Pity about the Goblet of Porridge though . . .'

'Aha!' said Edwina. 'What exactly can you tell us about the goblet's disappearance? It was Edward, wasn't it? *He* stole it. Didn't he? Come on, admit it.'

'Edward?' Percy shook his head. 'I don't think so. I was just coming back from changing my shirt when Edward and Ella came riding past on a battlecat, and they certainly didn't have the Goblet of Porridge with them. I asked them where they were going and Edward said nowhere . . .'

'Nowhere,' Edwina breathed.

'Very interesting,' said Randalf, tugging at his beard. 'So it *must* have been the jeer-leaders who stole the Goblet of Porridge . . .'

'Percy? Percy! Who is it?'

Two more heads appeared at the trapdoor.

'Mum, Dad,' said Percy excitedly as his parents stepped up on to the bridge, 'it's my headmaster. And my friend Joe from school. And this is Norbert, who does the dinners, and Veronica, the headmaster's secretary bird.'

'Very pleased to make your acquaintance,' said Nodding Ned, nodding.

'Any friends of Percy's are always welcome here,' said Lazy Susan. 'Oh, my goodness! What have you done to that carpet?' she said, her gaze falling on the soggy stair-carpet in Norbert's arms. 'Here, give it to me. Let me hang it up for you.' She took the carpet from Norbert, carried it across to the side of the bridge and hung it over the balustrade. 'It'll be dry in no time.'

'Well, we're not going anywhere until it is,' said Randalf.

'Then you must join us for a spot of lunch,' said Lazy Susan. 'I've got a lovely mangelwurzel tart with turnip custard and all the trimmings.'

Nodding Ned nodded.

'And you're all very welcome,' said Percy. 'Even what's-her-name.' He frowned. 'Where is she?'

Everyone looked around, but Edwina Lovely was nowhere to be seen.

'Too sneaky by half, that one,' said Veronica.

'She calls me Numbutt,' said Norbert.

'She gives me the creeps,' said Joe.

'I know what you mean,' said Randalf. 'And she's a little too bossy for my liking.' He rubbed his tummy and turned to Lazy Susan. '*Mangelwurzel* tart, did you say? With turnip custard and *all* the trimmings?'

Nodding Ned nodded enthusiastically.

After what could only be described as a veritable banquet of root vegetables of every shape, size and description, served by their generous hostess on an enormous revolving table, Joe was feeling rather sick. And it wasn't just the food . . .

Although his big sister had run off with a barbarian to goodness knows where on the back of a battlecat, at least Joe now knew that they weren't part of this gang Edwina had gone on about. According to Percy, those strange jeer-leaders were acting on their own in stealing the goblet. Edwina had been wrong to accuse Edward of being their leader.

What did she have against the handsome barbarian anyway? Joe wondered.

The thing was, now that Edwina had run off, he couldn't even ask her. The Goblet of Porridge, the jeer-leaders, Edward, his sister Ella, Edwina – *all* of them had disappeared. It made his head swim and his tummy gurgle. And the food wasn't helping . . .

The mangelwurzel tart looked like a cowpat and tasted of mud, while the turnip custard smelled of old wellington boots. As for the trimmings, these turned out to be various jellies in the shape of vegetables that wobbled to and fro as the table slowly turned. Joe took one mouthful of the Brussels sprout jelly and immediately regretted it.

The others had no such misgivings. Randalf and Norbert joined in with the Throwback family with gusto.

Meanwhile, Veronica hopped around the table pecking contentedly at pumpkin seeds and pastry crumbs.

'If you'll excuse me,' said Joe, 'I think I need a little bit of fresh air.'

'Excellent idea,' said Randalf, sitting back and patting his mouth with a napkin. 'I think I'll join you. See how the flying carpet's coming along. There's no time to waste. We've still got that goblet to find. Now, where could those jeer-leaders have got to? We've got some serious detective work to do!' He got up from the table. 'Norbert, put down that spoon. And Veronica, hop on to my hat.'

'Your word is my command, Fatso,' said Veronica sarcastically, landing on the brim of his pointy hat.

'Thank you so much,' said Norbert to Lazy Susan. 'That turnip custard was delicious. It tasted just like wellington boots. You must let me have the recipe.'

Randalf shook hands with Nodding Ned, who nodded, and patted Percy on the head. 'See you back at Stinkyhogs next term.'

And with that, they left the Throwbacks' cosy cabin and stepped back on to the bustling bridge. Joe closed the trapdoor of number 25 and followed Norbert and Randalf over to the balustrade, where Lazy Susan had hung the carpet to dry. A short, wiry goblin with a long, thin, drooping moustache was sitting a little way off, his legs dangling over the side of the bridge as he stared glumly at the water below. Lost in thought, he didn't look up as Randalf prodded the soggy carpet with his staff.

'Still a little damp,' he observed, 'but that soak in the Enchanted River has brought out its colours beautifully.'

Joe looked at the carpet. The wizard was right. The once drab brown stair-carpet was now a rich shade of blue, with an intricate border of interwoven leaves, fruits and flowers in an array of exquisite colours.

'It's beautiful,' he said.

'Thank you,' whispered the carpet in a small, breathy voice.

'You can talk!' said Joe in surprise.

'That's all we need,' chirped Veronica. 'A talking stair-carpet.'

'Yes,' muttered Randalf to himself. 'Budgies, carpets . . . Whatever next?'

'Thank you, O great magician of large yet dainty feet,' whispered the stair-carpet, 'for your great wisdom in dunking me in the waters of yonder river, thereby washing away all those years of dust and grime. Why, I feel like a completely new carpet – fresh, fragrant and so, so pretty . . . *Tra-la-la-la-la-la* . . .'

'Oh, great,' said Veronica sarcastically. 'A talking, *singing* stair-carpet.'

'*Tra-la-la* . . .' The carpet fell abruptly quiet. 'I don't *believe* it,' it whispered in a small, outraged voice. 'I'd know those feet anywhere!'

It rose a couple of inches from the balustrade and hovered in mid-air, quivering with indignation. Joe, Randalf and Norbert turned and, for the first time, noticed the weedy-looking goblin sitting with his legs dangling down over the side of the bridge. The goblin looked up, his mournful expression changing to one of surprise.

'Randalf? Randalf, is that you?' said the goblin.

Randalf frowned. 'Do I know you?' he said uncertainly.

'Of course you do,' said the goblin. 'Isn't my voice familiar?'

'Horned Baron!' exclaimed Randalf. 'I didn't recognize you without your horned helmet!' He strode across to him, his hand outstretched. 'How *are* you, my dear chap?'

The Horned Baron's face slumped as he stared down at his dangling feet, the waters of the Enchanted River flowing far beneath.

'Not so good,' he said.

Behind him, Joe heard the carpet harrumph. 'Serves him right for using me as a stair-carpet in his rotten old castle for all those years,' it complained. 'He treated me like a doormat and walked all over me,' it whispered bitterly.

The Horned Baron didn't seem to hear it. His bony body began to shake. His thin moustache trembled and his eyes welled up with tears.

'When I hung up my horned helmet and stepped down from the throne to begin my new life with Fifi, I'd never been so happy. With our beautiful little trapdoor cottage, a turnip patch of our very own and the best humorously shaped vegetable stall in the whole of Trollbridge, who wouldn't be happy? Oh, but now it's all ruined.'

'It is?' said Randalf.

'Utterly,' the Horned Baron said bleakly, and wiped his nose on a grubby handkerchief. 'For Fifi's heart has been stolen by another.'

'It has?' said Randalf.

'Yes!' said the Horned Baron, reaching into his smock and pulling out a dog-eared letter. He flourished it theatrically. 'I have the proof here in my hand. I intercepted the post-elf. '*Dearest Hrothgar,*' he read out in a tearful voice, '*my hero, my life-saver, I'll bring everything you asked for, plus a little something of my own. I want this to be really special.* Look!' he said, waving the letter under Randalf's nose. 'She even underlined the *really special* bit!'

'She did?' said Randalf.

'And there's more!' the Horned Baron wailed. '*I'll see*

you at your place at the usual time. And remember, on no account is Walter to learn of this! With thanks, love and kisses, Fifi. 'Thanks!' the baron moaned. 'Love!' he groaned. '*Kisses!*' He buried his head in his hands. 'I've *lost* her!'

'I'm sure it's not as bad as you think,' said Randalf, patting the Horned Baron on the shoulder.

'It is. It *is* . . .' insisted the Horned Baron miserably. 'Hrothgar! That's a barbarian name. What if he's tall and dark and handsome?'

'Looks are overrated,' said Randalf.

'And rich. What if he's rich?'

'Money isn't everything,' said Randalf.

'And muscles. Great big muscles . . .'

'But you have brains, Horned Baron,' said Randalf.

'And a helmet! What if he's got the largest and most magnificent horned helmet in all of Muddle Earth?'

'*Aaah*,' said Randalf. 'I see your problem. Still,' he said brightly, taking the Horned Baron by the arm, 'you mustn't do anything silly.'

He helped him down from the balustrade.

'Humph,' whispered the carpet huffily. It rolled itself up tightly and leaned against Joe.

Just then, the Horned Baron let out a stifled cry and shrank back behind Norbert. 'Shh,' he hissed urgently. 'It's *her!*'

'Who?' said Norbert.

'Haven't you been listening?' chirruped Veronica

as a tall, elegantly dressed troll maiden sashayed over the bridge towards them.

She wore a broad-brimmed hat covered in flowering courgettes and carried a large wicker picnic basket on one arm. She was concentrating so intently on the shopping list she held in her gloved hand that she didn't notice the small group on the bridge as she passed by.

'Has she gone?' whispered the Horned Baron a moment later, and stepped out from behind Norbert. He turned to Randalf. 'Do you know what? I'm almost tempted to put on my horned helmet once more and return to the castle . . .'

'To Stinkyhogs?' Randalf squeaked.

Veronica landed on Joe's shoulder and chirruped in his ear. 'If he does, then Fatso's going to be looking for a new job.'

'O floor-covering of colourful delight, unfurl if you please,' said Randalf. The stair-carpet obeyed. They all jumped aboard, and Randalf tapped the carpet with his staff. 'Follow that troll!'

With a mighty roar, the magnificent pink-striped battlecat bounded through the forest. Its muscles rippled beneath its sleek pelt as it swerved this way and that, at one with the sinuous movements of its rider.

The barbarian princess sat back in the saddle and twitched the reins in her black-fingernailed hands. In answer, the battlecat swung to the left and ran full tilt towards a sparkling pool of crystal-clear water. Without hesitating, it sprang from rock to rock across the mirrored surface of the pool. Looking down, the barbarian princess caught the fleeting reflection of a powerful battlecat and its graceful rider.

She tugged on the reins, instantly bringing the battlecat to a halt on a mossy boulder. She leaned forward and examined her reflection.

Ella's eyes widened with astonishment. She hardly recognized herself. Staring back at her was a noble barbarian princess, confident and poised, and in perfect control of an extraordinary mythic beast. It felt wonderful, exhilarating, and so natural. It was as if this person had been inside her all along, but trapped and ignored and struggling to get out.

She sat admiring her reflection for several minutes before the low, impatient growl of her battlecat interrupted her thoughts.

'OK, Pinky, time to head back,' Ella agreed.

She twitched the reins, and the battlecat set off once more through the forest. They bounded down the steep wooded slopes, past the mighty waterfall, its spray forming rainbows in the sunny mountain air, and out across the alpine meadow beyond. Crouching in the lush pasture, head down and loppy ears drooping, a giant battlerabbit was grazing intently on the sweet grass, while its rider sat, arms folded, upon its back.

'Hello, Wayne,' said Ella as she trotted past. 'Just taken Pinky out for his early-morning ride.'

'Oh, hello, Ella,' said Wayne, looking up shyly. 'I've been trying to take Benjamin out for his early-morning hop, though we don't seem to have got very far.'

'Never mind,' said Ella, tickling Pinky between the ears. 'See you later.'

Ella pulled up next to the tents and jumped down from Pinky's back. She removed his bridle, unbuckled the saddle and tickled him under the chin.

'Who's a good pussycat?' she said. 'Time for breakfast.'

Pinky purred and nuzzled against her for a moment,

before trotting over to join the other battlecats, who were gathered in a circle around a giant saucer, slurping yak milk.

'Good morning, young Ella,' said Deric the Red, emerging from his yak-skin yurt. 'By the tinkling bells of Olaf the Pixie's boots, you're every inch the barbarian princess!' he exclaimed. 'Why, only last night as we feasted, I was saying to Quentin of the Really Large Spoon how impressed I was with you.' He smiled. 'I think you're ready.'

'Ready?' said Ella excitedly.

'Yes,' said Deric the Red. 'Ready to enter the Great Hall!'

He clapped an arm around her shoulders and led her along the broad path through the alpine meadow, away from the cluster of yak-skin yurts and the contented purrs of the breakfasting battlecats, and towards the magnificent wooden building at the centre of the valley. As they approached, Ella looked up. The Great Hall towered above them, tall and majestic, its onion-domed towers gleaming in the sunlight.

From every nook and cranny, the carved heads of barbarian gods and goddesses stared down. Wotulf the Stormbringer, cheeks puffed out and mouth forming an O, clutched an egg-whisk in one clawed hand. Beside him, Freya the Beardy, her plaited whiskers spreading out like branches of a fir tree, cradled a mixing bowl in the crook of her arm and stirred the cake-mixture inside with a hand in the shape of a wooden spoon. The other gods of Asgard were all there too – Gudrun, Igor, Luptoft and Lokki, Beverley, Bruce, Lionel and Stephen – all clutching their immortal implements of culinary prowess. Even Olaf the Pixie, prancing imp of the afterlife, was represented. Carved in seasoned pine, the tiny bells on his pointy-toed boots had been lovingly depicted, along with his twenty-three little fingers, each one sticky with pancake batter.

Deric the Red strode up to the pillared entrance of the hall, raised a clenched fist and *tap-tappety-tapped* demurely on one of the two huge black-hinged doors.

'By the eggy whisk of Wotulf the Stormbringer,' he bellowed, 'we seek admittance to the Great Hall!'

From inside came the rasp of heavy iron bolts being drawn back and the jangle of chains being removed. A key turned, a latch lifted, and the door creaked slowly open. Deric stepped aside and ushered Ella into the hall.

It took a few moments for Ella's eyes to become accustomed to the gloom. Flaming torches cast a dim, flickering light over the vast interior. The black-and-white-tiled floor was strewn with straw, while heavy timbers formed impregnable, windowless walls which rose up to a vaulted roof of joists and beams high overhead, where fruit-cake bats and cookie ravens flitted to and fro.

Ella followed Deric the Red past a vast brass stove, the length of a broomball pitch, which stood against the wall to her right. Its surface was studded with enough hobs and hot-plates to accommodate a hundred pots and pans, while beneath, a row of gleaming doors concealed ovens big enough to bake a hundred cakes at any one time. At the stove, barbarians wearing pinafores and oven gloves were busy at work, stirring batter, beating egg whites and pouring cake-mixture into buttered cake-trays, the feathers on their winged helmets drooping in the heat.

'Greetings, Ella!' called Rulf Son-of-Rulf.

'Welcome to the Great Hall at last,' chuckled Glenda Daughter-of-Glenda.

'Coming through,' said Nigel Nephew-of-Nigel,

rushing past with a trayful of steaming chocolate-chip meringues.

'You'll have to excuse Nigel,' said Deric the Red dramatically. 'He's taking part in the teatime challenge.' He took Ella by the arm and steered her away. 'Come with me,' he said.

Beyond the stove, they came to a huge round table. There was a hole in the middle, in which stood a gilded high-backed throne, upholstered with red velvet. Around the outer circumference of the table stood a ring of three-legged stools. And on one of the stools sat a small, fussy-looking individual with white bouffant hair and a neatly trimmed beard.

'That's Quentin of the Really Big Spoon,' Deric the Red whispered to Ella, stopping at the far side of the table. 'He's our cake druid. We'd better wait here . . .'

In front of the cake druid the place was set with a cup and saucer, a teapot, a milk jug and a sugar bowl with winged tongs, all standing on lace doilies. He held a large wooden spoon in his hand, which he raised and waved.

'Let the challenge begin,' he said grandly.

At his words, three big, burly barbarians lumbered over to the table, elbowing and barging into each other in their eagerness to get there first. Forming a disorderly line, they shoved their plates under the cake druid's nose.

'Gentlemen, gentlemen,' Quentin chided them with a wave of his large wooden spoon. 'How many times must I tell you? Presentation is half the battle!'

The barbarians took a step back and looked at Quentin expectantly. The cake druid inspected the cakes on the plates before him. He poured himself a cup of tea, took a sip and placed the cup back on the saucer.

'Well?' said the barbarians, craning their necks forward and trying to trip each other up.

'You can't rush these things,' said Quentin, picking up the first cake.

It was a squashed-looking Victoria sponge. Quentin sniffed it tentatively, then took a cautious bite.

'Somebody's been overdoing the strawberry jam again, hasn't he, Wulfgar?' he said.

He picked up the second cake.

'Rock cake, Gawain? Really? Do you think that's wise?' Quentin rapped it sharply with his big wooden spoon. 'Suitable for target practice rather than teatime, don't you think?'

He turned to Nigel Nephew-of-Nigel's chocolate-chip meringue.

'Intriguing,' he said. He picked the meringue up. 'And so light.' He took a bite. 'Mmm, and really not too bad at all. Mind you, it's still far from the standard required in the Big Barbarian Bake-Off. You've got a lot of work to do, young Nigel. Now, clear the table, all of you.'

'Yes, Quentin. Thank you, Quentin,' the three barbarians chorused, and bowed clumsily.

They picked up their plates and tea things and carried them towards the back of the hall. In the flickering

shadows, Ella could just make out the towering outline of the biggest pile of washing-up she had ever seen. Plates were piled on plates, dishes stacked on dishes, platters, pots, pans and bowls heaped in tottering towers and staggering steeples that almost defied belief.

'Impressive, isn't it?' said Deric following Ella's gaze. The barbarians added their plates to the mountain of washing-up and headed back to the stove. 'Nobody has done any washing-up since the days of King Marthur,' he added.

'But why?' said Ella.

'Because of *that*,' said Deric, pointing to the far corner of the Great Hall.

A shaft of light cut through the air at an angle from a window high up in the roof and fell upon a golden-handled sword that was embedded in an ancient cake.

'The Sword in the Scone,' said Deric the Red. 'For it is written, he who pulls the sword from the scone shall become the rightful ruler of the Round Kitchen Table – and has to do all the washing-up.'

As Ella watched, a group of barbarians approached the scone. The largest, a fearsome warrior with a big black beard, spat on his palms and rubbed his hands together. He braced himself on powerful legs and, biceps bulging, seized the handle of the sword and . . . gave it a little tug.

With a theatrical sigh, the mighty barbarian released his grip on the sword handle, stood up straight and wiped the back of his hand across his brow.

'It's beaten me,' he groaned, rolling his eyes and staggering backwards.

His fellow warriors exchanged awkward looks. One examined his fingernails, another shuffled his feet, a third turned a shade of deep red.

At the Round Kitchen Table, Quentin the cake druid looked up and sighed.

'It's remarkable how difficult these big strong barbarians have found it to pull a sword out of a crumbly cake,' he said. 'Isn't it, Deric?' he added pointedly.

Deric the Red blushed furiously. 'This is Ella, Cake Druid,' he said, changing the subject. 'The barbarian princess I was telling you about. Brilliant at battle-roaring, superb at swordplay, astounding at axe-throwing, and a natural battlecat-rider. I think she's ready for the ultimate challenge.'

'Baking a cake?' said Quentin, in tones of hushed awe. 'Step forward, my child.'

He rose from the table and picked up his really big spoon.

'Kneel,' the cake druid told her.

Ella did as she was instructed. Quentin reached out and tapped her with his large wooden spoon, first on one shoulder, then on the other, and finally on the top of her head.

'Go forth and bake,' he intoned.

This was easier said than done, Ella soon realized as she set about the business of barbarian baking. She'd never been much good in the kitchen at home, and here in the Great Hall she was no better. Standing at one of the trestle-tables beside the great stove, Ella was really struggling.

Deric had suggested she attempt iced cupcakes, a barbarian favourite. He took her to the recipe cupboard and selected an ancient parchment, dog-eared and spattered with cake-mix.

'The icing can be tricky,' he said, handing her the recipe, 'but for a barbarian princess like you, Ella, it should be a piece of cake!'

The first egg she tried to crack open exploded in her hand. So did the second. And the third. After half a dozen attempts, she had just about enough egg, not to mention shell, to continue the recipe. Next, she mixed sugar and yak butter together with a three-pronged fork until she was covered in sticky grease. When she sifted the flour it billowed up in a white cloud that made her sneeze, and when she added the milk, she knocked over the milk-jug and soaked the front of her dress.

After what seemed like an eternity of whisking and sieving and creaming and stirring, Ella had finally managed to produce a claggy gloop of cupcake mixture. She dolloped it messily into a row of parchment cups set out on a tray, as Deric the Red looked on, frowning.

'How's that?' said Ella uncertainly.

'Yes, well,' said Deric, eyeing the mess, 'I suppose even the most promising barbarian can't be good at everything.' He shook his head. 'You'd better get them into the oven and hope for the best.'

At the huge stove, where barbarians were coming and going with trays bearing cakes of every description, Deric pulled on an oven glove and opened a door. With a heavy sigh, Ella placed her cupcakes inside. Deric slammed the door shut.

'You might as well take your dirty dishes over to the washing-up pile while you're waiting,' he said, striding off.

Ella returned to the trestle-table to find a couple of black-feathered cookie ravens squabbling over her mixing bowl. They were hugely fat birds, with no necks and bloated bodies supported on thin, spindly legs. Their heads were encrusted in so many layers of dried cake-mix that they appeared to be wearing lumpy, biscuit-like helmets. As Ella watched, the cookie ravens buried their heads inside the bowl and scraped at the sides with their stubby beaks.

'Shoo! Shoo, you stupid creatures!' cried Ella irritably, and flapped her hands at the birds.

With raucous cries of what sounded like 'More, more, ever more!' the two ravens took to the wing. Puffing and panting, they flapped with considerable difficulty up to their roosts in the rafters.

Ella stared down disconsolately at the mess on the table. Drifts of flour mingled with heaps of sugar, eggshells floated in pools of spilt milk, and clusters of claggy cutlery lay beside upended measuring jugs and mixing bowls.

'Need some help?' came a familiar voice.

Ella turned. Edward Gorgeous was standing there, his shirt unbuttoned to the waist and a deathly pallor to his handsome face.

'Oh, Edward,' said Ella. 'I really thought I was good at this barbarian princess business. But I never imagined I'd have to master battlecat-riding *and* cake-baking,' she complained sadly.

Edward smiled and swept her up in his arms. 'No good crying over spilt milk,' he said gently. 'I'm sure you'll get the hang of it eventually.'

'Thank you, Edward,' said Ella, cheering up. 'So, while I've been breaking eggs and spilling milk in here, what have you been up to?'

'Nothing much,' said Edward with a shrug of his broad shoulders. 'Just hanging out in the woods.'

He looked more handsome and brooding than ever. Ella trembled in his arms.

'Edward . . .' she began.

'Benjamin! It's my Benjamin!' came a shout.

All eyes turned towards the doors of the Great Hall, which had just swung open. Wayne the Bunnyrider stood in the entrance, his winged helmet askew and straggly moustache trembling with emotion.

'He's in the meadow, lying flat on his back, shaking from ear-tip to tail. It's his thumb! It's been sucked!'

From every corner of the Great Hall came horrified gasps. Ella turned to Edward, eyes wide.

'I left him for a minute, that was all, happily chewing the grass. And the only other person in the meadow was –' Wayne's eyes darkened as his gaze fell upon Edward Gorgeous – '*him!*'

'Oh, Edward!'

The barbarians closed in around Edward and Ella, brandishing dripping egg-whisks and crumb-flecked cake-forks. With one arm wrapped protectively around Ella's shoulder, Edward turned to confront the mob.

'It wasn't me!' he protested. 'I didn't do it.' He turned to Ella beseechingly. 'You do believe me, don't you?'

Ella returned his gaze, her eyes full of doubt. 'Oh, Edward . . .'

Quentin the cake druid pushed his way through the crowd of glowering barbarians. He pointed at Edward with his really big spoon.

'Seize him!' he ordered. 'And clap him in irons!'

Two burly barbarians dropped their cooking utensils and obeyed. They grabbed Edward Gorgeous by the arms and frogmarched him away.

'Oh, Edward!!' Ella wailed.

Deric the Red appeared at Ella's side, scratching his ginger beard ruefully. Ella turned to him, tears in her eyes.

'I just don't know what to do,' she said. 'I came here with Edward because I thought it would be a wonderful adventure. And it has been – up until now. He's got his problems, but I thought he was getting over them. With my help. But now he's got himself into terrible trouble . . .'

'It's worse than that,' said Deric darkly, as an acrid smell filled the air. 'You've burned your cupcakes.'

'And another thing,' said the Horned Baron, warming to his theme. 'Her voice. Fifi has the most enchanting voice. It was the first thing I noticed about her. I'll never forget that sunny morning. I was a young goblin, footloose and carefree, and taking in the sights of Trollbridge, when I heard the most beautiful voice. It was coming from a turnip patch. I parted the turnip leaves and there, standing in front of me, was a vision of loveliness . . . .'

Perched on Joe's shoulder, Veronica rolled her eyes. 'I'm not sure how much more of this I can take,' she muttered.

'Shh, Veronica, he'll hear you,' Joe whispered.

He was sitting on the fourth step of the stair-carpet as it flew through Trollbridge. Below Joe, Norbert was back on the naughty step, while above, on the top step, Randalf and the Horned Baron sat side by side. The wizard's head was beginning to nod as the baron droned on.

'It was love at first sight! And Fifi felt the same

way. But our love was doomed from the start, for I was betrothed to another. Ingrid . . .'

Veronica shuddered.

'That summer in the turnip patch was the most wonderful of my young life, but Ingrid's mother, Gertrude, put a stop to all that. Then years later, I heard that enchanting voice again in *Mucky Maud's Custard Club* in Goblintown. It was Fifi, and I knew I couldn't lose her a second time. That's why I left Ingrid, the castle and ruling Muddle Earth behind, and ran away with Fifi –' he put his head in his hands and sobbed – 'and now she's running away from *me*!'

Joe held on tight as the stair-carpet swerved round a root-vegetable stall and swept over a barrow piled high with pumpkins. Ahead of them, disappearing through the toll gates, was the love of the Horned Baron's life, Fifi the Fair.

'She's getting away,' the Horned Baron cried, nudging Randalf in the ribs. 'Can't this thing go any faster?'

'Never seen those bloomers before in my life . . . What? What?' said Randalf, waking up with a start.

'Faster! Faster!' insisted the Horned Baron.

'Yes, certainly,' said Randalf, gathering his wits and tapping the stair-carpet with his staff. 'If you wouldn't mind, dear carpet.'

'Anything for true love,' it whispered back. 'Despite myself, I found the Horned Baron's story really quite moving.'

It soared up into the air, over the gate-towers of Trollbridge, and out across the swede fields and turnip patches beyond. Below them, Fifi was making her way along a winding path that followed the twists and turns of the Enchanted River. Just after a potato field, she came to a yak-skin yurt that was pitched on the riverbank. As she approached, the tent-flaps were thrown open and a barbarian warrior stepped out.

He was colossal, his huge shoulders clad in a black bearskin, his barrel-chest encased in a chain-mail shirt and his tree-trunk legs wrapped in cross-laced fleece to the knee. The sun played on the enormous helmet on his head, gleaming on its burnished bronze surface and glinting on the tips of its magnificent horns.

The Horned Baron turned pale.

With a sweep of one hefty, muscle-bound arm, the barbarian ushered Fifi inside the yak-skin yurt and disappeared after her. The tent-flap dropped back into place.

Up on the stair-carpet, Randalf and the Horned Baron exchanged looks.

'Of course, we could go in there and teach that barbarian a lesson,' said Randalf.

'Errm . . . yes, yes,' said the Horned Baron.

'But perhaps we should listen outside before we go rushing in,' said Randalf.

'Good idea,' said the Horned Baron.

'Scaredy-cats,' Veronica whispered in Joe's ear.

'Lovely stair-carpet,' said Randalf, 'hover above that tent as quietly as you can, if you'd be so kind.'

'Certainly, O great magician,' whispered the carpet, and swooped down towards the yurt.

As they approached the top of the tent, they heard the sound of voices coming from inside.

'Magnificent!' Fifi's voice rose in excitement. 'Absolutely magnificent!

'Do you really think so?' came a deep, booming barbarian voice. 'You're not just saying that?'

'Oh, no, Hrothgar,' said Fifi breathlessly. 'When I say magnificent, I really mean it. They're so curvy, for a start,' she went on. 'And so deliciously pointy.'

'Yes, they are,' Hrothgar agreed. 'I am rather proud of them.'

'And that's not all,' said Fifi. 'The finish, it's so flawless! I don't know how you manage it!'

'Years of training,' said Hrothgar modestly. 'But it's sweet of you to say so.'

'I could just stand here all day admiring it,' said Fifi. She gave a little laugh. 'But if I did that, Walter would be sure to find out and that would ruin everything! Talking of which, I really must get back home before he misses me . . . Oh, but what's this?'

'It's paint. For your nails,' said Hrothgar smoothly. 'It's all the rage. A barbarian princess called Ella started it. She turned up in Nowhere with black fingernails, and now all the maidens are painting theirs the same colour. I thought you might like it,' he said.

'How very thoughtful of you, Hrothgar,' said Fifi. 'Anyway, I must dash.'

'You heard her, comely carpet of splendour,' hissed Randalf. 'Get us back to Trollbridge at the double.'

They soared off. The Horned Baron looked back over his shoulder as the yurt receded into the distance.

'Black fingernail paint!' the Horned Baron raged. 'Did you hear that? *Black fingernail paint!* Just wait till she gets home! I'll have something to say to her about black fingernail paint – *and* horned helmets!'

'Randalf,' said Joe excitedly, scrambling up to the top step. 'Randalf, that barbarian knows where Ella is.'

'Yes,' said Randalf. 'Nowhere.'

'But she's got to be *somewhere*,' said Joe, confused.

'Nowhere is a place, Joe,' chirruped Veronica from Joe's shoulder. 'It's off the edge of the map, where all those barbarians in nasty winged helmets live.'

'And that's where Ella is?' said Joe. 'We must go there.'

'First things first, Joe,' said Randalf. 'We're searching for the Goblet of Porridge, remember?'

'I know,' said Joe. 'But couldn't we go to Nowhere first to find my big sister? *Please*, Randalf . . .'

'Oh, if you insist.' Randalf sighed. 'But then we search for the jeer-leaders. Is it a deal?'

'It's a deal,' agreed Joe, relieved.

'We'll set off just as soon as we've dropped the Horned Baron at his cottage in Trollbridge,' said Randalf.

'Number 16, Northside Archway,' said the Horned Baron bleakly.

The Horned Baron's cottage was a pleasant little timber cabin hanging from the underside of the bridge beneath a neatly painted trapdoor. It had two bedrooms, one bathroom with a maplewood hot tub and a watering-can shower, and a spacious sitting room with double windows set into the floor, through which the gently flowing waters of the Enchanted River could be seen. Fifi had furnished the cottage tastefully with wheelbarrow chairs upholstered in floral fabrics, and sideboards and cupboards beautifully constructed from antique mangelwurzel crates. It was in one such cupboard that the Horned Baron was frantically rummaging.

'Where *is* it?' he fumed. 'I know it's here some-where . . .'

Joe watched from one of the wheelbarrow chairs as the contents of the cupboard flew across the room. A bag of assorted marbles. A green muffler with *I Love Trollbridge* stitched into it in red letters. A copper tankard stamped with the name *Mucky Maud's Custard Club*. A rubber duck. A wind-up gas-frog. And a portrait of a humorously shaped turnip labelled *Gertrude* . . .

'Can't we go now?' asked Joe, looking across at Randalf in the other wheelbarrow chair.

Norbert stood behind him, holding the rolled-up carpet.

'The sooner the better,' said Veronica, dodging an old slipper as she flew across the room and landed on Randalf's shoulder.

'We can't leave him like this,' said Randalf. 'Not until Fifi gets home. The poor fellow's clearly distraught . . .'

Just then, from the depths of the cupboard there came a triumphant cry.

'There you are! At last! How I've missed you!' The Horned Baron turned round and stepped from the cupboard, the large horned helmet his butler had returned to him in his arms. He put it on. 'That's better,' he said. 'Now I feel like a ruler again. Powerful. Ruthless. With an iron fist and a heart of stone!'

He strode over to the potting-shed table, pulled up a chintz-covered crate and sat down. He folded his arms and glared up at the trapdoor at the top of the stairs. Moments later, there was the *trip-trap* of approaching footsteps. The trapdoor opened and a billy goat poked its head inside.

'Get out!' bellowed the Horned Baron.

The billy goat's head disappeared and the trapdoor slammed shut.

After a few moments the trapdoor opened again and this time Fifi the Fair stepped through. She descended the stairs, her large picnic basket clutched protectively in her arms.

'I see we've got guests,' she said brightly. 'How lovely.' She paused. 'Why, Walter, you're wearing your helmet. Are you feeling all right?'

The Horned Baron drew himself up to his full height, which was helped by the chintz-covered crate on which he now stood.

'What's in the basket?' he demanded imperiously.

'It's nothing, Walter,' she said. 'I've just been doing a little shopping, that's all.'

'A little shopping, eh?' said the Horned Baron, his eyes glaring from the depths of his horned helmet. He shot out an arm and pointed at the basket. 'Open it!' he commanded.

'Walter,' said Fifi. 'Haven't we forgotten to say *please*?'

'OPEN IT!'

Fifi took a step back. 'I was hoping it would be a surprise,' she said with a rueful smile. 'But since you insist . . .'

'I DO!'

Fifi removed the chequered cloth that covered the basket. She reached inside and removed a cake. It

was large, round and covered in flawless icing. With its curling horns of spun sugar and glaze of glistening butterscotch, the cake was a perfect replica of the very helmet the Horned Baron was now wearing. In exquisite piped icing-sugar lettering were the words *HAPPY BIRTHDAY, WALTER*.

There was a long silence, during which the Horned Baron's furiously pointing finger fell to his side.

'Absolutely magnificent . . .' he mumbled sheepishly as he remembered Fifi's words in the yak-skin yurt. 'Flawlessly finished . . . Deliciously pointy . . .'

Fifi reached out with black-fingernailed hands and placed the birthday cake before him. The Horned Baron stared. Fifi caught his gaze and held up her hands.

'Do you like them?' she asked. 'I painted them specially. For you, darling Walter.'

'So you *do* love me,' said the Horned Baron, sitting back down on the chintz-covered crate.

'Of course I do, silly,' said Fifi, smiling. 'You're the only one for me, Walter, you know that. With or without your helmet.'

'But I thought you didn't like me wearing it,' he said meekly.

'Only because of the way you thought you had to behave when you had it on,' she said. 'As I've always told you, Walter, it's not the helmet that's important, it's the goblin inside.'

'So I can wear it again?' he asked eagerly.

'Of course you can,' she replied. 'I know how much you missed your helmet, which is why I had Hrothgar the barbarian cake-maker bake you this birthday cake . . .' She smiled sweetly. 'Shall we?'

The Horned Baron removed the helmet and placed it

carefully beside him. He looked up.

'Yes, please!' he said excitedly.

Fifi reached out and gripped him tenderly by the ears.

'*Happy birthday to you,*' she sang sweetly. '*Happy birthday to you. Happy birthday, dear Walter . . .*'

She pushed his face down into the soft, gooey fondant of the helmet-shaped cake.

'*Happy birthday to you!*'

The Horned Baron let out a long, contented gurgle of delight and sat back up, his face covered in sweet, sticky cake.

'Just like the old days at the Custard Club,' he purred.

'How romantic,' whispered the carpet in Norbert's arms.

The little cloud drifted across the clear blue sky. Catching a gust of wind high above the Perfumed Bog, it enjoyed a pleasant billow in the scented breeze. Drifting on towards the Enchanted Lake, the cloud dallied over the choppy waters, luxuriating in the rising vapours as they plumped it up deliciously. White and fluffy, it moved on, choosing a gust here, a breeze there, an occasional zephyr or two, as it wandered lonely as a cloud – which, since it was indeed a cloud and the sky was remarkably clear, wasn't surprising.

Somewhere over the Musty Mountains, it was browsing the air currents, trying to make up its mind which one to select, when something caught its attention. It was bright and colourful and rippled delightfully as it made its way across the sky. It reminded the cloud of the kites it loved to play with over Goblintown. It broke up into little puffs of pleasure at the memory, before pulling itself together and setting off on a stiff wind towards the beautiful object in the sky ahead.

'Can't think what happened to Edwina,' said Randalf sleepily. 'Still, that's that Golden Towers lot for you. All over you one moment, then drop you like a hot fairy-cake the next.'

'Mmmm, hot fairy-cakes,' said Norbert, from the naughty step. 'Delicious! Though I do like lukewarm goblin-tarts. And I'm very partial to cold ogre-rusks. But snugglemuffins are my favourite, whatever the hotness. You like my snugglemuffins, don't you, Joe?'

'Y . . . Yes,' said Joe distractedly and shivered. 'Is it just me, or is it getting a bit chilly?'

'It's that cloud,' whispered the carpet. 'It's been hovering over us for ages. And every time I change course, it follows.'

'Oh, yes, so it is,' said Randalf, stifling a yawn. He climbed to his feet and began waving his staff over his head. 'Go away, you silly cloud,' he shouted.

On the brim of Randalf's hat, Veronica pulled her head from under her wing. 'What's all the fuss, Fatso?' she chirped.

'Go on! Shoo!' shouted Randalf.

Above them, the cloud darkened.

'Go *away*,' Randalf insisted, 'you foolish fogbank!'

Rain began to fall.

'Desist, you ridiculous cumulus!'

The cloud grew thunderous and the rain got harder.

'Well done, Fatso,' said Veronica sarcastically.

'Now you've hurt its feelings.'

'Nonsense!' said Randalf, continuing to brandish the staff above his head. 'It's just a stupid cloud. It doesn't have feelings.'

Flashes of lightning fizzed inside the rapidly blackening cloud and a shower of hailstones clattered down.

'Ouch! Ouch! Ouch!' protested the carpet.

Joe and Norbert cowered together on the naughty step while Veronica sought shelter in the folds of Randalf's cloak. The wizard sat back down and pulled his pointy hat down low over his head.

'Stop it, you naughty nimbus!' he squeaked.

There was a flash of lightning and a clap of thunder.

'Oooooaaaaawww!' screeched the carpet, and sped off across the sky at breakneck speed, a twisting trail of pungent smoke unravelling behind it.

The cloud gave chase.

In its panic the carpet had lost its stair shape and was now a long, flapping streak of woven blue. Randalf, Norbert and Joe had tumbled off the back of the carpet and were clinging on for dear life to its tasselled tail.

'Whoah, there!' gasped Randalf. 'Calm yourself, O stair adornment of woven splendour! *Whoah!*'

The stair-carpet slowed down, bunching along its length as it did so until it had regained a semblance of its old shape. Wheezing and puffing, Randalf was able to clamber back on board once more and resume his seat.

Norbert and Joe followed. The ogre eyed the wizard, his triple eyes narrowing.

'Shouldn't *you* be on the naughty step now, sir?' he said.

Veronica popped her head out of the folds of Randalf's cloak. 'Norbert's right, you know,' she said.

'Shut up, Veronica!' said Randalf hotly. He looked round, smoothing down his beard and gathering his cloak around him with as much dignity as he could muster. 'Thank goodness for that,' he said. 'I think we've given that imbecilic cirrus the slip.'

A single snowflake fluttered down and landed on the tip of Veronica's beak.

'Don't speak too soon, Fatso,' she said.

They all looked up. There, hovering above them, was the cloud. It looked bigger and darker and more furious than ever. A second snowflake fluttered delicately down. And a third . . .

Then, with a great muffled *whumpf*, the cloud dumped a whole blizzard of snowflakes down on their heads.

'It's freezing!' squealed the carpet, shivering so violently that Joe almost fell off his step again.

Beside him, Norbert was frantically bailing handfuls of

snow from the carpet. On the top step, Veronica had disappeared back into Randalf's robes, as the wizard brushed snow from the brim of his pointy hat.

Whumpf!

The blizzard intensified. The snow piled up faster than they could brush it away.

Whumpf!

It settled on their heads and shoulders until they resembled snowmen, and rapidly built up to form drifts that avalanched down the steps.

Whumpf!

'I can't feel my tassels,' moaned the carpet weakly.

It sagged and groaned beneath the weight of snow.

'O car . . . car . . . carpet of de . . . de . . . delight,' Randalf stuttered through chattering teeth. 'Ge . . . Ge . . . Get us ou . . . ou . . . outta here!'

'Prepare for an emergency landing,' whispered the carpet.

'How do we do that?' Joe shouted through the blizzard.

'Just lie down on the naughty step,' replied the carpet.

Joe and Norbert shovelled snow off the naughty step as Randalf slipped and slid down the stairs to join them. They lay down.

'Careful, Fatso!' squawked Veronica. 'Don't squash me!'

The carpet swooped down, rolling itself up tightly as it did so. It fell in a tumbling spiral out of the sky before hitting the ground and bouncing once, twice, three times, and beginning to unfurl. At the centre of the carpet, Joe, Norbert and Randalf were spun round and round. As it finished unrolling, they shot off the end and kept on rolling until, with a *splodge*, they came to an abrupt halt.

High in the sky, the cloud broke up into misty wisps of frustration, before recovering its composure and pulling itself together once more. With a shrug of its fluffy billows, the little cloud drifted huffily away in search of less contrary playmates.

'Gingerbread?' said Joe, sniffing the wall they'd crashed into on landing.

'It's a little stale,' said Norbert critically. 'Not like my snugglemuffins . . .'

'Who's that eating my house?' came a sing-song voice.

Randalf and Joe climbed slowly to their feet and dusted cake crumbs from their shoulders while Norbert took another mouthful of gingerbread wall. Joe looked around. They had crash-landed in a clearing in the middle of Elfwood, and smashed into an extraordinary fairy-tale house.

Its walls were made of gingerbread, with round yellow windows and a lozenge-shaped door. The pitched roof was covered with red and black tiles and edged with twists of translucent candy guttering. White icing had been piped over the walls and around the windows and door, to form intricate patterns of hearts, diamonds

and squiggly lines, while the garden path was paved with green, sticky-looking pastilles.

'Yuk!' exclaimed Norbert, who had just scooped a dollop of white icing from a wall and tasted it.

'It's *Dr Greenteeth's Big-Burp* toothpaste.'

Everyone turned to see Eudora Pinkwhistle standing in the lozenge-shaped doorway.

'Headmaster!' the witch exclaimed, her frown disappearing as her gaze fell on Randalf. 'How nice of you to drop in like this.'

'"Drop" is right!' Veronica's head popped out from the folds of the wizard's cloak. Her scarf was askew and her little bobble hat had slipped down over one eye. She spotted the witch's cat, Slocum, slinking out from the doorway and licking her lips. Veronica's head disappeared again. 'It gets worse and worse,' came her muffled voice from the depths of Randalf's robes.

'Ignore Veronica,' said Randalf. 'It's lovely to see you.

We were just on our way to Nowhere on our flying stair-carpet when we experienced a little turbulence . . .'

The stair-carpet, which had rolled itself up and tucked itself quietly under Randalf's arm, gave a little shiver.

'But we mustn't intrude,' he said. 'After all, it is the school holidays. If you'll excuse us, we'll be on our way . . . Norbert! Put down that roof tile!'

'*Burp* . . . Yes, sir. Sorry, sir,' said Norbert, reaching up and pushing the tile back into place. 'It tastes horrid anyway.'

'Really?' said Eudora sternly. 'The elves adore *Menthol Murphy's Liquorice and Aniseed Squares.* But headmaster, I can't let you rush off like this. Come in for a nice cup of tea.'

'If you insist,' Randalf sighed reluctantly.

'Oh, I do, I do, headmaster,' said Eudora, ushering them inside. 'You must tell me all the news from Stinkyhogs. Have you recovered the Goblet of Porridge? Is Roger the Wrinkled still cross with you? When does the new term start – if it *is* going to start, that is? And did I hear you were heading for Nowhere? Why, what a coincidence . . . But I'm forgetting my manners,' she said, 'bombarding you with all these questions. Do sit down and I'll put the kettle on.'

The stale-gingerbread house was far smaller inside than it looked from the outside. Randalf, Norbert and Joe sat bunched together on a lumpy sofa, while behind them Eudora Pinkwhistle fussed about at the tiny stove.

'Ooh, no! Stop it! Oh no! No, no, no, no. Stop it! Stop it! That tickles . . . Ha ha ha ha ha!'

As the kettle came to the boil, Eudora removed it from the stove and poured the steaming water into a brown teapot.

'The water's from the Babbling Brook,' she explained. 'Nice and quiet once it's been boiled.'

She poured cups of tea and handed them round. Then, taking down a cake-tin from an extremely small dresser in the corner, she turned and smiled.

'Fairy-cake, anyone?'

They reached into the cake-tin in turn.

'They're delicious!' Norbert exclaimed, swallowing three of the little cakes in one go.

'Yes, really excellent,' agreed Randalf.

Joe bit into his fairy-cake uncertainly. But despite the witch's stale gingerbread house, he had to admit her fairy-cakes were really very good.

'I'm so glad you like them,' said Eudora, drawing up a small rocking chair and sitting down opposite them. 'I've been practising all holiday. I'm entering the Big Barbarian Bake-Off in Nowhere. So you see, *I'm* going there too!' She frowned. 'Why are you going there anyway? On the trail of the missing goblet, perhaps?'

'Well, yes, sort of,' Joe broke in. 'But it's my sister Ella *I* want to find, and we heard that she's in Nowhere. She ran away with Edward Gorgeous after the broomball match . . .'

'Edward Gorgeous,' said Eudora Pinkwhistle. 'Such a polite young man. A little quiet, certainly, but a pleasure to teach. Don't you agree, headmaster?'

She leaned forward in the small rocking chair until her knees were touching Randalf's. She fluttered her eyelashes.

'So what do you think of my little house, headmaster?' she asked, leaning even closer as she changed the subject. 'Don't you just adore it? I have to admit, I had my doubts about Giggle Glade when I first moved here. My, but you should have seen the state of this place! A dreadful little teddy had been living here in an awful wooden shack. Well, of course I tore it down and started again. Completely transformed it into what you see around you. The elves simply can't get enough of it!' She held out the teapot in one hand and proffered the cake-tin with the other. 'More tea, headmaster? More cake?'

Just then, Slocum leaped up on to Randalf's lap and started sniffing at his cloak. From deep inside the folds of material came a muffled cry of outrage.

'Get that creature away from me!'

Joe gathered a protesting Slocum in his arms and, squeezing past Randalf and Eudora, got up from the sofa. 'Shall I put the cat out?' he said.

'That would be sweet of you,' said Eudora.

Joe crossed to what he took to be the front door and opened it. There, on the other side, was an iron staircase that led down into a cavernous basement. From the top of the stairs, Joe could see dozens of elves. They were

dashing around in circles, chattering in high-pitched elf voices as they kept repeating the questions they'd been asked so that they wouldn't forget them.

'Goggle, goggle, goggle, goggle, goggle . . . How many muckles in a pipsqueak?'

'Goggle, goggle, goggle, goggle, goggle . . . What's the colour of Roger the Wrinkled's beard?'

'Goggle, goggle, goggle, goggle, goggle . . . Who *is* the fairest of them all?'

At the far end of the room, other elves were arriving and leaving through a trapdoor in the ceiling, sliding down a long pole one way and climbing up a dangling rope-ladder the other. At the centre of the room, hovering above the floor at the end of a heavy iron chain, was a large leatherbound volume, the name *Muddlepedia* emblazoned on its spine. One by one, the elves approached the book, riffled through its pages, repeating their questions as they did so, until they came to the answers they were searching for.

'Two and a half . . . goggle, goggle, goggle. Depending on how squeaky the pip is.'

'Pink on Tuesdays . . . goggle, goggle, goggle. White on Wednesdays and soggy at bathtime.'

'Not you . . . goggle, goggle, goggle, Baroness Ingrid.'

Repeating their answers over and over, they turned away and headed for the dangling rope-ladder. In Joe's arms, Slocum squirmed and miaowed excitedly.

'Not that door, young man,' Eudora called from

the rocking chair. '*That* one.'

'Sorry,' said Joe, feeling foolish. He closed the door and headed for an identical one opposite and let Slocum out. 'If you don't mind me asking,' he said politely, 'what's going on down in the basement?'

'Oh, it's a little sideline of mine. I call it the Muddle-Wide-Web. And those are my inter-elves.'

'An absolute marvel,' said Randalf, nodding enthusiastically. 'Miss Pinkwhistle gave Stinkyhogs one of her goggle boxes. Ask it any question you like and the inter-elf inside pops out and goes off to find the answer.'

'It runs itself really,' said the witch modestly. 'Elves love dashing about – almost as much as they love stale gingerbread and throat-lozenges. Which reminds me. I must get that cough-candy guttering seen to . . .' She turned to Randalf. 'Do have another fairy-cake, headmaster.'

'Oh, I've had more than enough, thank you, Eudora,' said Randalf, picking up the carpet which was nestling at his feet. 'We really should be on our way, if we're to get to Nowhere by nightfall.'

'You're absolutely right, dear headmaster,' agreed Eudora. 'Dyson! Dyson! Over here, broom. We're leaving this instant.' She opened the front door. 'Slocum! Here, kitty, kitty, kitty . . .'

From the folds of Randalf's cloak came a muffled voice. 'That's it!' it said. 'I'm never coming out now!'

Delia finished buffing her nails and picked up the ornate mirror with its filigree handle and seashell-decorated frame. With her other hand she picked up a pair of curling tongs and delicately applied them to the wispy eyelashes of first one eye, then the other. She blinked seductively.

'Who's a pretty little thing?' she cooed to herself and gave a girlish giggle.

She put down the hand-mirror and curling tongs and reached out for the tray of teacakes. Plump and round, and with criss-cross indentations on the top, the teacakes were cinnamon-scented and speckled with currants, raisins and slices of candied peel. She eyed the dainty cakes appreciatively.

'I'm an artist,' she cooed. 'Mistress of the meringue, guru of the gateau, diva of the drop scone . . . Those fools! They've never appreciated my genius. But I'll show them!' she exclaimed, her eyelashes fluttering.

She skewered a teacake with a three-pronged toasting fork and held it aloft.

'Now for the finishing touch,' she whispered.

Opening her great purple-scaled jaws wide, she exhaled a dazzling plume of flame, twirling the toasting fork expertly as she did so. Three blinks of a dragon's eye later, her mouth snapped shut.

The teacake was golden-brown with twists of cinnamon-scented steam rising from its toasted centre. Delia the dragon smiled.

'Perfection,' she breathed.

The pink frog crouching on the broad mauve lily-pad let out a little *gribbit* and expanded.

'*Whiffle-piffle! Whiffle-piffle!*' it croaked quietly.

It opened its powder-blue eyes and blinked several times in rapid succession before shutting them tightly again.

'*Whiffle-piffle! Whiffle-pip-pip-pip!*' it croaked, expanding some more. '*Whiff-whiff-whiff-WHIFF!!*'

Its glistening pink body swelled to five times its normal size and its blue eyes bulged open, giving the gas-frog a look of startled surprise.

'*WHIFF-WHIFF-WHIFF . . .*' BANG!

A cloud of pink gas plumed up and hung for a moment in the perfumed air. Then, with a *plip, plip, plop, plop,* a thousand tiny tadpoles rained down into the bog-pool below.

The now empty lily-pad trembled and began to rise slowly from the surface of the water. Two eyes, a nose, a mouth and chin appeared, followed by a thin, scraggy neck and sloping shoulders. As the lily-pad rose higher a round body supported by thin stilt-like legs emerged, dripping, into the pink-tinged light. Two stick-like arms, as thin as the stilt-like legs, reached up and adjusted the lily-pad hat.

'Greetings, little pongpoles,' the perfumed bog-man said appreciatively in a gurgly, water-down-the-plughole kind of voice.

He reached out a long thin arm and stirred the tiny tadpoles in the water around him affectionately, before turning and plunging his other arm deep into the pool. He felt about in the muddy waters for a moment. Then, with a grunt of effort, he pulled his arm out again. In his hand was a small leather suitcase, lightly crusted with bog-barnacles and trailing fronds of pond-slime.

Swinging the suitcase merrily, he set off, striding on his stilt-like legs through the Perfumed Bog.

'See you later, pink stinky hogs! So long, exploding gas-frogs! Goodbye, little pongpoles!' he burbled in his gurgly, gargly voice. 'Old Peat's off to seek his fame and fortune!'

The sleek battlecat strained at its harness as it pulled the covered chariot over the rolling grassland, past Harmless Hill on one side and, far in the distance, the Sandpit on the other. Seated in the chariot, wearing an impressive horned helmet and bearskin coat, was a hulking barbarian. On the chariot's canvas covering, painted in large black Gothic letters edged in gold, was the name *HROTHGAR the HUNGER SLAYER*, while beneath, in a small fussy-looking script, were the words *Barbarian Baker and Peripatetic Patissier*.

'Whooah there, Sweetfang!' Hrothgar the Hunger Slayer bade his battlecat, pulling on the reins and bringing the chariot to a halt. 'By the Spooned Hand of Freya the Beardy, what have we here?'

In the shadow of Harmless Hill, behind a petal-covered trestle-table, stood four fairies. They wore black singlets decorated with white skull polka dots,

tattered black tutus, stripy black-and-white tights and heavy black boots. At their shoulders were translucent gossamer wings that shimmered in the bright sunlight.

'Greetings, barbarian warrior,' said the fairies' leader, who was tall and willowy, with long green hair and a pale complexion. She raised a jug in one hand and a tulip-shaped glass in the other. 'Can we offer you refreshment? Sparkling daisy dew, freshly made. Only a muckle a glass.'

She poured a yellow cordial from the jug into the glass and held it out. Her three companions gathered round. The first had a shock of purple hair, the second a magenta bob, while the third had straggly braids of bleached white. They looked at the barbarian expectantly.

'Don't mind if I do,' said Hrothgar, leaping down from his chariot and flipping a brass coin on to the table. He reached to his belt, unhooked his drinking horn and held it out. 'But I'm a barbarian and we drink only from these.'

The fairy with the green hair emptied the glass into the drinking horn and topped it up to the brim from the jug. Hrothgar raised it high.

'In true barbarian fashion, I give you this toast,' he announced, his even white teeth flashing in a dazzling grin. 'May your petals glisten as brightly as Olaf the Pixie's twenty-three fingers and your facial hair grow as luxuriantly as Freya the Beardy's!'

The four fairies exchanged looks as the barbarian put the drinking horn to his lips and drained it in one go. He wiped his mouth flamboyantly on the back of his hand.

'That was excell—'

Like a mighty pine tree falling in the mountain forests of Nowhere, the hefty barbarian warrior toppled forward and hit the ground with a resounding thud. Pesticide the flower fairy tossed back her green hair and smiled malevolently.

'Looks like we're in business, girls!'

'Are you sure you wouldn't like to ride up here with me, headmaster?' said Eudora Pinkwhistle. 'For there's room on my broom for two. And broom-riding is so, so exhilarating!'

She hovered above the top step of the flying stair-carpet on her broom, Dyson. Her cat, Slocum, nestled in her lap.

'That's very kind of you, Eudora,' said Randalf

sleepily. He yawned. 'But I'm more than happy where I am.'

'So am I,' came a muffled voice from his robes.

Joe and Norbert were sitting side by side halfway down the stair-carpet as they flew high over the Musty Mountains on the way to Nowhere.

'And this is one of my favourites,' Norbert was saying, pointing at a particularly grubby and well-thumbed page of his recipe book. 'Upside-down cake. You make it standing on your head.'

Joe smiled as the ogre turned the page. 'And this is jumping-up-and-down cake. You make it jumping up and down. And this one,' Norbert said, 'is cartwheel cake.'

'Don't tell me,' said Joe, and laughed. 'You make it turning cartwheels.'

'No, Joe,' said Norbert, puzzled. 'It's a cake the size of a cartwheel.'

The pair of them ducked down as Eudora Pinkwhistle came swooping over their heads and sped off into the sky ahead. She turned round and waved.

'Catch me if you can, slowcoaches,' she giggled.

The Great Hall of the barbarians of Nowhere towered high above the cluster of yak-skin yurts in the lush alpine meadow. From the forested slopes of the surrounding mountains came the raised voices of barbarians calling words of encouragement.

'Good luck, Nigel!'

'You can do it, my son!'

'Break an egg!'

Nigel Nephew-of-Nigel steered his battlecat out of the forest, across the green meadow, and stopped in front of the arched doorway of the Great Hall. He leaped from his steed and strode up to the formidable black-hinged doors. He raised a clenched fist and rapped politely. The doors opened.

'It is I, Nigel Nephew-of-Nigel, here to claim my place in the Big Barbarian Bake-Off.'

'Enter, Nigel Nephew-of-Nigel,' said a voice from the shadows.

Nigel stepped inside and the doors slammed shut.

High in the sky, there came the sound of mighty wingbeats, growing louder as a purple dragon emerged from the clouds overhead and descended towards the Great Hall. It landed in front of the black-hinged doors, reached out a taloned claw and tapped lightly on the wood. The doors opened.

'Hello, dear thing. My name's Delia Dragonbreath and I'm here to enter your marvellous Barbarian Bake-Off.'

'Enter, Delia Dragonbreath,' came the voice from the shadows.

Folding her wings neatly and gathering up the coils of her tail over one arm, she ducked her head and stepped inside. The doors slammed shut.

Just then, what looked like a spinning mauve cartwheel came rolling down the mountain slope and burst out from the trees. It was followed moments later by a tumbling boulder. The two of them bowled across the meadow, past the yurts, and crashed one after the other against the doors of the Great Hall. The boulder unfurled stick-like arms and stilt-like legs and climbed to its feet. It swept up the cartwheeling lily-pad hat and placed it on its head.

The doors opened.

'Peat the Perfumed Bog-Man at your service. I'm here to seek my fame and fortune in this here Barbarian Bake-Off of yours.'

'Enter, Peat the Perfumed Bog-Man,' said the voice.

'Much obliged,' said Peat, loping inside.

The doors slammed shut.

A little while later, a covered chariot pulled by a striped battlecat drew up outside the Great Hall. A tall figure in an impressive-looking horned helmet and a floor-length bearskin coat climbed down from the

chariot and tottered over to the doors. It reached out a mittened hand and knocked.

The doors opened.

'*Ahem*,' said a soft, high-pitched voice, which changed suddenly to a low, gruff one. 'It is I, Hrothgar the Hunger Slayer,' the voice growled through a heavy black beard that slipped to one side, only to be pushed back into place by the mittened hand. 'We're here . . . I mean, *I'm* here, to enter the Big Barbarian Bake-Off.'

Two green eyes blinked from the shadows beneath the impressive horned helmet.

'Enter, Hrothgar the Hunger Slayer!' the voice replied.

Arms outstretched and helmet wobbling, the barbarian lurched inside. The doors slammed shut.

Ten minutes came and went. Barbarians on battlecats emerged from the surrounding forest and made their way to their tents. Wood was chopped and cooking fires were lit. Kettles were boiled, teapots were filled and sandwiches passed around, while at their giant saucer, battlecats gathered to slurp stiltmouse milk.

From high over the treetops a witch on a broom appeared and circled the onion towers of the Great Hall, before swooping down to land at the black-hinged doors. She rapped on them briskly.

The doors opened.

'Miss Eudora Pinkwhistle of Ginger Gables, Giggle Glade. I wish to enter your Big Barbarian Bake-Off.'

'Enter, Miss Eudora Pinkwhistle,' said the shadowy voice.

With Dyson under her arm, she bustled inside the Great Hall and the doors slammed shut behind her. As they did so, a stair-carpet came into view. It descended rapidly out of the sky and came to a hovering halt a few inches above the lush meadow-grass in front of the yak-skin yurts.

Randalf, Norbert and Joe stepped from the stair-carpet.

'Well done, dear carpet of incomparable comfort,' said Randalf.

'Yes,' said Veronica, appearing from the folds of his cloak, 'you certainly gave that old witch and her nasty cat the slip.'

'It's so nice to be appreciated,' whispered the carpet, rolling itself up and snuggling under the wizard's arm.

Breaking away from the others, Joe ran up to a barbarian who had just emerged from a tent.

'Excuse me,' he said, 'but have you seen a tall barbarian princess? Fair hair. Black fingernails. Can be a bit sulky. Her name's Ella, and she's travelling with a boy called Edward . . .'

'By the Whiskers of Miffy the Magnificent!' exclaimed the red-bearded barbarian. 'But of course I have. She's one of my best pupils. The name's Deric the Red, by the way.'

He shot out a big meaty hand. Joe shook it.

'I'm Joe,' he said. 'Ella's younger brother.'

'Pleased to make your acquaintance, Joe Brother-of-Ella,' said Deric the Red warmly. His expression darkened. 'I'm afraid I've got some bad news. Edward and Ella have been clapped in irons.'

'Clapped in irons!' Joe exclaimed.

'Clapped in irons?' repeated Randalf, arriving at Joe's side.

'Sounds serious,' said Norbert behind them.

'It is,' confirmed Deric, nodding gravely. 'When Edward was accused of thumbsucking, Ella lost her temper with our cake druid. She tipped a bowl of pancake batter over his head, and that's about as serious as it can get.'

'So where exactly are they now?' said Joe.

The barbarian turned and pointed at the towering, onion-domed building at the centre of the meadow. 'In there,' he said.

'Well, we shall go in there and *un*clap them at once,' said Randalf. 'Then, my dear Joe, we really must get on with our quest for the Goblet of Porridge!'

'I'm afraid you can't,' Deric explained. 'Only barbarians and contestants in the Big Barbarian Bake-Off are allowed inside the Great Hall.'

'Then it's simple,' said Randalf.

'It is?' said Joe.

'Yes,' said Randalf, eyeing the frayed recipe book clutched in Norbert's hands.

A wizard, an ogre and a boy strode up to the black-hinged doors of the Great Hall. The wizard raised his staff and thumped loudly on the weathered timber.

The doors opened.

'Steady on,' came an indignant voice from the shadows.

'We're the Stinkyhogs Snugglemuffin Squad,' the wizard announced. 'We're here for the Big Barbarian Bake-Off.'

'Enter, Stinkyhogs Snugglemuffin Squad,' said the voice. 'And just be careful with that staff of yours.'

The three of them stepped inside.

The door slammed shut.

9

It was the smell that struck Joe first. That and the Great Hall's enveloping warmth. The air was sweet and spicy, the delicious aroma of baking biscuits and browning pastries mingling with the acrid tang of woodsmoke.

High above his head, in the shafts of dust-flecked light that penetrated the latticed windows of the onion-domed towers, Joe could just make out the silhouetted shapes of birds perching in the roof-beams. The hall was vast, with a large round table at its centre and what looked like a mountain of dirty dishes behind it.

As Joe followed Randalf and Norbert across the straw-strewn floor, he wondered how and where to begin the search for his sister. Ahead of them, the small fussy-looking individual who'd opened the black-hinged door raised his large wooden spoon and pointed.

'Excellent, excellent,' said Quentin the cake druid. 'You seem to be the last ones. You'll find everything you need just over there. Oven gloves. Big spoons. Pots and pans. And all the ingredients you could possibly need.'

In front of the biggest stove Joe had ever seen stood five tables, each one piled high with cooking utensils. Stacked on the floor in front of them were sacks of flour, baskets of eggs, and jars, jugs and pitchers brimming with yak-milk, butter, icing sugar, baking powder and candied fruit of every description.

At the first table stood a beefy-looking barbarian in a winged helmet and a crisp white apron with the letter N embroidered on the front. Towering above him at the next table was an enormous purple-scaled dragon, two thin wisps of smoke coiling up from her flared nostrils as she admired her reflection in the back of a ladle. At the third table a peculiar individual in a huge mauve hat stood on spindly legs pouring yak-milk from one measuring jug into another and back again. The heavily bearded barbarian at the next table along stood stiffly to attention, his thick bearskin coat buttoned up to the neck despite the warmth of the hall. Beside him, Eudora Pinkwhistle raised a hand and waved.

'Coo-ee, headmaster! Over here!' she trilled. 'So you're entering the bake-off too. How thrilling! The table next to me is free. Now, what are you going to bake? Do tell.'

'I don't intend to bake anything,' said Randalf with dignity. 'My assistant, Norbert, here is going to impress us all with his snugglemuffins. Aren't you, Norbert?'

'Doesn't that make you *Norbert's* assistant?' piped

up Veronica, and flapped from the brim of the wizard's pointy hat on to Joe's shoulder before Randalf could swat her away.

'Randalf, Norbert,' Joe whispered as they took their places at the table and the cake druid turned away. 'Can you keep them distracted while I look for Ella?'

'No problem,' said Randalf, pulling up a stool and settling himself down. 'I'm sure Norbert's snugglemuffins will be extremely distracting. Won't they, Norbert?'

'I'll try my best, sir,' said Norbert, ruefully eyeing the dragon who was blowing smoke rings, and the bog-man who was juggling droplets of milk.

In the middle of the hall, Quentin the cake druid emerged through the hole at the centre of the Round Kitchen Table and sat down upon the throne. He placed a colossal egg-timer in front of him, and waited as barbarian spectators filed into the hall. Pulling up stools and benches in a broad semicircle behind the table, they sat down and looked at the cake druid expectantly.

With a flourish, Quentin turned the egg-timer over. 'Let the Big Barbarian Bake-Off begin!' he announced.

A great cheer rose from the barbarian spectators as the contestants rushed over to the pile of sacks, baskets and jars and scooped up armfuls of ingredients, before returning to their tables. Joe slipped quietly away, skirting round behind the ovens and keeping to the shadows as he began his search of the hall.

All eyes were on the unfolding drama of the bake-off. Delia the dragon cracked a dozen eggs open with a swish of her tail. Pete the Perfumed Bog-Man sent three plumes of yak-milk up into the air like a fountain and caught them again in a measuring jug. Eudora drew gasps of appreciation as, with a click of her fingers, she set a dozen egg-whisks beating. Meanwhile Nigel was making steady progress sifting flour with one hand and measuring out baking powder with the other. Hrothgar, on the other hand, seemed to have shrunk to half his height and was dithering over a mixing bowl, his black beard trailing in the pancake batter he was attempting.

All eyes, that is, except for those belonging to a large black fruit-cake bat that was hanging upside-down from the rafters high above. Its eyes were fixed firmly on Joe as he ducked and dived along the walls of the Great Hall, peering into its nooks and crannies. Behind the mountain of dirty dishes, just to the right of a mouldy-looking lump of cake with a sword stuck in it, Joe came to the top of a flight of stairs. A sign on the wall with an arrow read, *Dungeons this way*.

'The dungeons,' said Joe.

'Yes,' said Veronica, 'the perfect place to clap someone in irons.'

Joe followed the arrow down the stairs. It was dark and dank, with the sound of dripping water echoing up from the gloom. He reached out a hand. The walls felt cold and slimy to the touch. Arriving at the bottom of the stairs, Joe made his way along a low, narrow passageway towards the dim outline of a door. As he approached, he saw that it was thick and nail-studded and, curiously for the door to a dungeon, slightly ajar.

With a trembling hand, Joe pushed at the heavy door. It swung slowly open on creaking hinges. Taking a deep breath, he stepped inside . . .

And found himself in a small, cosy sitting room, with charming floral wallpaper and a thick yak-wool carpet. Two high-backed armchairs upholstered in matching p a i s l e y fabric were positioned in front of a small fireplace which was framed with elegant green and white tiles. Ella sat in one chair and Edward sat in the other. Each wore delicate bracelets of blue-grey iron, with fine chains linking them to wafer-thin metal collars at their necks.

'Clapped in irons!' exclaimed Veronica. 'Clapped in jewellery more like!'

'It's just for show,' said Edward languidly from the chair. 'We've given our word we won't escape until we've served our time. The cake druid sentenced me to four days for thumbsucking, and Ella got two days for pancake-battery, didn't you, Ella?'

But Ella wasn't listening. 'Joe!' she cried, jumping up from her chair. 'What are *you* doing here?'

'I could ask you the same thing,' said Joe hotly. 'I've been looking for you all over Muddle Earth! What's been going on? Why did you run off? How do you think we're ever going to get home if you go disappearing like that?'

'Home?' said Ella, a faraway look coming into her eyes. 'You know, Joe, I'd almost forgotten home.' She paused. 'Edward had to disappear, and I couldn't let him go alone. He was in danger. He needed me . . .'

'Needed you?' came a screech from behind them, and everyone turned to see a large fruit-cake bat standing in the doorway, its wings flapping. 'Needed *you*!' it screeched again.

It hunched over and drew its wings over its head. Then, seeming to unfold itself, it rose up to human height and swept back its wings once more, which were now the folds of a black cloak, to reveal a young girl, pale-skinned, black-haired and lovely.

'Edwina!' groaned Edward.

'Ooh!' cried the barbarians. 'Aah!'

'Ooooh!'

'Aaaaaaah!'

With a flick of her tail, Delia the dragon tossed a treacle tart, crimped at the edges and exquisitely latticed with pastry strips, high into the air. She opened her jaws and sent a plume of flame up to meet it. Then, holding out a scaly paw, she caught it in her talons. It was toasted to perfection.

'By the Apron Strings of Lionel the Timid!' a barbarian bellowed.

'By the Measuring Thimble of Stephen the Stumpy!' roared another.

'By the Leaky Buckets of Beverley the Bountiful!'

Peat the Perfumed Bog-Man had conjured up five columns of spinning icing. Each of them danced on the tips of the long stick-like fingers of his left hand while he conducted them with his right. As the barbarian spectators exclaimed in wonderment, the bog-man slowly closed his hand, bringing the twisting spirals of caramel, chocolate, vanilla, raspberry and lemon icing together in a marvellous striped pillar. He clicked the fingers of his right hand. The spinning pillar of icing jumped across to the five-tier gateau that stood before him and decorated it with wavy piping and ornate rosettes.

Nigel Nephew-of-Nigel paused for a moment to admire the spectacle before returning to his chocolate-chip meringues. His once crisp white apron was now spattered with egg-white, icing sugar and chips of chocolate, so that the embroidered N was barely visible. The strain on his face was clear as he pulled on his oven gloves, knelt before the stove and removed a steaming baking tray.

The barbarian held up his meringues in triumph.

'Nigel! Nigel! NIGEL!' roared the crowd.

Eudora breezed past, a line of fairy-cakes flapping after her like little ducklings.

'Up on the silver cake-stand,

my light and fluffy darlings,' she cooed.

At the table next to her, Hrothgar the Hunger Slayer appeared to have fallen asleep. He was slumped forward, the arms of his bearskin coat hanging limply at his sides and his horned helmet resting against his mixing bowl. Not that any of the crowd noticed as the witch, the bog-man, the dragon and the home favourite, Nigel, continued to delight them with their cake-making skills.

Nobody noticed Norbert either as he quietly put the finishing touches to his snugglemuffins. Drenching some with icing sugar and sprinkling others with hundreds and thousands, he hummed softly to himself under his breath. Beside him, perched on the stool and basking in the heat of the oven, Randalf was fast asleep.

On his throne in the middle of the Round Kitchen Table, Quentin tapped the glass of the colossal egg-timer.

'Five minutes to go!' he announced.

'Yes, Edward, it's me,' said Edwina, her lovely eyes flashing. 'Did you really think that you could escape from me? Haven't you learned by now that wherever you go, however hard you try to hide, I shall always find you in the end? Golden Towers, Stinkyhogs, Nowhere . . . I've tracked you down every time, and I always will, because our love can never die!'

'Love?' said Edward. 'It isn't love, it's obsession. You're crazy . . .'

'Crazy!' screeched Edwina. 'Crazy? If I am, it's because of you! Oh, Edward, why can't you accept what you are, what I made you? All those years ago in your uncle's castle . . .'

'Whatever,' said Edward.

'Yes, Whatever!' Edwina cried. 'When I turned you into a vampire, I thought that we would be together forever, roaming Muddle Earth, sucking thumbs for eternity. But no. You had to go and spoil things by running away, denying your true nature, sucking the thumbs of stiltmice and rabbits and little woodland creatures, when you could have feasted upon the delicious digits of royalty with me . . .' Her eyes narrowed. 'It was me. I sucked that battlerabbit's thumb, just to get you into trouble. And I'd do it again. I'd do anything to make your life a misery. I want you to suffer as I have suffered . . .'

'You're mad, Edwina!' said Edward, tearing the delicate shackles from his wrists and neck and flinging them away. 'You tricked me. I've never had any feelings for you, and I never will.' He turned to Ella, who had pulled off her own chains, and took her hands in his. 'Whereas Ella, here . . .'

'Ooh, Edward,' said Ella, gazing into his gorgeous eyes.

'Her!' screeched Edwina, her shoulders hunching. 'You're choosing *her* over me?' She gave a deranged cackle of laughter. 'We'll see about that!'

With a snarl, she threw herself at Ella, her eyes flashing blood-red and lips parting to reveal two sharp white fangs. But Edward was too quick for her. He sprang forward, putting himself between Ella and the enraged vampire. Edward and Edwina crashed into one another, sending the high-backed armchairs flying. They fell to the floor and wrestled on the thick yak-wool carpet in a flurry of flapping cloaks and flashing fangs.

'Run, Ella! Run!' Edward cried as he struggled to pin Edwina down.

'You heard him!' cheeped Veronica. 'Let's get out of here!'

Joe grabbed his sister by the arm. He pulled her from the dungeon and dragged her up the stairs. 'Come on, Ella,' he told her urgently. 'We'll get help from your barbarian friends.'

'But Joe,' she protested, as they reached the top of the stairs. 'Edward needs me . . .'

She pulled away and turned, only to be confronted by the black-caped figure of the female vampire looming up at her. No longer lovely, Edwina's deathly white face was contorted and hideous, drool dripping from her bared fangs as she grabbed at Ella with long claw-like fingers.

Ella screamed.

Joe looked round desperately. There in front of him was the golden-handled sword sticking out of the stale cake. Without a second thought, he grabbed it and turned back to see Ella locked in a frenzied struggle with Edwina. The vampire had his sister's wrist in her grasp and was about to sink her fangs into Ella's thumb.

Taking a deep breath, Joe swung the sword . . .

As the broad silver blade sliced through the air, flashing in the flickering torchlight of the Great Hall, Edwina shot out a claw-like left hand and caught Joe by the wrist. With a scream of fury, she dropped Ella and, with her right hand now free, prised the sword from Joe's grip and hurled it contemptuously away.

The sword sailed high up into the air in a twisting arc and was about to tumble back again, when a green-haired fairy in a black tutu and stripy tights swooped down on fluttering wings and caught the sword in a gloved hand. Giggling quietly, the fairy darted back into the shadows at the far end of the hall, where her three companions were waiting.

Not that Joe noticed any of this. He was too busy trying to escape from Edwina's vice-like grip, which tightened as she raised him up by the wrist until his toes were barely touching the floor.

'Why, Joe,' Edwina said in a soft, cooing voice laced

with menace, 'I thought we were friends.' She licked her lips and brought Joe's clenched hand towards her mouth.

'Leave him alone!' Ella cried as she leaped on to the vampire's back and sent all three of them sprawling to the floor.

With a scream of rage, Edwina released her grip on Joe and clawed Ella from her back.

'I'll teach you to mess with Edwina Lovely, barbarian girl!' she hissed. 'And don't think you're going to end up undead like Edward. Oh no, I'm going to suck your thumbs until there isn't a drop of blood left in your entire barbarian body. Then you'll be dead, dead, *dead*!' she screeched.

Her lips opened to reveal her two gleaming white fangs. Snarling, she raised Ella's hands to her mouth.

Joe scrambled to his knees, staring in helpless horror.

'No!' he cried and reached out for the only thing to hand – the ancient stale scone.

Breaking off a chunk of the crumbly cake, he threw it at Edwina, hitting her squarely in the face.

'Mffll bllchll,' spluttered Edwina, coughing and choking.

She released her grip on Ella and shot up into the air in a flapping frenzy. As Joe and Ella watched open-mouthed, Edwina writhed and squealed and clutched at her throat. Her face contorted. Her skin wrinkled, her eyes dimmed and her lovely hair lost its sheen and fell from her head, leaving her scalp bald and pitted. Round and round she flew, faster and faster, until . . .

Ploff!

Edwina Lovely exploded in a cloud of grey dust.

Far below, the contestants in the Big Barbarian Bake-Off had been carefully placing their creations on the Round Kitchen Table for judging. Eudora Pinkwhistle had arranged her adorable little fairy-cakes in nests of spun sugar on the tiers of an elegant cake-stand. Nigel Nephew-of-Nigel's chocolate-chip meringues were balanced in a spectacular pyramid on a square oak platter, while Delia Dragonbreath had set her three treacle tarts spinning like plates on the end of three flexible willow rods and was preparing to give their delicate sugar glaze a final toasting. Next to her at the Round Kitchen Table, Peat the Perfumed Bog-Man was putting the finishing touches to his whirlpool and waterfall gateau. It was an astonishing five-tier cake which featured, along with its wavy piping and floral rosettes, a bubbling pool of chocolate which cascaded down its sides and collected in the honeycombed bottom tier.

Back at the workbenches, Hrothgar seemed to have disappeared completely. His bearskin coat lay crumpled on the floor, the impressive horned helmet by its side. Norbert, meanwhile, was on his knees beneath the workbench painstakingly picking up and rearranging the tray of snugglemuffins that Randalf had just knocked to

the floor in his sleep. Above the wizard's head Veronica was flapping and chirping in a desperate effort to wake him up.

'H . . . Help! J . . . J . . . Joe! In d . . . d . . . danger!' she squawked in panic.

From high above came the sound of an explosion.

'What on Muddle Earth was that?' said Eudora with a start that sent several of her fairy-cakes fluttering from their nests.

'Sounded like an exploding gas-frog,' said Peat the Perfumed Bog-Man, puzzled, as Edwina Lovely's empty cloak fluttered down and settled over his head. 'Who turned out the lights?' he exclaimed, flailing with his stick-like fingers and accidentally sending a plume of molten chocolate from his gateau shooting up into the air.

It hit the dragon in one of her long-lashed eyes.

In her shock and surprise Delia shot out a jet of flame that set Nigel's pyramid of chocolate-chip meringues on fire. The barbarian let out a cry of alarm and jumped back, sending Eudora's cake-stand toppling off the edge of the table. All of a flutter, the fairy-cakes fled from their nests and careered into the whirlpool and waterfall gateau, knocking it over. A tidal wave of molten chocolate swept across the table, knocking aside Delia's willow rods and launching the spinning treacle tarts into the air. With a *splat! splat! splat!* the tarts hit three barbarian spectators in the front row full in the face, as the chocolate tidal wave broke over the horrified cake druid, who was sitting on his throne, his big wooden spoon in one hand and colossal egg-timer in the other.

'This is an outrage!' Quentin exclaimed. '*Mmmm.*' He licked his lips. 'This chocolate is absolutely divine! But this is still an outrage!'

He stared down at the Round Kitchen Table. Peat the Perfumed Bog-Man's whirlpool and waterfall gateau had collapsed completely and was now a soggy mess in a pool of congealing chocolate. Next to it, Nigel Nephew-of-Nigel's pyramid of chocolate-chip meringues had burned down to a pile of smoking ash, while three wilted willow rods, set in the chocolate, were all that remained of Delia Dragonbreath's treacle-tart display. Marooned in the sticky goo, Eudora Pinkwhistle's bedraggled fairy-cakes lost their enchantment one by one and stopped flapping their cakey wings.

From the rafters high above, the fruit-cake bats and cookie

ravens came
spiralling
down through
the air. They
landed on the
table and fell
upon the ruined cakes
as the shocked contestants
looked on.

'I'm afraid I'm going to have to disqualify the lot of you,' Quentin announced with as much dignity as he could muster as he wiped chocolate sauce from his face.

Behind him, the barbarian spectators groaned with disappointment.

'What, even me?' came a voice.

All eyes turned to the ogre, who was lumbering across to the Round Kitchen Table, a tray clutched proudly in his hands. Following behind was a sleepy-looking wizard with a rolled-up carpet under one arm and a flustered budgie on the brim of his hat.

'In danger? Joe?' Randalf yawned. 'But here he comes now. Joe, Veronica here seems to have got herself in quite a state . . .'

'It's all right, Veronica,' Joe reassured the budgie as he caught up with the wizard. 'The danger's over.' He brushed scone crumbs from his sleeves and struggled to catch his breath. 'I found Ella and Edward!' he announced. 'But then Edwina Lovely found us! She was a *vampire*, Randalf, and she was in love with Edward!'

Ella appeared from out of the shadows at the back of the hall. She was flushed and dishevelled, her barbarian braids falling loose and her tooled-leather breastplate dented and scratched. Leaning on her for support was Edward Gorgeous, looking paler than ever. He was hunched over, his arms folded tightly across his chest, and the cuffs of his billowing white shirt soaked in blood.

'She attacked us in the dungeon,' Joe continued. 'Edward tried his best to hold her back . . .'

'She was too strong for me,' groaned Edward.

'But I threw a lump of stale cake at her and the next thing I knew, she exploded!'

'Exploded, eh? Well, fancy that,' said Randalf distractedly as he looked past Joe at the Round Kitchen Table, where Norbert had just placed his tray of snugglemuffins. 'Always thought there was something not quite right about that girl . . .'

The cake druid inspected the ogre's cakes.

'I have to admit these are really quite eye-catching,' Quentin was saying, prodding the brightly decorated snugglemuffins with his big wooden spoon. He reached forward and picked one up as Norbert watched him intently, his triple eyes blinking with excitement.

'Oooh!' went the barbarian spectators.

Quentin took a bite. 'Delicious,' he pronounced.

'Aaaaah!' went the barbarian spectators.

'Well,' said Quentin, 'it seems we have a winner after

all! Errm . . .'

'Norbert the Not-Very-Big,' said Norbert shyly.

'Norbert the Not-Very-Big!' Quentin announced.

'Hooray!' cheered the barbarian spectators, throwing their winged helmets in the air and stamping their feet.

'Who'd have thought it?' said Randalf. 'Good old Norbert . . . Of course, he couldn't have done it without my help.'

'Yeah, yeah, Fatso,' said Veronica, who had regained her composure and was back to her old self. 'Of course he couldn't.'

'Shut up, Veronica.'

'As the winner of the Big Barbarian Bake-Off,' Quentin announced grandly, 'you, Norbert the Not-Very-Big, have earned the right to attempt to pull the fabled sword from the legendary scone . . .'

'Oooooh!' muttered the barbarian spectators, exchanging knowing looks.

'The ancient scone that none other than King Marthur himself baked all those years ago to his very own recipe, the gorgeous Scone of Garlic!'

'Aaaaah!' the barbarian spectators chorused.

'Garlic,' said Joe, and sniffed the crumbs on his sleeve. 'That would explain what happened to Edwina.' Another thought struck him. He turned to Edward and Ella. 'Did he say something about a sword?'

'Come, Norbert,' said Quentin, clapping an arm round the ogre's shoulder and leading him towards the back of the hall. 'The sword in the scone awaits you, for it is written that he who pulls the sword from the scone shall become the new and rightful ruler of the Round Kitchen Table . . .'

'Ooooh!' muttered the barbarian spectators as they followed them.

'*And* do the washing-up.'

'Aah.' They nudged each other and sniggered behind the cake druid's back.

'But what is this?' Quentin thundered, stopping in front of the crumbled remains of the garlic scone, the sword nowhere to be seen. 'This is an outrage!' He spun round, his hands on his hips. 'Who has pulled the sword from the scone?' he demanded.

Joe blushed furiously.

'It wasn't us,' said the barbarian spectators.

'And it certainly wasn't any of us,' said Delia Dragon-breath, looking round at the other contestants. 'Was it?'

They all shook their heads.

'And *we* were clapped in irons,' said Edward weakly, taking Ella's hand. 'We didn't see a thing. Do you want us to go back to the dungeon?'

'No, no,' said Quentin. 'The dungeon's only really there for show. In fact, I'm surprised you stayed in it as long as you did. Anyway, this is far more important,' he said, waving his big wooden spoon in agitation. His gaze fell on Joe. 'What about *you*?'

Joe turned even redder. 'Errm . . .'

'It's not Joe the Barbarian you should be concerned about,' Veronica piped up, hopping from Randalf's hat to Joe's shoulder. She flapped a wing in the direction of the workbenches. 'It's the owner of *those*!'

Everyone stared at the bearskin coat and the horned helmet lying on the floor. Quentin's eyes narrowed.

'Hrothgrar the Hunger Slayer,' he said slowly. 'It seems we've found the culprit.'

'Or rather, we *haven't* found him,' a barbarian spectator commented. 'Because he's not there.'

The other barbarian spectators nodded sagely.

'This is an outrage!' Quentin exclaimed. 'Without the sword in the scone, we can't find a ruler of the Round Kitchen Table, and that means the washing-up will never get done!'

'Perhaps *I* might be of assistance,' said Peat the Perfumed Bog-Man in a soft, burbly kind of voice.

'You?' said Quentin.

'With the washing up,' said Peat, nodding his mauve lily-pad-hatted head towards the great mountain of washing-up in the shadows at the back of the hall. 'Allow me.'

'Yes, yes, allow him!' chorused the barbarians eagerly.

'Well, if you're quite sure you can handle it,' said Quentin uncertainly.

'Oh, I won't have to handle it,' laughed Peat. 'Follow me, everyone.'

Peat led them outside and pulled the doors of the Great Hall shut behind him. Then, with a high-pitched gurgling cry, he threw back his head and raised his long arms in the air. He danced about on the spot in a strange loose-limbed jig, then thrust out his bony fingers and began to sing.

'Burble, gurgle, splish and splosh!
Whirl and flow and scour and wash . . .'

High up at the top of the valley, the waterfall which cascaded down the mountainside began to tremble. As Peat chanted, his hands cupped and his fingers wiggling, the waterfall began to rise. It reared up from the mountain pool into which its waters normally fell and swayed to and fro in mid-air like a snake being charmed. Then, with a mighty whoosh, the waterfall arched high in the sky and flowed down on to the rooftops of the Great Hall. It gushed over the tiles and in through the windows of the onion-domed towers.

And as the enchanted
waterfall continued to flow
in an uninterrupted stream
into the hall, from inside
there came the sound of
sloshing and splashing and things
clattering about as the whole
building slowly filled with water.
Peat's long arms spun round and
round like the sails of a windmill
in a gale as his dance became
increasingly animated and his
singing grew louder and louder.

'*Pot and platter, spoon and cup!*
Easy goes the washing-up!'

Out from the top of the onion-domed towers came a
soggy flock of fruit-cake bats and cookie ravens, hooting
and cawing indignantly. They circled the Great Hall
several times before flying off towards the distant treetops.
Behind them, the water gushed from the windows of the
towers as the hall filled to the roof.

Peat raised his left hand and clicked his fingers,
sending the waterfall back to its mountainside, then raised
his right hand. He turned to face the two huge black-
hinged doors. Quentin the cake druid, the barbarians, the

contestants, Edward, Ella, Joe and Randalf stood open-mouthed, while on the wizard's pointy hat, Veronica stood open-beaked.

Peat clicked the fingers of his right hand.

With a resounding crash, the mighty doors of the Great Hall flew open and a torrent of water burst out. In a roiling, boiling, bubbling flood, it swept everyone off their feet and out across the alpine meadow. Rolling head over heels, Joe was carried along by the swirling current before coming to rest beside a drenched yak-skin yurt, which had twelve dripping battlecats clinging forlornly to its roof. All around, in shrinking pools and rapidly disappearing puddles, bedraggled barbarians flopped about like beached fish as the water drained away.

Joe climbed to his feet. So did the barbarians. And the contestants. *And* the cake druid. They all stared in amazement at the cutlery,

crockery and cooking utensils that had been washed out from the open doors and now lay in a heap in front of the Great Hall.

The mountain of washing-up was clean and sparkling, and already beginning to dry in the warm sunshine.

Quentin raised his big wooden spoon moistly and tapped Peat the Perfumed Bog-Man on both shoulders before kneeling at his feet.

'Long live King Peat of the Round Kitchen Table!' he proclaimed.

'Long live King Peat! Long live King Peat!' the barbarians cheered, their happy voices echoing round the valley as the flock of fruit-cake bats and cookie ravens began to return overhead.

'*Long live King Peat!*'

'Edward? Edward!' came Ella's concerned voice. 'Edward, speak to me!'

Joe turned from the washing-up to see his sister kneeling down beside Edward Gorgeous, who was lying motionless on the grass. A damp-looking Randalf sat a little way off, deep in conversation with the rolled-up stair-carpet, Norbert by his side.

'The first time I was pleased, but this is simply going too far,' the carpet was complaining. 'I mean, I'm a carpet. I'm meant to be swept. Occasionally beaten. But not soaked! It's not good for me . . . *Atishoo!*'

Edward Gorgeous sat up. His eyes were bright and his skin had a healthy pink glow to it.

'I feel wonderful!' he said. 'And so, so hungry! I haven't felt like this in years.'

He got to his feet and hugged Ella delightedly.

'You mean . . . you need to suck a thumb?' said Ella uneasily.

'No! That's just it!' Edward exclaimed. 'This is different. This is real hunger. *Normal* hunger!'

'Snugglemuffin, sir?' said Norbert helpfully, opening his large fist to reveal a rather mushy-looking cake.

'Yes, please!' said Edward, seizing it and devouring it greedily. 'Oh, I'd forgotten just how delicious food tastes.' He turned to Ella. 'I . . . I think . . . I think I'm cured!'

'That's what enchanted water can do for you,' said the carpet. '*Atishoo!* But one can have too much of it . . . *Atishoo! Atishoo!*'

'Oh, Edward,' Ella breathed.

'Oh, Ella,' Edward replied and pulled her close.

Joe turned away, embarrassed. Big sisters! One minute they're moping about in their bedrooms painting their nails black, the next they're riding off on battlecats to Nowhere. And then there was this soppy stuff to contend with. It was all such a pain . . .

Joe stopped. He blinked. He could scarcely believe his eyes. There in the distance, looming up on the horizon at the far end of the valley, was a large walled castle. It hadn't been there when they'd arrived, Joe was certain of it, and it looked so solid and forbidding, with its stone walls and high towers, it couldn't have been built overnight.

Could it?

Joe stared.

Then something else caught his eye. It was a small lamp-post that had emerged from the wooded mountainside, its light glowing dimly. It scuttled towards the castle on stubby mechanical legs. As it approached, the drawbridge lowered. The lamp-post trotted inside.

'Randalf! Randalf!' Joe shouted. 'The lamp-post! I've just seen the lamp-post!'

'Where?' said Randalf.

'There!' said Joe, pointing at the castle.

Randalf nodded. 'Whatever,' he said.

Beneath Harmless Hill, the four flower fairies sat in the flickering candlelight, their gossamer wings fluttering at their backs. In front of them, on a small, moss-covered stone table, next to a tiny battered vessel, lay a golden-handled broad-bladed implement.

'The fools! The fools!' laughed Pesticide, wiping a

couple of crumbs from the blade. 'We've grabbed the Goblet of Porridge and swiped the Sword in the Scone right from under their noses. And the best bit is, they have no idea who we really are!' She swept back her green hair and fluttered her gossamer wings. 'Nor what we've actually stolen!'

She reached out and stroked the objects on the stone table with a gloved hand.

'The Plant Pot of Power,' said Nettle, her eyes gleaming.

'And the Trowel of Turbulence,' added Thistle reverently.

'And now for the third of the lost treasures of Harmless Hill,' breathed Briar-Rose. 'The greatest of them all . . .'

'The Acorn of Abundance!' Pesticide declared.

'And where shall we look for it?' they all asked her.

'In the forests of Nowhere?' suggested Nettle.

'Or in the orchards of Trollbridge?' offered Thistle.

'Or the glades of Elfwood?' said Briar-Rose.

'To find it, we must follow the light,' said Pesticide.

'The light?' they chorused. 'The light of what? The sun? The moons? The stars? . . .'

'No,' said Pesticide dramatically, sweeping back her long green hair. 'The lamp-post.'

Book Three

Pesticide the Flower Fairy

Prologue

Deep, deep under the ground, in the vast vaulted fairy caverns beneath Harmless Hill, it was breakfast time. At one end of the forty-foot table sat Queen Titania, on her throne of living willow wood with its luxuriant garlands of fragrant flowers. At the other end sat King Oberon, on his leatherette reclining chair with its built-in footrest.

'Pass the acacia honey, Ron,' said his queen in a voice as soft and melodious as dewdrops dripping from dandelions.

'What's that, Tania, my love?' said King Oberon, without looking up from the sports section of the *Fairy Times*.

'The honey, Ron,' Queen Titania said in a voice as

light and gentle as a summer breeze in a flower meadow.

'The what?' muttered King Oberon, his gaze fixed on the fairy-football results.

'The acacia honey!' Queen Titania shouted in a voice capable of stunning a stiltmouse at a hundred yards. 'I want it! NOW!'

From high up in the vaulted ceiling came the fluttering of wings as four prim-faced elderly fairies swooped down on to the table. Pushing and jostling one another in their eagerness to please, they seized the silver honey pot at King Oberon's elbow and flew with it to Queen Titania's side. Cooing and clucking, they set the honey pot down and began fussing over the buttercup croissant on their queen's silver plate.

'A spoonful of honey dripped over it? . . .'

'Or shall we cut it in two and spread the honey inside? . . .'

'Or cut it into tiny pieces so you can dip it in the honey yourself? . . .'

'Or we can do it for you . . .'

'Thank you, Peaseblossom. Thank you, Cobweb. Thank you, Moth, and you, Mustardseed. That'll be all . . .' She waved them away. 'Put the spoon down, Peaseblossom. Leave the croissant alone, Cobweb. I said, *leave* it, Moth. *And* you, Mustardseed. Drop the butter-knife . . .' The queen's voice rose in irritation as the fairies continued to fuss and flutter around her. 'I said, *that will be all*! Now, shoo! Shoo, the lot of you!'

With prim little exclamations and tiny tutting sounds, Peaseblossom, Cobweb, Moth and Mustardseed flew back to their velvet cushions high up in the vaulted ceiling. Queen Titania sat back exhaustedly in her willow throne and sighed.

'Ron,' she said. 'Put the newspaper down. We need to talk.' She folded her arms. '*Ron!*'

At the other end of the table, King Oberon lowered the *Fairy Times* and scratched the hairy belly that protruded from his stained vest.

'Yes, dear,' he said obediently. 'What about?'

'Our daughter,' said Queen Titania.

'What's she done now?' he said wearily.

'That's just it, Ron,' said the queen. 'She hasn't *done*

anything. That school she insisted we send her to – now she says she doesn't need to go back. And as for that camping trip of hers, it turns out she didn't have permission to borrow that chariot after all. I had to deal with a very angry barbarian who kept going on about his missing horned helmet and bearskin coat. And since she got back, all she ever seems to do is mope about in her room with those dreadful friends of hers. And have you seen the state of her room? I looked in the other day, quite innocently, and she got absolutely furious with me. Took her mittens off and waved those awful fingers at me. I'm telling you, Ron, it sent shivers down my spine. Oh, when I think back to her christening . . .'

'Now, don't go upsetting yourself, Tania, my love,' said King Oberon. 'Fairy-tale christenings *can* go wrong. It was just one of those things. Look on the bright side. She could have grown up blue-eyed and beautiful, only to prick her finger on a spindle and fall asleep for a hundred years.'

'Yes, but Pesticide is such an unfortunate name,' said Queen Titania.

'That's the trouble with wicked fairy godmothers, my love,' said King Oberon, shaking his head. 'But as curses go, Pesticide could have done far worse. So long as she remembers to keep her mittens on, she'll be fine.'

'But she's *not* fine, Ron,' Queen Titania protested. 'You and I both know it. She's . . . Oh, hello, darling,' she gushed, blushing as crimson as a field poppy when she spotted her daughter standing in the doorway of the immense cavern. 'I didn't see you there. Daddy and I were just talking about you, weren't we, Ron?'

Pesticide shrugged and stared at her parents from beneath her fringe of acid-green hair. Her black eyeliner matched her black blouse edged in black spiderweb lace, which went perfectly with her black tutu with its carefully ripped black trim, her neatly laddered black tights and her extra clompy, blacker-than-black boots.

'I'm going out,' she said.

'Out, dear?' said Queen Titania, her voice as lilting as a lark in a lilac tree. 'Out where?'

'Just out,' Pesticide mumbled as she inspected a stray thread at the cuff of one of her black mittens. She looked up. 'Dad,' she said. 'How many aints are there in Elfwood? I goggled it on the inter-elf but I'm still waiting for an answer.'

'Aints?' said King Oberon. 'What on earth are you asking about aints for? That's old old fairy magic, that is. Best left well alone. You'll be asking me about the Trowel of Turbulence next.'

'Oh no, the inter-elf told me all about the trowel *and* the plant pot *and* the . . .' She clamped a mittened hand to her mouth to stop herself. 'Doesn't matter.' She turned on her heels and stomped sulkily off.

'Oh, Ron!' Queen Titania wailed. 'What *are* we going to do with her?'

From the four corners of the cream-coloured castle, ivory white turrets sprouted. Dozens of them. Some were short and squat, others tall and elegant. Some were square, some were round, while some were twisted, like sticks of white barley sugar. All were topped by pointy spires of pale alabaster from which faded calico pennants fluttered.

Set high up in the crenellated walls of the castle were small shuttered windows and cross-shaped arrow-slits, while at its base was a broad arched doorway. Above it, chiselled into the white marble, were the words *University of Whatever*.

The drawbridge to the castle was down and resting on the dusty ground.

'The lamp-post!' Joe called back over his shoulder as he ran on to the drawbridge. 'It went this way!'

Behind him, by some considerable distance, came Norbert, galumphing over the meadow grass. Randalf bounced about on his shoulders, struggling to hold on to his hat. Above them both flew Veronica, her small blue wings a blur of rapid movement. Further back still strolled Edward and Ella, hand in hand and gazing into one another's eyes.

'Wait, Joe! We don't have time for this!' shouted Randalf. 'We've got to find the Goblet of Porridge, remember?' He waved at him agitatedly. 'Stop! Stop! You have to ring the castle's bell first, or it'll think you're an invader!'

Joe paused on the drawbridge and turned. 'What bell? Who'll think I'm an invader? ... *Whoooah!*'

There was a resounding creak and a clatter of chains, and Joe disappeared from view as the drawbridge slammed shut.

'Joe! Joe!' squawked Veronica, flapping towards the castle and disappearing through one of the narrow arrow-slits. Just then, a klaxon sounded.

'That's torn it,' said Randalf as Norbert came to an abrupt halt in front of the castle gate.

On the wall beside the raised drawbridge was a silver doorbell. Beneath it, in small, spiky, difficult-to-read writing, were the words *Castle Admittance Device*, followed by a list of instructions in writing that was even smaller and harder to read.

(a) Raise hand and extend forefinger.

(b) Place said forefinger on circular button marked 'press'.

(c) Apply pressure with aforementioned digit.

(d) Retract said aforementioned digit and await response.

WARNING : INVADERS WILL BE REPELLED!

Edward and Ella approached.

'This place brings back memories,' said Edward with a shudder as he stopped next to Norbert and Randalf, and looked up.

Beside him, Ella gave a puzzled frown. 'Where's Joe?'

Randalf looked down at her from Norbert's shoulder. 'I'm afraid . . .' he began as, from inside the walls, there came the sounds of clanking cogs and grinding gear-wheels. 'Joe has invaded the castle.'

Just then, from high above their heads, there was a loud *WHUMPH!* and a plump vacuum-cleaner bag came sailing over the crenellated walls. It landed at their feet and burst open, sending a cloud of dust billowing into the air and coating the four of them from head to foot. From beneath Randalf's arm the rolled-up stair-carpet gave a choked little gasp.

'Oh! Dust! My worst nightmare . . . Sleepy. *So* sleepy . . . *Zzzzzzzzzz.*'

One by one, Norbert, Randalf, Ella and finally Edward slumped to the ground. There was a second *whumph* and a duvet and four pillows came fluttering gently down. The pillows slipped beneath the sleepers' heads while the duvet settled over their sleeping bodies. Stitched into the duvet cover and pillowcases in small hard-to-read letters were the words *Defeated Invaders Aftercare Kit*, followed by the instructions '(a) Sleep Well' and '(b) Don't Call Again'.

With a hydraulic hiss and a wheezing of steam pistons, the castle rose up on four gigantic mechanical legs and began to march across the landscape. In a matter of moments, the entire pearl-white edifice had plodded over the horizon and disappeared.

Randalf rolled on to his side and snuggled into his pillow. Next to him Ella and Edward gently snored, while Norbert's shoulders slowly rose and fell as he sucked his thumb.

'Mummy,' he murmured contentedly.

'I say, you there!' came a querulous voice. 'Yes, you. With the budgie.'

Joe looked up from the dusty flagstones. As the drawbridge had risen he'd been pitched into the castle and now found himself lying in the middle of a courtyard.

Veronica had just landed on his shoulder.

'Has the castle repelled the invaders?' the querulous voice enquired.

A tall, thin, balding man with silver-rimmed spectacles and a long flowing robe edged with white ermine came hurrying towards Joe and Veronica from the opposite side of the courtyard. A fat black Labrador padded along behind him, panting heavily.

'Invaders?' said Joe, climbing to his feet.

The man strode over to one of the arrow-slits in the wall and peered out. 'Ah, yes, seems it has. Sleeping like babies. Mechanical castle, one; invaders, nil. Well done, Whatever! Jolly good show.' As the castle began to judder and lurch alarmingly, he turned to Joe and stuck out a hand. 'Lord Asbow,' he said, pumping Joe's arm up and down. 'You must be the new man in Experimental Woodwork. Fluffy, is it? No, that was the last one . . .'

Beside him, the fat Labrador broke wind loudly.

'Joe,' said Joe, trying to ignore the appalling smell. 'Joe Jefferson.'

'Good to have you on board,

Jefferson,' said Lord Asbow. 'I say, what a splendid pet,' he added, and nodded at Veronica. 'Beautiful plumage.' He patted the Labrador's shoulders. 'Why don't you two join me and Daemian here in the Senior Common Room for a nice cup of dust?'

Veronica winked at Joe, who nodded uncertainly. He looked around, but there was no sign of the lamp-post. This strange person seemed to have mistaken him for someone else, but at least he seemed friendly. The castle gave another lurch. The whole place appeared to be moving.

'Yes, errm, thank you,' said Joe. 'We'd love to, but . . .'

'Excellent,' said Lord Asbow, taking him by the arm and propelling him across the courtyard, through a door and into the first of a maze of corridors. They turned right, then left, then left again, then climbed a flight of stairs, then descended another flight of stairs and turned left again . . .

'Oh, you'll soon get the hang of the place,' said Lord Asbow airily as he saw the look of confusion on Joe's face. 'And until you do, I'm happy to show you around.'

They came to a tall whitewashed door, bearing the sign *Senior Common Room Door – Instructions for Use*, followed by a column of tiny writing, numbered 1 to 37. Seizing the handle, Lord Asbow opened the door with a flourish and ushered Joe and Veronica inside.

The Senior Common Room of the University of Whatever was full of balding professors wearing silver-rimmed spectacles and long, flowing ermine-edged robes just like Lord Asbow's. Each of them had a different pet. There was a pink-eyed mouse, a neurotic looking gerbil, a guinea pig that was losing its fur, a plump duck, a tortoise with *Daemian* written on its shell in white paint, and a small goldfish in a glass bowl.

Lord Asbow removed an ermine-edged gown from a hook behind the door and handed it to Joe.

'Here, try this one on for size, Jefferson,' he said, 'and let's see about that cup of dust.' He looked up. 'I say, Mrs Couldn't-Possibly, two cups of your finest dust, if you'd be so kind.'

A tall, elegant woman with clear blue eyes and silky blonde hair the colour of sun-ripened barley came sashaying across the room. She stumbled slightly as the sleepy-looking wombat following her stepped on the hem of her silk dress.

'Certainly, Lord Asbow,' she said with a smile.

She turned to a pair of silver pot-bellied urns that stood on a sturdy oak sideboard beneath a complicated diagram covered in arrows and annotations.

She held a bone-china cup beneath the first urn's spout and turned the tap. Dust trickled into the cup like the sands of an upturned egg-timer. She turned to the second urn and added boiling water, then repeated the process with the second cup. With a gently steaming cup of dust in each hand she returned to Lord Asbow and Joe, almost tripping over her sleepy wombat as she did so.

'Oh, Daemian,' she chided, 'do try not to get under my feet.'

'Thank you so much,' said Lord Asbow.

'My pleasure,' said Mrs Couldn't-Possibly. 'I vacuumed it up fresh this morning from the roof of the west tower. Finest sunrise dust.'

'Mmm, delicious,' said Lord Asbow, as the fat Labrador at his side began licking the sleepy wombat's face. 'Daemian! Leave Daemian alone!' Lord Asbow scolded, prodding his Labrador with his foot. The appalling smell returned. He went over to a battered-looking leather sofa on which a balding professor with silver-rimmed glasses and long robes was sitting, a goldfish bowl beside him. 'If you wouldn't mind moving your pet, Professor Quedgely.'

'Yes, Lord Asbow. Sorry, Lord Asbow,' the professor said, picking up the glass bowl and climbing to his feet. 'Come on, Daemian,' he said, gazing fondly at the goldfish swimming round lethargically in the green-tinged bowl, 'time to change your water.'

Lord Asbow sat down on the sofa and patted the

cushion next to him. 'Take the weight off your feet, Jefferson.'

On Joe's shoulder, Veronica leaned across and whispered in his ear. 'I think we've got them fooled. Just remember to call me Daemian while I think of a way to get us out of here.'

Joe nodded and sat down next to Lord Asbow. He took a sip from the cup. The pale greenish liquid tasted delicious – sweet and fizzy and full of strange and wonderful flavours that Joe had never tasted before. He drained the cup in one go. He felt wide awake and full of energy.

'Real pick-me-up, sunrise dust,' said Lord Asbow. 'Unlike sunset dust, which can make you sleep for a week. Especially if you don't dilute it . . . Ah, I see you're admiring the portrait of our founder,' he said, following Joe's gaze.

The wood-panelled wall on the opposite side of the Common Room was covered with gold-framed portraits of all shapes and sizes. There was a square painting of a red-faced professor with a plump piglet tucked under one arm, and a tall thin painting of a worried-looking professor clutching a hefty python, while between the two of them was an oval-shaped painting of a short-sighted professor wearing thick glasses and with a speckled hen perched on his head . . . But what had caught Joe's eye was the large opulently framed portrait that had pride of place above the mantelpiece.

It showed a portly individual in a bottle-green bowler

VLAD THE TICKLER

hat and an oversized orange suit with a garish red check. The large yellow daffodil in the buttonhole of his lapel was squirting a jet of water, while his flamboyant bow-tie appeared to be revolving. In one hand was a glowing lantern; in the other, a pink feather-duster.

'Vlad the Tickler,' said Lord Asbow proudly. 'A fascinating character. He arrived here quite unexpectedly through a portal . . . Do you know what portals are, Jefferson?'

'Well, actually . . .' Joe began.

'Let me tell you,' Lord Asbow continued without a pause. 'Awkward blighters, portals. Things fall into them, things fall out of them. And all quite without warning. One of those things just happened to be our illustrious founder. Muddle only knows where *he* came from, but he was a real eccentric. His hobby was tickling people,' said Lord Asbow, pointing at the pink feather-duster in Vlad the Tickler's hand.

'But he was very popular in Muddle Earth,' he went on. 'And he must have liked it here because he stayed, and fell in love with a barbarian princess, Heidi the Gorgeous, and built this mechanical castle for her.' Lord Asbow pointed at Vlad's other hand. 'He was carrying that lantern when he first stumbled through the portal. He put it down on the soil on this side, and the next thing he knew, it had grown into a splendid lamp-post . . .'

'Lamp-post!' Joe exclaimed, nearly dropping his teacup.

'Yes,' said Lord Asbow matter-of-factly. 'A rather jolly little *walking* lamp-post. Because it grew in the magic earth at the entrance to the portal, the lamp-post and the portal are linked. Wherever the lamp-post goes, the portal follows. And as I said, they're awkward blighters, portals. Spoilt children are forever dropping out of them, putting on crowns and calling themselves kings and queens . . . It's all such a dreadful bore!'

'I've seen the lamp-post,' said Joe excitedly. 'It's somewhere in the castle.'

'Is it?' said Lord Asbow with a sigh. 'That means the portal's here too. Take my advice, Jefferson, and watch your step. Last time the portal was here, your predecessor allowed one of his most remarkable inventions to fall into it. It was unforgivably careless of him!' Lord Asbow frowned. 'He left us no choice but to impose the harshest punishment of all. We separated him from his pet, Daemian the hamster, and expelled him from the university. And you know what that means,' he said darkly.

'I do?' said Joe.

'Separated from our pets, Jefferson, we are condemned to become werecreatures every triple full moon. Werebudgies, werelabradors, wereducks, weregoldfish, and in Fluffy's case, a werehamster. No, Mr Fluffy had only himself to blame.' He shrugged. 'Goodness knows where he is now.'

'I think I might know,' Joe muttered under his breath.

Lord Asbow's eyes took on a faraway look. 'Mr Fluffy's

flat-pack wardrobe!' he breathed. 'An extraordinary, wondrous thing. Just think of it, Jefferson, an entire wardrobe, but in pieces and packed into a cardboard box as flat as a barbarian's pancake, together with the most detailed instructions ever devised. And a handy little tool to put it together.' Lord Asbow shook his head. 'All lost in a moment down that wretched portal. Goodness knows where it went.'

'I think I might know,' Joe muttered a second time.

'What's that, Jefferson?'

'Nothing,' said Joe, climbing to his feet and stepping over Lord Asbow's panting Labrador. He crossed the room to the portrait and peered closely at a shadowy figure in the background. It was Edward Gorgeous.

'That's Vlad the Tickler's nephew, Edward,' said Lord Asbow, who had followed him across the room, together with his decidedly smelly Labrador. 'History doesn't record what happened to him . . .'

'I think I might know,' Joe muttered for the third time.

'. . . unlike his uncle,' Lord Asbow went on, 'who lived to a ripe old age and founded this university. But shortly afterwards he was accidently trodden on by the building when somebody pulled the wrong lever. Ever since then, we at the University of Whatever have devoted ourselves to the discussion, study and writing of instruction sheets and manuals for absolutely everything, *whatever* it is, so that no such mistake should ever be made again.'

Lord Asbow laid a hand on Joe's shoulder as his fat Labrador broke wind once again. Veronica dived for cover inside Joe's robes, while Joe held his nose and tried not to breathe.

'But enough of all this, Jefferson,' said Lord Asbow. 'Let me show you to your woodwork laboratory.' He paused and sniffed the air. 'What on Muddle Earth is that smell?'

'I think I might know,' said Joe.

*M*ulti-Stepped Circular Elevation Structure, the notice read. *Instructions for use: (a) Hold handrail securely and place right foot on first step. (b) Place left foot on second step. (c) Place right foot on third step . . .*

Joe shook his head as he followed Lord Asbow up the spiral staircase. Everything in the castle – from doorknobs to window catches, bell pulls to banisters – seemed to have a notice attached to it, with ridiculously detailed instructions. And try as he might, Joe couldn't stop himself from reading them, no matter how pointless they turned out to be.

Veronica's head poked out from the folds of Joe's robes. 'Where are we?' she whispered.

'Climbing a multi-stepped circular elevation structure,' Joe whispered back. 'To the top of one of the towers.'

'Here we are,' announced Lord Asbow brightly as beside him Daemian the Labrador wagged his tail and looked up expectantly at the door in front of them, which bore the notice *Experimental Woodwork*. Lord Asbow threw open the door and ushered Joe inside. 'I'll leave you to it, Jefferson, old chap. Make yourself at home. If you need anything, I'll be in the Senior Common Room,' he said, turning on his heels and heading back down the staircase, followed by Daemian. 'You know where to find it,' his voice floated back. 'Down the stairs, second left, third right, fourth left, eighth right, right again, left again, right again . . .'

Joe looked around. He was standing in a cluttered workshop. Strange, unlikely-looking woodwork tools lay scattered across low, squat workbenches. There were crocodile saws and three-headed hammers, corkscrew mallets and duck-billed pliers, musical chisels, steam-driven drills and a humpback sanding machine that slouched in the corner. The walls were papered with complicated diagrams of wardrobes and cupboards and chests of drawers, while the floor was strewn with sawdust

and wood-shavings. A small golden hamster popped its head up out of the wood-shavings and fixed Joe with a beady-eyed stare. The next moment it shot across the workshop, through Joe's legs and out through the open door.

'Blast! You've let the hamster out!' said a portly professor with a manky grey parrot perched on his shoulder. He stepped into the workshop. 'The name's Munderfield,' he said, 'the new experimental woodwork professor. And you are?'

'Jefferson,' said Joe. 'The experimental . . . errm . . . errm . . . instruction-notice professor!'

'Oh, really?' said Professor Munderfield. 'Jolly good show. And don't worry about the hamster. I'm sure it'll find its own way back. Separated from its owner, poor thing. Bad business. Perhaps you've heard about it?'

'Yes, I have,' said Joe, edging towards the door. 'It's awful. I couldn't imagine being separated from Daemian here,' he added, tickling Veronica under her beak.

Veronica nodded theatrically.

'Yes,' said Professor Munderfield uncertainly, as he pulled a handkerchief from the pocket of his robes and wiped fresh parrot droppings from his lapel. 'I couldn't imagine it either.'

Joe backed out of the door and headed down the stairs.

'I don't think he suspected anything,' said Veronica. They reached the bottom of the staircase. 'Now, which way shall we go?'

'Let's try this way,' said Joe, turning to the right and setting off along a dimly lit corridor.

He took a left turn, then a right turn. Then another right turn . . . He found himself in a small courtyard and looked up. Above him were crenellated battlements, with stone steps leading up to them. Above the battlements, the ivory towers of the university rose up.

'This place is weird, even for Muddle Earth,' said Joe.

'You can say that again,' said Veronica. 'The rest of us stay as far away from it as we can. Which isn't always easy, with the whole place travelling around the way it does. And it attracts the weirdest types, who seem to like it here. Thumb-sucking vampires. Pet-loving werepeople. Zumbies. Poltergeese. Black bunnies called Binky . . . And you just went rushing inside, Joe, before Randalf or I could stop you.'

'I know. I'm sorry,' Joe said apologetically, 'but I saw –' he pointed – '*that*!'

The lamp-post had just appeared. There it was above them, skipping merrily along the battlements. Its light twinkled brightly as it broke into a little tap dance.

'Wait! Stop!' Joe shouted. He bounded up the stone steps that led to the battlements, two at a time. 'Come back!'

The lamp-post reached the end of the walkway and leaped across to the roof of the nearest tower.

'Careful, Joe,' warned Veronica, taking to the wing

as Joe sprinted along the battlements, his ermine-edged robes flapping.

He launched himself into the air after the lamp-post, and landed on the top of the tower just as the moving castle lurched to one side.

'Whooooah!' Joe cried out with alarm, sliding down the roof-tiles towards the edge of the tower.

A hand shot out, seized the hem of his robes and hauled him back from the brink. Joe looked up. Mrs Couldn't-Possibly was smiling down at him. She was wearing a floral-patterned pinafore, a pair of ermine-edged rubber gloves and a mask, which she had pulled aside. Next to her stood a large upright vacuum cleaner, a sleepy-looking wombat draped round its handle.

'Careful there, Professor Jefferson,' she said, helping him to his feet. 'Turret-jumping can be dangerous when the castle's on the move. Didn't you see the notice?'

The castle was lumbering over a rocky landscape of cliffs and crags on its huge mechanical legs. *Clunk! Clunk! Clunk!* Its footfalls echoed through the Here-Be-Dragons Mountains as its walls trembled and its turrets swayed. Behind Mrs Couldn't-Possibly, the lamp-post did a little somersault and jumped on to the adjacent tower. The air around it seemed to ripple and there came the sound of distant voices.

'Joe! Ella! Time for lunch!' It was Joe's dad's voice. 'Honestly, where have those two got to?'

'Don't ask us!' the twins called back. 'We haven't seen them anywhere.'

It was the portal back to his world. Joe felt a pang of homesickness in the pit of his stomach. He had to admit he'd had fun in Muddle Earth, what with the broomball match and the cake-baking competition, and helping Randalf. But, it seemed, life was continuing back home without him – his parents were back, the twins had been let in, lunch was ready and on the table . . . If only he could get the lamp-post to stop and listen, then perhaps it would come with him, and he and Ella could finally get back to where they belonged.

'I was just doing a spot of vacuuming,' Mrs Couldn't-Possibly was saying. 'Sunrise dust gathers on the east sides of the towers,' she explained. 'Sunset dust gathers on the west . . .'

But Joe wasn't listening.

'Come back, *please*!' he shouted as he threw himself after the lamp-post and landed on the top of the next tower in a cloud of dust.

'Careful, Professor Jefferson!' shouted Mrs Couldn't-Possibly. 'That's the *west* side! *Sunset* dust!'

Too late. Joe breathed in the twinkling particles and instantly fell asleep.

'Joe!' Veronica squawked as Joe fell from the tower and tumbled through the air. 'Joe!'

'Hello, clouds! Hello, mountains!' trilled the young dragon as he flapped his wings and flew across the sky. He swooped down lower and landed beside a mountain lake. 'Hello, flowers!' he said, thin wisps of smoke curling from his nostrils.

Eraguff the eager-to-please dragon carefully picked the tiny mountain blooms, some white, some pink, some pale yellow, that were growing in the rocky cracks and crevices. When he had gathered a small bunch, he raised it to his nose and sniffed their delicate fragrance.

'*Atishoo!*'

A jet of flame shot from his nostrils and instantly incinerated the pretty flowers.

'Oh dear! Not again!' said Eraguff, dropping the blackened remains of the bouquet. 'Sorry, flowers. Silly me.'

Just then, a solitary green-scaled dragon with flame-red wings and a sinuous tail of copper and bronze came gliding into view. Eraguff looked up and waved.

'Coo-ee! Uncle Alan! It's me, Eraguff! Isn't it a beautiful morning? I was just picking some flowers for my nest. They do brighten the place up, don't you think? And they're *so* pretty. Though I have to be careful, what with my allergies . . . Uncle Alan? Uncle Alan? Can't you stop, Uncle Alan? . . .' He lowered his hand and his shoulders slumped. 'Oh, obviously not.'

Eraguff blew a sad little smoke ring out of the corner of his mouth as, studiously ignoring him, the green-scaled dragon flew past on his majestic red wings.

'Likes to keep himself to himself, does Uncle Alan,' called Eraguff to a purple dragon that was just passing overhead. 'Coo-ee! Miss Dragonbreath. It's me, Eraguff!'

'We all do,' said the purple dragon sternly as she continued on her way.

Eraguff sighed. 'Oh, well,' he said to no one in particular. 'I might as well go and tidy my nest.'

With a flap of his beige wings, the young dragon took to the air, his grey scales drab and dull in the early morning sunshine.

'Goodbye, flowers! Goodbye, lake!' he trilled as he headed off towards a nearby mountain top.

Two minutes later, he spiralled down out of the sky and landed lightly on a messy collection of stubby branches, tangled twigs and tattered scraps of material that was balanced precariously on the top of a high rocky crag. Folding his wings and coiling his tail, Eraguff settled himself down and began tidying the nest. After half an hour, every single branch, twig and scrap of material had been carefully rearranged.

The nest looked exactly the same.

'That's better,' said Eraguff.

He picked up a pair of antique knitting needles and turned to the balls of wool, yarn and twine in his collection, all of them made by unravelling the threads of scrap material: abandoned curtains from Goblintown, discarded vegetable sacks from Trollbridge, mislaid snuggly-wugglies from the Ogre Hills, yak-wool duvets from Nowhere . . . in fact anything that had blown off a washing line, fallen from a passing cart or been accidently left by a mountain lake; Eraguff swooped on them all – so long as they were bright and colourful.

Humming a cheerful little tune, Eraguff selected a ball of cerise sisal and resumed knitting the endless stripy scarf that filled the centre of his nest in multicoloured coils. *Click-clack, clickety-clack* went the knitting needles.

'*Binky the Bunny, Binky the Bunny,*' he sang. '*He's big and black, and loves his honey . . .*'

CLUNK! CLUNK! CLUNK!

Eraguff stopped knitting and looked up as a shadow fell across his nest. It was that castle again, picking its way through the Here-Be-Dragons Mountains.

'Hello, castle!' Eraguff trilled.

As the castle rocked and swayed from side to side, a tiny figure fell from the top of a tall tower and came tumbling down through the air . . .

. . . and landed in the soft coils of Eraguff's knitted scarf.

CLUNK! Clunk!

Clunk!

The castle stomped off into the distance, over the mountain tops and far away.

Eraguff looked down. 'Hello . . . whatever you are,' he said.

'Zzzzzzzzzzzz,' came Joe's reply.

Joe yawned and stretched, then looked about him. He was high up, with an unbroken view of mountains stretching away in all directions as far as the eye could see.

'Where am I?' he mumbled sleepily.

He was tangled up in what appeared to be an enormous woolly scarf at the centre of a mess of twigs and branches.

'In my nest,' came a voice from above, 'in the Here-Be-Dragons Mountains.'

Joe looked up to see a large dragon with dull grey scales and dingy beige wings swoop down and land on the edge of the nest.

'And I must say it's lovely to have visitors.'

'Is it?' said Joe.

'Oh, yes,' said the dragon. 'You've no idea how lonely it can get up here in the mountains. Thank you so much for dropping in.'

'Dropping in?' said Joe.

'Yes, you fell off that moving castle of yours. You must be a professor,' he said, nodding at Joe's ermine-edged robes. 'Lovely material, by the way.'

'Yes,' said Joe, puzzled, as he looked down at the clothes he was wearing. 'I . . . I must be.'

His head felt as if it had been packed full of cotton wool and he was finding it difficult to collect his thoughts.

'My name's Eraguff,' said the dragon. 'What's yours?'

Joe frowned. What *was* his name? Joshua? No, that didn't sound right . . . Jeremy? Julian? . . . *Joe*. Yes, that was it.

'Joe,' he said.

'Delighted to meet you, Joe!' exclaimed Eraguff. 'Can we be friends? Can we? *Can* we?'

'Yes, I suppose so,' said Joe, trying to concentrate.

'We can pick flowers and paddle in the lake and roll up balls of wool,' the dragon gushed. 'And I can take you for a ride on my back! Oh, we're going to have such fun!'

'Yes, but first,' said Joe, 'there's something I have to do . . . At least, I think there is. But I can't quite remember what.' He scratched his head. 'I'm trying to get back home . . . That much I do remember, but I can't remember where home *is*!'

'The moving castle?' suggested Eraguff.

'No, not the castle,' said Joe. What was wrong with him? He still felt so sleepy. He yawned. 'But I'd know it if I saw it,' he said. 'I'm sure I would.'

'Then climb aboard,' said Eraguff, eager to please.

He crouched down and spread his beige-coloured wings wide. 'And we'll see if we can jog that memory of yours!'

Joe jumped to his feet and scrambled on to the dragon's back.

'That's it,' said Eraguff. 'Now, hold tight and try not to worry . . .'

'Worry about what?' said Joe as Eraguff flapped his wings and took to the air.

'Oh, nothing really,' said Eraguff cheerfully as he wobbled alarmingly from side to side. 'It's just that I've never actually taken anyone for a ride on my back before. And I dare say it'll take a bit of getting used to.'

The dragon swooped down unsteadily, before soaring back into the air on trembling wings. Still wobbling, he

made his ungainly way across the sky, while Joe clung on for all he was worth.

'This is fun, isn't it?' Eraguff called back.

'It is?' said Joe.

All at once, a gust of wind caught the dragon and sent him hurtling off towards a nearby mountain top in a flurry of flapping wings and billowing smoke. At the last moment, just as Joe was certain they were going to crash, Eraguff managed to steady himself and clear the jagged top of the mountain with inches to spare. On the other side, the dragon glided down and landed on a narrow ledge in front of a cave entrance.

'Phew, that was close,' said Eraguff, a couple of small smoke rings rising from his nostrils. 'But I think I'm getting the hang of it.'

'Do you mind keeping the noise down,' boomed a voice from inside the cave. 'Some of us are trying to sleep on our treasure hoards.'

The large, disgruntled head of a green-scaled dragon emerged from the cave and blinked twice.

'Uncle Alan!' trilled Eraguff.

'Oh, it's you,' said Uncle Alan grumpily. 'I might have known.' His eyes narrowed. 'And what on Muddle Earth have you got on your back?'

'This is Joe,' said Eraguff proudly. 'He's my friend.'

'Friend?' said Uncle Alan, eyeing Joe. 'You mean you're not going to eat him?'

'*Eat* him?' said Eraguff. 'Of course not.'

'Then you won't mind if I do,' said Uncle Alan, licking his lips.

'I think it's time to leave,' said Eraguff quickly, and launched himself back into the air.

Beating his wings as fast as he could, the dragon flew off across the mountains, leaving Uncle Alan at the cave entrance behind them, grumbling about being woken up by foolish nephews who played with their food.

'Don't mind Uncle Alan, Joe,' said Eraguff. 'I'm sure he didn't mean it.'

They flew on, high above the mountains and out across the dusty plains beyond. In the distance, Mount Boom and the Musty Mountains came into view, and far beyond that the surface of the Enchanted Lake glittered in the warm sunshine.

Eager to please as ever, Eraguff called back over his shoulder. 'Are you all right back there, Joe?' he said. 'Sitting comfortably? Now, you just give a shout if anything jogs your memory.'

The morning sunlight played on the turrets and spires of Stinkyhogs School of Wizardry, casting long shadows across the empty courtyards and deserted broomball pitches. The corridors were quiet, the carpetless staircase was still, while the sound of silence was deafening in the classrooms, dormitories and halls. No goblin grumbles, no barbarian maiden giggles, no *pitter-patter* of massive ogre feet or *rumble-gurgle* of troll tummies. It was the school holidays and nothing was stirring, not even a mouse . . .

Except, that is, for Mr Fluffy, who had just emerged from his nest of shredded exam papers in the corner of the teachers' room. Nose twitching and little eyes twinkling behind steel-framed spectacles, Stinkyhogs's woodwork teacher trotted over to the window and looked out. In the courtyard below stood the wooden hamster wheel, its rungs worn and scratched from heavy use.

'Phew,' he sighed. 'I'm glad that's over . . .' Mr Fluffy removed the stubby pencil from behind his ear and pulled a small leatherbound diary from his tweed jacket. He thumbed through its pages, looking for the next likely triple full moon and put large question marks against several dates. '. . . for now,' he said darkly.

He turned away from the window and surveyed the roomful of empty armchairs. With a little sigh, he selected one and slumped down into it, lost in thought. So lost in thought, in fact, that he didn't notice the dingy dragon through the window, circling high in the sky, flapping its beige wings and wobbling unsteadily as a figure clung to its back.

The seven brightly painted houseboats bobbed about on the Enchanted Lake. There was a half-timbered mansion, a white-stucco villa, a bungalow with portholes, a log cabin, a thatched cottage, a tin shack and an elegant town house, each one perched in its own wooden hull.

'Morning, Melvyn,' called Ernie the Shrivelled, throwing open one of the lattice windows of his thatched cottage and sticking his head out.

He waved to the flamboyant wizard in the mauve robes who had just sashayed through the doorway of the white-stucco villa and was swanning about on the deck.

'Morning, Ernie,' he called back. 'Morning, Bertram. Morning, Boris.'

Bertram the Incredibly Hairy in the log cabin and his brother, Boris the Bald, in the tin shack waved back from their windows.

'Morning,' called Eric the Mottled from the top storey of his half-timbered mansion. 'Morning, Roger. Morning . . . errm . . . errm . . .'

'Morning,' sighed Colin the Nondescript, and pulled his head back through the porthole of his bungalow.

On the deck of his elegant town-house boat, Roger the Wrinkled, head wizard of Muddle Earth, blew on his freshly varnished nails.

'Hmm . . . I'm not sure that black suits me,' he mused. 'But I'm a slave to fashion.' He adjusted his leopard-print dressing gown as he lay back in his deckchair and kicked off his shiny red patent leather court-shoes. The

shoes were certainly eye-catching, but they did give him such terrible blisters. The last time he'd worn them, he remembered, was at the Goblet of Porridge broomball match . . . Which reminded him, where *had* Randalf got to? He'd promised to find the missing Goblet of Porridge and return with it. But that was ages ago. And since then, not a word. It really was very irritating.

Roger reached out and took a sugared bonbon from the little dish on the table next to him. He popped it in his mouth.

If Randalf didn't find the Goblet of Porridge soon, well, what choice did Roger have? As its most eminent wizard, not to mention ruler, Muddle Earth looked to him to set standards. No, there was really no question about it, mused Roger, reaching out for another bonbon. He would have to close Stinkyhogs School of Wizardry for good.

He settled back contentedly in his deckchair and closed his eyes – which was why he didn't see the dragon, high in the sky, circling the lake once, twice, three times, before flapping off in the direction of Elfwood.

In the depths of Elfwood, the talking trees of Giggle Glade kept silent and listened intently to the ancient tree shepherds in their midst, who were grumbling to each other.

'She's back,' creaked Mistletoe Mary.

'I didn't know she was away,' rustled Knotty Sue. 'What with those nasty little elves coming and going all hours of the day and night.'

''Ere comes one now,' grumbled Trev the Trunk.

'One hundred and eleven, one hundred and twelve, one hundred and thirteen . . .' squeaked the elf as it wandered past. 'Goggle, goggle, goggle.'

'Irritating creatures,' bristled Needles.

'She must have got back last night,' Mistletoe Mary was saying. 'I saw the lights on in that ridiculous gingerbread house of hers.'

There was the sound of rustling leaves as Lichen Larry folded his branch arms across his trunk. 'Well, all

I can say is, Giggle Glade was a lot more peaceful before *she* moved in.'

Butch Canker and the Sawdust Kid nodded in agreement, dislodging several roosting batbirds as they did so.

'To be sure, to be sure,' agreed Mossback Murphy.

'Oh, listen to us lot,' said Bert Shiverwithers in a weatherbeaten voice as dry and tough as seasoned wood. 'We sound like a bunch of weeping willows. And we ain't!'

'No, we ain't!' came an orchard of voices.

'*We ain't beeches or birches or blackthorns,*' they sang out.

'*We ain't maple or poplar or lime; we ain't ashes or aspens, we ain't elms, we ain't oaks, we ain't chestnut or walnut or pine!*'

'So, what are we?' Bert Shiverwithers cried.

'*We're aints! We're aints! We're aints!*'

High over Elfwood, a dragon flapped slowly across the afternoon sky.

The warm afternoon sun shone down on the scented gardens of Golden Towers Finishing School for Little Princes and Princesses. Situated to the east of Goblintown in the gently rolling countryside of verdant hills and wooded dales, where there were definitely no dragons, Golden Towers prided itself on its wonderful grounds and gardens.

The little princes and princesses were in the middle of a game of emu croquet under the stern gaze of their teacher, Big Lady Fauntleroy.

'Hold your emu by the body, not the head, Prince Caspian,' she instructed. 'And Prince Adrian, aim at the armadillo, dear, not Prince Toby. That's the way . . .'

The princes and princesses were trying to hit their croquet balls, which were curled-up armadillos, with their mallets, which were emus, in order to send them rolling through hoops, which were hoops.

'And as for you girls,' their teacher said impatiently, her three chins trembling, 'stop gawping at the clouds and pay attention to the game . . .'

Princesses Camilla, Cecily, Guinevere and Araminta were staring up at the sky open-mouthed, while their emus wandered about, pecking at the camomile lawn in search of worms, and their armadillos snuffled into the rose bushes.

'But, Miss!' said Princess Araminta, pointing.

'I shan't tell you a second time,' warned Big Lady Fauntleroy.

On the terracotta terrace, the kings and queens of Golden Towers were taking afternoon tea.

'One lump or two?' said Queen Lucy.

'Three,' neighed the centaur in a black cummerbund and bow-tie.

Queen Lucy picked up three sugar lumps with the silver tongs and fed them to the centaur.

'Thank you, your highness,' said the centaur, and placed a silver platter of cucumber sandwiches on the terracotta table.

'I've got some bad news,' said King Peter.

'Mfffll blcckmm?' mumbled King Edmund through a mouthful of cucumber sandwich.

'Worse than that, I'm afraid, Edmund,' said King Peter, shifting uneasily in his golden deckchair. He turned to Queen Susan and Queen Lucy, his face taut with foreboding. 'It's the lamp-post. It's escaped.'

'Escaped!' exclaimed Queen Susan.

'You mean it's fwee?' gasped

Queen Lucy. 'Again! How fwightful!'

'Fllmmch!' spluttered King Edmund.

'It was Thragar Warspanner and his barbarian broomball team,' said King Peter with a shake of his head. 'We put them up in the east wing. Remember, Lucy?' he added accusingly.

'Well, we couldn't have had howwid barbawians in the main part of the castle,' Queen Lucy said defensively. 'Could we?'

'That's as may be,' said King Peter, 'but they've gone home now. The thing is, the east wing is where we locked up the lamp-post. I went down there this morning, only to find the trapdoor to the attic open. The lock had been broken. While they were here, one of the barbarians must have gone searching for plunder. You know what barbarians are like . . . The long and short of it is, the lamp-post has escaped. It's out there somewhere, wandering about – and you all know what *that* means!'

'The portal!' gasped Queen Susan. 'Out there, with the lamp-post . . . wandering about . . . But we could fall into it by accident and end up back—'

'I'm *never* going back!' burst out Queen Lucy defiantly, thumping the terracotta table with a little fist. 'Back to our old life – to that howwid old school with its howwid old teachers and its howwid old lessons . . . I'm a Queen of Golden Towers!' she sobbed, 'a beautiful faiwy-tale school that's just the way a school is meant to be.'

'There, there, Lucy, old thing,' said King Peter. 'Don't go upsetting yourself. We'll find that lamp-post and when we do . . .'

'Mwwbbl ffmmwwl bwllch!' said King Edmund, tossing his cucumber sandwich aside and helping himself to a handful of Turkish delight.

'That's right, Edmund,' said King Peter. 'We'll stomp all over it!'

'A dragon?' Big Lady Fauntleroy's imperious voice floated across from the camomile lawn. 'Where?'

'There, Miss,' came a chorus of princesses' voices.

Sure enough, high in the sky above Golden Towers Finishing School for Little Princes and Princesses, situated to the east of Goblintown in the gently rolling countryside of verdant hills and wooded dales, where there were definitely no dragons . . .

. . . was a dragon.

Eraguff and Joe had been flying all day. High over the Musty Mountains they had wobbled and dipped. Low over the Enchanted Lake they had spiralled and stuttered. Teetering and tottering, they had passed over the treetops of Elfwood and out across the Perfumed Bog beyond. Beneath the arches of Trollbridge and over the smoking towers of Goblintown, Eraguff had made his wobbly way, with Joe hanging on to his back for dear life. Finally, swooping round in a broad arc, they had narrowly avoided crashing into the high turrets of a golden castle, before heading back towards the wilderness of Nowhere.

And as they had flown, the effects of the sunset dust slowly wore off and Joe's head had begun to clear. By the time they were high over the barbarians' alpine valley, he was back to his old self.

'I say, what a splendid piece of cloth!' Eraguff exclaimed, spotting a duvet on the ground far below him. He flapped his wings so excitedly that he almost knocked Joe from his back. 'It could be just the thing for my nest.'

He swooped down for a closer look.

'Randalf! Norbert! Edward!' Joe cried out, seeing the sleeping figures in the alpine meadow below. 'Ella!'

The four of them were tucked up cosily beneath a plump duvet, their heads nestling on silk pillows. Eraguff came in to land next to the duvet with all the grace and poise of a stinky hog falling off a perfumed tussock. Joe climbed unsteadily from the dragon's back and shook the sleeping wizard by the shoulders.

'Those are *my* toffee apples!' spluttered Randalf, waking up with a start and sitting bolt upright.

Beside him, Edward, Ella and Norbert looked up sleepily from their pillows.

'Good evening, everyone,' Joe said. 'Time to get up!'

'I won't tell you again, Mum,' shouted Pesticide. 'Keep out of my bedroom!'

Pesticide the flower fairy stomped into her cavern bedroom and stormed over to the moss-covered table. Behind her, the ornately carved fairy-rune door slammed itself obediently shut.

'And *stay* out!'

Pesticide turned to the other fairies, who were seated at the table, and rolled her eyes.

'My mum's just as bad,' Nettle consoled her. 'She barged in and caught me painting my nails black last week and confiscated my nail varnish.'

'That's nothing!' said Thistle, her shock of purple hair bristling. 'When my dad found out I'd spray-painted my wings, he grounded me for a week!' She fluttered her translucent gossamer wings with their stencilled black skulls indignantly. 'I mean, what does he think *he* looks like, with those gaudy great butterfly wings of his and those rose-petal robes . . .' She smoothed down her tattered black tutu. 'That floral look is *so* over. But just try telling *him* that . . .'

'I know,' sympathized Briar-Rose, pouting as she touched up her black lipstick, 'but what can you expect from that lot? Lolling about on their flower beds, fussing over who gets to hold the hem of Queen Titania's gown, or which of them has the honour of pouring King Oberon's nectar . . . There's got to be more to life than that.'

'There is,' said Pesticide fiercely. 'There's a whole world out there just waiting for four flower fairies like us with the brains and talent to go and find what we want – and take it!'

All eyes turned to the moss-covered table where the Plant Pot of Power stood next to the Trowel of Turbulence.

'Two down and one to go,' said Pesticide, her intense green eyes glittering. 'Briar-Rose, remind me, what do we know about the Acorn of Abundance?'

Briar Rose turned to a wooden box that stood on a mahogany dressing table beside the ornate eight-poster bed, which was covered in lush flowering bindweed and creepers. Stamped on the front of the box, beside a small sliding door, were the words *Goggle Box*. Briar-Rose tapped on the lid with black fingernails and the door slid open. Two beady elf eyes peered out through the slit.

'So, what do we know about the Acorn of Abundance?' asked Briar-Rose.

'Flat, acorn-shaped and made of metal, the so-called Acorn of Abundance is one of the three enchanted objects of old old fairy magic that, once upon a time, were sold in a jumble sale and scattered to the three corners of Muddle Earth,' a squeaky elf voice told them. 'My enquiries have revealed that over the years the acorn has been used as a pastry-cutter, a door-wedge and a tool for removing the stones from centaurs' hoofs, before ending up in a goblin carpenter's toolbox. He found the acorn's flat shape was ideal for nestling in the palm of his hand and its stubby stem was perfect for tightening screws . . .'

'Yes, yes, a screwdriver,' said Briar-Rose. 'Get on with it!'

'Ahem.' The elf cleared its throat petulantly and continued. 'My further enquiries revealed that the acorn found its way into the Experimental Woodwork laboratory of the University of Whatever. There it was included as a tool in a flat-pack wardrobe which inadvertently fell through the portal marked by Vlad the Tickler's wandering lamp-post, which is currently back in Whatever Castle. So, if you want the acorn you'll have to break into the castle, find the lamp-post and go through the portal to Muddle only knows where. So there!'

The door slid shut.

'It's our biggest challenge so far,' said Nettle.

Thistle nodded. 'Much harder than disguising ourselves as jeer-leaders to get into Stinkyhogs . . .'

'Or dressing up as a big barbarian baker to get into

the Great Hall of Nowhere,' added Briar-Rose.

'You're right,' said Pesticide. 'It's not going to be easy, which is why we're going to need help.'

Just then, the ornately carved fairy runes on the door sparkled.

'There's an elf outside,' the door sang softly. 'Shall I let it in?'

Pesticide nodded and, with a click, the door unlocked itself and swung obediently open. The elf ran in.

'Goggle, goggle, goggle,' it squeaked as it gambolled over to the mahogany dressing table, opened the lid of the goggle box and jumped inside.

There was the sound of whispering and the sliding door at the front of the box slid open and a squeaky elf voice sounded.

'There are sixty-three and a half aints in Elfwood.'

Queen Titania glided down the curved marble staircase and into the vaulted throne room beneath Harmless Hill.

Above her head, Moth, Mustardseed, Cobweb and Peaseblossom fluttered and fussed, as they attended to her tall swaying hairdo. The queen's golden hair was piled high in a shimmering beehive, held in place with bramble combs and rose-thorn pins, and resplendent with interlaced garlands of peonies and sweet peas. Moth and Mustardseed were spraying clouds of pungent perfume over the backcombed tresses from small crystal bottles while, with little silver shears, Cobweb and Peaseblossom snipped and shaped the fern fronds and foliage that sprouted from the top.

On either side of Queen Titania, young Daisy and Dewdrop walked in step, fanning their queen with cabbage leaves. In front, Pollen skipped ahead, her gossamer wings quivering as she scattered rose petals in Queen Titania's path. Behind the queen, dainty Cloudburst and pretty Sprinkle watered the trailing grass train of her dress from tiny watering cans, while at the hem little Bluebell and Fuchsia took turns to carry it.

'Ron, my love. There you are,' Queen Titania cooed as King Oberon entered the throne room through a door at the opposite end.

Behind him, a scrum of brightly robed courtiers jostled for position at his shoulders. Each one clutched something different – a stool, a cushion, a goblet, a jug, a cheese and pickle sandwich – which they waved in the air.

'Take the weight off your feet, sir?'

'Nice comfy cushion?'

'Goblet of nectar, your highness?'

'Top you up, sir?'

'A bite to eat?'

'Tania,' said King Oberon, ignoring them. 'I made you this.'

He held up a pudgy fist as he strode towards his queen, his stained vest stretched tight across his wobbly belly.

'Oh, Ron!' she said, giving a melting sigh. 'It's exquisite! The workmanship is divine! It's more dazzling than diamonds, more sumptuous than gold. Who needs rubies or emeralds when we have riches like these?'

'Thought you'd like it, love,' grunted King Oberon as he fastened the daisy chain he'd just made round Queen Titania's swan-like neck, before taking her by the hand and leading her towards their thrones.

Queen Titania sat down upon her garlanded throne of living willow wood while, next to her, King Oberon

flopped into his leatherette reclining chair, as his courtiers extended the footrest and offered him his sandwich. Queen Titania's attendants fluttered prettily about her, several of the younger ones pulling lutes and recorders from the folds of their beautiful floral robes and beginning a lilting lullaby.

At that moment there was a rumbling sound from above, followed shortly after by a resounding *crash* that made the walls of the throne room tremble.

'Pesticide!' said Queen Titania in exasperation, her beehive hairdo swaying alarmingly. 'How many times have we told her not to slam the front door? And where can she be going *now*?'

'Search me, Tania, my love,' said King Oberon, scratching his belly.

'Oh, Ron,' Queen Titania wailed, and waved her hands towards the courtiers and attendants who were fluttering, fluffing, flapping and fussing tweely around them. 'Why, oh why, can't Pesticide be more like them?'

Pesticide, Thistle, Briar-Rose and Nettle flew up into the clear blue sky. Behind them, the front door to Harmless Hill, a great turf-covered slab of earth, hovered above the cavernous opening in the hillside. Turning in mid-air, her gossamer wings a blur of movement, Pesticide clapped her mittened hands together.

'Slam!' she commanded. The turf door came crashing

down, sealing the entrance to Harmless Hill, its grass blending in seamlessly with that surrounding it. Pesticide giggled and turned to the others. 'It drives Mum and Dad wild when I do that,' she said.

'Oh, loooook,' gushed Thistle. 'A baby stiltmouse. How sweeeeet.'

The others rolled their eyes. Below them on the crest of Harmless Hill, a small fluffy mouse with big blue eyes and extraordinarily long thin legs was tottering towards a daisy.

'Oh, no!' Thistle exclaimed. 'Watch out!'

She swooped down towards the baby stiltmouse as the daisy reared up and opened its gaping jaws, displaying a mouthful of savage fangs.

'Stop it, you naughty flower!' Thistle shouted as she landed between the stiltmouse and the killer daisy.

She pulled off a mitten and reached out her hand. But it was no ordinary fairy hand. It was green and covered in tiny needle-sharp prickles. The daisy hesitated, drool dripping from its open mouth.

'I'm warning you,' Thistle told the flower sternly.

Behind her, the baby stiltmouse gave a little squeak, the killer daisy lunged and Thistle slapped the flower on the top of its petalled head.

'Stop it!' she commanded.

With a yelp of pain, the daisy shrank back and buried its head in its leaves, while the baby stiltmouse tottered over to the safety of its family mousehole.

'Come on, Thistle!' 'Stop mucking about!' 'We've got work to do!' the other flower fairies chorused.

'All right, sorry,' said Thistle, flying after the others as they set off across the sky. 'Oh, I wish I could have a sweet little baby stiltmouse of my own,' she said sadly, pulling her mitten back on, 'to pet and to stroke . . .'

The four flower fairies followed the road, past the Sandpit to their left and Trollbridge to their right, and over the Enchanted River. Flying on, Pesticide in the lead and the others following, they eventually came to a signpost at a fork in the road. The flower fairies landed beside it and looked up. There were three signs on the post pointing off in three different directions.

OGRE-HILLS – dusty, rocky, drab; I wouldn't go there if I were you, read the first.

TROLLBRIDGE – dirty, noisy, bustling; I wouldn't go there either, read the second.

ELFWOOD – absolutely enchanting place, full of trees.

Go there! (In fact it's where I came from before they cut me down and turned me into this stupid signpost.)

Briar-Rose pulled off a mitten to reveal a hand that had five long curved thorns for fingernails. She crouched down and began carving her name into the wooden post, with skilful flourishes.

The other flower fairies exchanged meaningful looks.

'When you're quite finished, Briar-Rose,' said Pesticide testily, 'perhaps we can get on.' She glanced back at the signpost and pointed. 'Elfwood's that way.'

'Uh, yeah, sorry, guys,' said Briar-Rose, blushing. 'Sometimes I just can't help myself . . .'

The others had already set off and, with a flap of her gossamer wings, she hurried after them.

'Briar-Rose,' she murmured sadly. 'Such a pretty name.' She sighed. 'For someone with such ugly fingers.'

They flew on, following the road as it skirted round the edge of the Perfumed Bog. To the south-west, shimmering in the afternoon sun, were the low, rounded humps of the Ogre Hills, while to the south-east, still no more than a distant smudge on the horizon, was the vast sprawling forest of Elfwood.

'I'm tired,' whined Nettle. 'My wings feel as though they're about to drop off.'

'Here we go again,' said Pesticide, frowning beneath her fringe of green hair. 'Nettle's complaining again. Honestly, Nettle, why are you always so *weedy*!'

Tears welled up in Nettle's eyes. 'I can't help it,' she

said in a little voice. 'It's just the way I am.'

'All right, no need to cry about it,' said Pesticide. 'I suppose it wouldn't hurt if we stopped for five minutes . . .'

'Oh, goodie,' said Nettle, cheering up. 'Look, there's the perfect spot, just there!'

Leaving the others, she flitted over to a pink hillock nearby, which was sticking up above the fragrant mud of the Perfumed Bog. She came fluttering down to land cross-legged on the ground.

'Aah, that's better,' she said, as she folded her wings behind her. 'But I'm so hot!'

Nettle pulled off her thick woolly mittens and leaned back. As her hands touched the surface of the pink hillock it trembled, and an almighty glugging squeal filled the perfumed air. The next moment, the hillock shot up into the air, sending Nettle sprawling in the mud.

'*Wheeee! Wheeee! Wheeee! Wheeee!*' came the anguished squeals as the most enormous pink stinky hog the flower fairies had ever seen went hurtling off across the Perfumed Bog.

'Well done, Nettle,' said Pesticide sarcastically, hovering above her. 'When you've finished your little mudbath, we'll be on our way.'

Thistle and Briar-Rose sniggered.

Sitting up to her waist in the gloopy perfumed mud, Nettle stared down at her hands. The black nail varnish looked cool but could not disguise the

nasty sting in her fingertips.

'It's not my fault,' she sobbed, pulling her mittens back on.

'There are sixty-three and a half aints in Elfwood,' said Pesticide, 'and we can't find a single one.'

She broke off a piece of cough-candy tile and popped it in her mouth.

The sun had been low in the sky when the four flower fairies had finally reached the fringes of Elfwood and entered the forest. They had begun their search as the shadows had lengthened, the sun had set and two of the three moons of Muddle Earth had risen up to take its place. Several hours later – and after endless frustrating conversations with the talking trees of Elfwood – Pesticide and her gang were no nearer to finding the aints than when they'd started. Finally, well past midnight, they had stumbled into a large glade with an eccentric gingerbread house at its centre.

Pesticide broke off another piece of cough-candy. A light came on, a spun-sugar window flew open and a head poked out.

'Who's that nibbling at my little house?' came a sing-song voice.

The head disappeared back inside.

'It's Miss Pinkwhistle,' spluttered Pesticide, nearly choking on the piece of cough-candy. She turned to the others. 'Just act normal. She'll never recognize us without our hoodies. Let me do the talking . . .'

A moment later there came the sound of a latch being lifted and Eudora Pinkwhistle, her hair in curlers and wearing a black nightdress, stepped out on to the liquorice veranda.

'What are you doing here?' she demanded, then paused. Her eyes widened as her gaze fell upon their gossamer wings. 'Why, but you're flower fairies!' She wagged a finger at Pesticide's companions. 'That windowsill is *not* for you, it's for the elves.'

'Sorry,' said Nettle, Thistle and Briar-Rose guiltily, dropping their pieces of gingerbread.

'It's stale anyway,' Nettle whispered to the others.

'Honestly, flower fairies,' Eudora muttered under her breath. 'So, why *are* you here?' she asked.

The four flower fairies exchanged looks. Pesticide stared down and shuffled her feet.

'Actually,' she began hesitantly, 'we've come to Elfwood to look for the aints.'

'The aints!' Eudora exclaimed and laughed extravagantly. 'Why, my dear little flower fairy, you don't mean to say you believe in *aints*? They're only to be found in fairy tales. But then again . . .' she added, with a condescending little giggle. 'I suppose you *are* fairies.'

Blushing furiously, the four flower fairies glared back at her. Eudora didn't notice.

'Aints,' she repeated, clasping her hands together and rising up on the balls of her feet. 'The tree shepherds of legend, forest keepers of myth, arboreal sentinels of the wild woods . . .'

Pesticide rolled her eyes. Thistle sighed. Briar-Rose examined her mittened hands.

'It's like being trapped in one of her lessons,' Nettle muttered.

'Shh!' hissed Pesticide sharply.

'According to fairy lore, the aints were a race of leaf-covered giants who looked after the trees of the forest,' Eudora went on, 'though if you ask me, they sound absolutely ghastly! Stomping around all day bossing saplings about and bullying bushes. Got far too big for their roots apparently and were told off by the fairy king and queen. Been sulking ever since, or so the fairy tales would have us believe – though as I say, *I* don't believe they ever existed in the first place.' She gave a tinkling laugh. 'So, you see, you've wasted your time coming to Elfwood. Now, run along, all of you. I'm sure it's well past your fairy bedtime. Your fairy mummies and daddies must be wondering where you are.'

'Well, *her* mum and dad are Queen Titania and King Oberon, so *she* can stay up as late as she likes,' Nettle piped up. She nudged Pesticide. 'Go on, tell her, Pesticide.'

'You mean, you're Ron and Tania's daughter!' Eudora went pale.

'Yeah,' said Pesticide sulkily. 'So what?'

'Oh . . . oh, nothing, my dear,' said Eudora. She smiled. 'Now, take a little piece of my house for your journey, and off you fly. And when you get back home you really shouldn't worry your parents about where you've been, or who you've seen,' she cooed. 'It can be our little secret.'

Pesticide shrugged and turned away. 'Come on, girls,' she said.

The four of them trooped back across the clearing and into the forest.

'Do you think she's right?' said Nettle glumly. She slumped down on a mossy bank and leaned back against a gnarled tree-trunk.

'You mean that it's all just a stupid fairy tale?' said Thistle, sitting down beside her. 'I dunno.'

Briar-Rose sent a pebble scudding over the

forest floor with a moody kick of a clumpy black boot.

'But we looked it up on the inter-elf!' stormed Pesticide, 'so it *must* be true . . .'

She plonked herself down on the ground and hugged her knees to her chest. Briar-Rose sat down next to her.

'I mean, that old story that Peaseblossom, Cobweb, Moth and Mustardseed used to tell us, I never took it seriously,' she said. The others shook their heads in agreement. 'But then I got that goggle box, and the inter-elf said that the lost treasures of Harmless Hill really did exist.' Pesticide's green eyes gleamed.

'It said that the Plant Pot of Power was being used as a stupid old trophy for that ridiculous broomball game . . .'

'And it was,' said Nettle. Briar-Rose and Thistle nodded.

'It said that the Trowel of Turbulence was stuck in a mouldy old cake in the middle of Nowhere . . .'

'And it *was*!' the three of them chorused.

'The Acorn of Abundance – the most magical, the most magnificent, the most important of them all – is almost within our grasp.'

Pesticide looked up, her eyes blazing. 'And now this! No aints in Elfwood.' She hung her head. 'No aints anywhere.'

Pesticide climbed to her feet and began pacing back and forth, her mittened hands clasped behind her back.

'Oh, if only aints *did* exist. Just think what we could

do together. With our brains and their brawn, we could unite the lost treasures of Harmless Hill once more, and if we did *that* . . . Just imagine!'

Pesticide flung her arms wide. Nettle, Thistle and Briar-Rose sprang up, their wings fluttering.

'We could rule the whole of Muddle Earth if we chose to!' said Pesticide. 'And the aints could keep everyone else in line – and they could be as bossy as they liked and *we* wouldn't tell them off,' she declared, carried away by the thought of it all. 'Not ever!'

'Feisty little thing, ain't she?' came a rustly voice.

'Talks a lot of sense,' said another. 'I like what she's been saying.'

'Almost reminds me of the old days . . .' sighed a third voice.

'Steady on,' cautioned a fourth. 'Let's not get carried away.'

'I agree with Trev, she does talk a lot of sense.'

'And certainly knows her old old fairy magic by the sound of it.'

'To be sure, to be sure.'

The four flower fairies looked around.

'It's the trees,' said Nettle wearily. 'They've got an opinion on everything . . .'

'Except when you ask them if they've seen any aints,' said Briar-Rose hotly. 'I bet if you asked that chestnut over there, it'd soon shut up. Or that elm. Or that oak . . .'

'I ain't a chestnut!'

'I ain't an elm!'

'And I ain't an oak!'

'And we ain't either!' came an orchard of voices.

'*We ain't beeches or birches or blackthorns,*' they sang out. '*We ain't maple or poplar or lime; we ain't ashes or aspens, we ain't elms, we ain't oaks, we ain't chestnut or walnut or pine!*'

'So, what are we?' bellowed the oak tree that claimed not to be an oak tree.

'*We're aints! We're aints! We're aints!*' came the full-throated reply.

Pesticide took a little step backwards, her mouth open and eyes wide with

astonishment. 'So you *do* exist . . . We've been looking for you all over Elfwood.' She frowned. 'Why didn't you tell us some of you were aints and not just trees?'

'Why should we?' said the aint who looked like an oak tree sulkily. 'That's no one's business but ours.'

His ivy-clad trunk was broad and gnarled, the bark thick and ridged with age. Two rheumy eyes stared down at Pesticide from deep-set canker-ridden knot-holes, and below them, plate-like fungus fringed the dark jagged opening that was his mouth. He folded two massive branch-like arms with a creak of wood and a rustle of leaves, sending dozens of small beetles scurrying for cover across the broad expanse of his chest.

'But why *wouldn't* a magnificent tree shepherd like you not want to make himself known?' Pesticide asked, fluttering her eyelashes. 'I mean, you're so distinguished-looking, if you don't mind me saying so.'

'Yes, well, I do what I can,' he said, his foliage trembling with pride. 'Try to stay in shape.' He lifted a great rooty foot, shook clods of earth from it, then stomped it down. 'You know. Running on the spot. Waving my branches about. That sort of thing . . . Mind you,' he added, with a twinge of discomfort, 'it's not easy. What with the ivy and the fungus, not to mention the beetles – ooh, they get right under my bark! Itch like mad, they do . . .'

'You poor thing,' said Pesticide, removing her mittens to reveal two elegant, long-fingered hands of chemical blue. 'Let me see what I can do.'

She reached out to the base of the aint's trunk and touched a stem of ivy that was growing there. The green leaves turned black, one after the other, spreading up the trunk and out on to the branches until every last clump of ivy had shrivelled and fallen to the ground.

'Ooh, that feels wonderful,' said the aint in astonishment.

'Now, how about that horrid fungus of yours?' said Pesticide. 'Lean closer.'

With a creaking and groaning, the aint brought his gnarled and knotty features close to Pesticide's outstretched fingers.

'And we'll see about that canker at the same time,' she said.

Her fingertips were a blur of blue as they fluttered over the aint's face and the fungus and the canker fell away.

'I haven't felt this good in years,' said the aint, straightening up.

'Now for the beetles,' said Pesticide triumphantly, tickling the aint's trunk-like tummy.

A shower of dead beetles fell from the thick ridged bark and tumbled to the forest floor below. The aint gave a deep groan of satisfaction.

'How can I ever thank you?' he said, thrusting out a branch-like hand. 'Bert Shiverwithers at your service, leader of the Giggle Glade Mob.'

Around the flower fairies the aints came to life. They

pulled their great rooty feet out of the ground, flexed their branch-like arms and nodded their leaf-covered heads in greeting as they introduced themselves.

'Lichen Larry,' wheezed an aint that looked like an old birch tree, his white bark mottled with thick brown and orange blotches. 'Ooh, thank you!' he exclaimed as Pesticide's blue fingertips banished the lichen from his bark.

'Mossback Murphy, my dear. Delighted to meet you,' said his neighbour, an aint who resembled an ancient hazelnut tree, his bark so thick with moss it looked like a green fur coat.

Pesticide's nimble fingers turned the moss brown and the ancient aint shrugged it from his shoulders.

'Phew,' sighed Mossback Murphy. 'It was hot under that lot.'

Butch Canker and the Sawdust Kid introduced themselves next. They were a couple of elm-like aints in need of attention. Pesticide obliged, sending showers of elm-beetles falling from their trunks.

'Stone the crows, I feel like a young tree shepherd again,' said Butch Canker, his bark gleaming.

Mistletoe Mary and her friend Knotty Sue, who

looked like beech trees, had bunches of mistletoe cleared from their limbs, while Trev the Trunk – who resembled a horse chestnut – was extremely glad to get rid of a bad case of toadstools. Needles, looking like a pine tree, had several hard-to-get-at nests taken care of, while Stumpy, who looked like a small Christmas tree, was relieved to say goodbye to a particularly stubborn squirrel who had taken up residence in a knot-hole.

The small grey pest had run off squealing when Thistle, Nettle and Briar Rose had removed their mittens and touched its bushy tail.

'Why, you lovely, lovely flower fairies, you,' said Fungus O'Foyle, a sycamore-like aint who had been patiently waiting his turn and was now being helped by all four flower fairies at once.

Pesticide took care of the fungus covering his bark, while Briar-Rose and Thistle pulled an old wasps' nest from his branches, and Nettle chased a woodpecker away.

The aints of the Giggle Glade Mob gathered round the flower fairies, their eyes aglow with gratitude and admiration.

'. . . Seven. Eight. Nine. Ten . . .' Pesticide counted,

a blue finger pointing to the aints one after the other. 'Eleven,' she announced. 'So where are the other fifty-two and a half aints?'

'I have a sneaking suspicion *I'm* the half,' said Stumpy tetchily. 'Just wait till I catch up with that cheeky little inter-elf!'

'The other aints are in other parts of Elfwood,' Bert Shiverwithers informed Pesticide. 'There's the Babbling Brook Boys over by the babbling brook,' he said, with a wave of a branch-like arm. 'And the Dingly Dell Gang down in the dingly dell. And then there's the Wild Wood Crew.' He spread his branches wide. '*They're* all over the place.'

'They're mad, that lot!' nodded Lichen Larry approvingly.

'They certainly are,' said Bert Shiverwithers, 'and I'm sure they'd like to meet you, Pesticide. In fact all the gangs would. Stumpy, spread the word. We're calling a moonlight branch meeting.'

Stumpy stomped across to the nearest tree. 'Moonlight branch meeting,' he whispered out of the corner of his mouth. 'Giggle Glade. Pass it on.'

'Ooh,' said the tree. 'Did you hear that, Audrey? The aints are calling a moonlight branch meeting here in Giggle Glade. Pass it on.'

'Deirdre! I say, Deirdre!' Audrey called to her neighbour. 'A moonlight branch meeting. Giggle Glade. Pass it on.'

'Malcolm! Oh, Malcolm! Coo-ee! . . .'

The voices grew softer as the message was passed from tree to tree, spreading out to the farthest reaches of Elfwood.

A little while later, with the two full moons bathing the forest in dappled moonlight of purple and yellow, the ground beneath the flower fairies' feet began to tremble. *Stomp! Stomp! Stomp!* The heavy footfalls of tramping aints echoed through the forest.

'Mind out, Deirdre, here they come!'

'Watch out, Malcolm!'

The trees surrounding Giggle Glade began to shuffle out of the way, leaving broad avenues down which the approaching tree shepherds stomped. The first to arrive, down an avenue to the north, were the Babbling Brook Boys, a gang

of stooped willow-like aints with long trailing branches and gnarled straggly roots. Next came the Dingly Dell Gang, broad and stocky and covered in ivy, tramping into the glade from an avenue to the south. Finally, with the earth shaking and the forest trees swaying, the Wild Wood Crew burst on to the scene from all directions.

'Watch where you're going!'

'There's no need to shove!'

'An *excuse me* would be nice!'

The trees of Giggle Glade complained bitterly as the huge lumbering aints, tall and broad as ancient oaks, barged their way past them.

'So, what's this all about?' growled the leader of the Wild Wood Crew.

'Mad Marion,' said Bert Shiverwithers.

'Bert? Is that you?' said Mad Marion. 'Why, I hardly recognized you! You're looking so . . . handsome.'

'Meet my new friend, Pesticide,' said Bert, smiling broadly. 'She can do the same thing for you. Can't you, Pesticide?'

'It would be my pleasure,' said Pesticide, reaching out and withering the rash of mushrooms that sprouted from Mad Marion's trunk.

'And that's not all,' Bert went on, his voice becoming louder as he turned to the other aints. 'Pesticide and her friends have a plan. She says that with their brains and our brawn, we could rule the whole of Muddle Earth! We could boss everyone around as much as we liked,' he boomed. 'And they wouldn't tell us off. Not ever!'

'But what about Ron and Tania?' whispered one of the Babbling Brook Boys anxiously.

'King Oberon and Queen Titania are my parents,' Pesticide declared loftily, 'and they let me do whatever I want!'

'Oooooh!' went the aints, clearly impressed.

'Your days of sulking are over,' she told them. 'After all, why mope about here in Elfwood, allowing your roots to grow gnarled and your bark to become mossy? Why let the grass grow under your feet and the mistletoe clog your branches, when there's a great big world out there, just waiting to be bossed around? And with my help, you aints are just the ones to do it!'

She raised her arms high in the air and wiggled her chemical blue fingers.

'Today, Elfwood!' she cried. 'Tomorrow, Muddle Earth!!'

Her voice dropped. 'But first,' she said, her eyes narrowing beneath her fringe of green hair, 'there's something I want you to do for *me* . . .'

'Joe, it's you!' said Randalf, stifling a yawn. 'I was having the most extraordinary dream. I was being fed toffee apples by a pink stinky hog . . .'

He stopped, his eyes widening with alarm.

'Joe,' he whispered urgently. 'Don't move a muscle! There's a dragon right behind you, and it's staring straight at us . . .'

'Yes, I know,' Joe began.

'And it's a big one too! Huge, and mean-looking. And wild. Yes, wild, with horrible blood-red eyes! And it's drooling, Joe, out of the corner of its hideous twisted snout . . .'

'Oh, how rude!' exclaimed Eraguff. 'Joe, do you know these people?'

Joe turned and laughed. 'Yes, Eraguff, I do. Randalf, Norbert, and Edward here, are my friends. And this is Ella, my sister.' He patted the dragon on the neck. 'And *this*,' he said with a big smile, 'is Eraguff.'

'Your sister, did you say, Joe?' Eraguff took a step forward and extended a dull grey scaled hand. 'Enchanted to meet you, Ella.'

Ella threw the duvet aside and jumped back in alarm. Beside her Edward scrambled to his feet and stood protectively between her and the dragon. Norbert, meanwhile, had grabbed Randalf and was clutching him tightly to his chest.

'Can't . . . breathe . . .' gasped Randalf. 'Put . . . me . . . down . . .'

Eraguff looked hurt. 'I don't mean any harm,' he said. 'I only want to help. Anything I can do, just say the word. I'm always eager to please. Ask anyone . . .'

'That's right,' said Joe. 'Eraguff here has been extremely helpful from the moment I fell out of the University of Whatever . . .'

'You fell out of the University of Whatever?' said Randalf, struggling from Norbert's grasp and pushing the ogre away.

'Yes,' said Joe. 'Over the Here-Be-Dragons Mountains.'

'The Here-Be-Dragons Mountains?' said Randalf.

'Yes,' said Joe. 'And I landed in Eraguff's nest.'

'In Eraguff's nest?' said Randalf.

'Yes,' said Joe. 'Veronica and I were chasing the lamp-post . . .'

'The lamp-post?' said Ella.

'Veronica?' said Randalf. He frowned. 'And where is Veronica now?'

'So far as I know,' said Joe, 'she's still in Whatever. But I can't be certain. The lamp-post kicked sunset dust in my face and I fell asleep. That's when I toppled off the castle and landed in the nest.'

'That sunset dust of theirs is notorious,' Randalf agreed. 'I haven't slept so deeply in years.' He yawned expansively. 'I did try to warn you about the castle, Joe, but you just went rushing in. Terrible place, the University of Whatever. Mr Fluffy told me all about it when I appointed him woodwork master at Stinkyhogs. The dons treated him quite disgracefully. Apparently, they threw him out over some silly little mix-up or other . . .' He clasped a hand to his brow. 'Oh, and poor, dear Veronica. To think of her, all alone in that terrible place!'

'We must find her, sir,' said Norbert, tears welling up in his triple eyes.

'*And* the lamp-post,' said Ella, clasping Edward by the hand and giving him a knowing look.

'Then it's agreed,' said Randalf. 'Our Goblet of Porridge quest will have to wait yet again. We must find the moving castle!' He turned to the rolled-up stair-carpet that lay half covered by the duvet. 'O woven conveyance of airborne wondrousness, prepare for take-off, if you'd be so kind.'

The wizard tapped the carpet lightly with his staff, and with a little yawn, it unfurled, rose up and formed itself into steps. Eraguff gave an astonished gasp.

'Oh, but you're gorgeous!' he exclaimed, a flurry of smoke rings rising from his nostrils. 'Such quality! Such workmanship! Such rich colours!!'

'How sweet of you to notice,' the carpet breathed as it hovered in front of the drab grey dragon with the beige wings. 'It's so delightful to be admired.'

'Climb aboard, everyone!' Randalf interrupted, taking his seat on the top step of the flying carpet.

Norbert, Ella and Edward followed him.

'Come on, Joe,' said Ella, holding out a hand.

'I'll ride on Eraguff,' said Joe, turning to the dragon. 'If you'll have me.'

Eraguff's eyes glistened with emotion. 'You mean you'd rather ride on my back than on that exquisite tapestry?'

The stair-carpet cooed.

'I'd be honoured, Joe,' the dragon said. He paused as his eyes fell on the discarded duvet and pillows lying on the ground. 'And if nobody wants those,' he said, 'perhaps you could put them on my back. They'll make my scales more comfortable for you, and the material will look lovely in my nest . . . Though not as lovely as the beautiful tapestry,' Eraguff added.

The stair-carpet cooed again.

'Yes, well, if you're quite finished,' said Randalf from the top step, once Joe had arranged the duvet and pillows on the dragon's back, 'then perhaps we can get on.'

He tapped the stair-carpet which, with a little sigh, flew up into the air. At the same time, Eraguff beat his beige wings and took off.

'Now, where shall we start?' said Randalf.

'How about following those large moving-castle footprints down there?' Eraguff suggested helpfully.

'Ah, yes,' said Randalf, looking down at the muddy imprints in the grass of the alpine meadow far below, and the clumps of flattened trees that led through the wooded mountains beyond. 'Well done, that dragon!'

Eraguff beamed with delight and Joe had to cling on tightly as the dragon set off enthusiastically, the carpet following close behind.

'You might not be colourful,' said the stair-carpet, as they flew over the dusty plains of Nowhere, 'but you fly beautifully.'

'Thank you,' Eraguff replied, looking back and trying not to wobble. 'And so do you.'

On the top step of the stair-carpet, Randalf was already fast asleep. Further down the steps, Edward and Ella, locked together in deep whispered conversation, had eyes only for each other, while Norbert was busy examining the contents of his findy bag.

'Something from a barbarian's blouse,' he said, dropping a small yak-horn button into the bag. 'And something from a barbarian's pocket,' he said, adding a hairy gobstopper.

With the others occupied, and the dragon and the stair-carpet chatting happily, it was left to Joe to keep an eye on the trail of footprints on the ground below. But he too was having a hard time staying awake. The rolled-up duvet and pillows he was sitting on were so comfortable and the rhythmic beats of Eraguff's wings so hypnotic, that Joe's head was beginning to nod.

Flap! Flap! Flap!

'And I particularly like those little blue and yellow flowers in your border.'

'Oh, you noticed . . .'

Flap! Flap! Flap!

'And something pebbly from inside a barbarian's boot . . .'

Flap! Flap! Flap!

'It'll be OK, Edward, you'll see.'

'Will it, Ella? Will it?'

Flap! Flap! Flap!

Joe's chin came to rest on his chest. His eyes were closed and his breathing was steady.

Flap! Flap! . . .

WHUMPH!

Joe's eyes snapped open.

He was falling. Around
him, the others were falling too.

Randalf, arms flailing and mouth
opening and shutting like a surprised goldfish, was to
Joe's left. Ella and Edward, clasped in a desperate embrace,
were spiralling down through the air to his right, while
just below them, Norbert tumbled over and over, as the
contents of his findy bag scattered in all directions.

WHOOOSH!

A scaly hand caught Joe by the arm. Another grasped
Norbert by the seat of his pants, while a coiled tail lassoed
Edward and Ella.

'He-e-e-e-elp!' came Randalf's despairing cry as he
disappeared into a cloud and out the other side, the
ground hurtling up to meet him.

Swooping down, Eraguff lunged and caught the wizard in his jaws. Randalf found himself staring down a cavernous black tunnel fringed with jagged teeth.

'*He-e-e-e-elp!*'

Wobbling and weaving and tilting wildly from side to side, Eraguff flapped his beige wings for all he was worth. With all the elegance and agility of a stiltmouse dodging a killer daisy, the dragon came unsteadily in to land, his back legs pedalling furiously.

'*Oof!*' he grunted as his scaly belly struck the ground, and he skidded to a halt on the green turf.

'What happened?' gasped Joe. He felt the dragon's grip on his arm loosen.

'Mffll wppllf,' began Eraguff. He opened his mouth, and Randalf flopped on to the grass like a bedraggled lazybird that had just been rained on. 'Something flew into us,' Eraguff said, clearing his throat.

'Don't eat me,' Randalf whimpered weakly. 'Please don't eat me . . .'

'Eat you?' said Eraguff, looking hurt. 'I don't want to eat you. I just saved your life. And quite frankly, it's left me with a nasty taste in my mouth.'

The dragon uncoiled his tail and set Ella and Edward gently down, before releasing his grasp on the seat of Norbert's trousers.

'My findy things!' Norbert wailed, peering into his empty bag. 'Now I'll have to find new ones.'

'Honestly, Norbert, pull yourself together!' said Randalf, climbing to his feet with as much dignity as he could muster and wringing dragon drool from the hem of his robes. 'Nasty taste, indeed!' Randalf told the dragon. 'I'll have you know this cloak was fresh on last month.'

'Oh, oh, oh,' came a plaintive little voice from behind them.

Everyone turned to see the stair-carpet twisted up in knots and bulging in the middle like a python whose lunch had disagreed with it.

'You poor thing!' Eraguff exclaimed, rushing over and helping the carpet to unwind.

'Came out of nowhere!' it gasped. 'Black and flappy and shaped like a carpet sweeper!'

Disentangling itself, the stair-carpet rolled up tightly and scuttled behind the dragon on the tips of its tassels. There on the grass sat Eudora Pinkwhistle in a black cloak and crumpled witch's hat, clutching her broom, Dyson, in one hand and a black leather satchel in the other.

'Well I never,' she said. 'Fancy bumping into you, headmaster.' She giggled girlishly. 'We really can't go on meeting like this.'

'Miss Pinkwhistle,' said Randalf. 'You really should look where you're going.'

'But headmaster,' said Eudora cheerfully, 'I could have sworn that you were asleep when we had our little accident.'

'Nonsense!' said Randalf. 'I'll have you know I was busy scanning the landscape for the giant footprints of Whatever Castle.'

'Oh,' said Eudora, clapping her hands together. 'How intriguing! Why ever were you doing that? Do tell.'

'Well, if you must know,' said Randalf importantly, 'we're on a mission of mercy to rescue my familiar, Veronica, from that awful place.'

'Really!' exclaimed Eudora. 'You've lost your familiar. Oh, you must be beside yourself with worry, you poor dear wizard. I left my Slocum at home to mind the elves, but I don't know what I'd do if he ever went missing. You must let me help – and I won't take no for an answer.'

'There's really no need, Miss Pinkwhistle,' Randalf began.

'No, no, I absolutely insist!' said the witch. She reached into her capacious satchel and pulled out a tea tray with a teapot, milk jug, sugar bowl and a set of cups and saucers neatly arranged on it. 'Now, I'm sure we could all do with a nice cup of tea to settle our nerves after our little collision,' she said. 'I know I could.'

A tartan rug and a plate of shortbread appeared from the depths of the bag next, and soon everyone was sitting cross-legged in a circle sipping tea and nibbling biscuits.

'Joe?' said Ella, putting down her teacup. 'We've been talking, Edward and me.'

Now what? thought Joe, putting down his own teacup with a sigh. As if it wasn't enough that he and his big sister were stuck here in Muddle Earth, and were still no closer to getting home than when they'd first fallen through the portal, now she had fallen for Edward – and seemed determined to discuss it with him. I mean, how embarrassing was *that*?

'It's about the lamp-post,' Ella went on, taking Edward's hand and squeezing it.

'What about it?' asked Joe.

'We've made a decision,' said Edward Gorgeous, his dark eyes intense with emotion.

'When we find it,' said Ella, 'and step through the portal, Edward is coming with us.'

'There's nothing for me here in Muddle Earth,' said Edward, shaking his head. 'And now I'm no longer a thumbsucker, I want to start a new life.' He paused. 'Ella's told me all about where you come from,' he continued, his eyes growing wide. 'About traffic lights and bendy buses,' he breathed. 'And the music of the pop and the moving pictures of the tee vee. It all sounds wonderful!'

Ella smiled at Edward and gave him a hug.

'Edward could go to college,' said Ella. 'And after that he could get a job, and then when we're older we could . . .'

'College!' spluttered Joe. 'But . . . but I saw the portrait. Of you. And your Uncle Vlad in Whatever Castle. You must be . . .' Joe hesitated. 'How old *are* you?'

'I'm the same age as Ella,' Edward replied. 'The age I was when Edwina sucked my thumb. But I'm cured now and free to live a normal life, to grow up, to fall in love . . .'

'Yes, yes,' said Joe. 'Spare me the gruesome details.' He shrugged. 'It's OK with me, but first we've got to find the lamp-post.'

'Me?' came Eudora's tinkling voice. 'I was just on my way to Goblintown, headmaster – or can I call you Randalf?'

'Headmaster will be fine,' said Randalf.

'I know a charming goblin there, Randalf,' she said, ignoring him. 'Makes all my goggle boxes for me. You know, the inter-elf really has been a great success. But of course, Randalf,' she said, leaning closer and patting his arm, 'you don't need to worry. I would never dream of leaving Stinkyhogs. Not while *you're* the headmaster.'

Eudora pressed the plate of shortbread on him, which Randalf waved away.

'But that hasn't stopped me working on my little ideas,' Eudora said. 'Would you like to see my latest one?'

She reached into her black satchel and pulled out an

elf that was dressed in a tight-fitting suit with a peaked cap perched on its head. It was sitting on a miniature broomstick.

'I call it the me-elf,' said Eudora proudly, 'and it's going to revolutionize the inter-elf. With these little enchanted broomsticks, the elves can travel twenty times as fast, so you can get answers to your questions twenty times as quickly.' She flapped her hands excitedly. 'And I'm going to get Grubley to make me lots and lots of tiny broomsticks, which I can enchant, because everyone who's anyone is going to want a me-elf.'

She popped it back into her satchel.

'But all that'll keep, Randalf,' she said. 'For now I shall give my undivided attention to helping you find that dear little budgie of yours.' She smiled. 'More tea?'

'No, thank you,' said Randalf weakly.

Clip-clop, clip-clop, clip-clop . . .

The sound of hoofs clomping across the marble floor echoed round the throne room of Golden Towers. A centaur in a black bow-tie and cummerbund clattered to a halt, tossed his mane and bowed to the kings and queens, who were lounging about on their velvet couches. Queen Lucy was flicking through a tattered old exercise book, the name *Lucy Pevensey-Bay – Form 2B* written on its cover in neat handwriting. King Peter and King Edmund were midway through a game of marshmallow chequers, which Edmund was losing as he couldn't resist eating his own pieces. Queen Susan, meanwhile, was having her toenails painted black by her two faun attendants.

'Your royal highnesses,' the centaur announced, 'I bring news of the lamp-post.'

'At long last,' drawled King Peter.

'About time,' yawned Queen Susan.

'Mmmppl flmmbbpl,' mumbled King Edmund.

'I agwee, Edmund, it *is* a welief,' squeaked Queen Lucy.

'I've travelled far and wide,' the centaur declared. 'I've trotted to Trollbridge, galloped to Goblintown, pranced across the Perfumed Bog and show-jumped through the Ogre Hills, but it was only when I was cantering past the Musty Mountains that I finally saw it.'

'Yes?' said King Peter.

'Spit it out,' said Queen Lucy. 'No, not you, Edmund!'

'Whatever Castle,' the centaur announced. 'It was just sitting there in the foothills, and as I approached it, I saw the lamp-post.'

'Where?' King Peter demanded.

'High up on the battlements,' the centaur replied. 'I'd have tried to catch it, but that would have meant getting inside the castle, and you know how touchy they are about visitors.'

'We'll soon see about that,' said King Peter darkly. He reached into the pocket of his velvet dressing gown and removed a shiny gold muckle, which he gave to the centaur. 'You've done very well, Fetlock.'

'Thank you, your majesty,' whinnied the centaur with a bow.

'Now, if you could just tell Big Lady Fauntleroy to gather all the little princes and princesses in the stables. I'll be with them presently,' said King Peter.

He turned on his heel and strode from the throne room and down the sweeping staircase beyond. Pausing only to pluck a flaming torch from the wall, he continued down into the very depths of the castle. There, the flickering light fell upon a studded oak door with heavy hinges and a massive iron lock. Reaching inside his dressing gown, King Peter pulled out a tiny silver key and placed it in the lock.

He turned it once, twice, three times. There were three soft clicks followed by a long grinding noise, a loud grating noise, and a curious clunking sound that built up into a deafening cacophony as ancient cogs and gears and pulley-wheels slowly turned. With a gentle sigh, the studded oak door swung open on its heavy hinges and King Peter stepped inside.

The stone chamber was cavernous, with thick cobwebs curtaining its corners. In the middle of the dusty floor was a small pile of gold coins. King Peter walked over to it and bent down. He tutted softly and shook his head.

'The last of the fairy gold,' he muttered to himself as he filled the pockets of his velvet dressing gown.

He stood up, the gold muckles clinking, and stared down at the bare stone floor.

'Oh, well,' he sighed. 'It's all in a good cause.'

He turned and left the empty treasure chamber,

without bothering to lock the door behind him.

'He *bit* me!'

'Don't make a fuss, Ganymede,' said Big Lady Fauntleroy. 'You know what awful tempers they have.'

'Miss! Miss! The saddle strap won't do up. He's too fat.'

'Well, if you will keep feeding him sugar lumps, Camilla, what do you expect?' Big Lady Fauntleroy sighed. 'Do hurry up, children. King Peter will be here any minute.'

No sooner had the words left her mouth than King Peter came striding into the stables, three leather purses clutched in his hand.

The stables of Golden Towers were bright and airy, the walls whitewashed and the mosaic floor strewn with fresh sweet-smelling straw. Over each of the nine neat wooden stalls that divided the stables hung a little board, upon which was painted a name in small decorative letters: *Candy, Dimples, Merrylegs, Topsy, Turvy, Tutti-Frutti, Tinker, Patches* and *Frank*.

In the stalls themselves, nine furious little unicorns with rainbow-coloured manes and tails pawed the ground and kicked out with their hoofs as the princes and princesses attempted to put saddles on their backs. Pails of water were upended, bales of hay were sent flying and saddle soap, curry combs and grooming brushes

were scattered in all directions. As the last saddle was buckled and the final bridle secured – despite Candy's best efforts to bite Princess Araminta, and Merrylegs's attempts to kick Prince Rupert – King Peter stepped forward and raised his arms.

'If I could have your attention,' he drawled. 'Big Lady Fauntleroy will split you up into three groups. I shall give each group one of these,' he said, holding the leather purses up in the air. 'Now, listen carefully all of you . . .'

'That means you, too, Prince Ganymede,' said Big Lady Fauntleroy sternly.

'The future of Golden Towers depends on you.' He looked down at the row of expectant faces staring up at him. 'This is what I want you to do . . .'

Osbert the Obstinate rolled over on his bed of gravel and adjusted the boulder he used as a pillow. He pulled the coarse blanket up under his chin and tried to get comfortable. The blanket had once been a sack for mangelwurzels in Trollbridge and was grit-caked and scratchy. But it was all he had.

That, and his snuggly-wuggly, of course.

Osbert cuddled his pink cloth piglet, nuzzling up against its fraying fabric. It only had one ear, had lost half its stuffing and smelt of ogre dribble, but it felt wonderfully soft. As he stroked Pooper Pig, Osbert began to drift off to sleep . . .

'Osbert? Osbert!'

Osbert groaned and opened one of his three eyes as the dream faded away.

'What is it?' he roared.

His cave in the rolling dusty expanse of the Ogre Hills wasn't bad as far as ogre caves went. Of course, it didn't have any furniture to speak of, just a boulder for sitting on and another boulder for sitting *at*, and a third boulder for using as a pillow, or a footstool, or anything else that took your fancy. But it was quiet and secluded and an ogre could shut himself away from the hectic hustle and bustle of life in Ogre Hills, especially if he had a nice big boulder to use as a door.

Unfortunately, Osbert didn't have one of those, though he was saving up for one. In the meantime, there was nothing in his doorway but a great big hole through which anyone could shout.

'There's somebody here who wants to see you,' shouted the voice.

Osbert groaned again and climbed to his feet, narrowly avoiding grazing his head on the rough ceiling of his cave as he did so. He stomped over to his doorway and, stooping down, stepped outside.

'See? What did I tell you? He's a big 'un, ain't he?'

The voice belonged to none other than Horace the Hefty, who was standing outside the cave, his hands on his hips and a broad smile on his big ogre face.

'Oh, excellent, excellent,' replied a small voice and, looking down, Osbert saw three princesses in red riding jackets. They were seated on three pretty little unicorns.

'How lovely!' Osbert exclaimed, reaching down and attempting to pet one of the unicorns on its rainbow-maned head.

With an indignant snort, the unicorn bit him on the thumb.

'Ouch!' Osbert yelped.

'You have to watch out for Candy,' said the little princess who had spoken before. 'She bites,' she added unnecessarily.

The princess reached into the purse she was clutching, pulled out a shiny gold muckle and stared up at Osbert. He was one of the biggest ogres she'd met so far in the Ogre Hills.

'You're just what we're looking for,' she said. 'How would you like to earn this lovely gold muckle?'

'Oh, please, Daddy! Pleeeeease!'

'But Guinevere, princess, I can't just drop everything because you ask me to.'

Bolgar Bloodhatchet shook his wing-helmeted head.

It wouldn't do. It wouldn't do at all. First there were the battlecat trials in the Forest of Doom and straight after that the great wickerman bonfire to organize.

And as if that wasn't bad enough, the barbarian clan of the Snarling Wolf were hosting the Barbarian Maiden Arm-Wrestling Championship this solstice – and it looked as if things could get ugly. Matilda Oxbellow had gone out of her way to insult Ethelbertha Gooseneck, saying she had hands like a Trollbridge turnip masher, and besides, black nail varnish was against the rules. Ethelbertha had told her dad and now the whole clan of the Screeching Eagle was up in arms and threatening to cause trouble at the event.

That was the trouble with barbarians. They were too hot-tempered and quick to take offence for their own good.

But what could you expect, thought Bolgar Bloodhatchet, when they were brought up in clans with names like Bellowing Bear, Charging Elk and the less fearsome, but no less argumentative, clan of the Angry Beaver?

That was why he had sent his own little bundle of joy, the apple of his eye, his darling daughter, Guinevere, away to school.

It hadn't been an easy decision, and he wasn't afraid to admit that even a big tough barbarian clan leader like himself had shed more than a couple of tears as he'd dropped his little princess off at the gates of Golden Towers school. But he knew that she would receive the finest education there in indolent lolling, divine reclining, sighing, pouting and being exquisite.

And he hadn't been disappointed. Each time she returned home for the holidays, she was even more of a little princess, poised, polite and very hard to say no to.

'Pleeeeease, Daddy,' Princess Guinevere repeated.

She had ridden into the clan's camp in Nowhere and tied the reins of her rainbow unicorn to the tent pole of her father's yak-skin yurt. Her two companions, Prince Rupert and Prince Ganymede, had done the same. Never mind that Bolgar was in the middle of a very important meeting of the Custard Pie War Party; his daughter had walked straight up to his carved yak-horn throne and stamped her little foot.

'Golden Towers needs your help, Daddy,' she had said.

Bolgar Bloodhatchet had patiently explained just how busy he was. He'd told her and her two friends about the battlecat hunt, the wickerman bonfire, the barbarian maiden arm-wrestling championships, and even how complicated it was securing a good supply of custard powder at short notice. She had listened to his excuses, and then tried to get round him with that special way of hers.

'*Pleeeeeeease*, Daddy.'

'I'm sorry, princess, but Daddy's just too busy.'

Princess Guinevere reached into the folds of her cloak and produced a purse. She held it up and shook it. The unmistakable sound of jangling gold coins filled the tent.

Princess Guinevere smiled. 'Perhaps this will change your mind,' she said sweetly.

Lionel Firebelly circled high over the Here-Be-Dragon Mountains. With powerful beats of his deep crimson wings, Lionel sought out strong updraughts of air as he steered a zigzag course across the sky with swishes of his emerald-tipped tail. The sunlight played on the rich bottle-green scales of his back and on his burnished copper underbelly. The jagged ridge of bony plates that ran down his back from the top of his head to the tip of his tail stood out ruby-red against the bright blue of the sky.

Swooping down in order to take advantage of the glassy surface of a mountain lake, Lionel admired his reflection. The magnificent wings, the iridescent scales, the wonderfully sinuous tail . . . and all so thrillingly, eye-catchingly bright and colourful!

What a magnificent specimen of a dragon he was, thought Lionel, doing a triple back-loop followed by another swooping fly-past to catch his reflection in the lake once more.

Soaring back high into the sky, he exhaled a great jet of flame from his nostrils in pure joy at his own splendour.

Surely no other dragon could possibly complete with Lionel Firebelly when it came to sheer good looks, he thought to himself proudly.

Not that he'd ever dream of allowing them to try. That was why he liked to keep himself to himself and not have anything to do with those other dragons with their gaudy wings and overpolished scales.

They were all such show-offs, thought Lionel primly, or at least they would be if they ever got together – which they almost never did because, like Lionel, most dragons kept themselves to themselves.

He flew on, careful to make sure that he kept a good distance between himself and the other dragons circling the skies over the Here-Be-Dragon Mountains. Just as he was about to head back towards his comfortable cave, with its admittedly small but pleasingly glittery hoard of treasure, Lionel spotted something far below.

It was bright and shiny and glinted enticingly in the sunlight. Folding his crimson wings and arching his emerald-tipped tail, Lionel dived down towards the tempting object. Moments later, he landed on the boulder-strewn valley floor below.

There, sitting on a rock, was a gold muckle.

Lionel let out a little cry of delight together with a couple of perfectly formed smoke rings and reached for the coin – only for it to be snatched away by a small pampered hand.

'Not so fast,' came a haughty childlike voice.

Lionel looked up. Three little princes, each of them dressed in red riding cloaks and clutching the bridle of their own rainbow unicorn, stood in a line staring back at him.

Prince Caspian held the coin between a thumb and forefinger.

'If you want this gold muckle,' he said, 'you'll have to earn it.'

Golden Towers Finishing School for Little Princes and Princesses was a hive of activity. The battlements were thronged with barbarians in winged helmets and tooled-leather breastplates, busy unpacking yak-skin backpacks and unrolling fleecy sleeping bags. Swords, shields, battleaxes and large sacks marked *Custard Powder* littered the stone walkways and clogged the battlement steps.

'By the whiskers of Freya the Beardy!' roared their leader, a huge barbarian with a curling black beard. 'Get the saucepans on the fire. And don't let the milk boil over!'

In the courtyard below, seven enormous ogres were sitting around the beautiful marble fountain, soaking their enormous feet and nuzzling their snuggly-wugglies.

'Whoops!' said an ogre as he accidentally knocked the head off the marble statue of a water nymph riding a dolphin. 'Silly me!'

He picked up his pink fabric pig and rubbed it against his stubbly cheek.

'You're much more cuddly than that marble mermaid, Pooper,' he said.

High above the courtyard, perched on each of the four golden towers of the castle, were four dragons eyeing each other critically. The crimson-winged dragon with the bottle-green scales and emerald tip to his tail on the north tower snorted scornfully and stuck his nose in the air. On the south tower, a dappled mauve and pink dragon with distinctive striped wings pretended not to notice as she filed her talons with a lump of pumice-stone. Meanwhile, the dragons on the east and west towers were engaged in a staring contest to see which of them would blink first. The east-tower dragon spread her magnificent yellow wings for maximum effect, while the west-tower dragon puffed out his gaudy turquoise chest in response.

'Hmm, you're looking good, Lionel,' said the dragon on the north tower to himself.

'Nobody's got wings like yours,' the east-tower dragon told herself.

'This tail's to die for,' the west-tower dragon congratulated himself.

'Rise above it . . .

Rise above it all, Cynthia,' murmured the dragon on the south tower.

Over the main gate was a covered balcony that jutted out from the castle wall. The little princes and princesses were seated along it on small cushioned stools with seat belts. Big Lady Fauntleroy sat behind them in what looked like a barber's chair, while in front were four padded thrones in which sat the kings and queens of Golden Towers, strapped securely into place. King Peter looked down from the balcony at the ornamental gardens and landscaped grounds stretching out before them, then turned to the others.

'Ready?' he asked.

Queen Susan nodded.

King Edmund grunted.

Queen Lucy smiled thinly. 'Weady,' she said.

King Peter turned back and reached for the heavy iron lever that was bolted next to the brass steering wheel in front of him. He seized the lever and shoved it firmly forward.

There was a *rumble* and a *clang* and a resounding *clunk!* and the whole castle began to shake.

'Can't see them anywhere,' sighed Eraguff, flapping his beige wings as he hovered unsteadily above the rolling grasslands north of the Musty Mountains.

'Nor can I,' admitted Joe.

To his right, the stair-carpet fluttered in mid-air, Randalf, Norbert, Edward and Ella all scanning the ground below. To his left, Eudora Pinkwhistle was perched on her broomstick, Dyson, and doing the same. The aerial collision had knocked them badly off course and they had lost the trail of footprints they'd been following.

'Hang on a minute. What's that?' Eudora's voice rang out. She pointed. 'Over there!'

A little way off, heading away across the prairie, were the smudgy imprints of a pair of giant mechanical feet.

'Footprints!' exclaimed Eraguff and Joe together.

'Well done, Eudora,' said Randalf, suppressing a yawn. 'Now, let's try not to lose sight of them again,' he said, settling back down on his carpet step. His head began to nod.

They set off on the trail of the footprints, which headed in the direction of the mountain range on the horizon. They flew on through the late afternoon and some time later, as the sun was sinking low in the sky, found themselves in the stale canyons and stuffy valleys of the Musty Mountains. As they rounded a tall pointy peak, Eudora let out a little squeak.

'The castle!' she cried out. 'We've found it.'

There, stepping daintily over a ravine, was a beautiful building of white stone with elegant carved battlements, a shady courtyard and four golden towers at its corners around which were coiled sleeping dragons. Powered by a vast invisible engine that shuddered and thrummed in the very depths of the castle, its two great mechanical legs of shiny, oiled brass wheezed and hissed as they strode on through the mountains.

'Oh, no,' groaned Joe as he stared in disbelief. 'That's not Whatever. We've been following the wrong castle!'

'It's Golden Towers!' exclaimed Edward, sitting up on the flying carpet, 'or as I once knew it, when it belonged to my Aunt Heidi, Whoever Castle.' His eyes misted over. 'But that was all so long ago.'

Eudora looked at him quizzically from her broomstick, then reached into her satchel and drew out the me-elf. Holding it up to her mouth, she whispered into the elf's ear before throwing it into the air. The me-elf hovered for an instant above her head, then whizzed off on its tiny broomstick and disappeared into the distance.

Far ahead, the castle of Golden Towers descended the mountainside and began marching across the broad plain on the other side of the Musty Mountains. Joe, Eraguff, Eudora and the flying stair-carpet followed. Out over the plain, it soon became clear that the castle was following footprints of its own, and before long a second castle came into view. It was sitting motionless in the middle of the dusty plain, the great disc of the Enchanted Lake shimmering in the distance behind it.

'Whatever!' Joe shouted from Eraguff's back.

On the stair-carpet, Randalf woke up with a start, while Norbert stared, his triple eyes wide with surprise.

'*Two* castles?' he said and scratched his head.

Just then there came a whistling, whizzing sound as the me-elf on the tiny broomstick came hurtling back and landed on Eudora's outstretched arm.

'Goggle! Goggle! Goggle!' it trilled. 'Whoever Castle was built by Count Vlad the Tickler for his wife, Heidi the Gorgeous, when she had finally had enough of being tickled and chased with a feather-duster. Furthermore, Countess Heidi decided to turn Whoever Castle into a refuge for any over-tickled denizens of Muddle Earth, *whoever* they might be.'

The me-elf paused for breath, adjusted its cap, then continued.

'Just like Whatever Castle, Whoever Castle was built with the treasure trove that Count Vlad had dug up, creating a hole now known as the Sandpit. Originally, the towers of both castles were tiled with slate quarried from the banks of the Enchanted River. Dust settling on these magic rooftops at dusk and dawn became the legendary sunset and sunrise dust. After falling into disrepair, in recent times the empty castle of Whoever was taken over by the self-appointed kings and queens of Muddle Earth, who replaced the slate tiles with burnished gold when they turned the castle into the Golden Towers Finishing School for Little Princes and Princesses . . .'

'Thank you, that was fascinating,' said Eudora enthusiastically as she stared at the two castles ahead. Golden Towers had stopped in front of Whatever Castle and was now in the process of sitting itself down.

Eudora shoved the me-elf back into her satchel, its head disappearing inside with a little squeak. 'I wonder what *they're* up to?' she murmured, bringing her broomstick to a hover.

'I don't know,' said Joe, as Eraguff slowed down beside her, 'but I have the feeling we're about to find out.'

'Oh dear,' said Randalf from the top of the stair-carpet. 'I do hope there isn't going to be any unpleasantness. For Veronica's sake . . .'

At that moment, a loudhailer emerged from the covered balcony above the main gate of Golden Towers. A voice rang out.

'Professors of Whatever! We are the Kings and Queens of Golden Towers, and we believe that you are harbouring an escaped lamp-post. We demand that you let us in to claim it!'

'My apologies,' came a loud but polite voice in response, 'but we do our best to discourage visitors here at the university. So, if you wouldn't mind turning round and going away, we'd be awfully grateful.'

'Well, if that's the way you want to play it,' said King Peter hotly, 'then you leave us with no choice . . .'

'Oh, howwid old teachers like you make me so cwoss!' added Queen Lucy crossly.

'I'm sorry you feel that way,' came Lord Asbow's voice from the battlements of Whatever, 'but I'll have to leave matters up to the castle now. It's fully automated to repel invaders.'

As Joe watched, there came a loud *whumph*, then another, and another, and another, in rapid succession, as four plump vacuum-cleaner bags shot out of a row of nozzles set into the rotating top of the castle's central tower. They sailed up, high over the battlements of Whatever Castle, before coming hurtling down towards the gleaming rooftops of Golden Towers.

'Sunset dust!' bellowed King Peter.

'Dwagons, attack!' commanded Queen Lucy.

From the four corners of the castle came deep throaty roars as the four dragons uncoiled themselves and sprang into action.

The crimson-winged dragon with the bottle-green scales launched himself from the roof of the north tower and, lunging to his right, caught the first plump vacuum-

cleaner bag that was tumbling down out of the sky. At the same time, the mauve and pink dragon with the striped wings dived down from the south tower and plucked a second vacuum-cleaner bag out of the air, inches above the cobblestones of the courtyard below. Spreading her wings, she soared up into the air.

Meanwhile, spiralling down from the east tower like a streak of summer lightning, the yellow-winged dragon scooped up the third bag in both arms and hugged it to her chest.

The fourth dragon, in the meantime, had executed an elegant triple back-loop and lassoed the incoming fourth vacuum-cleaner bag in the coils of his tail, and was spinning round to circle the golden spire of the west tower. He puffed out his turquoise chest with pride.

'Bwavo!' Queen Lucy exclaimed.

High above the castle, the dragons hovered for a moment, their gaudy wings lit up by the evening sun. One after another, they tossed their vacuum-cleaner bags up above their heads. Then, opening their jaws wide, the dragons sent jets of flame billowing after them.

The next moment, the darkening sky was lit up by a series of spectacular explosions as the fire engulfed each vacuum-cleaner bag in turn. Showers of pink and gold and blue sparks crackled and fizzed.

'Oooooh . . . Aaaaaaahhhh!' came voices from the courtyard and turrets of Golden Towers.

On the battlements opposite, the professors of the

University of Whatever looked at each other in dismay.

'Oh dear,' said Lord Asbow. 'Perhaps we should try that again.'

From the covered balcony of Golden Towers, Queen Lucy's voice rang out. 'Barbawians, attack!'

A hundred wing-helmeted heads popped up above the walls of the castle and the air filled with raucous battle oaths.

'Mighty Wotulf, make my flan fly true!'

'Curdle not my custard, Freya of the Flaxen Beard!'

'By the tinkling of your pixie boots, little Olaf, guide my pie!'

Bolgar Bloodhatchet drew himself up to his full height and raised a fist above his head. In response, the massed clans of the Custard Pie War Party leaped to their feet.

The clan of the Screeching Eagle balanced the broad discs of their *tartes de crème* in the palms of their hands, while the clan of the Bellowing Bear gripped the crenellated edges of their whipped vanilla pies in trembling fingers. Beside them, the clan of the Charging Elk and the clan of the Snarling Wolf cradled their custard flans and steaming sweet quiches in the crooks of their muscle-bound arms as the clan of the Angry Beaver wiped away crumbs from the corners of their mouths and tried to hide the nibbled corners of their custard turnovers.

'Fire!' bellowed Bolgar Bloodhatchet and dropped his fist.

A hundred custard pies flew through the air towards Whatever Castle. They whistled over the heads of the cowering professors on the battlements and splattered against the central tower, clogging the row of nozzles at its rotating top as they did so. The tower stopped rotating and the vacuum-cleaner bags that were about to shoot out of its nozzles exploded within its ivory walls with muffled *whumphs*.

The tower shuddered, and from deep within, there came the sound of grinding gears and clashing cogwheels. The tower rattled and shook. Then, after a series of stifled bangs and crashes, it abruptly fell still.

'I say!' exclaimed Lord Asbow, his outraged voice mingling with the howls of his Labrador. 'That wasn't very sporting! But throw as many custard pies as you like, you're still not coming in!'

'Pwepare the battewing wam!' Queen Lucy gave the command.

In the courtyard, the biggest of the seven ogres put his pink fabric pig in his pocket and lay on the ground. Stooping down, the other ogres – three on one side, three on the other – gently picked him up and tucked him securely under their massive arms. As the gates of Golden Towers swung open, the ogres stomped through them carrying their companion head first. Gathering speed, their huge feet throwing up clods of earth, the ogres thundered towards the raised drawbridge of Whatever Castle.

'*OOOF!*' grunted the ogre battering ram, to the accompaniment of splintering wood and breaking hinges, as his huge head smashed into the door.

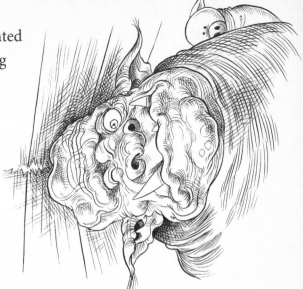

'*OOOF! OOOF! OOOF!*' the battering ram exclaimed as his companions swung him repeatedly at the disintegrating timbers.

CRASH!!

The drawbridge collapsed and, dropping the battering ram, the other six ogres stormed into the castle.

'You're much more cuddly than that wooden drawbridge, Pooper,' the ogre battering ram muttered as he pulled his snuggly-wuggly from his pocket and followed the others inside.

From his vantage point on Eraguff's back, Joe had watched as the siege of Whatever Castle had unfolded. He had never seen anything like it. Hovering by his side, Eudora had shared his fascination.

'Masterful use of dragons,' she said. 'Clever deployment of barbarians. And the ogre battering ram was a lovely finishing touch. That Queen Lucy is quite the little general!'

'That's as may be, Miss Pinkwhistle,' said Randalf, calling across from the stair-carpet, 'but we're here to rescue Veronica.' He raised his staff and tapped lightly. 'O carpet of aerial delight, if you wouldn't mind landing on yonder castle tower, we can begin our search.'

'Certainly, O great magician,' the stair-carpet whispered, shaking its tassels and speeding off towards Whatever Castle, the witch following close behind on her broomstick.

'Randalf! Eudora! *Wait!*' cried Joe. 'Watch out for the sunset dust!'

But they didn't hear him. The stair-carpet swooped down on to the top of a tall tower at the back of the castle and landed in a cloud of dust. Eudora and Dyson landed next to it.

'Ella! Edward! Cover your mouths!' called Joe as first Randalf, then Norbert fell fast asleep and slumped from their steps on the carpet. 'We're coming to get you!'

Eager to please, Eraguff beat his wings and raced forward, just in time to scoop Joe's sister and her boyfriend from the dusty carpet, itself now gently snoring. Looking back over his shoulder, Joe saw Eudora crumple beside Randalf, her snoozing broom in her arms.

'Over there,' Joe said, pointing to the battlements, now empty of professors, who were streaming down the steps that led to the courtyard.

Eraguff landed gently and set Edward and Ella on the

ground. Joe jumped from his back.

'You're getting better and better at this, Eraguff,' he complimented his friend, patting him on the neck. He turned to the other two. 'It's OK,' he said. 'You can breathe now.'

But Edward wasn't listening. He was staring at the gleaming ivory towers, a haunted look in his eyes.

'This place,' he murmured. 'It brings it all back to me. It was on these very battlements that Edwina Lovely tricked me into letting her suck my thumb.' He shuddered.

'Oh, Edward,' said Ella. 'That was the past. It's the future we must think of.' She turned to Joe. 'We've got to find that portal . . .'

Just then, from far below in the courtyard, came a shrill voice. 'Stand back, wiff-waff! And make way for my big bwother, King Peter!'

Joe peered down to see the kings and queens of Golden Towers step through the castle gate. They strode into the cobbled courtyard, where the crestfallen professors of the university awaited them, their pets fluttering, fidgeting and breaking wind around them. King Edmund and Queen Susan were carrying a large net between them. Queen Lucy had a lasso coiled over her shoulder, while King Peter was holding a sack of cement in one hand and a sturdy catapult in the other.

'We've come for the lamp-post,' he said. 'And we're not leaving without it.' He brandished his catapult. 'I'm going to smash its light bulb,' he said fiercely. 'And set its feet in concrete in the basement of Golden Towers,' he added, flourishing the sack of cement. 'That way, the portal will be locked away where it can't do any harm!'

'And we shall never have to weturn to that howwid school ever again!' Queen Lucy added with a stamp of her foot.

Lord Asbow stared back at King Peter unhappily. 'This really isn't the way we do things here at the university,' he protested. 'I'm afraid you're going to have to pay for a new drawbridge. And Muddle Earth only knows how much it'll cost to repair the dust-catapult . . .'

'Peter. It's over there,' hissed Queen Lucy urgently and pointed to the far corner of the courtyard.

All eyes turned in the direction of her pointing finger. And there, in the shadows cast by the stone steps that led up to the battlements, sat the little lamp-post, its wrought iron legs neatly crossed one over the other and its light bulb dimmed.

Lord Asbow shrugged. 'If it means you'll go away and leave us in peace, then take the confounded thing,' he said, 'though in my opinion, you have the most appalling manners for royalty.'

The kings and queens ignored him. With the net raised, Queen Susan and King Edmund tiptoed towards the lamp-post from one side, while King Peter put down the sack of cement and approached from the other side, his catapult raised and loaded. Queen Lucy crept stealthily behind him, uncoiling the lasso as she went.

From the battlements above, Joe, Ella and Edward looked on helplessly. Joe shook his head. If the kings and queens destroyed the lamp-post, he and his big sister would never get home. Behind them, Eraguff's ears twitched.

'What's that?' the dragon whispered.

Joe stared. In the shadows to the left of the sleeping lamp-post, he thought he detected the slightest of shimmers in the air, like a net curtain twitching in a summer breeze. And the faintest of smells – a mixture of boiled cabbage and floor polish. And a sound, so soft Joe might almost have been imagining it – the sound of distant voices in a classroom somewhere chanting their nine-times table.

'It's the portal!' Joe exclaimed, then frowned. 'Though it doesn't sound or smell like it leads to our house . . .'

King Edmund, Queen Susan and Queen Lucy crept as close to the lamp-post as they dared, net and lasso at the ready, before pausing and looking over to their older brother for a sign. King Peter raised the catapult, closed one eye and took aim at the lamp-post's light bulb.

Suddenly, the lamp-post burst into dazzling light.

'Oh!' gasped King Peter, dropping the catapult and shielding his eyes.

'Oh!' gasped Queen Lucy, blinded for an instant and tripping over King Edmund's pudgy foot.

'Oh!' gasped Queen Susan. The lamp-post leaped up and whisked the net out of her hands and encircled the four of them.

'Mppllffwb!' protested King Edmund indignantly as the net tightened and he was squashed up against his brother and sisters.

Joe watched the lamp-post hook the bulging net with one foot and twirl it around. Then, with a low chuckle, it kicked out and released one end, sending the kings and queens tumbling into the shadows. Like four pebbles dropping into a pool, Peter, Edmund, Susan and Lucy created ripples in the air as they fell into the portal and disappeared from view.

With its light bulb glowing brightly, the lamp-post gave a little hop, skip and jump before sprinting off across the courtyard, over the broken drawbridge and out of the castle.

'Oh, no!' wailed Ella.

'It's getting away!' cried Edward.

'Not again,' moaned Joe.

Eraguff leaped up and took to the air. 'Don't worry,' he called back eagerly. 'I'll catch it.'

Before Joe could say anything, the dragon had flapped over the castle walls and was gone.

From the top of the tower above him, Joe could hear a chorus of snoring as Randalf, Norbert and Eudora slept on, oblivious to all the excitement. Meanwhile, down below in the courtyard, Lord Asbow and the professors watched the bemused ogres shuffle apologetically out of the castle.

'Sorry about all the mess,' said Osbert the Obstinate. 'Lovely soft Labrador, by the way,' he called as he put back the shattered boards of the drawbridge behind him as best he could.

Moments later, one by one, the propped-up timbers of the drawbridge fell down again as the earth began to tremble.

STOMP! STOMP! STOMP! STOMP!

The towers swayed. The glass rattled in the windows. And pastry crumbs danced on the cobblestones of the courtyard as it shook.

Lord Asbow sighed heavily and rolled his eyes. 'Now what?'

'They did *what*?' Big Lady Fauntleroy gasped, her three chins wobbling.

'They just disappeared. All four of them,' Osbert the Obstinate repeated. He scratched his head. 'One moment they were there, the next moment they were gone.'

'Gone,' Big Lady Fauntleroy echoed in a shocked voice. She sat down heavily on one of the empty thrones that stood on the balcony and grabbed the large brass steering wheel for support. 'They must have fallen through the portal. Of course, that was always the danger. I warned them, but their minds were made up.' She shook her head sadly, then looked around, suddenly aware that all eyes were on her. The little princes and princesses perched on their padded stools at the back of the balcony, their lower lips trembling. The seven ogres, the largest one with a purple bruise beginning to form on the top of his head, stood in a cluster by the door. Above them, lining the battlements, a hundred barbarians in winged helmets looked down on the balcony, their faces grim and questioning. On the four towers perched the four gaudily coloured dragons, impatiently blowing smoke rings as they watched Big Lady Fauntleroy through narrowed yellow eyes.

'And now they're gone.' She shrugged her large shoulders. 'So I suppose that's the end of that.'

Her plump fingers drummed on the brass steering wheel as a thought came into her head. With the kings and queens no longer there, Golden Towers Finishing School for Little Princes and Princesses would need new leadership.

'But Big Lady Fauntleroy,' said one of the little princes, 'what are we going to *do*?'

Big Lady Fauntleroy's eyes sparkled and her chins wobbled. 'That's *Headmistress* Fauntleroy to you, Prince Adrian,' she announced proudly.

STOMP! STOMP! STOMP! STOMP!

Startled plumes of flame shot from the open mouths of the dragons, while a low murmur spread through the ranks of the barbarians on the battlements. Down on the balcony, the ogres' triple eyes bulged with astonishment, and the little princes and princesses almost fell off their stools in surprise. On the padded throne, Headmistress Fauntleroy gripped the brass steering wheel and stared.

Advancing towards them across the rolling plain was what appeared to be a forest. Except this forest had feet – big gnarled rooty feet, one hundred and twenty-eight of them, pounding on the plain as they approached the two castles.

STOMP! STOMP! STOMP! STOMP!

As the forest drew near, the individual trees could be seen more clearly. They were huge. Towering chestnuts, mighty oaks, rough-barked pines and swaying willows. Bright twinkling eyes stared out from knot-holes, and bark-fringed mouths gaped open.

'*We ain't beeches or birches or blackthorn, we ain't maple or poplar or lime; we ain't ashes or aspens, we ain't elms, we ain't oaks, we ain't chestnut or walnut or pine!*' sang the Giggle Glade Mob, the Babbling Brook Boys, the Dingly Dell Gang and the Wild Wood Crew in unison.

'*We're aints! We're aints! We're aints!*'

STOMP! STOMP! STOMP! STOMP!

On the balcony of Golden Towers, Headmistress Fauntleroy grew pale.

'I think its time we were on our way,' she said.

On the towers, the four dragons nodded. On the battlements, the barbarians quickly agreed, while the ogres clattered down the steps from the balcony to the courtyard and attempted to hide behind the marble fountain.

'Singing trees,' gasped Osbert the Obstinate, hugging his pink fabric pig tightly to his huge chest. 'Scary!'

The headmistress grabbed the iron lever beside the steering wheel and pushed it forward, while the little princes and princesses tightened the straps on their padded stools. With a hissing of pistons and a grinding of gears, Golden Towers rose up on its mechanical legs and began trotting off across the plains.

In the branches of the mighty oak-like aint who was striding out in front, four flower fairies peered through the leaves.

'Let it go,' Pesticide commanded. She pointed to Whatever Castle. '*That's* the one we want!'

From the battlements of Whatever Castle, Joe, Ella and Edward looked on in horrified fascination as what appeared to be huge walking trees burst into the courtyard below. The professors seemed equally dumbstruck as the trees surrounded them. Hugging their pets and gazing up at the gnarled, knotty faces leering down at them, they whimpered softly.

Clutching his Labrador around its ample belly, Lord Asbow found his voice. 'Oh dear, not *more* visitors,' he moaned.

'Come on, you two,' Joe whispered urgently as he dashed off along the battlements towards the nearest tower.

But before Ella and Edward could follow, they were grasped by the willowy arms of one of the Babbling Brook Boys who had crept up the steps to the battlements.

'Put me down! Put me down!' protested Ella, struggling as the willow passed her to his companions below.

Seconds later, the pair of them found themselves on the cobbles of the courtyard beside the trembling professors and their pets, surrounded by trees.

'Do I know you?' Lord Asbow asked, distracted for a moment from his and his fellow professors' predicament. 'You're not Stibbing and Chate from the Blueprints and Pie Charts Department by any chance?'

Before Ella or Edward could answer, an imperious voice sounded from the branches of the tall oak towering over them.

'Professors of the University of Whatever, your castle is ours!'

The four flower fairies burst from the foliage and fluttered down to land on the cobblestones below.

'The jeer-leaders!' Edward gasped.

'But you've got wings!' exclaimed Ella.

'No speaking unless you're spoken to!' boomed the towering oak. 'Stand up straight and stop that shuffling!' he added bossily.

'Thank you, Bert Shiverwithers,' said Pesticide, tossing back her green hair and folding her arms. She eyed Edward and Ella dismissively. 'Oh, if it isn't the broomball captain and his barbarian girlfriend,' she sneered. 'Shouldn't you be in some stupid class or other back at Stinkyhogs?'

Lord Asbow gave Ella and Edward a quizzical look.

Pesticide turned away. 'Still, who cares?' she said, pacing backwards and forwards in front of the professors. 'I've got far more important things on my mind, such as the lamp-post . . .'

'Not you as well,' groaned Lord Asbow.

Pesticide ignored him. 'We have to find the lamp-post because we wish to enter the portal. The two objects already in our possession will guide us to the third. We need to retrieve the flat-pack wardrobe you professors so carelessly allowed to fall into it.'

'That was Mr Fluffy's fault,' Lord Asbow muttered.

'For included in that flat-pack,' Pesticide continued, 'was a seemingly insignificant tool for tightening screws. Flat, made of metal and shaped like an acorn. You professors had no idea of its true value, unlike we flower fairies.'

Ella frowned and reached into the pocket of her black cut-off jeans.

'Because, rather than a simple screwdriver,' Pesticide went on, 'that tool was none other than the fabled third object of the old old fairy magic . . .' She paused for dramatic effect. 'The Acorn of Abundance!'

'Well, if you're looking for the lamp-post,' said Lord Asbow loftily, 'I'm afraid you're out of luck. It ran off just before you arrived.'

'Out of luck?' said Nettle.

'Ran off?' said Thistle.

'*Just* before we arrived?' groaned Briar-Rose.

'Then we must follow it!' Pesticide cried, flapping her wings and hovering just above the cobblestones. 'Which way did it go?'

'Not a clue, I'm afraid,' said Lord Asbow airily as an appalling smell rose up from the black Labrador in his arms. 'Tricky fellows, lamp-posts. It could be absolutely anywhere by now.'

Pesticide clenched her mittened hands in frustration. 'If I can't find the portal,' she screamed, 'then how on Muddle Earth am I ever going to get my hands on the

Acorn of Abundance?'

'This acorn you're wailing about,' said Ella, taking a step forward and pulling her hand from her pocket. 'Does it look anything like this?'

She opened her fist and there, resting in her palm, was the curious little tool she'd used to tighten the screws on the doors of the flat-pack wardrobe.

'The Acorn of Abundance!' exclaimed Pesticide, snatching it from Ella. She paused and looked up. 'But how did *you* get hold of this?'

'Well,' Ella began, 'I was—'

'Oh, who cares?' said Pesticide, turning delightedly to the other flower fairies. 'The important thing is, it's ours now – and we won't have to go chasing after that stupid lamp-post after all!'

Her gossamer wings were a blur of movement as she flitted around the courtyard excitedly.

'Nettle, Thistle, the Plant Pot of Power!' she commanded. 'Briar-Rose, the Trowel of Destiny!' She hovered in front of the oak-like leader of the aints. 'And Bert Shiverwithers, move everyone well back. You need plenty of space for old old fairy magic . . .'

Joe hadn't looked back as he'd run the length of the battlements and leaped through the open window of the nearest tower. He'd crouched down in the shadows inside and waited for Ella and Edward to join him, only to hear their shouts of protest as the weeping willow had carried them off.

What now? he wondered with a sinking feeling in the pit of his stomach. First Randalf, Norbert and Eudora had fallen victim to the sunset dust, and now Ella and Edward had been caught by a walking tree. And as for the lamp-post, they were still no nearer to finding it than when they'd started!

'Joe? Joe, is that you?' came a voice.

Joe looked around. He was standing in a familiar-looking workshop full of odd woodworking tools.

'Experimental woodwork,' he muttered. His gaze fell upon a small birdcage hanging from the ceiling. 'Veronica!' Joe exclaimed, rushing over and opening the door to the cage. 'What happened to you?'

Veronica hopped out on to his shoulder. 'You may well ask,' she said with feeling. 'When you fell off the castle tower, Joe, I tried to follow you, but a gust of wind blew me through a window, and I ended up in this preposterous excuse for a workshop. One of those crazy professors locked me up in that cage. He was convinced I was your pet and was determined to look after me until you returned. Wouldn't take no for an answer. I mean, me – a *pet*!' she chirped indignantly. 'Have you ever heard of such a thing?'

'It's good to have you back,' said Joe. 'But we're in big trouble . . .'

'That doesn't surprise me where Randalf's concerned,' said Veronica. 'What's he done now?'

'Well . . .' Joe began.

'Who's there?' came a rather timid-sounding voice, and a dishevelled, bespectacled figure stepped out of the shadows in the far corner of the workshop. He was holding a small golden hamster in his hands.

'Mr Fluffy?' said Joe. 'It *is* Mr Fluffy, isn't it?'

'Joe the Barbarian,' said Mr Fluffy. 'Weren't you off with the headmaster searching for the Goblet of Porridge? Did you have any luck?'

'No,' admitted Joe, 'not much.' He frowned. 'You used to work here, didn't you? You made that wardrobe, the flat-pack one . . .'

'Oh, the *Tumnus*! That was my best work!' Mr Fluffy

exclaimed, his beady eyes twinkling. His face fell. 'Until it fell into that portal. Unfortunate business,' he admitted. He gripped his hamster tightly. 'And they punished me for it. Lord Asbow and the others. But it's all right now, isn't it, Daemian? Those nasty old professors couldn't keep us apart forever, could they, boy?'

Mr Fluffy kissed the hamster tenderly on the head, his beady eyes misting with tears behind his wire-framed spectacles. He looked up at Joe and cleared his throat.

'I saw the castle walk past Stinkyhogs, and despite my disgrace, I just couldn't help myself. I knew I had to follow it if I was ever to be reunited with my Daemian.' He smiled. 'I sneaked in over the battlements while the castle was distracted by Golden Towers. And here I am.'

Just then, two branch-like arms burst through the open window of the workshop and weeping-willow fingers seized Mr Fluffy and Joe.

'Get off!' shouted Joe. 'Leave me alone!'

'It's all right, Daemian, I'll protect you,' wailed Mr Fluffy, pushing the little hamster into the top pocket of his tweed jacket.

'Resistance is futile,' came a bossy voice as the arms dragged Joe and Mr Fluffy across the workshop and out through the window.

Veronica flapped after them.

On the battlements outside, the enormous aint tucked Joe and Mr Fluffy securely under his arms, before turning on his root-like feet and descending the stone steps to the courtyard below. There it unceremoniously dumped the two of them on to the cobblestones next to a group of bewildered-looking professors and their pets.

'Found two more,' the aint informed Bert Shiverwithers. 'They were hiding in this torture chamber. Horrible, it was. Sawdust and wood-shavings all over the place,' he added with a leafy shudder.

'Joe, are you all right?' said Ella, as she and Edward helped him to his feet.

'No talking!' barked Bert Shiverwithers.

Joe straightened his robes. Veronica fluttered down and landed on his shoulder. Behind Joe, Lord Asbow leaned forward.

'Caught you in your workshop, eh, Jefferson?' he whispered. 'Bad luck.'

Joe smiled weakly. He looked around. The courtyard was full of the towering tree-like creatures, their knobbly knot-hole eyes all fixed on the four flower fairies with the interesting hairstyles standing at its centre. The one with green hair and a severe fringe seemed to be in charge.

'Nettle, Thistle. Put the Plant Pot of Power down there,' she instructed.

The two flower fairies – one with straggly braids of bleached white and the other with a shock of purple spikes – put the small battered-looking cup down on the cobbles.

Joe gasped. 'The Goblet of Porridge,' he breathed.

'Briar-Rose, the Trowel of Destiny,' said Pesticide.

The flower fairy with the magenta bob placed a silver object with a gold handle in Pesticide's mittened hand.

Joe's eyes widened. 'The Sword in the Scone,' he breathed.

Pesticide held up her other hand. Grasped in her mittened fingers was a flat metal disc. 'The Acorn of Abundance!' she proclaimed.

Joe gave a puzzled frown. 'The thing for tightening the screws in the flat-pack wardrobe?' he breathed.

In the centre of the courtyard, Pesticide crouched down in front of the plant pot and leaned forward. Carefully, she placed the acorn in the bowl of the pot. Then, with trembling fingers, she inserted the silver blade of the trowel into a narrow slit at the base of the pot and turned its gold handle. As she did so, there was a metallic *clink* and the acorn dropped down inside the stem of the pot, like a coin in a slot-machine.

'And all without instructions,' said Lord Asbow, impressed.

'Shhh!' hissed Bert Shiverwithers.

Pesticide straightened up and stepped back, her gossamer wings fluttering excitedly as the Plant Pot of Power began to tremble and shake. Suddenly, from deep within, a beam of silver light shot up into the air, followed by another and another and another, until the whole plant pot was glowing like a bright star.

Shielding his eyes and peering into the light, Joe could just make out silvery tendrils snaking their way over the rim of the plant pot and coiling down the sides. They grew thicker and more tangled as they enveloped the pot and the trowel, and spread out across the cobbles like the roots of a tree. Larger strands erupted from the centre of the pot and, plaiting themselves together, rose up into the air to form a shining silver trunk. Branches appeared, dividing and subdividing, and subdividing again, until Joe found himself staring at a tall glowing tree covered with rustling silver-foil leaves.

Around him, the professors gave out small gasps of disbelief and grasped their pets protectively.

'Old old fairy magic,' said Lord Asbow thoughtfully as yet another appalling smell rose up from his Labrador. 'Powerful stuff.'

Tiny gold buds sprouted at the tips of every branch and grew steadily in size until the entire tree was laden with clinking clusters of gold coins. Pesticide gave a little whoop of joy. She reached out a mittened glove and shook the silver trunk of the tree. With a metallic clatter, coins rained down on to the cobblestones to form a carpet of gold beneath the tree. In the branches above, more gold muckles sprouted to take their place.

'Rich! Rich!' Pesticide cackled, linking arms with Nettle, Thistle and Briar-Rose, and dancing round the fabled muckle tree of fairy legend. 'Rich beyond our wildest dreams!'

'We can buy anything!' laughed Briar-Rose. 'Black nail varnish by the barrelful . . .'

'And all the stripy black-and-white tights and big boots we could ever want!' chortled Nettle.

'We can be waited on hand and wing,' nodded Thistle. 'And never have to do what our silly old parents tell us ever again!'

'That's just the start,' said Pesticide darkly. 'Now that we're rich, with our friends the aints and this castle at our command, we can throw out those stupid wizards and rule Muddle Earth ourselves!'

'At *your* command, did you say?' said Lord Asbow, putting down his Labrador and stepping forward. 'I'm afraid, my young fairy, the instructions for operating the castle are extremely complicated and take years of careful study to master. I think you'll find that, when it comes to Whatever Castle,' he said grandly, '*I* am in command.'

'Then I command you to make it do what I want,' said Pesticide, stamping her foot.

'Out of the question,' said Lord Asbow firmly and folded his arms. 'And neither you, your gold muckles nor your big forest friends here can change my mind.'

'We'll see about that,' said Pesticide menacingly. 'Aints, seize them!'

The aints shot out branch-like arms and wrapped them round the terrified professors and their pets, pinning them to the spot. Joe, Ella and Edward found themselves in the clutches of a gnarled old aint that smelled of pine cones and mildew.

'Hold them still,' Pesticide hissed, pulling off her mittens to reveal her chemical blue fingers.

Behind her, the other flower fairies pulled off their mittens. Thistle's needle-sharp prickles bristled, Briar-Rose's long curved thorns glinted, and the tips of Nettle's black-nailed fingers glistened with venom.

'You *will* do as we say!' Pesticide insisted.

The four of them advanced towards Lord Asbow and the professors, their hands raised.

'Wait!' Mr Fluffy's voice rang out. 'There's a better

way to get them to do what you want.'

Pesticide paused and stared at the strange bespectacled figure in the tweed jacket who was in the clutches of a sycamore aint.

'Silence!' thundered Bert Shiverwithers.

'Wait,' said Pesticide, intrigued. 'Let him speak.'

'Take away their pets and lock them up,' Mr Fluffy blurted out, 'and the professors will do anything you say.'

'Fluffy! How could you!' exclaimed Lord Asbow, noticing the former experimental woodworking professor for the first time. He struggled in Bert Shiverwithers's woody grip. 'You traitor!'

'Release him,' Pesticide said. She smiled at Mr Fluffy and pointed towards the tree. 'I can be generous to those who help me,' she said. 'Take a gold muckle.'

Mr Fluffy bent down and plucked a gold coin from the heap of muckles beneath the tree.

'How could you stoop so low?' said Lord Asbow in a shocked-sounding voice.

Pesticide turned towards him, a wicked twinkle in her eyes. 'Now take away the pets,' she told the aints, 'and lock them up in the farthest tower.'

The courtyard filled abruptly with barking, hissing, croaking, quacking, squawking and splashing as the aints separated the pets from their owners. While half the aints held the distraught professors in their grip, the other half carried off the dogs, cats, toads, ducks, parrots and the small goldfish in a glass bowl.

'Daemian! Daemian! Daemian!' the professors chorused tearfully as they watched their pets disappear.

'Now,' said Pesticide, turning to Lord Asbow, 'are you prepared to do what I say?'

'Yes. Yes, I am,' whimpered Lord Asbow.

Above them, the three moons of Muddle Earth rose majestically in the evening sky and shone down upon the courtyard . . .

'I want those instructions and I want them now!' demanded Pesticide. 'You will show me how to operate Whatever Castle, how to make it walk, run, stomp on things that get in my way . . .' She frowned. 'What's wrong? Why are you looking at me like that?'

In Bert Shiverwithers's woody grip, Lord Asbow struggled and squirmed. Thick black fur was sprouting from his face and neck as his body expanded. His nose turned black and shiny and elongated into a snarling snout. His hands and feet curled into claws and a thick stubby tail sprouted from the seat of his trousers. As the purple, yellow and green moonlight bathed the courtyard, Lord Asbow raised his immense canine head to the sky and howled at the triple moons.

Moments later, the most appalling smell rose up from his monstrously bloated doggy body.

'Pfwooaarrh!' exclaimed Bert Shiverwithers, dropping the gigantic werelabrador and staggering back, his twiggy fingers clamped to his knotty nose.

Around him, in the moonlight, the other professors were undergoing transformations of their own. A corpulent ginger werecat spat and clawed at Lichen Larry, while a huge warty brown weretoad sprang out of Mistletoe Mary's horrified grasp.

The rest of the Giggle Glade Mob struggled with deranged weregerbils, pink-eyed weremice and enraged wereguinea pigs. Meanwhile the Babbling Brook Boys weren't faring much better, stumbling back under the attacks of squawking wereparrots and enormous quacking wereducks. Behind them, panic gripped the Dingly Dell Gang as a giant weretortoise with *Daemian* painted on its shell ran amok, barging the aints aside and snapping at their branches. In the middle of the courtyard, crammed into its bowl, an immense weregoldfish observed the unfolding chaos, one monstrous eye pressed up against the glass.

Pesticide and the other flower fairies huddled together beneath the muckle tree, their faces white with shock.

'What's happening?' whimpered Nettle.

'I'm frightened,' moaned Thistle.

'That goldfish, it's staring at me,' cried Briar-Rose.

'Bert Shiverwithers!' screamed Pesticide. 'Do something!'

Joe, Ella and Edward were dropped on to the cobblestones as the aint that had been holding them retreated with the others across the courtyard towards the gates. Joe felt a tap on his shoulder and looked up to see Mr Fluffy beaming down at him.

'You knew this would happen, didn't you, Mr Fluffy?' said Joe with a smile.

Mr Fluffy winked. 'It's a terrible thing for a wereperson to be separated from his pet, isn't it, Daemian?' he said, stroking the golden hamster that was peering out of the top pocket of his tweed jacket. 'Especially on a triple full moon.'

'He-e-e-elp!'

Joe turned to see the aints who had taken the pets come hurtling out of an arched doorway and back into the courtyard.

'We found the furthest tower,' babbled Mad Marion of the Wild Wood Crew, 'but when we opened the door, it was horrible!'

The aints of the Wild Wood Crew swept past and

headed after the others, who were getting into a tangle of roots and branches as they scrambled through the open gates. Echoing down the corridors of Whatever Castle came a cacophony of honking, banging and crashing, together with a monotonous chant of 'Cake! Cake! Cake!'

'Tower 101,' said Mr Fluffy ominously. 'It's where the poltergeese and the zumbies live. Not to mention . . .'

At that moment, through the arched doorway a strange phantom-like goose emerged into the courtyard, honking for all it was worth as it waddled on ghostly webbed feet. It was followed by a gaggle of others, clashing saucepan lids together and beating pots and pans with wooden spoons. Behind them, blinking into the bright moonlight, lurched a crowd of zumbies, portly undead cake-eaters, arms outstretched before them. Ancient crumbs encrusted their mouths and vintage jam stains streaked their woolly jumpers.

At the gates,

the aints let out creaking cries of dismay.

THUD! THUD! THUD!

Following the poltergeese and zumbies into the courtyard came a black rabbit of frightening proportions. It stood on the cobblestones, its paws clenched and furry face scowling as its bloodshot eyes surveyed the scene. Then taking three massive hops it bounded up to Bert Shiverwithers and nibbled on one of his branch-like fingers.

'Ouch!' he shrieked, shaking off Binky the Black Bunny. 'That's it! I'm not staying here to become rabbit food!' He shoved his companions out through the gates. 'Aints!' he roared. 'Back to Elfwood!'

With that, the Babbling Brook Boys, the Dingly Dell Gang, the Wild Wood Crew and the Giggle Glade Mob clumped off as fast as their big rooty feet would carry them. They didn't look back.

'Daemian!'

'Daemian!'

'Daemian!'

Inside the courtyard, the air filled with delighted cries as the professors' pets came tumbling from the arched doorway and ran, hopped, waddled, flapped and slid up to their owners. The instant Lord Asbow was reunited with his fat Labrador, he turned back to his former self, his claws retracting, fur disappearing and tail shrinking to nothing. In the middle of the courtyard, the pet goldfish in its bowl came sliding to a halt. The giant

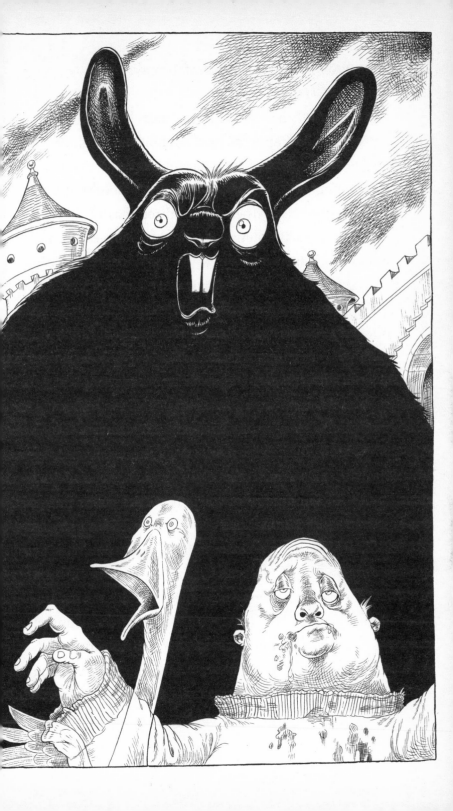

weregoldfish, its monstrous eye pressed against the glass of its own fishbowl, stared down at it. Moments later a decidedly damp Professor Quedgely picked up the bowl containing his pet goldfish and hugged it to his chest.

'Oh, Daemian,' he crooned.

Lord Asbow turned to the professors, who had all now resumed their human form. 'Munderfield. Round up the poltergeese, if you'd be so kind,' he instructed. 'Stibbing. Chate. Take care of the zumbies. They've had far too much excitement for one night, poor things. There's chocolate cake in the pantry. Give each of them a slice.' Lord Asbow turned to the enormous black rabbit. 'Now, Binky,' he said gently. 'Hop along back to your tower, there's a good bunny, and Professor Quedgely will find you a nice juicy lettuce leaf, won't you, Quedgely?'

Professor Quedgely nodded and, tucking his goldfish bowl under his arm, led the black bunny away.

Lord Asbow

looked at the flower fairies cowering beneath the muckle tree, at the gold coins strewn across the cobblestones, and at the wreckage of the drawbridge at the castle gate. He shook his head and turned to Joe.

'This is why we don't encourage visitors, Jefferson,' he said. 'They do so upset everyone. Werepeople, zumbies, poltergeese – *all* our residents. Poor Binky is going to be having nightmares for weeks . . .' He sighed. 'You see, Jefferson, when you've lived here as long as I have, you'll understand that Whatever Castle is a haven for those who find it difficult to fit in here in Muddle Earth . . .' His gaze returned to Pesticide and her friends, who were pulling on their mittens and looking shamefaced. 'As you obviously do, my dear young fairies,' he said meaningfully.

'Lord Asbow!' came a brisk businesslike voice. 'I found these three fast asleep at the top of a tower.' An elegant woman with blue eyes, blonde hair and a dozy-looking wombat under one arm came striding across the courtyard, with Randalf, Norbert and Eudora Pinkwhistle in tow. 'I revived them with cups of my sunrise tea.'

'Well done, Mrs Couldn't-Possibly,' said Lord Asbow, and sighed. 'This has certainly been quite a day for visitors!'

'Fatso!' came a joyful squawk, and Veronica burst from Joe's robes and flapped over to Randalf.

'Veronica!' said Randalf. 'I can't tell you how glad I am that you're safe. I've been so worried . . .'

'Have you? Have you really, Randalf?' Veronica cooed, landing on the wizard's shoulder and nuzzling against his ear.

A shrill fanfare of bluebell trumpets sounded in the night air and a magnificent sleigh of woven meadow flowers on a blackberry-bramble frame came gliding through the gates of Whatever Castle. It was drawn by a dozen giant dragonflies ridden by fairy attendants in petal robes and followed by two grasshoppers in matching barley-straw top hats, their bluebell trumpets now tucked neatly under their arms as they hopped. The sleigh came to a halt in front of the muckle tree and its occupants climbed out.

'King Oberon and Queen Titania of Harmless Hill,' one of the grasshoppers announced.

'Dad! Mum!' Pesticide exclaimed guiltily. 'It's not what it looks like – honestly!' She buried her head in her mittened hands and started to cry.

'It's precisely what it looks like, young lady,' said Queen Titania sternly. 'Can you imagine how I felt when I saw what you were up to in my magical viewing pool? Of course, we came at once to put a stop to it. Your father and I are very disappointed with you. With *all* of you. Aren't we, Ron?'

'Yes, Tania, my love,' King Oberon said, scratching his wobbly belly through his stained vest and looking unhappy.

Beside him, his queen drew herself up to her full

height in her exquisite gown of camellia petals, stitched together with spider-silk and studded with rosehips.

'A muckle tree! I mean, really, Pesticide! Untold riches! An endless supply of gold coins . . . How vulgar!' Queen Titania sighed. 'Isn't that right, Ron?'

'Yes, Tania, my love,' said King Oberon, fiddling with his wand.

'I mean, that's not the way we brought you up,' Queen Titania continued. 'We got rid of all that old old fairy magic at the jumble sale before you were born, and buried all that vulgar gold. After all, who needs it with the wealth of nature that we have at our fingertips?'

'That's just it!' wailed Pesticide, pulling off her mittens and waving her chemical-blue fingers at her parents. She put her mittens back on. 'What chance have I ever had to enjoy the wealth of nature when everything I touch withers and dies?'

'And everything *I* touch gets stung,' said Nettle.

'And scratched,' said Briar-Rose.

'And prickled,' said Thistle. 'Oh, all I've ever wanted is a sweet little baby stiltmouse to call my own, to pet and stroke . . .'

Beside Randalf and Norbert, Eudora Pinkwhistle gave a stifled sob. Queen Titania spun round.

'Eudora?' she said quietly. 'Eudora the wicked fairy godmother. Is that you?' Her voice grew louder and harsher. 'I might have known you'd be mixed up in this somehow. Wasn't it bad enough that you blighted these poor innocent fairies' lives, just because your invitation to their christening got lost in the elf-post?'

'I've never liked the elf-post,' said Eudora quietly. 'That's why I invented the inter-elf—'

Queen Titania ignored her. 'An innocent mishap, but you wouldn't listen to reason. All the other fairy godmothers were so kind with their gifts of beauty, sweet temper and grace. But not you. Oh, no. You had to fly into a rage and put that horrid curse on my daughter and her three handmaids. What was it again? *With your fingers, nimble and spry, everything you touch shall sicken and die. As for your handmaids, one two three, their touch shall hurt all those they see!* You remember, don't you, Ron?' she said, her voice breaking with emotion.

'Yes, Tania, my love,' King Oberon replied, nodding sadly.

'Oh, I'm so ashamed,' Eudora Pinkwhistle wailed, falling to her knees and clasping her hands before her. 'Forgive me! Until this moment, I hadn't realized how effective my curse had been. But you must understand, I was young. I was impetuous. And I had the most awful temper. But I'm so much better now,' she said, wiping her eyes and scrambling to her feet. She reached into her black leather satchel. 'Please, let me put it all right . . .' She pulled out her magic wand and waved it in the air. *'Before these fairies go from bad to worse, may this wand remove my curse!'*

The four flower fairies looked at one another as Eudora Pinkwhistle stepped back. Gingerly, first Nettle, then Thistle and then Briar-Rose pulled off their mittens and looked at their hands. The stings, the prickles, the thorns had all gone. Pesticide went last. She pulled off her black mittens and wiggled her fingers. They were now a delicate shade of pink.

'Oh, darling!' cried Queen Titania. 'Come and give Mummy a great big hug! You too, girls!' She opened her arms wide and Pesticide and the flower fairies rushed into them.

'I'm sorry, Mummy,' said Pesticide. 'We all are.'

'There, there, dear,' said Queen Titania. 'We can make a fresh start,' she added as she swept the four of them up in her arms and climbed into her fairy sleigh. 'Ron!' she called back. 'See to that dreadful tree!'

'Yes, Tania, my love,' said King Oberon, reaching out and touching the silver and gold muckle tree with the tip of his magic wand before jumping into the sleigh next to his wife.

As the dragonflies whisked the sleigh away Queen Titania shot Eudora Pinkwhistle a withering look. 'If I never see you again,' she called over her shoulder, 'it'll be too soon!'

The fairy sleigh disappeared through the castle gates and for a moment there was silence in the courtyard before, with a tinkling sigh, the muckle tree withered away, branches, trunk, roots, coins and all. Randalf rushed forward, Norbert at his shoulder, and stooping down, seized the battered old drinking vessel standing on the cobblestones.

'The Goblet of Porridge!' he proclaimed. 'I've got it! At last! My quest is at an end!'

Joe smiled sadly. 'I'm pleased for you, Randalf. Of course I am – but we're still stuck here in Muddle Earth.'

Beside him Ella and Edward exchanged miserable glances.

'And we're still no nearer to finding that lamp-post,' Joe went on.

'Don't worry,' said Randalf, patting Joe on the

shoulder. 'Something'll turn up. It generally does.' He smiled. 'Trust me, I'm a wizard.'

'That's what you always say,' said Veronica.

'Shut up, Veronica,' said Randalf affectionately, tickling her tummy.

'Coo-ee! Coo-ee! Up here!'

Everyone looked up. There, flapping over the battlements and coming in to land unsteadily on the cobblestones, was Eraguff the eager-to-please dragon. His grey scales glinted in the moonlight as he folded his drab beige wings. In his claws he clutched a plump duvet. Unfurling it with a flourish, the dragon revealed the lamp-post, its legs tied up with three knotted pillowcases and a fourth pillowcase pulled down over its hexagonal glass lantern.

'You see,' said Randalf. 'I told you something would turn up.'

'It tried to get away but I was too quick for it!' Eraguff exclaimed proudly, pulling the pillowcase off the top of the lamp-post to reveal its glowing lantern. Just beside it, in the circle of yellow lamplight, the air shimmered and rippled like a puddle in the rain. 'I hope you're pleased,' the dragon said eagerly, smoke rings rising from his nostrils and floating up into the night air.

'Oh, yes, Eraguff!' Joe said. 'Very, very pleased! Aren't we, Ella? Aren't we, Edward?'

They both nodded, their eyes bright with excitement.

Joe rushed up and, wrapping his arms around Eraguff's scaly neck, gave him a great big hug. The dragon purred with pleasure. 'I'm just happy that I was able to help,' he said.

'The portal!' Ella pointed to the rippling pool of light. 'It's right there. That means we can go home.'

Joe turned to Randalf. 'It *will* take us home, won't it?' he asked uncertainly. 'We don't want to end up somewhere else – somewhere even stranger than Muddle Earth . . .'

'Oh, I think so, Joe,' said Randalf reassuringly. 'You

see, worlds are like dandruff, remember? When you live in them for a while, bits of them stick to you. Bits of Muddle Earth brought you back here when you fell through the portal, and bits of your own world – from your own time and place – will pull you back when you step through the portal from this side.' He stroked his beard. 'Does that make sense?'

'N . . . Not really,' said Joe, and smiled. 'But I trust you. You're a wizard!' He hugged Randalf. 'I'll miss you,' he said. 'And you, Veronica,' he added, stroking the budgie's head.

'Good luck, Joe,' she chirruped.

'And me?' said Norbert, his three eyes blinking back his tears. 'Will you miss me?'

'Of course I will, Norbert,' said Joe, throwing his arms around the ogre. '*And* your prize-winning snugglemuffins!'

'Come on, Joe,' said Ella, who was holding Edward's hand. 'Before the lamp-post gets away again!'

Joe shrugged and he waved goodbye to everyone. 'Big sisters!' he laughed.

The air closed in around him as he stepped into the portal after Ella and Edward. Behind him, he was aware of the yellow glow from the lamp-post growing fainter. Soft fur coats brushed his face. They smelt of old ladies and banana skins. He pushed past them. The next moment he tumbled out of the wardrobe and found himself in his big sister's bedroom, sprawling on top of Ella and Edward.

There was a creak and a groan, and the three of them looked up to see the flat-pack wardrobe disassembling and packing itself away. Planks, doors, screws, hinges, dowelling rods, door handles and instruction leaflet all neatly arranged themselves back in the cardboard box, which flipped itself over and disappeared into the rippling air.

A distant cry of surprise echoed between the worlds. It was Mr Fluffy's voice.

'The *Tumnus*!' it was saying. 'It's back!'

'Hello, clouds! Hello, mountains!' trilled a magnificent young dragon with wings of iridescent lapis lazuli, scales of opalescent cinnabar and underbelly of sparkling sapphire. 'Hello, everybody!'

Eraguff, the most eye-catching dragon in the Here-Be-Dragons Mountains, landed gracefully beside the mountain lake. The other young dragons, who had been waiting patiently to catch a glimpse of him, broke into rapturous applause.

'Isn't he marvellous!'

'Yes, so handsome . . .'

'And so nice with it. Not at all vain.'

'Apparently, a witch waved a magic wand over him and he hasn't been the same since.'

Eraguff stretched his long sinuous neck and sent a

magnificent set of intertwining smoke rings coiling up
into the air. The young dragons trilled their approval.

'As I always say, it's important to try to please,'
Eraguff was pronouncing. 'Why, the best thing I ever did
was give Miss Eudora Pinkwhistle a lift back to Giggle
Glade when she lost her broom . . .'

With a sigh of satisfaction, headmaster Randalfus Rumblebore sat back in his big swivel-chair and eyed the Goblet of Porridge in the trophy case opposite. The honour of Stinkyhogs School of Wizardry had been restored, and he had Roger the Wrinkled's personally signed letter in his pocket to prove it.

A few gold muckles from the High Wizard and Ruler of Muddle Earth in appreciation for all his hard work would have been nice too, thought Randalf, but still, one couldn't have everything.

In the corner of the study, Norbert the Not-Very-Big was sitting cross-legged on the floor, his findy bag in his lap. He sighed heavily.

'I had so many marvellous things,' he grumbled, 'until I lost them all, falling off that silly carpet. Now I've only got these,' he said to himself, 'an old trowel and this acorn thingy.'

He placed the two objects on the floor in front of him. At the desk, Randalf clutched the arms of his big swivel-chair.

'Trowel? Acorn?' he said. He scrambled to his feet and seized the Goblet of Porridge from the trophy case. 'Norbert, if I might have a little word . . .'

Crash! Bang! Wallop! Squelch!

'Peter, I can smell boiled cabbage and floor polish. And is that the nine-times table I can hear?'

'Oh, Susan, we're back. And look at the clock on the cloakroom wall. Only five minutes has passed. That means we haven't dodged detention after all . . .'

'But Peter! That's why we climbed into that howwible bwoom cupboard in the first place! What is that awful smell . . . Oh, Edmund, you haven't, have you?'

The stair-carpet sighed with contentment.

'I'm so in love,' she whispered.

Dyson the broom continued sweeping her intricate border of interwoven leaves, fruits and flowers.

From the far end of the corridor, Lord Asbow approached. He stopped at the foot of the impressive marble staircase of Whatever Castle's central tower. Dyson the broom stopped brushing and flew down to meet him.

Sweeping Lord Asbow off his feet, Dyson carried him swiftly to the top of the stairs and deposited him on the marble landing. The broom gave a little bow and returned to his brushing.

'I'm so in love,' the stair-carpet whispered again.

'Who'd have thought it?' said Joe to himself, and turned from the window as the roar of Edward Gorgeous's motorbike died away.

The former thumbsucking vampire from Muddle Earth had taken to his new life as if he'd been born to it, finding a job and a flat and even buying a Harley-Davidson to go with his fashionable motorcycle jacket. Mind you, he could afford it with the money he earned as the hottest new actor on the scene. If Ella was to be believed, her boyfriend had just landed the lead role in the new movie *Moonlight* – something about a girl falling in love with a vampire.

It sounded absolutely ludicrous, thought Joe with a smile. Still, he had to admit, everything had turned out rather well in the end. Both in this world . . . and in Muddle Earth too!